Also by D. E. Stevenson

Miss Buncle's Book

Miss Buncle Married

The Young Clementina

The Two Mrs. Abbotts

The Four Graces

LISTENING VALLEY

D. E. Stevenson

sourcebooks
landmark

Published by Sourcebooks Landmark, an imprint of Sourcebooks, Inc.
P.O. Box 4410, Naperville, Illinois 60567-4410
(630) 961-3900
Fax: (630) 961-2168
www.sourcebooks.com

Originally published in 1944 in the United Kingdom by Farrar & Rinehart, Inc. This edition issued based on the paperback edition published in 1972 in the United States by ACE Books, an imprint of Holt, Rinehart, and Winston.

Library of Congress Cataloging-in-Publication data is on file with the publisher.

Printed and bound in the United States of America.
VP 10 9 8 7 6 5 4 3 2 1

Author's Note

The characters in this book are imaginary and have no relation whatsoever to any person who may happen by accident to bear the same name. Some of the places mentioned exist in fact, but Ryddelton is intended to present a composite picture of a Scottish border town and to reproduce the atmosphere with artistic rather than literal truth. Although *Listening Valley* is not a sequel to *Celia's House*, readers of the latter may recognize some of the characters in this novel and find themselves in familiar surroundings.

Part One

Chapter One

The House with the High Wall

Most people, looking back at their childhood, see it as a misty country half forgotten or only to be remembered through an evocative sound or scent, but some episodes of those short years remain clear and brightly colored like a landscape seen through the wrong end of a telescope. It was thus that Louise Melville was always to remember the house with the high wall and the adventure connected with it. Antonia was to remember it, too, but not so vividly, for really and truly it was Lou's adventure. Lou was the adventurous one.

The house with the high wall was within five minutes' walk of their own house (the house in which they had been born and in which they lived with their father and mother), but, whereas their own house was one of many, all exactly alike, and was situated in a square with a small and very sooty garden in front, the house with the high wall stood alone, surrounded by a solid gray stone wall and half hidden by trees. In the summer a laburnum flung careless streams of golden blossom over the top of the wall and a snow-white hawthorn tree filled the air with sweetness.

The children often walked around that way in the afternoon, and they used to linger as they passed the tall wooden door in the hope that it would open and give them a glimpse of the garden and the house, but Nannie did not approve of lingering here. She never said anything but always hurried them on…

Lou and Tonia did not ask why, of course, for they were aware that Nannie would not tell them. Nannie was an adept at the art of turning questions aside—questions that she could not or would not answer.

"P'raps an ogre lives there," Tonia said. "An ogre who eats children for his breakfast."

"Or p'raps a wicked magician who would turn us into frogs," countered Lou with relish.

They did not really believe in ogres and magicians, for they were sensible children, but it was fun to pretend to believe in these monsters of iniquity and it was an absorbing topic of conversation.

"Grown-ups are queer," said Tonia, referring to Nannie's inexplicable behavior.

"Yes," agreed Lou. "Yes, they get queer ideas. I think Nannie must have gotten a queer idea about the house with the high wall."

"Mother has it, too," said Tonia, nodding. "Mother wouldn't let me *look* at the house when we drove past yesterday."

One blustery day toward the end of March, the east wind was sweeping through the streets of Edinburgh, raising the dust in clouds and playing all sorts of impish tricks with the hats and skirts of the citizens. The children were out with Nannie as usual, but there was an unusual feeling in Lou's heart. Perhaps it was the sunshine and the breeze, or perhaps it was the fact that the flower shop windows were full of daffodils, showing that spring was really on its way. Whatever it was, Lou's heart felt light and her feet wanted to dance…and when she got to the corner of the high gray wall she took to her heels and ran. Tonia followed, of course, she always followed Lou, and Nannie was left panting along behind.

The children stopped at the big brown door and looked at each other, smiling.

"I won," said Lou, breathlessly.

"You—started—first," said Tonia, more breathlessly still.

"You could have started first if you'd wanted—"

"But I didn't know," began Tonia in reproachful tones.

At this moment the big brown door swung open and a lady appeared. She stepped out into the street and looked up and down—as if she were looking for someone. She was dressed in a soft blue coat with gray furs and a little hat made of gray feathers, but it was her face that riveted the eyes of Tonia and Lou; her face was beautiful. It was pink and white like the Dresden china lady in the drawing room cabinet, and her eyes were bright and brown and sparkling with life.

The lady stopped and smiled. "Two dear little mice!" she exclaimed. She might have said more—she looked as if she were going to say more—but Nannie was just behind and swept the children on.

"The idea!" said Nannie under her breath.

They talked about the lady all the way home, walking along in front of Nannie very sedately.

"What a lovely smell she had!" whispered Lou.

"It was violets," said Tonia, whispering back.

"She was like a picture—"

"Like a queen—that's what I thought."

"She called us mice."

"Because of our gray coats, of course."

For days on end they talked of nothing else, for the sudden appearance of the picture lady and her unusual beauty had kindled their imaginations; unfortunately they had been so entranced that neither of them had looked in through the open door, so the house with the high wall was as mysterious as ever—perhaps even more mysterious.

"She lives there, of course," said Lou. "It must be lovely if *she* lives there. How I wish I had remembered to *look*!"

Tonia said nothing for she was content with the mystery. It was pleasant to speculate, to make up stories about the garden and the house and the beautiful picture lady who lived there... but Lou was different. Lou always wanted to know.

It was the end of May or perhaps the beginning of June when Nannie went home for the weekend. She went home to see her mother who was "getting on" (as Nannie put it), and while she was away the children's mother looked after them and Maggie, the housemaid, put them to bed. Maggie was young and enjoyed having games with the children, so, although they were fond of Nannie, her absence was a pleasant change.

On Sunday afternoon, Lou and Tonia went down to the drawing room dressed in their best frocks—blue Liberty smocks, the color of their eyes. Mrs. Melville intended to have them with her for tea, but after about twenty minutes of their company she changed her mind, for they were in a tiresome sort of mood and she could not be bothered with them. If only one of them had been a boy, thought Mrs. Melville, looking at her daughters regretfully, or even if one of them were really interesting; they were both rather dull. The children of Mrs. Melville's friends were bright and entertaining and frequently made amusing remarks, but neither Lou nor Tonia ever said anything worth repeating.

"I think you might go upstairs and play with the dollhouse," suggested Mrs. Melville. "You'd like that, wouldn't you? And I'll tell Maggie to take your tea up to the nursery."

"Do you love Mother?" asked Tonia, as they toiled upstairs together.

"Why, of course," replied Lou in horrified tones. "It would be frightfully wicked not to love Mother. You love her, don't you?"

"Of course," said Tonia hastily…but did she? Perhaps she was frightfully wicked. How could you be sure?

"And Father," continued Lou in earnest tones. "You love Father, don't you?"

"Oh, of course," agreed Tonia. She hesitated and then added in a doubtful voice, "But we don't see him often, do we?"

"He buys your clothes, Tonia. He buys your food. You would starve if Father didn't buy you things."

"Yes, of course," said Tonia for the third time, but without much conviction.

They had arrived at the nursery. Tonia opened the dollhouse, but Lou ran across to the window and leaned out. There were bars across the window, but you could get your head between the bars—if Nannie was not there—and you could look down into the street, far below. People were walking along, dressed in their Sunday clothes, and it was amusing because you could see their hats and a dumpy sort of figure beneath. A dog ran across the street and a black-and-white cat sprang onto the railing of the garden and crouched there, spitting with rage. There was a hawthorn tree in the garden, and the afternoon sun was shining on the snow-white blossoms with a golden light.

"Let's go out," said Lou.

"Alone!" exclaimed Tonia in amazement.

"Why not?" demanded Lou. Her cheeks were suddenly pink, and her eyes were sparkling. Her very hair seemed full of excitement; a few moments ago it had been lying flat with boredom, but now her golden curls were bobbing and dancing as if they were alive. "What could happen to us, Tonia?" she continued. "I suppose you're frightened of getting lost or something. We *always* go for a walk in the afternoons—it's good for us. I'll take care of you," added Lou grandly.

Five minutes later the hall door opened, and two little girls in little blue frocks came out and walked sedately down the steps.

Nothing had been arranged about the direction of their walk, but neither of them showed any hesitation. They turned to their left and proceeded upon their way, hand in hand.

The wall was just as mysterious as ever, and the brown door was shut. Lou and Tonia walked past very slowly, turned at the corner, and walked back.

"It won't open," said Tonia, breaking the silence. "I know it won't open; I've got a sort of feeling—"

Lou said nothing. She reached up and pulled the bell. Far in the distance, there was a jangling noise that died away into silence.

"Lou!"

"I had to. I just *had* to, Tonia."

"But what will you say?"

"I don't know—but I *must* see inside," declared Lou breathlessly.

They waited for a few moments and then they heard foot-steps approaching and the door swung open…it was the lady they had seen before, the picture lady. Today she was all in pale gray with a string of pearls around her neck, and her dark hair was waved and curled.

The lady looked at her visitors in some surprise and then she smiled. "It's the two little mice!" she exclaimed.

Lou and Tonia were dumb. They walked into the garden, and the door was shut behind them. It was not a big garden, but it was even more wonderful than they had imagined, for it was full of sunshine and flowers. There was a paved courtyard with a pool in the middle, and all around the paved space was high rockery, covered with pink and yellow and purple flowers; they looked like colored waterfalls streaming down between the stones. At one side was a swinging garden seat with a gaily striped red and white canopy, and in front of it was a tea table with a white lace cloth and silver that sparkled in the sun. A fat lady was sitting in the swinging seat and a young man in white flannels was sitting near her in a deck chair, reading a paper.

Lou and Tonia stood there, hand in hand, and gazed about them.

"Good heavens!" exclaimed the young man, throwing down his paper. "Good heavens, where did you find them, Mother?"

"They're perfect," declared the fat lady, holding up a lorgnette.

"Yes, quite perfect," agreed the picture lady, laughing to herself in a pleased way. "I thought you'd like them, Daisy. Wasn't it clever of me to produce them for you on a dull Sunday afternoon?"

"It's never dull when you're about," declared the young man.

"It was very clever of you, Wanda," declared the fat lady.

"They're two little mice, you know," said the picture lady, nodding. "Two dear little mice."

"Not mice, Wanda," objected the fat lady.

"No," agreed the young man. "Aunt Daisy is right. They aren't mice. I can't quite make up my mind what they are— babes in the wood, perhaps."

"They're Alices in Wonderland," said Aunt Daisy, closing her lorgnette with a snap.

A short silence ensued. It was broken by the young man. "Can they talk?" he inquired in a grave, interested voice.

"I don't think so," replied the picture lady. "But they don't have to talk, do they? I mean, they're so entrancing to look at."

"Entrancing," agreed Aunt Daisy with a sigh. "And how fortunate they are! They *go together* so beautifully, don't they? One fair and one dark—and they both have dark blue eyes and rose-leaf complexions. When we were young, you were so much fairer."

"I couldn't help it, Daisy," said the picture lady regretfully.

Lou and Tonia had never heard this sort of conversation before (it was entirely different from the conversation of their mother's friends), but the whole adventure was so strange, so different from everyday life, that nothing would have surprised them.

"Of course we can talk," said Lou, waking suddenly from the daze into which she had fallen.

"They can talk!" exclaimed the young man in amazement.

"Perhaps they can eat and drink," suggested Aunt Daisy.

The young man immediately rose, produced two cushions, and, putting them on the broad stone rim of the pool, invited the children to sit down. The picture lady poured out two cups of tea and offered them a plate of chocolate éclairs.

"We usually start with bread and butter," said Lou, doubtfully.

"We always start with éclairs," said the young man gravely. "You see we haven't been very well brought up."

"Speak for yourself, Jack," interposed Aunt Daisy with asperity. "Your mother and I were *very* well brought up. We always started with bread and butter, didn't we, Wanda?"

"You can be *too* well brought up," replied her sister sadly. "I mean, you have so much further to backslide—"

"But respectability is so dull—"

"So difficult to achieve—"

"Who wants to achieve it?" asked Jack. "Give me chocolate éclairs every time."

The picture lady looked at him and smiled.

"Are they twins, I wonder," said Aunt Daisy suddenly.

"No, we aren't," declared Lou.

"They aren't twins." Jack nodded. "As a matter of fact, I was pretty certain they were not. The pretty one is the elder."

"They're both pretty," objected Aunt Daisy, "but of course I know what you mean. The fair one is more obviously pretty."

"She's adorable," said Jack.

"The dark one has better features," said his mother, "but you always prefer blonds."

"Except one," put in Jack, smiling at her affectionately.

"Sentimental nonsense," grumbled Aunt Daisy, handing in her cup for more tea.

Neither Lou nor Tonia had any sense of social obligation, so they sat and ate chocolate éclairs and made no attempt to join in the conversation of their hosts. They listened, of course, in a slightly dazed manner, and not much of it escaped them. It was very pleasant in the garden, warm and bright. Bees buzzed among the flowers, and an occasional car passed by outside the high wall and hooted at the corner. Presently, the church bells began to ring for evening service, and the picture lady rose.

"Are you going to church?" asked Lou.

She smiled and shook her head. "It's time for you to go home, isn't it?"

"Let's keep them," suggested Jack. "This is Liberty Hall. They would like to live here—"

"Yes, let's keep them," agreed Aunt Daisy.

"I'm afraid you can't," said Lou. "Mother might wonder where we had gone, and Nannie is coming home tomorrow—so you see—"

"I see," said Jack sadly.

Their hosts accompanied them to the door and shook hands with them. "Come back soon," said Jack.

"Nannie won't let them," said the picture lady.

Aunt Daisy laughed and said, "Oh, you know who they are!"

Lou and Tonia walked home in silence, for there was so much to think about that they had no words at all. It was not until they had regained the familiar haven of the nursery and had seated themselves upon the blue cretonne-covered window seat that they found their tongues.

"Her name is Wanda," said Tonia in a low voice.

"And Jack is her son," said Lou. "And the house is called Liberty Hall."

"She knows who we are," said Tonia. "How does she know, Lou?"

"I wonder," said Lou, frowning.

"They were laughing at us—"

"But not nastily—"

"Oh no—"

"All the same," said Lou slowly. "All the same…we *were* silly. Next time…"

Tonia nodded. She knew what Lou meant, for they were so close to each other that they needed very few words. Next time they went to Liberty Hall they must behave like Mother's friends. Tonia knew how they behaved because she and Lou were sometimes present at Mother's tea parties and were permitted to hand around the cakes. Mother's friends talked all the time; they talked about their children, their servants, and their clothes. It was quite different sort of talk.

"I don't think we could," said Tonia suddenly.

"What?" asked Lou, whose thoughts had strayed in a different direction.

"Talk to them," said Tonia with a sigh.

While they were out, Maggie had brought up the nursery tea and laid it on the table. There were two large mugs of milk, a pile of thick bread and butter, and several slices of nursery cake—very plain and uninteresting.

"I couldn't," said Lou, looking at it in disgust.

Tonia had not eaten as many éclairs as Lou, but she had eaten enough to make bread and butter distasteful. "I suppose we ought to," she said in doubtful tones.

"I couldn't," repeated Lou.

They were still looking at the spread and wondering what to do when Maggie returned to clear away.

"You've eaten nothing. Are you feeling well enough?" she inquired, looking at the children anxiously.

"We've had tea, thank you," said Lou with a grand air. "We called on a lady and she asked us to stay."

Lou did not hesitate to tell Maggie about their adventure, for Maggie was an ally. She was not like other grown-ups (who were apt to take strong views and were nearly always unreasonable). Maggie was young and friendly and amenable to suggestion. The story was a good one and Lou told it well, encouraged by the absorbed attention of her audience.

"Well now, did you ever hear the like!" exclaimed Maggie. "In the name of Fortune what will you think of next! You rang the bell as bold as brass and Mrs. Halley asked you in to tea!"

"Mrs. Halley—is that her name?" asked Lou.

"That's her name," replied Maggie, nodding portentously. "My cousin is there as kitchen maid and I've been there two or three times. It's a very comfortable place if you don't mind the goings-on."

"Goings-on?"

"Parties and the like. It's a gay house—not like here. I had the offer to go as housemaid, but Father put his foot down," added Maggie regretfully. "Father is all for respectability."

"What *is* respectability?" inquired Tonia. The word had intrigued her when she had heard it used by her new friends—and here it was again.

"Well, there now," said Maggie. "You're a funny one and no mistake. Respectability is living with your husband, quiet-like, and going off to bed at the proper time... And my goodness if it's not your bedtime this minute and me with the tea dishes to wash. You get started now," added Maggie, lifting the heavy tray with a swing of her strong young arms. "You turn on the bath and get your things ready. I'll be up in a minute—"

Chapter Two
Learning History

Nannie was not sorry when her short holiday ended and she found herself back in her own comfortable nursery, for Nannie's holiday was merely a change of work and a change for the worse. Nannie's mother lived at Ryddelton and took lodgers in the summer months. When Nannie went home, she spent her time washing and scrubbing and polishing until everything in the house was as bright and shining as a new pin—for that was the way she was made—and as Nannie was not very young and was unused to hard work, she was very tired at the end of it.

Nannie was small and rotund, she had rosy cheeks and bright brown eyes, and she always wore a crackly starched apron. Her name was Kate Dalrymple—like the lady in the song—and, to tell the truth, she was very proud of the fact that there was a song that might be said to be her exclusive property. Naturally enough, it was Nannie's favorite song; she sang it to the children and hummed it cheerfully as she laid the nursery meals. She was a cheerful person. When she was not busy with the hundred and one little jobs that fell to her lot, Nannie employed her time with crochet; she was always working out new patterns and murmuring the complicated directions under her breath. She made crochet mats for her mother's birthday, and crochet insertions for towels, and tablecloths with crochet lace, but her chief work, and one that employed her for months, was a set of crochet antimacassars for her mother's sitting room.

In spite of the holiday feeling that had prevailed in Nannie's absence, the children were delighted at her return and welcomed her warmly. Tonia was especially glad to see Nannie back, for she was more dependent than Lou upon Nannie's good offices. Tonia had the greatest difficulty in coping with buttons and shoe-laces—in fact, with anything that required nimble fingers—and Nannie understood this disability and was reasonably patient. Sometimes she grumbled, of course, and sometimes she seized Tonia's hands (which were very small and frail) and looked at them thoughtfully, but usually she just did up the buttons and tied the laces without any comment.

"Did you enjoy your holiday?" Tonia inquired.

"Not much. I'm getting too old for holidays," replied Nannie with dry humor.

"I suppose the lodgers were a nuisance," said Lou.

"Why does your mother have them?" Tonia wanted to know.

"To make money," replied Nannie, who was always more communicative when she returned from Ryddelton and less inclined to turn aside a straight question. "People have to make money so as to buy food and clothes; besides what would be the use of having a lovely house and not taking in lodgers? It's not like an ordinary house, you know," said Nannie proudly. "People come back there year after year; nice people, too."

"Why isn't it like an ordinary house, Nannie?"

"Because it belonged to your Great-Aunt Antonia, of course. I've told you half a dozen times."

"Did your mother buy the house?"

"Well, what a question. How would she have the money to buy it—and the furniture and everything? The house was given to her by old Mr. Melville, your grandfather, because she had been housekeeper at Ryddelton Castle for years and years. He gave it to her when old Miss Antonia died. That's what happened. He gave her a pension, too—but you don't understand all that."

"I do," declared Lou earnestly. "It's very interesting, Nannie. What did Grandfather do when he gave away his house?"

"Goodness! As if you didn't know! I've told you already it was old Miss Antonia's house. Your grandfather never lived there himself. He lived at Ryddelton Castle, a lovely big place about six miles out of Ryddelton. You've seen the picture of Ryddelton Castle hanging on the wall in your father's study, haven't you? Melville House—where my mother lives—is in Ryddelton, in the High Street. The family used to move into Ryddelton in the winter when the roads were so bad they couldn't get in and out to Ryddelton Castle. That's why all the big families that lived roundabout used to have houses in the town. Of course that was long ago. It's a very old house, you know. It's one of the oldest houses in the town. The front door opens right onto the High Street, but there's a nice bit of garden at the back."

"Why don't we live at Ryddelton Castle now?"

"Because…oh well, because your mother doesn't like the country. The castle was sold soon after Tonia was born. There now, that's enough…too much I shouldn't wonder," added Nannie under her breath.

It was at least sufficient to kindle the interest of Lou and Tonia, and they continued to pester Nannie with questions.

"Ask your father," said Nannie at last. "He was born and brought up at Ryddelton Castle. Perhaps he'll tell you about it."

It was not easy to carry out this suggestion, for their father was away all day at his office, and when he was at home he paid very little attention to his daughters and showed no desire for their company. However, Lou was of a persistent nature so she bided her time, and one evening when her mother was out and

Nannie was busy, she presented herself in her father's study, dragging a reluctant Tonia by the hand.

"We want to know all about Ryddelton Castle," said Lou firmly. "I want to know and so does Tonia—only she's rather shy. So will you tell us, please?"

"I suppose Nannie's been talking," said Mr. Melville, looking at his elder daughter and noting, for the first time, that she was a very good-looking child. "Well, never mind. There's no reason why she shouldn't talk—nothing to be ashamed of. It's a fine place. I never would have sold it if one of you had been a boy."

"Why?" asked Lou.

"Good heavens, that's obvious, isn't it? There's always been a Melville at the castle—ever since it was built hundreds of years ago. But what was the use of keeping it? Ella wouldn't live there."

"Mother?"

"Yes, your mother can't stand the country at any price. She couldn't get her bridge. There was no use keeping the place standing empty. Damned fine place it is. Sometimes I think I was a fool to sell it, but I got a good offer and I took it." He sighed and relapsed into silence.

"Is there a pond?" asked Tonia in a very small voice.

"A pond!" exclaimed Mr. Melville in disgust. "My good child, there's a river. That's better than a pond, isn't it? I'll show you some photographs if you like." He rose and took some large photograph albums off a shelf in his bookcase and handed one to Tonia.

Tonia dropped it.

"She can't help dropping things," said Lou, picking it up and putting it on the table.

"What d'you mean?" asked Mr. Melville. "Why can't she help it? Carelessness, that's what it is."

"No," said Lou earnestly. "No, she isn't careless. She just can't hold things with her hands."

"Holds things with her feet, I suppose," said Mr. Melville with heavy sarcasm. "Well, never mind. There's no harm done. No need to look so miserable about it."

The albums were full of photographs, and Mr. Melville turned the pages and expatiated on the glories of his ancestral home. He found his daughters a sympathetic audience. They listened with attention; they exclaimed at the right moment; they asked quite pertinent questions. Mr. Melville enjoyed himself, surprisingly, for he had loved Ryddelton Castle. Of course Lou and Tonia were Melvilles, so perhaps that was why they were so interested.

"That's the Rydd Water," said Mr. Melville. "It runs through the grounds quite close to the castle. I used to fish in it when I was a boy. And here's a photograph of the woods…and this is the garden. You can see the greenhouses in the corner. You've seen the big photograph of the castle, of course. I had it enlarged. There it is over the fireplace."

They turned and looked at it again—the square, solid-looking building with the tower (from which on a clear day you could see the English hills).

There was a picture of the town house as well, and Mr. Melville elaborated Nannie's information on the subject. Ryddelton was a gay little town in winter, when all the big families were congregated there. They had balls at the town hall and whist at each other's houses in the long winter evenings. Scarcely a day passed without some sort of party; there were lots of young people about.

They opened another album full of photographs of people, gentlemen in queer old-fashioned clothes, ladies in crinolines, family groups of children.

"She's like Tonia," declared Lou, pointing to a colored sketch of a young girl with dark curls and a rose-leaf complexion.

"Is she?" asked Mr. Melville doubtfully. "I don't see much resemblance. That's my Aunt Antonia when she was young."

"The one that lived in Melville House?"

"Yes, she lived there. She was my father's eldest sister. She was engaged to be married to a man called Arthur Dunne—one of the Dunnes of Dunnian—but he was lost at sea."

"Oh, poor Antonia!" cried Tonia in dismay.

Mr. Melville looked at her in surprise, for it seemed odd that she should be distressed over something that had happened so long ago.

"Did you ever see Aunt Antonia?" asked Lou, whose curiosity was as insatiable as that of the elephant's child.

"Yes," replied Mr. Melville, "I remember her quite well. I used to go to see her when I was a small boy, and she always gave me mixed cookies with little pieces of sugar on the top. She wore a silk dress and a lace cap with lilac ribbons, and the whole house smelled of lavender. I remember when she died," continued Mr. Melville in reminiscent tones. "I must have been about seventeen. It was a magnificent funeral. I never saw so many flowers in my life, and the carriages stretched all down Ryddelton High Street. Everybody knew her, of course."

"So then her house was given to Nannie's mother. I wonder why?"

"There were various reasons—reasons you wouldn't understand. There were rows in the family about it. My father was a hasty-tempered man, and he suddenly lost patience and made it over to Mrs. Dalrymple just as it stood, lock, stock, and barrel."

"Because Mrs. Dalrymple loved Aunt Antonia," said Tonia, nodding.

"How do you know?" asked Mr. Melville in surprise.

Tonia was silent.

"Well, can't you answer?" inquired Mr. Melville. "There's no need to look sulky. I'm asking you a plain question: How did you know?"

"I just—knew," said Tonia in a trembling voice.

Mr. Melville was irritated (it took very little to irritate him because he had inherited his father's temper and had taken no pains to improve it), so he shut the album with a bang and told his daughters to go back to the nursery.

"He was cross," whispered Tonia as they went upstairs together.

"Grown-ups are like that," said Lou in comforting tones. "They're nice, and you get on all right, and then suddenly they're cross."

"P'raps they get tired," said Tonia.

"Yes, because they're so old," agreed Lou.

Mr. Melville (aged a little over forty) would have been even less pleased with his offspring if he could have heard their remarks. As it was, he put the albums back on the shelf with very mixed feelings. He had enjoyed himself up to a point, but now he was upset and irritated. Why was that, wondered Mr. Melville. The children were such an odd mixture, a mixture of sense and imbecility. In Tonia the imbecility predominated. Perhaps it was because he saw the children so seldom that he found them a strain; he must see them more often...but did he want to see them more often? Mr. Melville was debating this point when Mrs. Melville came in—she had been to a bridge party, of course.

"The children have been here," said Mr. Melville crossly.

"Here?" asked Mrs. Melville in amazement.

"Yes, *here*. I can't think why you don't have them in the drawing room. Nannie can't be expected to keep them the whole time. As a matter of fact, I don't know how she stands it."

"She's paid to stand it—and I always have them down after tea."

"Not always—"

"Yes, always, unless I'm out or have people in to bridge."

"Which happens four days out of five!"

"They're much happier in the nursery. Nannie understands them."

"That's a nice admission!" cried Mr. Melville. "You don't understand your own children!"

"Neither do you," Mrs. Melville pointed out.

"I do. I've had them here for nearly an hour—"

"And you're as cross as a bear after it."

"I am not," declared Mr. Melville furiously. "I am not in the least upset. We got on very well indeed. Lou is quite sensible and amusing. She takes a real interest in things—in the family for instance—and that's more than you do."

"Good gracious, what a fuss!" said Mrs. Melville, yawning. "If you like having the children, have them by all means."

"You ought to have them."

"They bore me so dreadfully," complained Mrs. Melville. "I find them dull. If one of them had been a boy, it would have been different."

"What on earth is the use of saying that?" demanded Mr. Melville. "Of course it would have been different if one of them had been a boy—everything would have been different. You know perfectly well I wanted a boy."

"It wasn't my fault," declared Mrs. Melville, smiling.

"It *was* your fault," retorted her enraged husband. "There was no reason why we shouldn't have had another try. As a matter of fact, it isn't too late now—"

"You're mad!" cried Mrs. Melville, roused at last. "Nothing would induce me to have another child. I told you that after Tonia was born…"

Chapter Three
The Worst Boy in the School

There was a small kindergarten school at the end of the street, run by a maiden lady and her married sister, and every morning at nine o'clock Nannie took the Melville children to the door and left them there, calling back to fetch them at twelve o'clock precisely. Miss Mann and Mrs. Grant were quite unlike each other, the former was tall and thin and extremely conscientious, the latter round and fat and easygoing. Unfortunately neither lady had a way with children, so the school was noisy and ill-disciplined. It was not so bad when the small scholars were anchored safely to their desks, for Miss Mann was a good teacher and able to hold their interest, but when the break came the children spent their time chasing each other around the classroom, shrieking and yelling like maniacs, or ran helter-skelter to the changing room where they had left their schoolbags. These schoolbags contained a bottle of milk and some cookies that were consumed by their owners halfway through the morning—and to see the children fighting and jostling one another in the doorway in the effort to get the food, one might have imagined that they had come to school without any breakfast.

The Melvilles did not take part in this melee but stood aside and waited quite patiently until the coast was clear. They were not used to other children and disliked being jostled, and they found the noise and bustle somewhat alarming. Tonia was more alarmed than Lou. She had envisaged school as a place full of people like herself, but she soon discovered that she had nothing in common with her fellow students—nothing except size.

"Antonia and Louise *look on*," said Miss Mann to her sister. "They look on at school as if it were a pantomime."

"They're soft," replied Mrs. Grant. "But they're no trouble to teach. Antonia learned to read in six weeks. Her concentration is remarkable."

"They're too good!"

"I wish some of the others were like them. Bay Coates, for instance."

"Bay *is* a problem," sighed Miss Mann.

Bay was the worst boy in the school. He was a rebel from the top of his bright brown head to the tips of his toes. His eyes were bright brown, too—the color of an autumn beech leaf—and his teeth were very white and pearly in his suntanned face. He was small but sturdy. He wore a red kilt and a brown tweed jacket, and his knees were usually adorned with sticking plaster. Bay lived in the country—which accounted for his tan and perhaps also for his independent spirit. His people lived at Drumford, some miles out of Edinburgh, and Bay drove in with his father every morning. He usually arrived before the other children, which fortunate circumstance gave him the chance to prepare his jokes in private before lessons began. Bay's jokes were always different, for he had a fertile imagination. He brought frogs in his pocket and hid them in people's shoes. He substituted a white stone for Mrs. Grant's chalk (this was a great success, for it was most amusing to see the good lady trying to write with it on the blackboard). He produced a false nose and put it on when Miss Mann's back was turned and sat there, perfectly solemnly, while the whole class giggled and sniggered and could not do its sums.

Lou disliked Bay intensely, but Tonia had a sneaking sort of admiration for him. She did not admit it, of course, but there it was. Bay was brave, and he was very funny. You never knew what he would do next, and it was delicious to be shocked.

"Isn't Bay awful!" she would say to Lou as they walked home to dinner.

"He's simply frightful," Lou would agree. "He ought to be smacked, I think."

Perhaps she was right; perhaps Bay ought to have been smacked, but neither Miss Mann nor Mrs. Grant had the courage to attempt such drastic measures. They made him stand in the corner, of course, but this had little or no effect upon him; Tonia felt certain that the time he spent standing in the corner was used by the culprit to plan more subtle forms of mischief.

One morning Tonia discovered something wrong with her desk. It rocked backward and forward in the oddest manner whenever she leaned upon it. At first she could not imagine what had happened, but presently she found a little square of wood under one of the legs of her desk. She removed it surreptitiously and looked at Bay across the room. It was obvious, by the mischievous glance he gave her, that this was another of his jokes.

Quite early in their acquaintance Bay had discovered Tonia's weakness, and he made good use of this discovery. "Here, catch!" he would cry and throw something at her—a rolled-up pair of socks or a rubber ball. Tonia would grab at it feebly and it would slip through her hands and fall on the floor, and then he would laugh uproariously and call her "Butterfingers." But strangely enough, Bay's teasing did not distress Tonia; in fact, it gave her a feeling of importance when she found that he teased her more than the other children.

Nita's teasing was a different matter, for Nita had a different technique. She was past master in the art of getting others into trouble and remaining out of it herself. Nita was that shameless recreant, the teacher's pet; Miss Mann and Mrs. Grant liked her and praised her and she was held up as a pattern to her fellow students. "Look at Nita!" they would say. "Why can't you behave like her!" and the other children would look at Nita with something approaching hatred in their souls. There she sat, smug and complacent, enjoying the approbation she ill deserved. She was not very nice to look at, anyhow, for she was tall and very thin with a pale face and a self-assertive nose, and she wore her mouse-colored hair in two long plaits tied with green ribbon.

One day when the children arrived at school, they found that Bay had been up to his tricks again. Two figures had been drawn on the blackboard, one short and fat, the other tall and thin, and (so that there should be no mistake as to their identity) he had written beneath them in large letters: "MRS. CANT and MISS CAN."

The children were enchanted with this effort, but their teachers were not amused. Oddly enough Miss Mann was more upset than her sister. She made Bay stand in the corner for half an hour.

"He's getting worse," said Miss Mann to Mrs. Grant when the children had gone.

"Oh, I don't think so," replied Mrs. Grant comfortably. "It was just a joke—and rather funny, really. He's quite right, you know. I'm not a good teacher; I can't hold the children's interest like you can. Of course they know that, the little wretches."

"He ought to respect you. How are you going to keep order if the children don't respect you?"

"Bay respects nobody."

"That's just it!" cried Miss Mann. "We can't manage Bay. He's too much for us. We shall have to ask his father to take him away."

"Oh no, Margaret. His father is such a delightful man."

"That may be," said Miss Mann grimly. "But Bay is an imp. I'm terrified of what he will do next."

Several days passed without incident, and then something really terrible occurred, something none of the children would ever forget. It was eleven o'clock and the usual scrimmage took place in the changing room, the children searching for their schoolbags containing their lunches, but when the bottles of milk were produced, it was found that the bottles had been opened and topped up with ink that had seeped all through the milk in violet streaks. Bay's bottle was the only one that had not been tampered with, so there was no doubt as to the culprit.

"You wicked boy!" cried Miss Mann as she collected the bottles and emptied them into the sink. "You naughty, wicked boy. It's the most dreadful sin to spoil good food. Don't you know that there are children starving, children who never get milk like this to drink! There are children here, in this city, who would be thankful for milk like this—and you've ruined it. I can't deal with you, Bay. I shall take you around to your father's office—that's the only thing I can do. He'll have to deal with you; he'll have to take you away. You're too naughty for me." She was trembling with rage and fright—almost weeping—for it seemed to her that this was something abnormal. This was no ordinary childish prank.

Miss Mann could not take Bay to his father at once, for the other children must be considered, so she sent him into the back room to wait for her until she was ready. The half hour seemed very long, and not very much work was done, for teacher and class alike were upset and restless. Everybody was relieved when the time came to go home; hats and coats were put on with unusual quietness and rapidity.

Tonia was the last to leave (she always was, for it took her such a long time to button her coat and tie her shoelaces), and as she was hurrying after Lou she passed Bay in the passage. He was waiting for Miss Mann, standing there with his legs apart and his hands in his pockets and a scowl of bravado on his small brown face.

Tonia looked at him and hesitated. "Did you do it, Bay?" she whispered.

He made no reply, but his scowl became fiercer and he gave Tonia a little push that sent her stumbling against the wall... Tonia recovered her balance and ran on down the stairs after Lou.

"It was awful, Nannie," Lou was saying. "Miss Mann was terribly angry. Wasn't it a wicked thing to do? Miss Mann said, 'You're a wicked boy. I can't deal with you.' D'you think he'll be sent to prison?"

"I shouldn't wonder," said Nannie, hurrying them along.

"To prison!" exclaimed Tonia in dismay.

"Well, why not?" said Nannie. "Prison is the best place for wicked people, isn't it?" She smiled as she spoke, but Tonia did not see the smile and, as Bay disappeared from school and nobody knew what had happened to him, it was only reasonable to suppose that he was languishing in prison.

"With bread and water to eat," said Tonia to Lou in horrified accents.

"Well, he *deserves* it," replied Lou.

Tonia did not agree. The very idea of Bay in prison appalled her. She visualized him sitting upon a bench in a dank cell with bars across the window, and for several nights she dreamed of Bay and awoke in a cold sweat of terror. Fortunately this period of anxiety and misery came to a sudden and entirely satisfactory conclusion. Tonia had been to the mailbox at the corner to post a letter for Nannie. She was walking back to the house when she saw Bay coming toward her. Yes, it was Bay, and he looked exactly the same as usual. He was brown and fit, and his kilt swung from his hips with a jaunty air. The two children passed each other without stopping...and then Tonia paused and looked back. Bay was looking back, too, and when he saw that she had stopped, he began to walk toward her.

"Hallo, Butterfingers!" said Bay with a defiant air.

Tonia had one foot on her own doorstep, and this gave her confidence. "You didn't do it," she said.

"How d'you know," he demanded.

"Because," said Tonia, searching for words. "Because it wasn't funny."

Bay's toe was drawing circles on the pavement, and he was watching it intently. "I never said I didn't," he mumbled.

Tonia was silent, but her eyes had begun to smile.

"Well, is that all?" inquired Bay.

"Yes," retorted Tonia with unaccustomed spirit. "Yes, that's all—except that you're a very silly little boy."

She ran up the steps without a backward glance and slammed the door. She had gotten even with Bay.

Chapter Four
Growing Up

The years passed quickly. Lou and Tonia left Miss Mann's and were taught at home by a governess. Miss Fraser was conscientious and kind and saw to it that the children were well grounded. She taught them French and music as well as ordinary subjects. Tonia loved music and had a small sweet voice, tuneful as a bird's, but piano lessons were mixed pleasure. She was very anxious to learn to play the piano, for it seemed to her that to play the piano really well would be to attain the height of bliss, but, although she could learn the theory of music and could pick out any tune by ear, her hands were too small and feeble to compass the notes. Lou had practically no ear for music and—to tell the truth—did not care for it much, but she soon learned to play "The Joyful Peasant" and "Träumerei" and had gone on to Songs from Schubert while Tonia was still struggling hopelessly with five-finger exercises. Fortunately Tonia had a refuge from the trials and troubles of life. It was a place inside herself—a listening place—and when life pressed upon her too strongly, she could hide from her troubles and enjoy peace and quietness there. When Tonia went into her listening place, her small face became utterly blank and the sights and sounds of everyday life faded away into the distance. She had not much control of her comings and goings—that was the odd thing about it—and sometimes when Mother or Nannie was speaking to her, she would feel herself slipping away and the voice of authority would grow dim.

"That imbecile expression!" Mrs. Melville would complain. "Really, one would think the child was half-witted."

Nannie was a trifle more patient, but only Lou understood; for Lou was the only person who had been allowed into the secret.

"I can't help it, really," Tonia would explain. "I don't *want* to help it, of course, because I like going there; but, even if I wanted to, I couldn't."

"What do you see there?" Lou would inquire.

"Nothing—I listen," said Tonia vaguely. "It's sort of music—"

"Like Joan of Arc?"

"No, not like that a bit."

Lou sighed. She was a trifle jealous of the listening place, for it was the only thing they did not share. She had tried very hard to make a listening place for herself but without much success.

They shared everything else—lessons and walks and reading. They worked their way through Mr. Melville's library like a couple of bookworms. Mrs. Melville was one of those curious people who believe that any book bound in leather is a classic and that all classics are suitable for the young, so she put no constraint upon her daughters' activities. "My girls are tremendous readers," she would say as she shuffled the cards in her strong white hands and prepared to deal. "Dickens and Scott, you know..." She was still as keen as ever on bridge—they were playing auction now, of course.

❧

"Reading again," said Nannie one day as she came into the nursery. (They had tried to call it the schoolroom but without much success.) "Reading again—and in this light, too. You'll ruin your eyesight. That'll be the end of it."

Lou was curled up in the big basket chair and Tonia was stretched full length upon the hearth rug—these were their invariable positions—for Tonia's hands soon tired of holding a book and she found it much easier to lie facedown with the book on the floor.

"What else should we do?" asked Lou, stretching her arms above her head. "We don't know anybody to talk to. Why don't we know people, Nannie?"

"Why don't you know people?" said Nannie in a doubtful tone.

"Yes. Other girls know lots of people and go to parties."

Nannie was silent. She knew the answer, of course, but she had a queer feeling of loyalty to Mrs. Melville, and she would not criticize her. If Mrs. Melville had bestirred herself and asked the children of her own friends to tea, it might have helped a bit. As a matter of fact, Nannie had suggested this several times, but the suggestion had borne no fruit.

"Yes, Nannie. Yes, we'll see..." Mrs. Melville had replied in a vague sort of tone, and she had hurried off to her club.

"We don't know anyone," said Lou, thinking it over and looking rather surprised. "It seems odd, doesn't it?"

"We don't *want* other people," declared Tonia, raising her head from her book. "I think it would be a frightful bore if we had to go to parties."

Nannie looked at her. Nannie was not particularly clever, but she was sensible enough in her own way, and she felt certain that Tonia's attitude was unnatural. Tonia ought to want friends; she ought to want to go to parties like other girls. It wasn't— healthy, thought Nannie vaguely.

"It would be different if we lived at Ryddelton," said Nannie, thinking aloud. "You'd know everybody, and you'd have lots of friends. There are several nice families with children that live roundabout Ryddelton and have Christmas parties and Halloween parties—ducking for apples and all that. There would be tennis, too," added Nannie. "Tennis in the summer. But of course it's quite different in town. Nobody knows who you are—or cares."

"I wish we lived at Ryddelton," said Lou.

"So do I," agreed Nannie. "But we don't—and not likely to. The only way is to make the best of what you've got. Mrs. Melville knows lots of people and we could have a party. You ask her, Lou," suggested Nannie guilefully.

"It wouldn't be any good asking her," replied Lou with a sigh.

After this conversation Nannie worried more than ever, for she was aware that she would have to leave them soon, and what would happen to them, then? They did not need her as a nurse, for Lou was nearly eighteen, but they did need somebody to look after them and love them. I'll stay on as long as she'll keep me, thought Nannie ("she" was Mrs. Melville, of course), and as a matter of fact, thought Nannie, I'm pretty useful to her. She'd notice a difference if I wasn't here to look after things when she's out. Who'd see to the linen and do all the mending and wash the woollies and handkerchiefs, thought Nannie as she bustled about, doing all these things and a good many other things besides.

Soon after this incident Mrs. Melville was looking about for some way to economize, and her eye fell upon Nannie.

"It's ridiculous," she said to her husband. "The girls don't need Nannie any longer. Lou is eighteen."

"Nannie does quite a lot in the house," replied Mr. Melville.

"We can easily get on without her," said Mrs. Melville firmly. "I can raise Maggie's wages, and she can do the mending and look after the girls."

"Maggie is a bit of a fool," said Mr. Melville dubiously, but he might as well have saved his breath.

"And Miss Fraser can go, too," said Mrs. Melville in a thoughtful voice. "Yes, we shan't need Miss Fraser. We can spend the extra money on classes for the girls. They must learn dancing—and Lou is quite good at music. I shall arrange singing lessons for Lou."

"Tonia is only seventeen—" began Mr. Melville.

"She can have cooking lessons."

"It seems a pity," said Mr. Melville—quite patiently for him.

"Nonsense, Henry, it isn't any use bothering with Tonia. She's hopeless. She can't do anything well. She can't even pass a teacup without spilling it all over the floor, and the more I tell her to be careful the worse she is."

"But, Ella—"

"Besides," said Ella, continuing firmly. "Besides, you said yourself that you wished the girls weren't always poring over books. It will be good for them to go to classes and meet other girls."

Mr. Melville walked off to his club and spent the evening there. It was no use talking to Ella when she had made up her mind, but he was upset about Nannie. Nannie was the one remaining link with Ryddelton: she had been with the family for years, and her mother before her. They were old friends. He would give Nannie an annuity, of course, and she would go home to her mother. He would miss seeing her bustling about the house.

Lou and Tonia sat on the window seat in the nursery and saw Nannie depart. Their eyes were swollen with tears, and Nannie had forbidden them to come downstairs, for she knew that Mrs. Melville would be annoyed. It was Nannie's last injunction to her charges. "You can wave to me from the window," she said in a trembling voice—and hurried away.

"There she is," said Lou hoarsely.

They saw her black sailor hat disappear into the waiting taxi, and a white handkerchief waved wildly from the window as the taxi drove away.

"What are we going to *do*!" wailed Tonia, throwing herself into the old basket chair.

"I'll take care of you," said Lou. "I'll do up your shoes and everything. Don't cry, Tonia."

"You're crying yourself."

"I'm stopping," declared Lou. "It isn't any use…there now, I've stopped."

Lou was quite as fond of Nannie as her sister, but her nature was independent and resilient; besides, she had a plan that had come to her suddenly in the watches of the night. She had realized that when Nannie left she and Tonia would have complete liberty of action. Maggie was easily managed.

"Listen, Tonia," said Lou. "We can do anything we like. What do you want to do? I know what I want. Let's go about and *see* things, Tonia."

"What kind of things?"

"Places we've read about. Oh, I know we can't go far, but we don't need to. There are hundreds of interesting places at our very door."

This was an exaggeration, of course, but not a very serious one, for the stones of Edinburgh are steeped in history and romance. And Lou and Tonia, having read so much and discussed their reading together, were admirably equipped for a historical pilgrimage. At first they were a little frightened of their newfound liberty, but this phase was quickly over, and they spread their wings and wandered far afield.

Their first expedition was to the castle, and here they saw the small room where James the Sixth of Scotland was born and the window from which he was let down in a laundry basket. They visited St. Giles Cathedral—where Jenny Geddes had thrown her cutty stool at the bishop because she disapproved of his sermon. They discovered, among the grim buildings in the Royal Mile, narrow wynds that led to ancient mansions of graceful architecture, once occupied by Scottish nobility but now sadly degenerate. They saw Boswell's Court, where Dr. Johnson stayed, and they were interested in St. John Street, for it was here that James Ballantyne lived—James Ballantyne who printed and published the Waverley Novels. The novels had been written in a certain room in 39 Castle Street. Lou and Tonia stood for a long time gazing at this house with awe and were jostled considerably by the passersby, who had no idea what they were staring at.

They went and looked at Moray House, not far from the Tolbooth; it was strangely modern in architecture, though dating from the seventeenth century. From the balcony at Moray House, Argyll watched Montrose ride past on his way to his death and jeered at his fallen enemy. Perhaps Holyrood Palace was the most interesting of all; it was full of ghosts, some sad and some gay. They saw Queen Mary's small room, where Rizzio was murdered by the barons; they remembered the revels that had taken place in the big ballroom when Prince Charlie had stayed here on his way south.

These were only some of the places they saw and some of the things they remembered during this orgy of romance and history in which they indulged. It was Lou who grew tired of it first and began to look about for something different to do. "Do you remember Liberty Hall?" she asked Tonia in a casual sort of voice.

Tonia had almost forgotten, but not quite, and now the memory of that summer afternoon—so long ago—returned to her, and she saw in a flash the dazzling garden with its waterfalls of gay flowers.

"Why shouldn't we?" said Lou, coaxingly.

"Do you want to?" asked Tonia in some surprise.

"Yes," said Lou firmly. "Yes, I do. I want to go just once, and it wouldn't be doing anything wrong. How could it be wrong? He said we were to come back, didn't he?"

Tonia was sure it was wrong, but if Lou was determined to go it was not much use making objections. "Well, of course, if you want to," said Tonia.

"Maggie says she was divorced," continued Lou in a low voice. "Maggie says that's why Mother——"

"Oh!" exclaimed Tonia, opening her blue eyes very wide.

"Tomorrow," said Lou. "I don't have singing tomorrow, and you don't have cooking. It's a free afternoon."

Tonia had been hoping for another tour of Holyrood, but she gave it up without a murmur, and when tomorrow arrived, the two girls put on their best clothes and sallied forth to call upon Mrs. Halley.

On this occasion the brown door was opened by a maid in a white muslin apron, and Lou inquired a trifle breathlessly if Mrs. Halley were at home.

The garden looked quite different today, and Tonia was unreasonably disappointed (unreasonably because it was February, a month when no garden can be expected to look its best). But the house satisfied her completely, which was saying a good deal, for Tonia had expected the house to be perfect. They were shown into the lounge, a large, long-shaped room, with tall windows and a parquet floor covered with Persian rugs. The walls were cream colored and hung with mirrors that added to the almost dazzling brightness, and there were flowers everywhere, arranged with artistic effect in tall vases. The chairs and the large, comfortable sofa were covered with cretonne, and there were colored cushions—pink and green and brown. Last but not least a log fire burned briskly in the grate, sending long tongues of golden flame leaping up the chimney.

"Lovely," breathed Tonia, looking about her with interest.

"Like *her*," agreed Lou in a whisper.

They were silent after that, and presently Mrs. Halley came in. She looked almost exactly the same, for the years had been kind to her. Tall and slim and dark and perfectly dressed in a close-fitting frock of deep wine color, she could have passed for a woman of forty.

Mrs. Halley was somewhat surprised to find two complete strangers in her lounge, and even more surprised when they greeted her like a long-lost friend. They were extremely pretty girls, however, and Mrs. Halley liked pretty things, so she was quite pleased to see them—and said so.

"Jack said we were to come back," explained Lou. "Of course it's a *long* time, but we couldn't come before."

"It's ages," agreed Mrs. Halley, trying to think who on earth they could be. "It's simply ages. What have you been doing with yourselves?" she added, playing for safety.

"Lessons, mostly," replied Tonia, who had made up her mind to be as conversational as possible and not leave everything to Lou. "But of course we've finished with lessons now. We just have classes."

"And parties, I suppose," said Mrs. Halley, smiling. "Lots of parties. Did you go to the New Club ball the other night?"

"No," replied Lou. "No, we don't—I mean, we don't seem to know many people."

"We shall have to do something about that." Mrs. Halley laughed. "We often have parties."

Lou hesitated and looked at Tonia.

"You *must*," declared Mrs. Halley. "It will be lovely to have you. Jack is home on leave from India and he wants some young people to play about with. I can't think where he is at the moment."

"I'm here," said Jack, walking in through the French

windows. "Do you want me, Mother? I was just having a look at the car—Great Scott, it's the Alices!"

"The Alisons!" repeated Mrs. Halley in perplexed tones.

"The Alices in Wonderland," said Jack. "And they're grown up! Good Lord, how amazing! You called them mice, and they sat on the edge of the pool and ate chocolate cookies—"

"Éclairs," said Tonia.

"Éclairs it was," agreed Jack, shaking hands with them. "What fun this is! You're staying to tea, of course."

"Of course they are," put in Mrs. Halley.

Tea was a very cheerful meal, and everybody enjoyed it. When it was over, Jack suggested that Lou might like to see his den and carried her off in a masterful manner. Both girls were attractive and unusual, but he had admired Lou more than her sister, and he preferred one girl at a time.

"You'll come and talk to me, won't you?" said Mrs. Halley to Tonia. "We'll sit by the fire and have a chat. I like a log fire, don't you?"

"It's lovely," agreed Tonia. "But everything is lovely here."

"You'll come back often, won't you?"

"We'll try," said Tonia doubtfully.

Mrs. Halley laughed. "Don't tell your mother you've been here. She doesn't approve of me. I'm supposed to be a wicked woman, you know."

"I don't think you're wicked," declared Tonia stoutly.

"Not really wicked," agreed Mrs. Halley, laughing again. "Just unfortunate. You see, I married the wrong man. I was eighteen when I married Edmund Skene, and I knew nothing about life."

"Maggie said you were divorced," said Tonia, who, knowing nothing of social conventions, rushed in where angels might have feared to tread.

"Maggie was perfectly right," replied Mrs. Halley. "I don't

know who Maggie is, but she put the whole thing in a nutshell. I suppose you're shocked."

"No," said Tonia thoughtfully. "I may not know very much about it, but I've read *Anna Karenina.*"

"Without Mother's permission, I suppose."

"Oh, yes. At least if Mother had known what it was *about* she wouldn't have let me."

"Mother doesn't read."

"She plays bridge," explained Tonia.

Mrs. Halley nodded understandingly.

There was a short silence, and then Tonia said, "Anna had a dreadful time, didn't she?"

"I was a good deal more fortunate," replied Mrs. Halley, who felt that if Antonia Melville had the run of Tolstoy, there was little need to beat about the bush. "My husband wasn't an ogre. In fact, he was a very good, kind creature and he knew I couldn't help falling in love with Philip. He divorced me, and Philip and I were married. We were very happy indeed. Then poor old Edmund died and Jack came to live with us, which made it all quite perfect. Jack is my son by my first marriage."

Tonia had followed all this very carefully. She sighed and said, "I wish Mother knew you. If Mother knew you, she wouldn't mind us coming here."

"Oh, but she does know me," declared Mrs. Halley, smiling. "That's the whole trouble, really. Ella and I were at school together and hated each other like poison. I could have married Tiddles Melville if I had wanted, but instead I married Edmund, and—"

"Tiddles?"

"Your father," said Mrs. Halley, laughing heartily. "We always called him Tiddles. It's *very* naughty of me to tell you all this, but it's such fun—and really Ella deserves it. Ella ought to look after you properly. If I had two pretty daughters I would give up bridge and take them to dances. What fun it would be!"

Tonia was inclined to agree. She was fascinated by Mrs. Halley.

Lou and Tonia had a lot to talk about as they walked home together.

"Jack's name is really Skene," said Lou eagerly. "He's a captain in the Indian Army. He was telling me all about India, and he showed me photographs of his bungalow."

"Mrs. Halley used to know Father," returned Tonia with a chuckle. "She called him Tiddles. Isn't it extraordinary?"

"Extraordinary," agreed Lou. "I can't imagine Father *young*, can you?"

Chapter Five
Beautiful, Brilliant Lou

"Tonia, I want to tell you something!"

Tonia came back slowly from her dreams and pronounced herself awake and ready to listen, for she could tell by Lou's voice that it was extremely important. They were in bed; it was the place where their most intimate confidences were exchanged, for the two beds were so conveniently placed that if Lou lay upon her right side and Tonia upon her left their heads were very close together.

"Listen, Tonia," said Lou—quite unnecessarily, of course, for by this time Tonia was listening most intently. "Listen, Tonia, I've been there again—at Mrs. Halley's. I've been there several times."

"Lou! How?" asked Tonia in amazement, for she knew the hours of Lou's classes, which fitted in like pieces in a jigsaw puzzle.

"On my way back from singing. If I leave the class early and take a tram, I can go there quite easily. And why shouldn't I?" said Lou defiantly. "Why shouldn't I go and see my friends? They like me. I feel quite different when I go there—they *like* me, Tonia."

"But, Lou…"

"Mother doesn't do anything," continued Lou in an earnest

whisper. "I'm eighteen now, and I ought to be going to dances. *They* are having a dance tomorrow night, and they have asked me to go."

"Lou darling…" began Tonia, and then she stopped, for she did not know how to go on. It was all true, of course. Lou was grown up. Lou ought to be going about and enjoying herself, going to dances like other girls. Beautiful, brilliant Lou.

"I wish you could come too," said Lou with a sigh.

"But you can't go!" exclaimed Tonia. "Mother wouldn't let you—not *there*. Mother wouldn't *hear* of it."

"She won't," said Lou grimly.

"But, Lou…"

"Listen, Tonia, I *must* go. I want to go most frightfully. Jack will fetch me and bring me back in his car. Nobody will know."

Tonia was silent. She was appalled, for, unlike Lou, she was not of an adventurous disposition. She could not imagine wanting a thing so much that she would be willing—nay, eager—to take such risks to obtain it. And it *was* risky. Tonia envisaged a thousand calamities; she was shaking all over at the mere idea.

"Don't, darling," said Lou, stroking her arm. "Don't worry about it. Everything will be perfectly all right. And even if something went wrong and they found out, they couldn't do anything to me. It isn't fair," said Lou, vehemently. "It isn't fair to keep me at home and never take me anywhere. Other girls go to dances and have a good time—"

"Mrs. Halley said that."

"Yes, she did, and why shouldn't she say it when it's perfectly true?"

"I don't like it."

"But you'll help," said Lou confidently.

Of course Tonia would help. She would have died for Lou quite happily, and, when she saw Lou dressed for the dance in the pale pink frock, which Maggie had altered for her, she was bound to admit that Lou was really and truly grown up and ready for the fray.

"Darling, you're beautiful," she declared, kissing Lou very carefully so that she would not disarrange her golden curls. "There won't be anybody there as beautiful as you."

Lou slipped out of the house at ten o'clock (while her parents were listening to the wireless), and she was back at four. Her plans had been well laid, and she had carried them out successfully. Of course Tonia had not slept a wink. She had died a thousand deaths in six hours, but her fears and anxieties were all forgotten at the sight of Lou, and they hugged each other ecstatically.

"Oh, Tonia, it was marvelous!" declared Lou in an excited whisper. "Oh, how I wish you could have been there! I danced and danced. Jack dances beautifully. He introduced some of his friends to me. We went out into the garden between the dances. It was quite warm, and the moon was shining, and the garden was full of flowers. They had put out the swing seat; you remember the swing seat with the striped awning? I thought of the first time we went there—two little mice! Jack remembered it, too. He said we were the sweetest things he had ever seen."

"Mrs. Halley?" whispered Tonia.

"She looked lovely," replied Lou. "Black velvet and diamonds. Jack said, 'Mother is prettier than any of the girls—except one.'"

"He meant you."

"I expect so," said Lou, smiling.

"What else?" asked Tonia.

"They had cleared the lounge, of course. The floor was splendid. There was champagne for supper…and cold ham and tongue and salad and ices… Jack said…" She hesitated and then went on, "Jack wants me to go to tea tomorrow—it's today, really—and I can manage it if I miss my singing. Mrs. Halley wants you to come, too."

It was easy enough for Tonia to go to the tea party, for she did not have singing lessons; she had cooking classes instead, and nobody seemed to mind if you slipped out before the end. Mrs. Halley was waiting for her in the garden and greeted her very cordially, putting her arm through Tonia's and leading her to the swing seat.

"I wanted to see you particularly," declared Mrs. Halley. "I wanted to talk to you. I suppose you know what's happened?"

"What's happened!" repeated Tonia in alarm.

"A very natural thing, my dear. Those two have fallen in love with each other...yes, Jack and Lou."

Tonia gazed at her, wide eyed.

"I've seen it coming," continued Mrs. Halley. "As a matter of fact, Jack fell in love with Lou the first time he saw her, only of course she was too young. But she isn't too young now. She knows her own mind, does Lou, and I think all the better of her. I'm delighted, of course," said Mrs. Halley, nodding. "I love Lou. Who could help it? She's young and beautiful and gay and she's made of the right stuff...and Jack is a dear (why shouldn't I say it?). Jack will make her a very good husband."

"But, Mrs. Halley—"

"I know. That's the trouble. That's why I wanted to see you. What about the parents?"

"It's—they'll be—furious," said Tonia in a dazed voice.

"We've got to think," said Mrs. Halley seriously. "We must manage it somehow, you and I. What are we to do?"

Tonia did not know what they could do; the thing seemed hopeless, but Mrs. Halley was determined that somehow or other the course of love must be smoothed. Jack and Lou loved each other and nothing else mattered. She herself had given up a good deal for love's sake and had never regretted it—never once in twenty years.

"I wish I were respectable," said Mrs. Halley with a smile and a sigh. "I've never minded until now whether people wanted to know me or not. I've had a good time and enjoyed myself and I've made Philip happy."

Lou was as sweet as ever and even more beautiful, but she drifted away from Tonia; they were not quite so close together now. There was another interest in Lou's life. Lou was in love. She talked about Jack incessantly and Tonia listened. Tonia was a little puzzled about it, because, although she liked Jack very much, she could not see him as Lou saw him. He was friendly and kind, but he was not particularly good-looking; he was not the paragon that Lou imagined him. Sometimes Lou was as happy as a bird, and sometimes she would sit and dream with shadows in her eyes.

"Tell me what to do," she would say, seizing Tonia's hand. "I've never been frightened before, but I'm frightened now. I can't let Jack go back to India without me. I shall die if I can't marry Jack. Honestly, Tonia, I shall die."

Tonia believed her.

"Jack wants to speak to Father," continued Lou. "He wants to be properly engaged, but I'm too afraid. I don't mind a row, but if they stopped us seeing each other—"

"They would," said Tonia with conviction.

"It's so *silly*," declared Lou. "It's like *Romeo and Juliet*. Just because they don't like Mrs. Halley—"

"When you're twenty-one—" began Tonia, who had taken the trouble to look up the law of the land in her father's encyclopedia.

"But we can't wait all that time!" cried Lou, aghast.

There seemed no solution to the problem. Tonia considered

it in all its aspects and indulged in a good deal of wishful thinking. She envisaged Jack rescuing Lou from a burning house—their own house, of course. The crowd cheered as Jack staggered out, bearing the unconscious form of Lou over his broad shoulders. Mother was in tears, and Father strode forward and cried, "My boy, you have saved her life! How can I reward you?" Sometimes it was Mr. Melville himself who was in peril and was rescued by Jack. He fell into Duddingston Loch and was almost drowned, but Jack, who happened to be passing, rushed to his aid and brought him safely to shore. Mr. Melville was saved from runaway horses, as well, and from railway accidents. He had no idea of it, of course; to him life seemed much as usual. He noticed, once or twice, that his younger daughter was staring at him with a strangely intent gaze, but Tonia was always dreaming.

August came and Jack's leave was nearly over, but oddly enough Lou seemed more cheerful. "It can't be helped," she said, when Tonia tried to question her.

"It can't be helped!" repeated Tonia. "Whatever do you mean?"

"I've tried to talk to Mother," replied Lou. "I asked her about Mrs. Halley, and she simply went off the deep end." This was one of Jack's expressions, of course.

"I mean, what are you going to *do*?" Tonia inquired.

"What can we do?" asked Lou.

"I wish I could think of something."

"Don't worry, darling," said Lou, taking up her music case, which looked oddly bulky. "Don't worry at all. Just give me a big hug."

"You'll be back to tea," said Tonia, but Lou had gone.

Tonia thought about this conversation all the afternoon. It was unsatisfactory, and there was something odd about it. It wasn't like Lou to take things lying down, to accept the fact that she couldn't have what she wanted without making a proper fight for it...and why had she said not to worry? Of course Tonia was worrying.

When teatime came Tonia took up her position on the window seat to watch for Lou's return (she was determined to get to the bottom of the mystery, for that was what it was), and while she was still watching a car drove up to the door and Mrs. Halley got out and came up the steps and vanished into the house.

Mrs. Halley! What had *she* come for? Why had Mrs. Halley come *here?* Tonia hesitated for a moment and then ran out onto the landing and leaned over the banisters. She saw Mrs. Halley come up the stairs (escorted by Maggie) and disappear into the drawing room. There was silence. She was talking to Mother and Father. Now—they were both at home—what could she be saying?

Tonia was shaking all over. She felt so ill that she went back into the nursery and sat down in the basket chair. Lou had gone. She knew it as surely as if Lou had told her the whole thing. Lou had not told her because she did not want to implicate Tonia in the trouble that would ensue... What an appalling row there would be! Lou had gone. Perhaps she was married now; perhaps she was already on her way to London...with Jack. Tonia leaned back, her head against the cushion; the world seemed to crash about her ears.

∽✦∼

Meantime Mrs. Halley was enjoying herself in the drawing room. She was full of righteous wrath, and having decided that it was her duty to vent it upon the Melvilles she did not mince her words. She was in the enviable position of having nothing to lose, for Ella was her enemy already and Tiddles had never counted for much. The sound and fury of Tiddles signified practically nothing. She had discovered this interesting fact thirty years ago. Mrs. Halley informed her hearers that Jack and Lou had been married that afternoon and were on their way to London. Mr. Melville could go after them if he liked (she did not call him Tiddles). He could go after them and make a scene and have the marriage annulled. Lou was underage, so of course she had no right to be married without the consent of her parents. Mrs. Halley knew that, but it had not worried her in the least. She had helped them—aided and abetted was the term. She had helped to arrange the whole thing and would do the same thing again, for she was on the side of youth and love and romance. She had always been a rebel and gloried in the fact.

The Melvilles were so stricken that they found very little to say, and, drawing a long breath, Mrs. Halley continued. She told them they were stodgy and old-fashioned and selfish. They had neglected the girls, and they were lucky that nothing worse had happened. She told them this several times in slightly different language so that there should be no mistake about it. She finished by repeating that Mr. Melville could take any action he liked—he could go after his daughter and bring her home. It would be a juicy piece of scandal and lots of people would enjoy it. She didn't care what Mr. Melville did. Not a scrap. Why should she? She wasn't respectable, thank heaven.

Having said her say Mrs. Halley departed, leaving behind her a faint scent of violets.

Mr. and Mrs. Melville were speechless for a few moments. Mrs. Melville because she was so furiously angry and Mr. Melville because he could not help realizing that there was some truth in what had been said…and this was partly due to the fact that it was Wanda who had said it. He had always admired Wanda, and she was still a beautiful woman…and no less beautiful when she was angry and her fine eyes were flashing fire. He recovered from his daze to hear his wife's voice.

"That woman!" cried Mrs. Melville. "I would rather Lou had married the butcher's boy—"

"Why didn't you arrange a marriage with the butcher's boy?"

"It's no use talking like that. We must *do* something—"

"What can we do?"

"You stood there like a dummy. Why didn't you say something?"

"For the same reason that you said nothing, I suppose."

"That woman!" repeated Mrs. Melville. "She was at the bottom of it. She arranged the whole thing."

Mr. Melville was walking up and down the room.

"You'll make me scream," declared his wife. "Can't you think of something to do instead of prowling about like that?"

"No, I can't," he replied. "There isn't anything to do. It would make the most frightful stink if we *tried* to do anything. If you take my advice, you'll make the best of it."

"Make the best of it!"

"The girl is married. I suppose we ought to be thankful for that."

This silenced Mrs. Melville for a few moments, and her thoughts took a different trend. "The deceitfulness of it!" she said at last. "Where can Lou have met him? She never said a word about it—not a word... Tonia will know, of course," added Mrs. Melville, rising from the sofa. "Tonia must have been in it from the beginning."

Chapter Six
Lonely Days

It seemed strangely quiet when Tonia drifted back into consciousness, when the roaring rushing sound inside her head had died away. She found herself looking at the ceiling. It was the ceiling of her bedroom with the curiously shaped stain in the middle, which Lou had likened to the man in the moon. Tonia turned her head and looked toward Lou's bed. It was empty…everything came back to her with a rush.

A voice said, "She's coming around." It was Dr. Malcolm's voice.

"Am I ill?" she asked faintly.

"Not very," replied Dr. Malcolm reassuringly, and his kind, rugged face suddenly appeared above her head.

"Why have you come?" Tonia wanted to know.

"You fainted, that's all," he replied. "Your mother was a little worried, but you'll be perfectly all right soon. Just lie still and take your time," added Dr. Malcolm, patting her shoulder.

There was movement in the room. Mother's voice said, "You're sure it's nothing. She looked so dreadful…"

The voices moved away—out onto the landing, but they were still audible to Tonia's sharp ears.

"Light diet and complete rest," Dr. Malcolm was saying. "I'll look in tomorrow if you like, but it's not really necessary."

"Please do," said Mother's voice.

"She mustn't be worried, of course."

"No, of course not," said Mother. "But I just wanted to ask her…you see she and Lou…I mean, she must have known… such a shock to us…"

"Can't allow it," declared Dr. Malcolm. The voices were very faint now, for their owners were going downstairs. "Not now… We'll see in a day or two… No questions at all…"

Tonia lay in bed, and Mother and Maggie looked after her. Mother was very kind and attentive, which was difficult to understand, for Tonia had expected Mother to be angry. In a way Mother had every right to be angry, thought Tonia, watching the shadows move slowly across the ceiling. Mother was rather pathetic, really. She brought Tonia books to read—*The Daisy Chain* and *The Wide, Wide World*—and Tonia pretended to read them while Mother was in the room, but when Mother had gone she put them down and lay quite still and thought about all that had happened and tried to imagine where Lou was *now* and what she was doing.

The fact was Mrs. Melville had received a double shock, for she had no sooner heard from Wanda Halley that she had lost one daughter than she had gone upstairs and found her other daughter in a state of collapse. Tonia was lying in the basket chair looking exactly like death; it was some moments before Mrs. Melville was able to assure herself that the child was still breathing. Mrs. Melville was shaken to the core; her complacency was shattered—though only temporarily.

Presently Tonia rose from her bed and began to go about as usual, but she still felt rather queer. She felt as if she had lost part of herself—an arm or a leg or a piece of her heart. She had depended on Lou for everything, and Lou had gone and there was no savor in life. The days went by, dim and gray. If the sun shone Tonia did not notice it.

Jack and Lou had sailed to India, and from India letters began to arrive. Lou was happy. She was having a marvelous time: there were dances and picnics, and she had learned to ride. The station was full of young people, and they were all nice to Lou. It was difficult to write back to Lou in the same strain, for nothing seemed to happen to Tonia (each day was as dull as the one before), but somehow or other, letters were written and dispatched—loving, cheerful letters.

Tonia's only other correspondent was Nannie, who wrote to her at long intervals and gave very little news. Nannie was getting old now and was finding it difficult to carry on. "If I could get a girl to help me," wrote Nannie. "But I cannot afford a girl. It is just not easy to make ends meet sometimes." Tonia could read a good deal between the lines of this carefully phrased epistle, for she knew Nannie to be addicted to understatement, so if Nannie said it was not easy to make ends meet she must be having a bad time. Fortunately Tonia had some money in the Post Office Savings Bank—it was money that had been given to her from time to time and that she had been made to save. The interest had accumulated, and Tonia discovered to her amazement that she possessed nearly two hundred pounds. It was her own money, of course, so she could do what she liked with it, but all the same she felt a trifle guilty as she penned the withdrawal slip, for she was aware that her parents would make all sorts of objections if they knew of her intention. But I don't care, thought Tonia, signing with a firm hand and remembering as she did so a hundred and one things that Nannie had done for her, remembering Nannie's patience when she could not tie her shoes and how Nannie had sat up with her when she was ill.

The money was to be paid in pound notes (all of it, for this would save Nannie a lot of bother), and when Tonia received it, she packed the notes into a chocolate box and dispatched it by registered post. She was very happy now—happier than she had felt for months—and her only regret was that she would not see Nannie's face when the chocolate box was opened.

Nannie's letter arrived a few days later and was so grateful and loving and so incoherent (owing to the shock its writer had received) that Tonia shed tears upon it and carried it about with her for days until it fell to pieces and had to be burned.

"I am wanting to see you so much," Nannie had written. "Maybe I could tell you a bit of what I feel. I never was much of a hand at letter writing. Would Mrs. Melville let you come and stay with me for a week or two? It would be a nice change and it must be dull without Lou and I would give you old Miss Melville's room that looks out on to the garden at the back and gets the morning sun. I would be so pleased to have you, dear, but you know that."

Tonia considered the matter. It would be nice to see Nannie again, but was it worth the bother? Mother would be sure to make a fuss—and how Tonia hated fusses! All Tonia wanted was to be left in peace. She decided not to go.

Once Tonia had recovered from her indisposition and Mrs. Melville had recovered from her shock, the relations between them disimproved. Mrs. Melville decided that Tonia was "grown up" now; she must go about, she must come down to the drawing room and take her proper place in the house, but Tonia was a most unsatisfactory sort of daughter; she was silent and dreamy and had no talent for conversation. She disliked shopping and tea parties and escaped from social activities whenever she could. The old nursery was Tonia's refuge; she would sit there for hours, reading or dreaming or thinking about Lou. Sometimes Mrs. Melville would send Maggie to fetch her, not because she enjoyed Tonia's company, but because it was the right thing for Tonia to be there when visitors came to tea, and

Tonia would brush her hair and wash her hands and come down to the drawing room, obedient to her mother's command.

"I don't know what to do with her," complained Mrs. Melville to her husband. "She isn't like other girls, somehow. Lydia says *her* girls enjoy going out with her in the car and shopping and that sort of thing. Lydia's girls have plenty to say for themselves. They're amusing and bright. I wish to goodness Tonia were not so sulky."

"She isn't sulky," replied Mr. Melville.

"Well, silent, then," said Mrs. Melville. "I never know what she's thinking about."

"It's because you never bothered with them when they were young. They were always in the nursery. I told you at the time you were making a mistake, but you wouldn't listen. You're paying for it now."

"It isn't that, at all."

"What is it, then?"

"Tonia is…*queer*," declared Mrs. Melville.

"Nonsense!"

"It isn't nonsense. There really is something queer about her. Sometimes she behaves as if she weren't all there. She looks absolutely blank."

"She's dreamy."

"It's more than that. She must take it from the Melvilles, of course. We were all perfectly normal."

Mr. Melville rose in his wrath. "She's as normal as you are!" he retorted in violent tones. "In fact, she's a damn sight more normal. *She* isn't crazy about bridge. And let me tell you that my family…" and he proceeded to tell her (in detail and at length) of the excellences of the Melville connection.

It was a first-class row and Mr. and Mrs. Melville both enjoyed it, for the odd thing was that they really *did* enjoy a good row. They were fond of each other in their own way—a peculiar way, perhaps: they depended upon each other's loyalty, and if a third party had entered the lists they would have combined forces immediately and fought for each other tooth and nail, but when they were alone, or when nobody but Tonia was present, they enlivened their existence by quarreling incessantly. Fortunately, although both of them possessed hasty tempers and unruly tongues, neither of them was sensitive, nor sulky, so however fiercely they went for each other they soon came around and resumed their normal relationship and forgot all the hard things that had been said in the heat of battle.

Having failed to turn her daughter into a social success, Mrs. Melville gave up the attempt and returned to her bridge. She was out nearly every afternoon, and it became the usual thing for Tonia to be waiting for her father when he came in from the office after his day's work and for them to have tea together by the fire. She got on quite well with her father, for she took care not to irritate him, and he neither desired nor expected her to talk.

One day Mr. Melville brought a friend home to tea, a tall, good-looking man with gray hair. He was introduced to Tonia as "Mr. Norman" and he smiled at her kindly as he shook her by the hand. Apart from the conventional greeting he took very little notice of her, for he had come to talk business and he was pressed for time. Tonia poured out the tea and listened to the talk of stocks and shares and did not understand a word of it, but although the actual business was beyond her she realized quite soon that Mr. Norman was an important person. Father was slightly in awe of Mr. Norman and anxious to make a good impression upon him—anxious, also, to obtain his advice—it was rather odd to see father playing second fiddle.

"Very sound," said Mr. Melville when his guest had gone. "Norman knows the ropes. I got a lot of useful information out of him, and you behaved very sensibly, Tonia. Thank heaven you aren't a chatterbox!"

It was a new experience to be commended for silence, and, what was even more surprising, she had evidently gained credit from Mr. Norman, as well, for the next day she received a note from him enclosing four tickets for the New Club Ball, which was to take place shortly at the Assembly Rooms. The note was short and to the point and had evidently been dashed off in a hurry.

To make up for a dull afternoon—R. K. Norman.

"I can't go, of course," said Tonia with conviction.

"You can't go!" exclaimed Mr. Melville. "Of course you can go. Norman would think it very odd if you didn't go. It's dashed good of him to send you the tickets."

"We'll all go," declared Mrs. Melville. "I haven't danced for years, and the New Club is always a good ball. Perhaps Frank would like to make up the party. I'll ring him up."

"I don't want to go," said Tonia in agonized tones, for the prospect of meeting so many strangers, of dancing with them and trying to talk to them filled her with dismay.

"Nonsense," replied Mr. Melville. "You'll enjoy it. I'll stand you a new dress."

Chapter Seven
The Ball

"Such a lovely frock!" exclaimed Maggie, slipping the white net ball gown over Tonia's head. "You suit it, too."

"Do you think so?" asked Tonia. She was looking at herself in the pier glass and she was not particularly pleased with what she saw. Mother had chosen the dress and had insisted on white.

"It's a pity you're so pale and thin," said Maggie. "You don't eat enough, that's what. Maybe you'll look better when you've had a good dinner."

Tonia laughed mirthlessly.

"Now then," said Maggie, trying to be encouraging. "It's no use taking on about it. There's plenty of girls would give their eyes for a figure like you. It's fashionable."

"I look like a ghost."

"Not you. Maybe your arms are a bit skinny...and your neck. Will you wear your pink scarf?"

Tonia did not care what she wore, so to please Maggie she took the pink gauze scarf and wound it around her neck.

"Not like that," said Maggie. "I'll show you...that's a lot better. It gives you a bit of color."

"I wish I could go to bed instead," declared Tonia with a sigh.

"Nonsense," replied Maggie. "It'll be lovely, you'll see. I wish I was going in that lovely frock and everything. Just you make up your mind you're going to enjoy yourself, Miss Tonia. Remember what a fine time Miss Lou had at that dance she went to."

Tonia had been thinking of it before Maggie spoke. She had been thinking of Lou's appetite for adventure. If Lou had been here to go with her and sustain her, she would not have been so frightened.

Frank Melville was the fourth member of the party. He was a distant cousin and Tonia had only met him once before. She did her best to talk to him at dinner but it was difficult going, for they seemed to have nothing in common. She felt sure that Frank already regretted his acceptance of the invitation and was wondering how often he would have to dance with her.

The taxi was late in coming, and when the Melville party arrived the Assembly Rooms were already crowded. Tonia was dazed by the noise of talk and laughter; she clung to her mother's hand as they pushed their way through the throng. The principal room was enormous to Tonia's eyes. It was high and brilliantly lighted and divided in two by a thick red rope. The band was playing a fox-trot, and the floor was full of couples.

"We're late," said Mrs. Melville crossly. "I can't see Frank anywhere. Wait here and I'll try to find somebody for you to dance with."

Tonia was almost sick with fright. She stood in the doorway, but just at that moment the dance ended and she was swept into the vestibule by the crowd of dancers who were looking for seats outside. She found a corner and stood there, watching the people and listening to the snatches of conversation. "Not one left, my dear. You're much too late..." "No, I haven't seen her since we arrived..." "Sonia, how marvelous!" "I've been looking everywhere for you..." "What a crush..." "May I introduce..." "It's no use; she's sure to be booked up..." "Yes, isn't he appalling..." "Oh, I beg your pardon..." "Over near the band, in blue, with a rose in her hair…" "The last extra if you're going to be here…" "She's sweet, isn't she?" "Who told you that?" "Haven't you got one left…" "She wore it last year…"

Tonia's heart had ceased to thump uncomfortably, for she had discovered that she was invisible. Nobody saw her, nobody made the slightest attempt to speak to her, and it was evident that nobody was going to ask her to dance. This being so, she plucked up courage and was able to look about. The floor was covered with red carpets, and there were flowers and palms and mirrors, and among these glories the throng of black-clad men and girls in gaily colored frocks moved backward and forward in a constant stream. The girls interested her more than the men. They were nearly all pretty, but not one of them was as pretty as Lou.

Presently she heard the strains of another band and discovered that it was playing in the music hall and that more people were dancing there. The light was not so glaring in the music hall, and the whole place was decorated to resemble a Malayan village. It was hung with scenery depicting mountains and forests and blue sky, and there were grass huts around the edge of the dancing floor with seats in them. Tonia was quite happy now—if only Lou had been there she would have been completely happy—she sat down on one of the seats, leaning forward with one elbow on her knee and her cheek against her hand. It was like a play, thought Tonia, watching enthralled as the couples passed her talking gaily and suddenly, on reaching the dancing floor, melted together and swam off into a waltz.

She was so intent, so eager to see everything that happened, that she did not notice someone had stopped and was standing beside her and looking down, and as she had made up her mind that she was invisible she was considerably startled when she was addressed by name.

"Miss Melville," said a voice.

She raised her eyes and found that it was Mr. Norman.

"Oh!" exclaimed Tonia in surprise and alarm.

Mr. Norman looked a trifle taken aback; perhaps he had expected a warmer greeting since it was by his invitation Miss Melville was here. He was not to know that he had rent Miss Melville's comforting illusion that she was wearing an invisible cloak. He was silent for a moment, looking at her, and then he decided to persevere. "Tired of dancing?" he inquired with a kind smile.

Tonia shook her head. "I don't know anyone, that's all."

"Great Scott! Where is the rest of your party?"

"I don't know. It doesn't matter. I'd rather watch, really."

"It's amusing to watch," he agreed, sitting down beside her.

Tonia would much rather have watched alone, but she remembered that he had sent her the tickets, so she smiled at him. He looked very distinguished in his full evening dress with a white carnation in his buttonhole, and Tonia decided that even if she had not known he was "important" she would have guessed it at once from his appearance.

"You watch a good deal, don't you?" Mr. Norman said. "You're an onlooker and you see most of the game. This is a queer game, isn't it—a queer artificial way of enjoyment."

"It's artificial, of course," agreed Tonia, discovering to her surprise that she could talk to him quite easily. "It's artificial, but there's a great deal of tradition and history behind it."

"Why, of course there is! People have always danced since David danced before the Ark of the Lord...but you weren't thinking of that."

"I was thinking of Waterloo," admitted Tonia.

"You were! That's odd. I was thinking of it too. They danced while the enemy was approaching, didn't they?"

"Do you mean—"

"Yes." Mr. Norman nodded. "We're dancing and Germany

is making guns. But this is neither the time nor the place to talk of guns. What else were you thinking about?"

"Lou," replied Tonia. "She's my sister. She's married, you know, and I miss her terribly. If she were here it would be *quite* perfect. Everything is more fun with Lou."

"There are people like that—people who bring out the colors of life."

"Oh *yes!*" cried Tonia. "Yes, Lou's like that."

They looked at each other gravely.

"My mother was like that," said Mr. Norman. "Perhaps you think I'm too old to have a mother, but she was only eighteen years older than I. She didn't seem old because she understood things so well. She believed in me."

"Like Lou," breathed Tonia. "Lou never thinks I'm silly."

"Are you silly?" inquired Mr. Norman smiling.

"I do silly things."

"We all do."

"Yes, sometimes, perhaps, but not all the time like me."

There had been an interval during their conversation, but now the band began to play "The Blue Danube," and the floor was suddenly full of dancers.

"Shall we dance?" asked Mr. Norman. "I'm an old-fashioned sort of person, but I can waltz quite passably and I love this tune."

Tonia loved it too. She rose at once and the next moment he had swept her onto the floor. She had never danced with a man before, only with other girls at the dancing class, so dancing with Mr. Norman was a revelation to her. She felt like thistledown in his strong capable arms. He danced beautifully in a conventional, dignified manner and was able to suit his step to his inexperienced partner, so they got on very well indeed. Tonia's color rose and her eyes sparkled and she began to realize the enchantment of rhythm and synchronized movement—no wonder everybody looked so happy and gay. The band played splendidly and the swish…swish…swish of the dancers' feet provided an exciting accompaniment to the tune. When the dance came to an end, Tonia was eager for more and she clapped as heartily as anybody.

"There's a young fellow over there," said Mr. Norman as he slipped his arm around Tonia's waist and prepared to resume the dance. "I think he's looking at you. Is he one of your party?"

"It's Frank," replied Tonia. "Oh dear, I believe this is the one he said he would dance with me. Perhaps we had better stop," she added, her step faltering a little as she spoke.

Mr. Norman took no notice except to hold her more firmly.

"Doesn't it matter?" she asked.

"Not in the least," replied her partner. "The young man needs a lesson, I fancy."

Tonia had no idea what he meant by this enigmatic statement.

By the time the waltz was over Frank had disappeared, so Mr. Norman took her downstairs to the supper room and they sat down at a table in the corner. Mr. Norman seemed to know a good many people (he smiled and bowed to them but did not speak), and he seemed to know the waiters, too, for he obtained instant attention. It's because he's nice, thought Tonia as she listened to him talking to the waiter and ordering the food, and she contrasted his behavior with that of a very bombastic young man at the next table.

Tonia ate lobster and drank champagne, but Mr. Norman contented himself with a glass of beer and some crackers, explaining apologetically that this fare was more suited to his age and constitution.

"I can eat anything," Tonia replied.

"But you can't *drink* anything," said Mr. Norman, smiling at her and removing her glass. "It's extremely interfering of me, I know, but unless you have a fairly strong head I would advise you to confine yourself to two glasses of champagne."

"Oh!" exclaimed Tonia in surprise. "Yes, it's true. I feel a little funny already. What a good thing you thought about that, wasn't it?"

She felt slightly elated; the lights seemed more brilliant, the noise of chatter and laughter seemed to have grown in volume, and it was all tremendous fun. Even the sight of Frank, making his way toward them across the room, had no power to disturb her.

"You cut out my dance," said Frank, pausing by the table. "I couldn't find you anywhere."

"I forgot all about it," replied Tonia, smiling happily.

"You forgot!"

"Yes," said Tonia, nodding.

Frank Melville was not used to being forgotten. He looked at his cousin in surprise. He had thought her dull and uninteresting and rather plain, but he was forced to change his mind about her. "Oh, I see," said Frank in a doubtful sort of voice. "Oh well, it doesn't matter. I just came to tell you that your mother is looking for you."

"Is she?" said Tonia, unperturbed.

"She wants you to come," urged Frank.

"Well, you might just tell her I'm having supper with Mr. Norman," said Tonia, nodding at him kindly.

Frank hesitated for a moment and then departed to carry out her behest.

"That's the way to treat him," declared Mr. Norman, chuckling delightedly. "I said he needed a lesson, didn't I?"

They spent a long time over their supper and nobody disturbed them. Mr. Norman was a keen historian and was particularly interested in the history of Edinburgh. He found to his amazement that Tonia knew almost as much about the subject as he did and had visited various ancient houses that had now degenerated into appalling slums.

"Who took you to Michael Scott's house?" asked Mr. Norman, looking at her with his piercing blue eyes.

"Nobody," replied Tonia. "Lou and I went together. It was awfully dirty, of course, but the people were very nice to us."

"Don't go there again," said Mr. Norman.

Tonia looked at him in surprise. The conversation had re-aroused her interest in Edinburgh's history, and she had just that moment decided to make another visit to the place.

They danced once more when they had finished their supper, and then Mrs. Melville managed to find her daughter and dragged her away. Mrs. Melville was tired and cross, for she was not used to dancing and the evening had not come up to her expectations.

Mr. Melville had passed the time more pleasantly; he had made contact with an old flame who was still very attractive, and he had seen Tonia dancing with Norman and looking gay and pretty. "It was a splendid show," declared Mr. Melville with complacency as he climbed into the taxi and sat down beside his wife. "They did us well, didn't they? I saw you enjoying yourself, Tonia."

"It was lovely," Tonia said.

"I've been looking for you for hours," said Mrs. Melville. "Do you know it's nearly four o'clock?"

"I was dancing with Mr. Norman," replied Tonia. "He's nice, isn't he? He asked me to go to tea with him tomorrow. He has a collection of old glass bottles, and he said he would show them to me."

"What an extraordinary idea!" Mrs. Melville exclaimed.

"There's nothing extraordinary about it," retorted Mr. Melville. "Why shouldn't Tonia go to tea with him? I saw her dancing with him, and they seemed to be..."

"That's quite different from going to his house."

"Nonsense. It will do Tonia good to go out a bit."

"I don't prevent her going out."

"Well, don't prevent her, then," returned Mr. Melville tartly. "Norman is a very good fellow and useful to know. His sister lives with him—if that's any comfort to you. See that Tonia has something decent to wear."

Chapter Eight
Across the Dean Bridge

"I hope to goodness you'll behave yourself properly," said Mrs. Melville as she saw her daughter ready to go to the tea party. "Don't sit and dream and forget to talk, and don't spill your tea—you're so dreadfully clumsy—and, whatever you do, don't stay too long."

"How long?" asked Tonia meekly.

"You had better be home by half past five, but come away earlier if you see them getting bored…Oh dear, I'm not sure that hat suits you after all!"

"Shall I change it?"

"No, the green one is worse. I don't know why we can't find a hat to suit you. It's your hair, or something."

Tonia could not change her hair, so she sighed heavily and started off. She had been looking forward to seeing Mr. Norman again, but now she wished with all her heart that she had refused his invitation. As she walked down the street and across the Dean Bridge—where as usual a stiff breeze was playing tricks with the hats of the passersby—Tonia tried to think of things to say, but she could think of nothing that would not sound trite or absurd. Her hat was new. It had been purchased that morning, and Tonia had not liked it from the first. It was a different shape from her other hats and did not suit her at all, and it was tight and uncomfortable to wear. By the time she reached Mr. Norman's house she was so wretched, and so alarmed at the ordeal confronting her, that she hesitated upon the doorstep and contemplated flight. I could ring up and say I was ill, thought Tonia.

At this moment the door opened and a lady came out. She was "quite old" in Tonia's estimation, but she was extremely good-looking and smartly dressed.

"Oh!" she exclaimed, looking at Tonia in surprise. "Oh, are you…"

"Antonia Melville," said Tonia faintly.

"Goodness, you look about sixteen! I thought—but do come in. My brother is expecting you." She turned into the house and called out, "Robert, here's Miss Melville! I shall have to fly—"

Almost immediately Mr. Norman appeared from a doorway on the right of the hall, and Tonia was so thankful to see him that she ran forward holding out her hand.

He took her hand and drew her into the room. "This is delightful," he declared.

"But I didn't say good-bye to—to the lady," said Tonia, hanging back.

"She's in a hurry," replied Mr. Norman, smiling. "My sister, Janet, is usually in a hurry. She hasn't much idea of time."

The room was a perfect example of a bachelor's den; it was paneled and hung with sporting prints and furnished with large leather-covered chairs. There was a nice warm fire and a tea table in front of it.

"Do you like it?" inquired Mr. Norman, who saw her looking around.

"It's just right for you," replied Tonia thoughtfully. "I mean, it's big and comfortable."

"Big and comfortable," repeated Mr. Norman, laughing. "I knew I was big, and I'm very glad I'm comfortable. Would you like to take off your hat?"

Tonia was only too pleased to comply with this suggestion. She removed it and threw it onto a chair and gave her head a shake so that her dark curls fell into their natural positions.

"Now we're both comfortable," said Mr. Norman.

Tea was ready so they sat down, one at each side of the fire, and Mr. Norman poured it out. She had been afraid—just for a moment—that he would ask her to manage the teapot, but apparently he was quite used to managing it himself. A spaniel was lying on the hearth rug; he got up and sniffed at Tonia and wagged his tail in a friendly fashion.

"Gruff likes you," said Mr. Norman. "He doesn't approve of everybody. Janet says he's a most unfriendly dog."

"Does she live with you?" asked Tonia—meaning Janet, of course.

Mr. Norman understood. "Most of the time," he replied. "She and her daughter come and go as they please. Their spiritual home is London."

"She's a little like you."

"So people say. It's our noses, I suppose. Noses run in families, you know. Nita, my niece, has the Garland nose—quite a different variety of beak."

"Nita?" said Tonia. "There was a girl named Nita at school with me."

"Miss Mann's? Yes, that must have been my niece."

Tonia hoped Mr. Norman would not ask if she had liked Nita (I shall have to say yes, thought Tonia, gazing very hard at the fire), but fortunately he did not ask, and the moment passed and it was quite comfortable again.

The tea was extremely good, and Tonia did full justice to it. There were hot buttered scones, jammy cookies, and rich plum cake. Mr. Norman did not eat much himself; he talked and plied his guest with food and seemed perfectly happy. When they had finished they looked at the bottles, which were arranged in a big shallow cabinet with glass doors. There were dozens of them, all shapes and sizes, and they had come from all over the world. Their owner took them out, one by one, and told their history, and Tonia listened enthralled.

"You've been everywhere," she said at last, looking at him with something like awe.

"I like traveling," he replied. "I travel whenever I can get away from business."

"I've never been *anywhere*," said Tonia with a sigh. "I've read about places and sometimes I think I can imagine them…"

He was still taking down the bottles and showing them to her. There was one that was supposed to have belonged to Prince Charlie; he had found it in Skye. There was another that Dr. Johnson was said to have used when he visited Scotland. The bottles were all old and queerly uneven in shape, bulging in the wrong places. Some of them had crooked necks; others had bubbles in the glass.

"They look homemade," declared Tonia.

"They are, really," replied Mr. Norman. "They are hand-made—not turned out of a factory by the thousand. Janet thinks I'm mad to collect them, but they fascinate me. Take it in your hands," he added, holding out the gem of the collection, a squat gin bottle with a rakish lopsided appearance. "I like the feel of the glass; it's quite an unusual sort of feeling—"

"Oh no, I might drop it," said Tonia, putting her hands behind her back.

"Nonsense!"

"It isn't nonsense. My hands are no good."

"No good?" asked Mr. Norman in surprise.

"None at all," said Tonia, shaking her head sadly. "They're silly hands. I can't hold things with them, and I can't knit or sew or play the piano properly."

Mr. Norman put down the bottle and took her hands in his,

examining them carefully and flexing the fingers. They were small and frail and rather stiff, but they were beautifully made. There was something very pathetic about these silly hands. Perhaps that was why Mr. Norman dropped them so hastily.

"There doesn't seem to be much the matter with them," he said. "I'm not a doctor, of course."

"A doctor!" said Tonia in amazement. "Why should you be a doctor?"

"A doctor would know what to advise. I suppose you've tried massage and electric treatment."

"I haven't tried anything."

"But your parents—"

"Oh, they don't know," said Tonia. "I mean, of course they know my hands are silly, but…" she hesitated, for it was difficult to explain. She was just beginning to realize that it needed explanation. The fact was her parents had not bothered. Nobody had bothered. Everybody had just taken it for granted that she was clumsy and inept.

"How extraordinary!" exclaimed Mr. Norman, who seemed to understand things without being told. "Your hands ought to have been attended to when you were a child."

"Could anything have been done?"

"Of course. Far more wonderful things are done every day."

Tonia was silent. How wonderful it would have been if her hands could have been improved, if they could have been made into useful hands. "You know," she said slowly. "You know, I don't think I should be nearly so silly if my hands were like other people's."

At this moment the clock on the mantelpiece struck six. Tonia looked at it in dismay. "It can't be right!" she exclaimed.

"I'm afraid it is, but time was made for slaves—and Cinderellas," replied her host with a smile.

Tonia did not return the smile; she was pulling on her hat

and tucking her curls away with complete disregard for her appearance. "Oh dear!" she cried. "Mother said I wasn't to stay too long—"

"You haven't stayed too long."

"She said I would bore you," declared Tonia, wrestling with the handle of the door.

Mr. Norman said no more, for he saw it was useless. His guest was far too upset to listen. He came with her into the hall and let her out into the street. She was too upset to remember to shake hands with him or to thank him for her entertainment in the conventional manner. She just rushed wildly down the steps and made for home.

For a few moments Mr. Norman watched the flying figure, and then he shook his head very thoughtfully and went back into the house.

❦

It was a wet afternoon. Mr. Melville was hurrying home to tea and was thinking with pleasure of his comfortable chair and his nice warm fire and of his daughter—who would be waiting for him. Since the ball (which was now about a fortnight ago) Tonia had been different, "more human" as Mr. Melville put it to himself, and this only went to show how right he had been to make her go to the ball and to give her a new dress for the occasion. Ella had actually begun to grumble because she said Tonia was getting her horns out and was being difficult about her clothes, refusing to wear some hat that Ella had bought her and insisting on having a new coat and skirt. A little while ago Ella had been complaining that Tonia took no interest in clothes—some people were never satisfied.

Mr. Melville was thinking of these domestic problems and hastening along with his umbrella cocked at exactly the right angle to ward off the rain when he felt a hand on his arm, detaining him, and was surprised to find that the owner of the hand was Mr. Norman.

"Hallo, Norman!" he exclaimed. "What a hellish evening! Come and have a cup of tea—or something stronger."

"Come and have a cup of tea with me—or something stronger," suggested Norman smiling.

Mr. Melville accepted the invitation (for there were several things he wanted to know and Norman was a good fellow to keep in with), and the two men walked on together through the rain. The house in Belgrave Crescent was warm and comfortable, and Mr. Melville was favorably impressed with Norman's "den." It was exactly the sort of room he would have liked to have, thought Mr. Melville looking around, but it was not likely he would ever be able to afford it. Unlike his daughter, he made no comment but accepted a glass of whisky and soda and a very fine cigar and took up his position on the hearth rug. The fire warmed the back of his legs in a very comforting manner.

"Appalling weather," said Mr. Melville cheerfully. "The middle of March and still as cold as winter... By the way I bought those shares. It was good of you to give me the tip."

"They've done pretty well, haven't they?"

"They have, and they're still rising. I suppose I should hold on?"

"I should sell now if I were you. They won't go much higher."

"Think so?"

"Yes, take your profit and clear out. If you want another flutter, you might do worse than Warden and Miles."

"Warden and Miles," repeated Mr. Melville, nodding, "I'll see about it tomorrow. It's very good of you, Norman. Wish I could do something in return."

"You can," said Norman quickly.

Mr. Melville was slightly taken aback. He had made the

statement in a vague sort of way, and the last thing he had expected was to be taken literally. Besides, what on earth could he do for Norman? The fellow was rolling in money.

Norman was pouring out a drink for himself and making it a stiff one. "It's like this," he said at last. "I don't want you to feel you're under any sort of obligation to me…just because… because I gave you the tip to buy those shares."

Mr. Melville looked at his host in amazement. Norman was usually so sure of himself, so reserved and dignified and aloof. All sorts of odd ideas flashed through Mr. Melville's mind in the silence that ensued.

"I'm fifty-nine," said Norman at last, raising his eyes and looking back at his guest. "I'm perfectly fit, of course, and I don't really feel my age."

"I'm fifty-five," replied Mr. Melville, who was under the impression that this was the correct response.

Unfortunately Norman did not seem pleased with the response. He sighed and said regretfully, "Yes, I was afraid of it. I'm older than you are, Melville."

"But not much," said Mr. Melville kindly. "I mean, four years is neither here nor there."

"It's a good deal less than forty," agreed Norman.

Mr. Melville was even more bewildered now. He searched for something to say but could find nothing. The only thing he could do was to wait and see what Norman would say next… and Norman seemed in no hurry to say anything. He was lighting a cigarette and his hands were shaking.

At last, after a silence that seemed unduly long, Norman shook out the match and tossed it into the fire. "I had better tell you," he said. "It's no good beating about the bush. I want to marry Antonia."

"You want to—to marry—*Tonia*?"

"Of course I'm too old. I'm much too old and she's much

too young. If you tell me I'm a fool I shan't blame you. The fact is I love her—I enjoy her—and I'm pretty certain I could make her happy. I know as well as you do that there are all sorts of things to be said against it. I've said them to myself much more strongly than you're ever likely to say them, but there are several things to be said in favor of it. Antonia isn't an ordinary girl. She's mature in some ways and she's very adaptable. She has a beautiful nature, unselfish and sensitive. Life might bear upon her pretty hardly unless she finds someone who can understand her properly—she has no confidence in herself. Of course you know all this as well as I do."

Mr. Melville did not. He had not analyzed his daughter's character. He had realized that she was not quite like other girls—Ella always said she was queer—but he had never thought of her as having a beautiful nature or as being particularly sensitive.

He said, "Well, I must say...you've surprised me...I don't know what to say..."

"Of course," agreed Norman. "Naturally you're surprised. I don't want you to say anything until you've thought it over. The whole thing rests with Antonia herself, doesn't it?"

"I suppose it does," said Mr. Melville in a dazed manner. "And that being so, why did you—"

"Because she's so young," interrupted Norman. "I thought I would speak to you first. That's all."

"But, Norman, have you thought—"

"I've thought of everything. I may die and leave her a widow. Is that what you were going to say?"

"No," said Mr. Melville hastily.

"The settlements shall be exactly as you wish."

"It isn't that at all. I mean, I know that part of it will be all right."

"Perhaps you're thinking that she may meet someone of her

own age and fall in love. Well, in that case she can divorce me. I wouldn't stand in her way."

"Good heavens!" exclaimed Mr. Melville. "You can't mean—"

"It would be only fair," continued Norman in deliberate tones. "I've faced that—it's the worst snag, really."

"I'm thinking of you," declared Mr. Melville.

"Of me?"

"Yes, Tonia is just a child. She isn't like Lou, who has plenty to say for herself—Lou's an attractive minx."

"Perhaps she wouldn't attract me."

"Perhaps not, but—but I'm just wondering if Tonia would be able to—to—I mean, she isn't very capable."

"I don't need a housekeeper," said Norman somewhat grimly. "I have a very competent housekeeper, and I don't need a nurse either, thank heaven. All I need is a companion."

"Well, there you are!" exclaimed Mr. Melville, who was beginning to lose his temper. "Could Tonia *ever* be a companion to a man like you? It's absurd."

"I thought you might think it absurd," was the reply.

There was silence, and the clock struck six. Norman remembered Cinderella, and the remembrance made him smile. He said in quite a different tone of voice, "I hope you will give me permission to pay my addresses to your daughter, Melville."

Mr. Melville had regained control of his temper and he chuckled. "Sounds a bit old-fashioned, doesn't it? Things aren't done that way nowadays. Lou's young man walked off with her without so much as a by-your-leave." He hesitated—it was most extraordinary to think that this was "Tonia's young man."

"You haven't answered," Norman reminded him.

"Supposing I said no?"

"Ah, I wonder. I'm afraid I shouldn't take it as final. Have another drink?"

"I shan't say a word to Ella," said Mr. Melville, handing over his glass.

"Nor to Antonia."

"Of course not."

"You don't really...object?" inquired Norman somewhat diffidently. "I mean...I mean, you see my point. I shall take the very greatest care of her, you know."

"She's devilish lucky," declared Mr. Melville, looking around the comfortable room.

"And war is coming," added Norman thoughtfully.

"War? Do you think so?"

"I'm perfectly certain of it."

They talked about the prospects of war and of which nations were likely to stand up and fight. It was not until Mr. Melville was going away that Tonia was mentioned again.

"I suppose you'll want to—to take her out and all that?" said Mr. Melville doubtfully.

"Most certainly," replied Norman with a smile.

Chapter Nine

Alarms and Excursions

"What would I like to do?" asked Tonia in a surprised voice. She had been called to speak to Mr. Norman on the telephone and had arrived, somewhat breathless, to be confronted with this extraordinary question.

"It's wet," Mr. Norman pointed out. "If it hadn't been such a bad day we might have gone for a spin in the car to the country. Perhaps you would like to go to the pictures."

"There's a concert," Tonia said. "But perhaps you don't like concerts."

Mr. Norman liked concerts and said so. He was a little surprised to find that the concert Tonia had chosen was one being given by a young pianist of rising fame and consisted of works by Brahms and Liszt, but if that was what she wanted she should have it. He sent his clerk to get tickets and fetched Tonia at half past two. They were early at the hall, for Tonia was determined not to miss a single note, and they settled down comfortably and chatted until it began.

"If I could play Liszt's Fourteenth Rhapsody I should die happy," declared Tonia, looking at her companion with large dark blue serious eyes.

"It's a high ambition."

"It isn't an ambition at all. I mean, I know I never could

unless a miracle happened and I got new hands. An ambition is something you try for, something you hope for, isn't it?"

Mr. Norman's reply was drowned by the sound of clapping that greeted the appearance of the pianist. He was quite young and very dark with long hair and a foreign cut of countenance—not very prepossessing in appearance, but one forgot that the moment he began to play. He played like an angel with fire and tenderness. Liszt's most difficult passages flowed from the instrument with a glorious precision—each note clear and liquid as the song of a bird. Mr. Norman enjoyed it tremendously. He looked at his companion to see if she was enjoying it and noticed a very strange expression on her face. It was really a complete lack of expression, a complete and absolute blankness. Tonia's body was there but her soul was—somewhere else. He was slightly alarmed about her, and even more alarmed when the concert finished and Tonia did not return. He took her arm and piloted her through the crowd, found his car, and put her into it. He spoke to her several times during their walk, but she did not answer. It was not until he had started the engine and was moving off into the stream of traffic that Tonia awoke.

She heaved a long sigh. "Oh, it was lovely," she said.

"You're all right?" asked Mr. Norman anxiously.

"Quite all right," declared Tonia, smiling at him.

"Where were you, Antonia?"

"Was I silly?" she asked.

"You were just—not there."

"I was in my listening valley," she replied. "I used to call it my listening place until I read Blake's poem. Listening valley is better."

"Much better," agreed Mr. Norman.

"It isn't anywhere, really," continued Tonia, who was aware that Mr. Norman was interested and would understand. "It's inside myself. But lately I've begun to see it as if it were a real place."

"Perhaps it is a real place."

"A real place that I've never seen," said Tonia, thoughtfully. "That would be even queerer, wouldn't it?"

∾◦∽

My darling Lou, wrote Tonia. *I still miss you terribly much, but I am not quite so unhappy now because I have a friend. You remember I told you Mr. Norman had sent me tickets for the ball. I told you about it in my last letter and how I danced with him and Frank was angry. Since then I have seen him quite often. He asked me if he might call me Antonia, so of course I said yes. It would be ridiculous for him to go on calling me Miss Melville because he must be about Father's age, I should think. Somehow it makes me feel more grown up and important to be called Antonia. It's as if I were two people. When I am at home I am just Tonia and I do silly things, but when I am with Mr. Norman I am Antonia, and she is quite a sensible sort of person. We went to a concert one afternoon and another day we went to Queensferry in his car and had tea at the Hawes Inn. He has a marvelous car and drives very well—fast but carefully. Of course he is quite old, but he understands things almost as well as you do—which is rather wonderful, I think. I will tell you what he is like to look at: very tall and big with gray hair and blue eyes. He has lovely hands with long fingers. I like looking at them when he is driving the car. But all this does not really give you much idea of him. He is very distinguished looking. People look at him when he walks past and wonder who he is. Father says he is a brilliant financier. The other day Father said, "Are you going out with your friend, the brilliant financier?" It was a joke, of course. Father is quite different to me lately; he talks to me and asks questions and listens to the answers, as if I were important—if you know what I mean. He has given me fifty pounds to buy some new clothes.*

Tonia hesitated and stopped. What would Lou think when she read the letter? Would she think it queer? It *was* queer, really. Why does Mr. Norman bother with me, Tonia wondered.

"Frank has been here several times," continued Tonia. "He asked me to go to a dance with him and Mother wanted me to go, but Father said I was to do as I liked, so I did not go. I was rather surprised at Frank asking me because I did not think he liked me much. He rang up again this morning and asked me to go with him to the zoo, but fortunately I had arranged to go to North Berwick with Mr. Norman…"

❦

It was a glorious afternoon with a breeze from the east, keen and invigorating. The sea was a deep blue, the sky a lighter blue and cloudless; there was a hard line along the horizon as if it had been drawn with a ruler and a pencil. Against this line the islands stood out bold and rugged, so clear that you could see the bright green grass growing between the boulders. Mr. Norman and Tonia left the car at the harbor and walked along the East Bay toward a high escarpment of red rock. The tide was out. Small waves like snow-white frills broke upon the shore.

"Are you happy, Antonia?" asked Mr. Norman.

"Very happy," she replied. "It would be funny if I were not happy, wouldn't it? All this…" said Tonia, who had learned that she could prattle to Mr. Norman without being pulled up with a jerk and made to feel a fool. "All this is so lovely—the sea and the sky and the wind and you being so kind to me."

"You're kind to me," he replied with unaccustomed gravity.

"I am?"

"Yes, of course. You make me happy."

Tonia considered this. It was a new point of view. "But you

could have anyone," she said. "Anyone would like to come out in your car."

"But only you could make me happy."

"If you had met Lou," said Tonia with a sigh. "Lou is so interesting and amusing, so full of life and…"

"I don't want Lou," said Mr. Norman firmly.

Perhaps this was just as well, thought Tonia as they picked their way over a flat reef of slippery rocks. It was nice to feel that Mr. Norman was her own friend, her very own, not just a sort of overflow from someone else. "I hope you won't get bored with me," said Tonia suddenly, following out her train of thought.

"You might get bored with me," suggested her companion in a casual sort of tone.

"Never," said Tonia confidently.

"Are you sure?"

"Of course I'm sure."

"How much do you like me?" Mr. Norman wanted to know.

That was easy to answer. She smiled at him. "Oh, a lot," she said.

"Enough to marry me?" he inquired.

At first Tonia was certain she had misunderstood the words—the wind was blowing and the seagulls were making a terrific noise—but when she looked at him she saw by his face that she had heard the words correctly and he really meant them. She was dumb with surprise. She was distressed and embarrassed and rather frightened.

"Supposing we sit down in the shelter of this rock and talk about it," suggested Mr. Norman.

They sat down. Tonia stared at the seagulls with unseeing eyes. There was a lump of misery in her throat. She listened to Mr. Norman talking, but it was quite impossible to reply.

"Don't worry about it," he was saying. "We'll never speak of it again if you would rather not. You have only to say no, but

I hope you'll think about it seriously first. We like each other, don't we? We're happy when we're together and we understand each other so well. Of course I know I'm too old. I would give anything on earth to be the right age for you, Antonia."

He hesitated. There was so much he could offer her, but he did not want to bribe her. He could offer her travel—he knew she wanted to see the world. He could offer her jewels and furs and pretty frocks. He could remind her that she was unhappy at home—unappreciated—and that her life was dull and purposeless. Mr. Norman said none of this. He just waited. It seemed a long time to him.

"I don't...know," said Tonia at last, twisting her hands together. "I never thought...of getting married...to anyone."

"Think of it now," suggested her companion.

"I'm trying to think," said Tonia miserably. "Perhaps I'm frightened or something. It isn't that I don't like you."

"That's something, anyhow," said Mr. Norman, rather grimly. "We'll leave it like that, shall we? You can think it over. There's no hurry at all. Meantime perhaps you could call me Robert—unless you'd rather not."

Tonia felt it would be quite impossible to call him Robert, but she could not say so. She said nothing at all.

The day was spoiled, of course. The sky was just as blue, but it gave Tonia no pleasure at all; there was no pleasure in anything. They walked back to the car, and as they went, Mr. Norman—no, Robert—talked quite cheerfully of ordinary things. He told his companion about a bottle he had bought at a small shop in the Grassmarket...and presently Tonia made an effort and pulled herself together and answered him quite naturally; but it was not the same as before, and she couldn't, no, she simply couldn't call him Robert.

◈

It was late when Tonia got home and Mr. and Mrs. Melville had started dinner without her. She smoothed her hair and washed her hands and appeared in the dining room quite breathless with haste, looking and feeling extremely guilty.

"You're late," said Mrs. Melville. "Really, Tonia, I think you might make an effort to be on time for meals. We've finished our soup; you can have some fried sole. I wish—"

"I wish you would tell your cook to have the fat *boiling*," interposed Mr. Melville. "The fat should be absolutely boiling, with a blue haze rising from the pan, before the fillets are put in. Then the fish would be crisp and tasty instead of greasy and flabby—I can't eat this stuff."

"There's nothing the matter with the fish. You're too particular," replied Mrs. Melville with asperity.

Mr. Melville laughed mirthlessly.

"Why are you laughing, Henry?"

"Because, like all women, you are illogical. If the fat was boiling and there's nothing the matter with the fish, why add that I'm too particular?"

"You're far too particular…"

"I only want plain food properly cooked. That's not much to ask."

"Plain food is the most difficult to cook well."

"Have elaborate food, then," retorted Mr. Melville. "Have anything you like, only have it right. I'll eat anything."

"You said just now that you couldn't eat this."

"Anything if it's properly cooked," cried Mr. Melville with violence. "*Anything.* We pay the woman enough in all conscience. Why can't she cook?"

"She *can* cook—"

"You don't bother to keep her up to the mark, that's what's the matter."

"It's my fault, is it?"

"Of course. You do the housekeeping, don't you? If you can't spare the time, why don't you hand it over to Tonia?"

"Tonia!" cried Mrs. Melville. "I'd like to see the sort of hash Tonia would make of it."

"She couldn't do much worse than you," declared Mr. Melville. "You had better try her out. It would be good practice for her."

"Practice for what?"

"For when she has a house of her own, of course."

"Tonia isn't likely to be married."

"Lou is married—"

"A hole-and-corner affair. I pity her husband," cried Mrs. Melville wildly. "Neither Lou nor Tonia has ever taken the slightest interest in the house. Tonia is interested in nothing but books—*books!* She's cut out for an old maid."

Tonia listened to all this in silence. She ought to have become used to rows by this time. She ought to have learned that they never led to anything but were just sound and fury and blew over like thunderclouds leaving a clear sky, but Tonia was too sensitive. She felt the blows upon her own person—felt them far more keenly than the antagonists. Tonight she was not only frightened, she was angry as well, for the mention of Lou's name had the power to rouse her. So she suddenly broke into the discussion, saying in a loud and rather unnatural voice, "But I'm going to be married quite soon."

The remark certainly had the effect of stopping the fight. Tonia's parents were immediately silent, gazing at her. Her mother gazed at her with amazement and consternation, her father with a curious expression that was hard to read.

"To Robert," said Tonia, taking up the carafe and pouring out some water with rather an unsteady hand. "He asked me today on the beach at North Berwick. That's why we were—a little late."

"Are you sure you want to?" asked Mr. Melville. "I mean, Norman is an awfully good fellow, but he—he isn't young. You had better be quite sure, Tonia. I mean—"

"I'm quite sure," declared Tonia, and indeed she was, for at that moment Robert Norman seemed a refuge and a sure tower.

"But it's a splendid match!" exclaimed Mrs. Melville, gazing at her daughter with something like awe. "Robert Norman! I never thought for a moment...could he really have meant it?"

"What on earth are you talking about?" demanded Mr. Melville.

"I mean, Tonia is so—*so silly*. Perhaps she misunderstood. I can hardly believe—"

"It's you who are silly, Ella," interrupted her husband. "As a matter of fact, I know all about it. Norman spoke to me the other day."

"Spoke to *you*?"

"I'm the girl's father," said Mr. Melville with elaborate patience. "At least so I've been led to believe. I thought it very proper that he should speak to me. He was extremely nice about it. Of course the whole thing depends on Tonia. Nobody is going to force her into it."

"I've made up my mind," said Tonia firmly.

Mrs. Melville was still incredulous. "I can hardly believe it," she repeated, looking at Tonia as she spoke.

This had been Mr. Melville's own reaction when he had first heard of the affair, but he had forgotten that now. "Why can't you believe it?" he inquired. "Tonia is a very attractive girl—a thorough Melville. The Melville women all marry young—except poor old Aunt Antonia, of course. Yes, they all marry young. It's a tradition in the Melville family."

For once in her life Ella failed to rise to the bait.

Henry Melville drank two glasses of port after his dinner, for it was a special occasion, and then he rose and walked about the room. He was restless and he could not sit still. Presently he decided that the right thing to do was to go around and visit his prospective son-in-law. It was a dark night and there was rain in the chill wind as he crossed the Dean Bridge, but the house in Belgrave Crescent was pleasantly warm and Robert Norman's study as comfortable a place as you could wish for.

"Well, Robert," said Henry Melville (for he had decided that this was now the correct manner of address). "Well, Robert, here I am. I felt I had to come around—don't really know whether it's the right thing to congratulate you or what!" He laughed jovially. He was too excited to notice anything strange in his host's demeanor.

"I don't know, either," said Robert Norman doubtfully.

"I'm damned glad, anyway. Girls are a bit of an anxiety these days."

"Yes, I daresay."

"For instance, Lou took the bit in her teeth and bolted. It was perfectly all right, of course," added Mr. Melville, feeling he had been rather indiscreet. "I mean, she married the fellow—it was young Skene—but there was a sort of family feud and Ella was upset about it."

"So I gathered."

"Tonia's quite different, of course," added Mr. Melville.

"Yes," agreed Robert. He was still pretty much in the dark, so it was better to say as little as possible and let Melville ramble on.

Melville rambled on quite happily. He accepted a whisky and soda and a large cigar. "Tonia is *quite* different," he said. "She's quiet and—and obedient. She—but you know all that already."

"Yes…but you didn't say anything to her, did you?" inquired Robert anxiously. He was a little startled at the word "obedient."

"Say anything! Good Lord, no! It was Tonia who did all the saying. She came out with it quite suddenly at dinner. Created quite a sensation."

"What did she say?" asked Robert.

"She just said—in a matter-of-fact sort of voice—'Robert and I are going to be married quite soon.' That was all," declared Mr. Melville, laughing. "Ha-ha, that was all, but it was quite enough."

"She said that?" said Robert, trying not to sound incredulous.

"Just that. You should have seen Ella's face. I hadn't said a word to Ella, of course."

"I hope Mrs. Melville was pleased—"

"Oh yes, she was pleased. Who wouldn't be? It was just that she was surprised. The fact is Ella doesn't get on too well with Tonia, hasn't much opinion of her, you know…of course Tonia takes some understanding; she isn't everybody's meat," added Mr. Melville hastily.

"Yes—no," agreed Robert. He was feeling very bewildered, for he had made up his mind that Antonia was not for him. She had received his proposal with such amazement and had betrayed so much embarrassment and distress that he had decided it was hopeless. He had decided to let the matter drop and to try to win back her confidence. She should have his friendship if she did not want his love, and now it appeared that she did want his love, or at least his protection. He was astute enough to realize quite clearly that something must have happened to make Antonia change her mind. In a way that was a pity. It would have been more felicitous if Antonia had accepted him because she loved him and if he could have heard the news from her own lips, but you could not have everything in this very imperfect world, especially when you were nearly sixty. Quite suddenly, Robert was full of surging gladness. Nothing really mattered except that Antonia was his for the taking. He could make her happy, he was sure of it—he could give her the earth.

Robert seized Mr. Melville's hand and shook it heartily. "Of course you must congratulate me," he cried. "I'm the happiest man alive."

Chapter Ten

Honeymoon

"It's all a dream," said Tonia, as she stood at her husband's side and watched the coast of England fade and vanish in the evening mist. "It's either a dream or else I'm not me. Which is it, Robert?"

"Let's dream together," he replied.

"Let's not wake up," she added, slipping her hand through his arm. It was sheer happiness to be with Robert, for he was so strong and kind and so even tempered. He was never moody or cross, and you could say what you liked without weighing your words or wondering if he would understand. Tonia was no longer afraid of doing something silly (in Robert's eyes she could do no wrong), and, because she admired him so much, his belief in her gave her confidence and poise.

They were going to India for their honeymoon; they were going to see Lou, because this was what Tonia wanted more than anything and Robert was delighted to think that he could give it to her. But, although Lou was waiting at the end of the voyage, Tonia was not impatient, for the voyage itself was the most entrancing experience. There were long, slow, lazy days of sunshine and blue sky and calm blue seas and there were wonderful places to be seen (places Tonia had read about and dreamed of) and there were pleasant people on board who were eager to be friendly with the tall good-looking man and his young and pretty wife. Robert encouraged Tonia to join in the social life, for it was no part of his intention to keep her to himself. He noticed that many of their fellow passengers were imbued with the idea that Tonia was his daughter and this distressed him a little—though he was aware that it was unreasonable to be distressed. The mistake did not worry Tonia; she always put it right immediately, saying with an air of grave dignity: "I'm Mrs. Norman. Robert and I are married."

It was a halcyon voyage, and they were happy. Any qualms that Robert had felt faded and disappeared...and every day Tonia gained more self-confidence and laughed more merrily and put on weight.

"Do you think Lou will be the same?" asked Tonia one evening when they were walking up and down the deck together.

"Do you think you're the same?" inquired Robert quite seriously.

She was silent for a few moments. Of course she was different. Even her feeling for Lou had undergone a change. Lou had been her first, her only, friend—and now there was Robert.

"Take people as you find them," continued Robert. He was a trifle anxious about this meeting and was trying to save Tonia from disappointment. "It isn't very easy sometimes. Our natures are too apt to be possessive."

"I must wait and see," said Tonia thoughtfully. "I shan't expect too much...and I shan't ask for anything. That's what you mean, isn't it?"

"It's exactly what I mean," replied Robert.

❧

There was no need for Robert's anxiety. Lou was the same in every way that mattered. She was waiting on the steps of the veranda when the car drew up and in a moment the two sisters were in each other's arms, clinging to each other and babbling hysterically. Jack and Robert smiled at each other and shook hands.

"Better come in and have a drink," said Jack. "Better leave them to it. We shan't get any sense out of them for a bit."

"It doesn't look like it," agreed Robert. He liked Jack at once and liked him all the better because he was friendly and natural and treated one as a contemporary. Robert had a feeling that it was difficult for Jack to refrain from calling him "sir" but, if so, Jack managed to overcome the difficulty.

They had no sooner arrived than they were caught up in a whirl of gaiety, for Jack and Lou had definite ideas on entertaining guests. There were dances and picnics and evening parties at the mess and polo matches and race meetings. Robert had bought a car on his arrival at Bombay, and as it was a powerful car it increased their orbit of activities. "Let's go over and see the Whittakers," Lou would say, and Robert would discover that the town in which the Whittakers were stationed was about a hundred miles away.

Robert found the constant gaiety very tiring. He would have preferred a quiet visit with time to prowl about the native quarter and make interesting discoveries and purchases, but he did not want to spoil Tonia's fun, so he took his part in everything. He had believed himself perfectly fit and extremely strong, but it was an effort to keep up with the easy buoyant stride of youth. What Jack and Lou and Tonia accomplished without turning a hair required a big effort from Robert, but this was just one of the drawbacks of marrying a child, thought Robert a trifle ruefully. It was the first time Robert had felt his age, and he did not like it. He did not like it when Tonia asked him if he was tired, for he was determined to keep up with the others, so he merely replied that the heat bothered him a little and made a bigger effort to join in all the fun.

Robert got on splendidly with Jack and liked him more and more. Jack was not brilliant, perhaps, but he was sound and dependable—a good fellow in the best sense of the words. Lou was not quite so easy to get on with, Robert found. She was very pleasant to Robert, but he could sense an undercurrent of hostility beneath her friendly manner. He ignored it, of course, for it was the only thing to do.

"You like Lou, don't you?" Tonia asked. She asked him the same question several times, and each time Robert assured her that he liked Lou immensely, adding that she was beautiful to look at—which was perfectly true.

"Lou likes you very much indeed," said Tonia.

"That's splendid!" Robert declared.

Tonia was happy. She had Robert and she had Lou. It was extraordinary to meet Lou in this strange foreign land. The last time she had seen Lou was in the nursery at home, going off to her singing lesson with her music case under her arm, and now, here was Lou thousands of miles away! Here was Lou moving about the bungalow, perfectly at home, giving orders to the native servants and comporting herself as a memsahib should; but Lou, herself, was just the same—her face, her expressive hands, the way she turned her head suddenly, the way she crinkled her eyes when she laughed—all these things were familiar and dear. Yes, Tonia was very happy—she loved the bright colors of life and enjoyed the gaiety and friendliness with which she was surrounded.

"You know," said Jack one day, looking from his wife to his sister-in-law with admiring eyes. "You know there isn't a girl in the place to touch you two for looks. Don't you agree, Robert?"

Robert agreed most heartily.

"Yes," continued Jack. "I remember something Aunt Daisy said the first time you came to tea. She said, 'They go together so well.' It was true then and it's true now. Apart you're both extremely pretty and easy on the eye, but together you're irresistible."

It was a joke, of course, and they all laughed, but many a true word is spoken in jest, thought Robert. The two were alike in feature and complexion and they both had strangely deep-blue eyes, but Lou's curls were fair and fluffy and Antonia's were dark with a shade of auburn in their darkness. Lou was perhaps the more taking of the two, for she was gay and sparkled with life and energy, but Antonia's loveliness went deeper (Robert thought). There was more expression in her face. She was sometimes thoughtful and dreamy and sometimes eager and intelligent, but she was always gentle and full of spiritual grace. Now that she had filled out a little and lost that queer hunted look, Antonia was really beautiful, thought Robert, looking at her tenderly.

After dinner that same night Robert found himself sitting on the veranda beside his hostess. The moon was shining with unnatural brilliance and the scent of the jasmine, which hung in masses on the pillars of the veranda, was sweet and strong. They were alone—which was unusual—and Robert had a feeling that Lou had maneuvered skillfully for this *tête–à–tête*. He wondered what Lou wanted to say to him.

"I was angry with you at first," said Lou suddenly. "I suppose you wondered why—"

"No," replied Robert. "I knew why you were angry. I'd like to know why you have changed your mind."

Lou was silent for a few moments. He was going too fast for her and had put her out of her stride. She had rehearsed this conversation beforehand, but it was not going according to plan. "You're very clever," she said at last.

"I've had a good deal of experience," Robert pointed out.

"Experience doesn't always make people clever."

"Not always," agreed Robert, hiding a smile.

Lou hesitated. At last she said, "I thought at first you were too old for Tonia. I thought it was wrong of you to have married her, but you've made her happy, and that's all that matters."

"Not quite all that matters. It's important that we should understand each other, I think."

"I think so too," declared Lou. "That was why I wanted to tell you—"

"And that's why I want to tell you," said Robert firmly. "I married Antonia so that I could try to repair the damage done to her by you."

"Robert, what *do* you mean!"

"We're speaking quite frankly, aren't we?"

"You seem to be!"

"I thought that was the idea."

"But I don't understand," declared Lou. "Tonia and I have always adored each other!"

"You adored each other but not as equals. You made Antonia dependent upon you—"

"Robert, you must be mad!" cried Lou, who was completely taken aback at this reversal of the tables.

"You made her dependent upon you instead of trying to bring her forward and encouraging her to stand on her own feet, and then, quite suddenly, without the slightest warning, you went away and left her."

"You *are* mad," declared Lou.

"Those are the facts, Lou," said Robert in a quite pleasant tone of voice. "I don't for a moment suggest that you intended to make Antonia dependent upon you and then desert her and leave her to her fate, but that is exactly what you did."

"I loved Jack—"

"Of course, and you had every right to marry Jack. But you had no right to overshadow Antonia—"

"Did Tonia tell you that?"

"No, of course not," replied Robert. "She adores you and thinks you can do no wrong. You are quite perfect in her eyes. You were always so clever, so capable, so full of life. You could do everything well—and she could do nothing."

"How could I have helped it!" cried Lou.

"I think you could have helped it," replied Robert thoughtfully. "I think you're quite clever enough to have helped it. I think you could have given her more self-confidence instead of taking away the little she had. Something might have been done about her hands, for instance—"

"They've improved," said Lou quickly.

"I know," he agreed. "That shows their helplessness was largely psychological. She has gained a little confidence in herself. Of course I shall take her to a specialist when we go home, but I feel pretty certain he will find nothing wrong— nothing that massage and exercises won't cure."

"Robert, look here—"

"So that's why I married her," continued Robert, still in that pleasant easy tone. "I thought I should like you to know the facts, so I've told you. I love Antonia dearly. I love her more now than I did when I married her, which is saying a good deal, but I certainly would not have married her under ordinary circumstances—it wouldn't have been fair. She needed help so badly that I took the risk. That's what I meant when I said I had tried to repair the damage done by you."

"You wouldn't have married her!"

"No," said Robert firmly. "You see, Lou, in one way you were right—your feeling was right. It isn't natural for a man of my age to marry a young girl. There are all sorts of complications. For instance I shall be an old man when Antonia is still quite young—that's one of the dragons I have to face. I considered that and other possible eventualities very carefully; I faced them and weighed them in the balance. They weighed pretty heavily, of course, but not so heavily as Antonia's need of love and protection…so far everything is perfectly all right and we're both very happy." He had finished now. He lay back in his chair and lit a cigarette.

There was a very long silence. Lou was thinking. At first she had been angry, of course, but Robert had spoken so quietly and confidently that she was obliged to consider his words. He's straight, anyhow, thought Lou. She was straight herself and prided herself on her sincerity and on the fact that she liked plain speaking, so she could hardly complain that Robert had spoken too plainly. She considered his words. Perhaps there was just a tiny grain of truth in what he had said. Perhaps she had overshadowed Tonia a little and protected her and shielded her just a little too much. So you could be too kind, thought Lou in surprise, or was it more true to say you could be kind in a wrong way? All sorts of long-forgotten incidents sprang into Lou's mind, trivial incidents, perhaps, but all tending in the same direction: incidents at school, in the nursery, in the drawing room when Mother had visitors and she and Tonia went downstairs to hand around cakes, occasions when people had spoken to Tonia and Lou had replied. Yes, Lou had always gone forward herself and dragged Tonia after her. And Lou had felt pleased with herself, very pleased and complacent, because she was taking care of poor little Tonia. She had prided herself on being stronger and wiser than Tonia, on being able to do everything better than Tonia. She had actually prided herself on the fact that Tonia couldn't get on without her, and then Jack had appeared on the scene and she had left Tonia stranded.

"What a beast I am!" exclaimed Lou in a low voice.

Robert looked at his beautiful sister-in-law and smiled. "Just a little thoughtless, that's all," said Robert in a friendly tone.

It was while they were here with Jack and Lou that a lawyer's letter arrived addressed to Miss Antonia Melville. It had been following them about for some time before catching up with them. Somehow or other Tonia was frightened when she saw it, so she took it to Robert and asked him to open it.

"Read it and tell me about it," Tonia said.

Robert opened it and studied it thoughtfully. "It's about a legacy," he said. "I suppose it *is* intended for you. Who was Miss Kate Dalrymple?"

"That's Nannie! Oh, Robert, you don't mean Nannie is dead?"

"I'm afraid so," said Robert.

"Oh, poor Nannie!" exclaimed Tonia, gazing before her with wide eyes. "I meant to go and see her…and now it's too late. Oh, Robert, we could have done things for her, couldn't we? Why did I forget about her?"

"You didn't forget about her."

"Not really," agreed Tonia. "I just didn't think about her; it was horrid of me. Oh dear, I wish I had gone and stayed with her at Ryddelton. Nannie must have thought it so ungrateful."

"Nannie can't have thought you horrid and ungrateful; she has left you her house and everything in it. Hadn't she any relations of her own?"

"Her house at Ryddelton—to *me*!"

"Perhaps you ought not to accept it."

"Not accept it?"

"I mean, it seems rather odd," said Robert, frowning.

"It isn't really odd," replied Tonia. "You see, the house belonged to Great-Aunt Antonia. When she died grandfather gave it to Nannie's mother, so I suppose…"

"In that case perhaps it should go to your father, or to Lou."

"Nannie left it to *me*," said Tonia with more firmness than she usually betrayed. "Nannie wanted *me* to have it, Robert."

"I wonder why."

"I think I know why."

"Well?"

"I sent her...some money," replied Tonia. She said it thoughtfully, for it seemed such a long time ago, and Tonia had almost forgotten about the chocolate box and its unusual contents...but Nannie had not forgotten. Nannie had remembered and thought about her kindly and left her the house that had belonged to Great-Aunt Antonia. She explained the whole thing to Robert and Robert understood (he laughed when he heard about the chocolate box), and he agreed that under the circumstances Tonia had every right to the legacy, more right than anybody else.

"Your father may be annoyed," said Robert. "And of course you don't really need the house."

Tonia realized this, but all the same she intended to keep it, for the house meant a good deal to her (although she had never seen it), and Nannie had wanted her to have it. The house would be her very own, which was a pleasant thought.

"Very well," said Robert, when he saw that she was determined upon it. "I'll write to Phillips. He'll settle everything and see that the place is in good repair and thoroughly insured. He can arrange for a caretaker if necessary."

"And when we get home we can go and see it," added Tonia.

Chapter Eleven
War Experiences

The Normans went home more quickly than they intended, for there was war in the air. They flew part of the way and arrived at Hendon in August 1939. Robert had intended to retire from active participation in the affairs of his firm and make way for younger men, but this idea was quickly dissipated; the younger men were otherwise employed, and Robert was asked by his partners if he would take over the London branch, which meant living in London. In some ways Tonia was glad they were not going back to Edinburgh, for Robert had been right—Mr. Melville was very much annoyed when he heard that Melville House had been left to Tonia. Angry letters arrived, not only from him but from Mrs. Melville as well, and neither soft answers nor lengthy explanations had the power to turn their wrath. Ultimately Tonia was very busy finding a flat in London and moving in, so her parents' displeasure did not distress her unduly; in fact, Robert was surprised—and secretly amused—by the calm manner in which his young wife dismissed the subject.

London was still its old self—or very nearly—for the war was still in its infancy and, like an infant, seemed harmless and feeble. Robert was busy, of course, but he found time to take Tonia to concerts and theaters and to visit the zoo with her on a Sunday afternoon. Tonia was busy too. She was having treatment for her hands (Robert had insisted upon it), and she was studying music under the tutelage of an Austrian refugee. It was a happy period in Tonia's life, that winter of 1939. It would have been happier if she could have stopped thinking about the war.

Once they were settled in the flat they began to have visitors, and Mrs. Halley was the first, for she wanted to know all about Jack and Lou. Tonia liked having Mrs. Halley; she was a delightful guest and just as friendly and attractive as ever. Robert's sister, Janet Garland, was the next to visit them, and she was a very different kind of guest. Tonia was frightened of Janet, which made her clumsy and awkward. She was aware that Janet disapproved of her and thought her a fool. Perhaps it was natural that Janet should be prejudiced against Robert's wife, for, before his marriage, Robert had been extremely useful to the Garlands. Janet and her daughter could stay with Robert when they liked and use his house pretty much as their own, provided they did not overstep the limit of his patience (this was all the more convenient because Janet was a widow with large ideas and a small income); but now all that was changed and Janet and Nita were obliged to fend for themselves.

"I'm sorry, Robert," said Tonia when Janet had gone. "I'm awfully sorry. I really *did* try."

"I know," said Robert, smiling at her. "Perhaps you tried too hard. Janet is a bit difficult, and you started with a handicap."

"I feel a brute, Robert."

"You needn't, darling. I've settled some money on Janet, so she isn't a loser by our marriage and unless she's wildly extravagant she ought to be all right."

Soon after this Frank Melville came to stay for a few days. He had obtained a post at one of the ministries and had come to London to look for rooms. Tonia had not liked Frank very much and had been under the impression that Frank did not like her, but she was forced to alter her opinion. Frank was interesting and amusing and treated Tonia with consideration and friendliness; he was such a pleasant change from her last guest that Tonia was grateful to him. She came out of her shell and they had good fun together, and after some difficulty they found comfortable rooms for Frank, not too far away. He made a habit of dropping in and seeing the Normans, chatting to Robert or listening to concerts on the wireless with Tonia.

After the fall of France everything was different, for the war had suddenly taken on a new aspect and became more grim and ghastly every day. Calamities followed each other in quick succession, blows that would have seemed unbearable if they could have been foreseen. The gnawing anxiety was like a load upon one's shoulders—what would the outcome be? Could Britain hold out against the might of Germany, could she survive until she had gathered strength to meet this frightful enemy who had been preparing for so long? Robert Norman was doubtful of Britain's ability to hold on, not because he was unduly pessimistic, but because he had a clear grasp of the state of affairs in Britain and in Germany. He knew more than other people what we were up against. But he kept his fears to himself and did his job—and several other men's jobs—as well as he knew how. He had fought for Britain in 1914, and he would have liked to fight for her again. Patriotism was a real thing to Robert Norman.

Tonia had the same loyal feelings and these were intensified by the danger. She felt a curious elation. Churchill had said this was Britain's finest hour. She felt at one with the past and its traditions, akin to Raleigh and Nelson and Pitt and a hundred others who had saved their country in her hour of need. She was aware that Robert was anxious, for she knew him well by now, and she wondered what chance Britain had of weathering the storm. What would an impartial spectator give as the odds, a spectator on Mars (there were no impartial spectators on this planet)? He would not give much for Britain's chance of survival, because he would not know the men and women who inhabit the small proud island. He would not know of the queer wild streak that runs right through the British character—the dogged streak, which does not permit the Briton to envisage the possibility of defeat. We're unbeatable, thought Tonia with pride. We have our faults and failings, but we have the dogged streak. Each one of us has it, young and old and rich and poor—we know we can't be beaten.

There was much to do now. Tonia spent her days cooking in a canteen. Many of their nights were spent in the cellar with the other tenants of the flats while the guns roared and the bombs came crashing down on London. Robert wanted Tonia to leave London, but she refused to go, for she had work to do and was determined to stay and face the worst. She was all the more determined because Robert was not well. He was often tired and had lost a lot of weight; he was feeling the strain more and more.

"I'm getting old, that's what's the matter," said Robert one day, and, although he smiled as he said it, the smile was not very cheerful.

"Nonsense," cried Tonia. "You aren't old at all. Everybody is tired. You're working far too hard, and you don't get enough sleep."

Robert said no more, for he did not want to worry her, but he thought about it a good deal. He was getting old and Antonia was still very young. He had known this would happen, of course, but he had not expected it to happen so soon. If he could have retired and settled down in the country, he might have remained fit and hearty for many years. It was the war that was sapping his strength—this ghastly war. He would not complain, of course. He could not complain when thousands of men in the prime of their manhood were giving their lives for their country. In the last war Robert had served Britain with his body; in this war he was serving her with his brain. It was a pity that one could not dissociate the two, thought Robert sadly.

His Antonia was growing up very rapidly now and was more dear to him than ever. And she loved him, he knew that (it was evident in a hundred different ways), but she did not love him quite as he would have chosen. She had put him on a pedestal; she admired him and looked up to him and deferred to him in everything. Robert would rather have stood beside her on the level ground. Foolish, of course, thought Robert. Foolish to cry for the moon. He ought to be grateful for the joy and tenderness Antonia had brought into his life.

One night Tonia had been working late at the canteen and was on her way home, when the sirens began to howl. She hated the sound. The roar of the guns was terrifying, but the howl of the sirens did something horrible to one's inside… Tonia knew now what Joshua's people had felt when the men of Ai chased them: "…the hearts of the people melted, and became as water." Yes, that described it exactly, thought Tonia.

The sirens howled and the guns roared and barked and, far away, there was the sickening crash of bombs bursting. It was a bright night with a few scattered clouds in the sky—ideal conditions for a full-scale attack. Tonia hesitated on the edge of the pavement. She was anxious to get home to Robert, but perhaps it would be foolish to try, perhaps she had better take shelter somewhere. The question was *where,* and it suddenly became an urgent question, for the bombs were falling nearer and a house in the next street had burst into flames… People had started to run. They were running past her in all directions, calling to each other. "We might get a taxi!" somebody cried. "Not the tube. I couldn't, Harry!" exclaimed a woman's voice. "This way, this way—there's a shelter just around the corner!" shouted a man.

Tonia had turned to follow this man when she heard the

bomb coming—that unmistakable sound, that screeching, tearing, whistling sort of noise. Others had heard it, too; a mild stampede ensued and a man seized Tonia's arm, dragged her into an archway, and flung her on the ground. There was a deafening shattering crash like a thousand peals of thunder—it was the loudest thing that had ever happened...

⌘

"I don't think there's much the matter with this one," somebody said.

"I'll look at her in a minute," said another voice.

Tonia opened her eyes. Her head was buzzing and aching. She saw a man in a white coat bending over her and, beside him, a nurse with a pleasant friendly face. "Where's Robert?" Tonia said.

"I don't know. He's probably somewhere about," replied the doctor. "How are you feeling, yourself? Any pain?"

"No, what happened?"

"No pain at all?"

"No, I don't think so..."

"Keep her lying down for a bit," said the doctor and he hurried away.

"You lie still," said the nurse, patting her shoulder. "You'll be all right in a little—just lie still."

"Where am I?"

"In a first-aid post," replied the nurse.

Tonia lay still for a few minutes and then she raised herself on her elbow and looked around. She was lying on a mattress in a big empty garage. There were lights, bright unshaded bulbs dangling from the ceiling. People were moving about, talking, working, spreading more mattresses all over the floor; and a constant stream of stretcher-bearers poured in with wounded, putting the stretchers down, lifting the people onto the mattresses, and going away for more. Some of the people were moaning, some were talking rapidly in high unnatural voices, others were lying very still. Through all this confusion, the doctor and the nurses were moving about, soothing people and directing operations with unhurried calm. "Put her here, please." "Move that mattress. We must have a passageway down the middle." "There's a vacant mattress over there." "Dr. Strachey, this man needs immediate attention."

A child was lying on the mattress next to Tonia and sobbing in a hopeless sort of way. Tonia got up and bent over the child.

"I want Mummy," she said.

"Mummy will come soon," declared Tonia, and she knelt down and began to pat her shoulder. She found herself humming Nannie's song—"Kate Dalrymple."

"I want Mummy," said the child again, but this time in a drowsy sort of voice.

A nurse came up and said, "You've found her; that's good! Don't worry, she'll be all right. She'll be sent to the hospital when things calm down a bit, and you can go with her."

"She doesn't belong to me," Tonia said.

"Oh, doesn't she?" said the nurse, and she hurried away.

Things had been going smoothly until now, for the post was well organized, but now the wounded were arriving faster and there was no room for them. Things were getting beyond the capacities of the staff. More people poured in, wounded people supported by friends, wounded people carried in on stretchers. Tonia rose to her feet, for the child was asleep now, and she began to make her way to the door, stepping between the mattresses; but she had not gotten very far before she was swept into the struggle.

A woman called out for water and a nurse thrust a cup into Tonia's hands and pointed to the tap. Tonia fetched the water and helped the woman to drink it. Then somebody gave her an armful of bandages and told her to take them to Dr. Strachey, who was at the other end of the room.

"A three-inch bandage, please," said Dr. Strachey, holding out his hand. "The scissors now. Hold this a minute." Dr. Strachey had accepted her as an assistant as he would have accepted anyone who happened to be there. She went around with him after that, carrying the things he needed and fetching what he required, for this was something she could do and it relieved one of the nurses. She had learned first aid so she was not entirely ignorant, and Dr. Strachey was very patient with her. She was aware that she was not a *person* to Dr. Strachey. He never looked at her once. She was just an extra hand—not a very skillful hand, but a good deal better than nothing.

The things she saw as she went around with the doctor were dreadful beyond words, but she was still somewhat dazed, and the whole thing had happened so suddenly and was so unlike anything that had ever happened before that it seemed unreal to her. She was dreaming it; the sights and sounds were part of a nightmare, and soon, she would wake up and find herself safely in bed...

To add to the confusion and to increase the resemblance to a horrible dream, everyone seemed to have lost someone else. People wandered in from the street and moved hither and thither, looking at the wounded who were lying on the mattresses, or seized the arm of a passing nurse and besought her in agonized tones to tell them if she had seen their friends. Sometimes they found the people they were looking for and sat down beside them, patiently awaiting the doctor's verdict, but mostly they went away to try somewhere else. Their patience was very moving, Tonia thought. They were not angry or rebellious or demanding. No, they were just patient.

A woman was carried in. She had been rescued from beneath

a pile of fallen masonry and was covered with gray dust. She clutched Tonia's arm and cried, "Have you seen a little boy? A little boy with curly hair."

"Put her here," said Dr. Strachey. "Give me the hypodermic. I can't do anything at all…"

"Have you seen a little boy?" she asked, gazing up into Tonia's face. "Have you…seen a little…boy with…curly hair."

"You're all in," said the doctor, looking at Tonia suddenly. "Go and make some tea."

"I'm all right."

"Go and make some tea. It'll do us all good."

"Tea!" exclaimed the sister, who happened to be passing. "You'll find everything in the office."

Chapter Twelve
Making Tea

Tonia found a big urn in the office. There were some packets of tea on the table and a few cans of condensed milk.

The sister had followed her. "Have you got everything?" she asked. "I'll send a boy to help you. I saw a boy somewhere." She turned away, and then she hesitated and looked at Tonia in a bewildered sort of way. "Who are you?" she said.

"Who am I?" repeated Tonia stupidly.

"What's your name, I mean."

"Mrs. Norman."

"I suppose you belong to Lady Green's first-aid post."

"I don't belong anywhere," said Tonia.

The sister appeared quite satisfied with this extraordinary statement. She said, "I see. Well, you'll find a can opener in the drawer. Don't cut your fingers…"

"Don't cut my fingers!"

"Tin makes a very nasty cut," said the sister, and she disappeared.

Tonia laughed hysterically. It seemed so funny. *She mustn't cut her fingers…*

The boy appeared. He looked about thirteen years old; his hands and face were absolutely black and his clothes were in ribbons, but he smiled at Tonia quite cheerfully and asked what he was supposed to do.

"I wish we had some more tea," said Tonia. "There isn't much here—and there's no sugar at all. Where could we get some, I wonder."

"I know where there's a grocer," he replied and vanished.

All this time the guns had been banging furiously and bombs had been bursting all around, but Tonia had been too busy to notice them. She noticed them now, for she had nothing to do until the water boiled. She opened the door that led into the street and looked out. The sky was red. Houses were blazing. Three bombs fell some distance away, and a huge building crumpled and fell. One moment she saw its bulk, dark against the crimson sky, and the next moment it wavered unsteadily and, quite slowly, fell apart, crumbling, toppling, crashing with a noise like thunder. It isn't real, said Tonia to herself. You couldn't bear it if it were real.

Nothing was real—the hurrying people, the men with hoses shouting to each other, the streets slopping with water, the blazing fires, the acrid smoke eddying in the wind. None of it was real. It was the stuff nightmares are made of.

A man lurched past and leaned against the wall. He was merely a dark bulky shadow against the inferno. "The city is done for," he said in a hoarse voice. "All gone... St. Clement Dane's is like a furnace. I've just come from there. I'm trying to get home."

"You had better take shelter."

"My wife is having a baby."

"If you wait I'll give you a cup of tea."

"Tea!" exclaimed the man, and he laughed.

"I know, but I've nothing else."

He accepted a cup of tea and drank it standing there. He drank it quickly and handed back the cup. "How much?" he said.

"How much?" asked Tonia in surprise.

"How much money for the tea?"

"Oh—nothing," said Tonia. She watched him lurch away down the street. It seemed odd to think of money.

There were cups in the cupboard—all sorts of cups, most of them cracked or without handles. Tonia put them on a tray, filled them with tea and condensed milk, and carried them into the garage. The doctor and the nurses drank thirstily, for the acrid smoke that filled the air was parching to the throat. Some of the patients wanted it too and held up their hands for a cup.

"Don't give it to anyone without permission," said the sister. "Yes, that woman can have some. Leave the tray there and make some more. Put plenty of sugar in it."

The boy was in the office when Tonia went back. He had a sack full of packets of tea and sugar and cookies; he emptied it onto the table.

"How clever of you!" Tonia said. "I was afraid the shop wouldn't be open."

"It wasn't exactly open," said the boy. "I mean, it was… smashed open. Nobody was there so I just took the things." He gazed up at her as he spoke, his eyes very blue in his blackened face. "I just took them," he repeated. "I mean, nobody was there so I couldn't pay. Do you think it was all right? I didn't quite know what to do, you see. The walls were down. There was stuff lying about all over the place, tea and butter and bacon and everything all mixed up. It was horrible."

"I know, but it isn't real," said Tonia hastily.

He nodded. "We're dreaming, aren't we?" he said. "It's a pretty horrible dream. I shan't forget that shop in a hurry, you know."

"You soon forget dreams," she told him.

He was sorting out the packets now. "That's tea," he said. "I only took the whole packets, not the loose stuff. There might have been glass in it. The packets are sure to be all right, don't you think? Shall I fill up the urn with water?"

They worked away together, and while they worked the boy continued to talk. Tonia encouraged him to talk, for it was better for him and she found his talk soothing. "My name's Page," he said. "I'm at Eton, but of course this is the holidays. I'm fourteen—at least nearly. Dad and I were at the movies and Dad was called away—he's a doctor, you see—and he told me to go home, but I couldn't go home because the streets were all blocked. I tried, *really*. I don't quite know what happened… There was a fire. I got my hands a bit dirty… Do you think Dad will be angry? I did try to go home. I'm being useful, aren't I?"

"I couldn't possibly have managed without you."

"That's all right, then. I can tell Dad that."

The noise was frightful now. Bombs seemed to be crashing all around. The whole building rocked as if by an earthquake, and the lights swung backward and forward from the roof.

"It will be fun if the lights go out," said Page gravely. "As a matter of fact, I don't know why they haven't. I've got a flashlight, but it would be a bit difficult, wouldn't it?"

"Yes," said Tonia. She saw that he was a little frightened—and no wonder. For her part, she was almost sick with fright, but fright seemed to be affecting them in opposite ways, for Page was talking hard and she was almost incapable of answering.

"My brother's in the Guards," said Page, just a trifle unsteadily. "There's nobody like the Guards."

"I know," said Tonia.

"Nobody," repeated Page. "I expect if my brother was here he'd laugh like anything… This would be *nothing* to him, you know."

"Let's put in the tea now," said Tonia.

"I'm used to making tea," declared Page. "I do it at Eton, you see."

A nurse looked in at the door and said, "Are you getting on all right? Is it nearly ready?"

"Almost," replied Page. "The water was *absolutely* boiling."

There was a terrific crash. The light flickered, went out for a moment, and then came on again.

"There's something…queer about this," said Page. "It's—it's awfully queer, isn't it? I've never done anything like this before, have you?"

"No, never."

"I don't suppose there ever *was* anything like this before, except…d'you think Pompeii was like this?"

Tonia had not thought of Pompeii. "Perhaps, but not so noisy," she said, trying to speak in a natural voice.

"*That* was God, of course," said Page, as he took up a tray full of cups and led the way into the garage.

He was right, thought Tonia. Pompeii was God's vengeance and this was man's…

Quite suddenly the raid was over. The guns ceased firing and the sirens began to give the signal ALL CLEAR, taking it up all over the London area. "Whoo-eeee…" screeched the siren, and then another answered from a distance, "Whoo-eeee…" and the next moment they were all blowing, screeching like a chorus of fiends.

The night had seemed so long that Tonia felt it had lasted for weeks, so long that she had ceased wondering when it would end. Now that it was over she felt shaky at the knees and very, very cold. She leaned against the wall and tried to feel glad that she was alive, but somehow it did not seem to matter.

Page found her standing there. He had washed his face and hands, and she saw for the first time what he really looked like. His chubby face was very pale and there were dark shadows around his eyes. He ought not to have been here, thought Tonia in sudden dismay. He ought to be somewhere safe. He ought to be playing with toys...

"Good-bye," said Page. "I've got to go home now. It's been—it's been fun, hasn't it?" His lips were trembling a little as he spoke and he looked so young that Tonia wanted to kiss him.

They shook hands gravely.

"You've been splendid," Tonia said.

"Well, so have you," replied Page.

All this time the garage had been emptying. Patients were being carried out and put into ambulances, the walking wounded left with their friends, but there was a row of mattresses along the inner wall whose occupants were destined neither for the hospital nor home.

The nurses were clearing up as best they could. They were haggard and drawn, their eyes bloodshot and sunk in their sockets, their clothes stained and bedraggled.

"I'm finished now," declared Dr. Strachey. "Nothing more I can do, and there may be another show tonight. I'm going home—if I've got a home left. Anyone going my way? What about you?" he added, looking at Tonia as if he were seeing her for the first time.

"I'm going to Wintringham Square."

"I'll see you home if you like. Where's your coat?"

It was the last, but not the least, of all the odd things that had happened on that extraordinary night that Tonia had no coat and hat, nor had she the remotest idea when she had lost these garments. It did not matter, of course, but the mystery intrigued her.

"You *must* have a coat," declared the doctor. "You'll catch a chill. One of the nurses will find you a coat."

One of the nurses found a man's raincoat and wrapped it around her and tied a piece of bandage around her waist. "That will keep you warm, anyhow," said the nurse.

"All ready?" said Dr. Strachey. He opened the door and they went out together into the street.

It was broad daylight now. The fires were still blazing; tongues of flame were shooting out of the windows of a warehouse not more than a hundred yards away. There was a raw bitter smell in the air, a smell that caught your throat, and the streets were full of smoke and dust that drifted hither and thither and settled in the water underfoot. There were fire engines and hoses everywhere and crowds of people hurrying to and fro. Some of them had children in their arms; some were carrying furniture, which they had rescued from their burning homes. Furniture was piled up in the streets. Every now and then an ambulance drove by, and the muddy water sprayed from beneath its wheels. When you looked up at the houses, you saw the gaping windows with jagged pieces of glass, broken glass everywhere. It crunched and crackled beneath people's feet as they dug frantically among the ruins, while others stood by and watched them.

The darkness had been horrible but in daylight the scene was even worse. It was a desolate scene, an abomination of desolation. You could see the shattered houses, some of them cut in half as if with a knife, the rooms open to view and still full of domestic furniture. You could see the tumbled masonry, the blackened ruins that still smoked, the tottering walls, stark and naked in the light of day. And worst of all, you could see people's faces mirroring fatigue, horror, hopeless misery—faces set like stone or grimed with dirt and tears.

Dr. Strachey and Tonia walked along without saying very much, for they were beyond words. They went up one street and down another; some of the streets were closed because of the fires, or because of an unexploded bomb, or simply because they were blocked by masonry; but at last they arrived at Wintringham Square and found it still standing.

"It seems all right," said Dr. Strachey in surprise.

Tonia was surprised too. It was extraordinary to find that her home had escaped destruction.

They went upstairs together and opened the door of the flat, and Tonia ran in and called to Robert. She looked all over the flat, but Robert was not there, and his bed had not been slept in.

Dr. Strachey was waiting in the hall. He was leaning against the table, his face ghastly.

"You must have a drink," said Tonia. "My husband…but I don't know where he is!"

"He'll turn up all right," said Dr. Strachey in a flat voice. "I could do with a drink, really."

They went into the dining room and Tonia poured out some whisky. She said, "This is…war."

"It's war," he replied. "Worse than the trenches…such a horrible mixture of everyday life and fantastic horror…don't worry about your husband too much. I expect he's gone out to look for you."

"Poor Robert!"

"Lucky Robert to come home and find you safe."

"But I can't wait here—"

"Don't be silly," he replied. "You can't possibly search all London. The best thing you can do is to go to bed." He gave her two small pink pills and went away.

Tonia could not go to bed. How could she, when she didn't know where Robert was? She did not know if he was alive. She sat down on the sofa and thought about it and wondered what to do.

Tonia's head felt heavy. She rested it on a cushion and suddenly…she began to sink…down…down, down, deep down to the bottom of the sea. The fishes were swimming about all around her, looking at her. The water was green and cool and translucent. She looked up and saw a ceiling above her head, a yellowish white ceiling with a stain on it like the man in the moon. "The man in the moon came down too soon," said Lou. "Come on, Tonia, I'll take care of you…" Tonia rose and drifted out onto the landing and down the stairs with her fingertips resting on the banisters. The hall door was open and she drifted out…she was dancing now, dancing with Robert; the band was playing "The Blue Danube." A woman clutched her arm and cried, "Have you seen a little boy, a little boy with curly hair…with curly hair…with curly hair…" Now Robert had vanished and she was trying to find him; she was searching among the blackened ruins of a church—it was St. Clement Dane's. She could not find him. "Robert!" she cried. "Robert…Robert!"

⚬∞⚬

Someone was shaking her gently. Tonia opened her eyes and there was Robert looking at her; he bent over her and caught her in his arms, kissing her fiercely. She clung to him with all her strength.

Chapter Thirteen
A War Casualty

A year passed and then another. They were slow years and a great deal happened. London was bombed again and again, though mercifully never quite so badly. The armies moved forward and backward across North Africa. America came into the war. The Russians won the Battle of Stalingrad and surged forward in their millions against the common foe. At home in Britain the outlook changed from grim and dogged determination to a determination full of hope. Victory was possible. It was probable. It was certain if we could just hold on. The most spectacular event at home was the advent of the Americans; one saw them everywhere: in the streets, in tubes and buses, in theaters and restaurants, thousands of young Americans full of life and energy and enthusiasm. But there were other changes, too. There were more women in uniform; there was less food; there was less traffic.

Robert and Tonia were still in the flat (the windows had been broken twice, but otherwise it was undamaged), and Robert was busier than ever, for he was working for the Treasury now and carrying on his firm's business as well. His days were full, and he brought home papers and worked at them half the night. Tonia started to help Robert with the work he brought home, and she was so quick and intelligent that Robert suggested she come to the office. He made the suggestion in a tentative manner, but Tonia leaped at the chance, for she realized that this was important work—more important than cooking at the canteen—and if Robert really wanted her it was her duty to go. She was quite untrained, of course, but she was intelligent and conscientious. She could add and spell and write a clear letter, and, as most of the clerks had gone and had been replaced by incompetent girls, Robert found his wife's services invaluable. He could give her a letter to answer and say, "Tell them they can't do that. Tell them to send someone around to see me on Monday and I'll explain," and he could hurry away to a meeting knowing that the whole thing would be tactfully managed and the appointment arranged.

But although Tonia helped him more and more, assuming responsibility and arranging and rearranging his appointments, she could not take the heavy strain off his shoulders. He began to look very tired and older than his years; his step became slower and heavier.

"You ought to have a holiday," Tonia declared.

"How can I, Antonia? We're doing important work, you and I."

"You'll get ill," said Tonia. "Honestly, Robert, nobody could go on like this. Everybody has holidays except you."

"I haven't noticed you taking a holiday," replied Robert.

"But, Robert—"

"I can't," he replied with a worried look. "There's an important conference next week—perhaps after that."

She knew, then, that he was really feeling the strain, and she worried more than ever, though her days were now so full that she had not much time for worrying. The telephone never ceased ringing and Robert was in constant demand. Would Mr. Norman prepare statistics of this? Would Mr. Norman give his opinion on that? Could Mr. Norman see a representative of half a dozen different firms and unions? Could Mr. Norman come to a meeting at the Treasury? Robert was worried and badgered and run off his legs, but somehow or other everything was done and the conference was a success.

By this time, however, Robert was so exhausted both physically and mentally that there was no possibility of going away for a holiday—as Tonia had hoped. Robert lay in bed, looking like a ghost, too tired to sleep or eat.

"Thank goodness the conference is over," said Robert in a feeble voice. "I don't believe I could get up if I tried."

"I'll ask Dr. Strachey to come," said Tonia.

"Perhaps you'd better," Robert agreed.

Dr. Strachey had become a friend. He had called in to ask for Tonia after the "blitz" and, since then, they had seen him frequently. Tonia had a high opinion of him, for she had seen him at work and noted his calm confidence and competence. Robert liked him, too. They had had some long talks together. He came around at once.

"You know," said Tonia, when Dr. Strachey came out of Robert's room. "You know he's been doing too much. I've been dreadfully worried about him." She had been so worried about him that she was almost glad he was ill. It seemed queer, perhaps, but that was how she felt. It was a relief to have Robert at home, safely in bed, to be able to look after him and give him his meals at the proper time. She explained this to Dr. Strachey.

"I'm afraid he has carried on too long," said Dr. Strachey gravely.

"Do you mean he's *very* ill?" asked Tonia in alarm.

Apparently this was exactly what he meant, though he did not actually say so. He said he would like another opinion—a heart specialist—and added that he would send in two nurses so that Mr. Norman need not be moved more than was absolutely necessary.

Tonia went in and looked at Robert. She had been with him constantly, so she had not noticed the change in him as much as a stranger might have, but now, looking at him with new eyes, she saw how worn and haggard he had become.

"Antonia," he said, rousing himself with difficulty. "Perhaps you had better go down to the office…those returns should be ready today."

"You mustn't worry," declared Tonia. "You must rest. You've worn yourself to a shadow."

"I am resting."

"But you're worrying, Robert. Don't worry about the office. You'll be better soon and then you'll be able to see to everything."

"Did the doctor say that?"

"Yes, of course," replied Tonia, lying bravely.

"I thought he had more sense," said Robert with a faint smile. He was silent for a few moments and then he added, "Don't tell Janet. She would come by the first train. I'm not strong enough to bear Janet."

Tonia did not feel strong enough, either.

"I just want you," added Robert.

The two nurses arrived and took possession of the flat. They altered the furniture in Robert's bedroom, and they altered the hours of meals, and they asked for things that they happened to need so that Tonia found her time fully occupied in running messages to and from the shops. She did not mind, of course; she minded nothing if they could nurse Robert back to health, but this prospect seemed more and more doubtful. Some days Robert was better, other days he was worse, and the weeks dragged on interminably. The nurses moved about quietly— only their aprons rustled—and they spoke to each other frequently and at length in hushed whispers.

It was a dreadful time. Tonia could not have borne it if it had not been for Dr. Strachey, who came in every day and eased her burden. He did not try to buoy her up with false optimism but encouraged her to face the issue squarely.

"He may recover," said Dr. Strachey in answer to a straight question. "But he could never get really fit. He wouldn't like being an invalid, would he?"

"No," said Tonia doubtfully. "But I wouldn't mind. I mean, I would rather have Robert—"

"Don't give up hope. Miracles sometimes happen, but it's better to face the music, isn't it? Of course I don't talk to all my patients' relations so frankly, but I know you. I know you can take it."

"I'll try," said Tonia making an effort to live up to his opinion of her.

"He's a war casualty," continued Dr. Strachey. "He's been wounded in battle—think of it like that. The success of the conference is largely due to his genius for finance. A fellow who was there told me that Mr. Norman did magnificent work both before the conference, preparing the figures, and during the conference as well. He saved the situation several times by his quick, clear grasp of the essential and his extraordinary tact."

"It wore him out," said Tonia huskily.

"He's a war casualty," repeated Dr. Strachey.

This talk helped Tonia a good deal, for it removed the feeling that Robert had worn himself out to no purpose, that the sacrifice was in vain…and Tonia needed all the help she could get, for it now became obvious that Robert was going very quickly down the hill. Tonia could see it for herself only too clearly.

It was a Sunday evening when the day nurse came to Tonia and said that Mr. Norman wanted her. "He's a little easier now, but don't let him talk too much," she said.

Tonia went in. She felt numb with misery. She was long past tears. The bedroom window was wide open and the evening sunshine filled the room with golden light. The bells were ringing for evening service. They had started to ring again after their long years of silence, and their sound took Tonia back to her childhood and her old home.

Robert was lying very still, propped up with pillows, his face turned toward the door. He smiled at Tonia when he saw her and moved his hand a little. She went forward and took his hand in hers.

"Don't grieve, darling," said Robert faintly. "I'm happy—quite comfortable and happy. I want to talk."

"You shouldn't talk," she whispered.

"I want to...and there isn't much time...the bells, darling. Isn't it nice to hear the bells?"

She sat down beside him and waited.

"You've been wonderful," he said, after a little silence. "You've given me the happiest years of my life. Nobody could ask more than five years of happiness."

"I can't bear it," she said.

"I know," he replied. "I know it's hard, but it's better this way. I've thought about it so much. I've always dreaded growing old...and being a bother to you."

"Don't, Robert..."

"I've thought about it so much..."

"Robert—don't leave me. Promise you'll be with me—wherever you are."

"How can I?" said Robert thoughtfully. "And even if I could it wouldn't be right. Someday you will find—somebody else—"

"No, Robert—oh, no!"

"You're young—so beautifully young—all life before you. Don't be frightened of life. It's good. Make friends with life, Antonia."

She pressed his hand.

"Make friends...with life," said Robert faintly.

The bells had stopped ringing now and Robert's eyes were shut. He was asleep and breathing more easily. Perhaps he was better. Perhaps he was going to stay with her after all…but Robert did not stay.

Chapter Fourteen
Patience and Politeness

Tonia was alone in the flat except for a woman who came in every day. It was curious to be alone and have nothing whatever to do, but she was so miserable that she did not want other people. She was dismayed when she received a telegram from Janet Garland saying that she and Nita would come on Tuesday. How long would they stay, Tonia wondered, but it was no use wondering that. Janet was Robert's sister so she must be welcomed as warmly as possible and Nita must be welcomed too. Janet's last visit had not been a success, but Tonia felt older now and less in awe of Janet, so perhaps she would manage better this time. As for Nita, Tonia had scarcely seen her since they had been at school together—Nita was an unknown quantity.

They arrived and were welcomed, and the morning after their arrival they were all in the lounge together. Janet was sitting in Robert's chair reading the paper. Tonia had a curious feeling about Robert's chair. It was a silly feeling, of course, but she wished Janet had chosen to sit somewhere else. She also wished (most unreasonably) that Janet did not resemble Robert. She was like him in some ways, but so very unlike him in others.

"You will have to give up the flat and go home to Edinburgh," Janet said.

"Yes, but not till August," replied Tonia. "We took the flat until the end of August."

"And then Edinburgh, I suppose."

"I haven't really thought about it."

"What about your work?" asked Nita, taking up the paper her mother had dropped and glancing at it casually.

Tonia explained that her work was at an end. She had been Robert's private secretary, and now somebody else had taken over the work Robert had been doing, and he would have his own secretary—probably an experienced one. She explained it all carefully, but she was aware that before she got to the end the attention of her audience had wandered. Neither Janet nor Nita was really interested in what she did. Nobody was interested in what she did; that was the hardest thing to bear.

"I'm rather surprised," said Janet, looking at her young sister-in-law with a disapproving air. "I must say I'm rather surprised to see that you aren't wearing black. Of course I know it isn't the fashion nowadays, but it seems very odd to me."

"He wouldn't like it," said Tonia in a low voice.

"It shows respect," said Janet. "Respect for his memory."

"Don't be silly, Mother," said Nita, looking up from a letter she had begun to write at Robert's desk. "Nobody wears black now, and it wouldn't suit Tonia—she would look frightful."

"That isn't why—" began Tonia, and then she stopped. For one thing they were not listening and, for another, she could never make them understand. Let them think what they liked. What on earth did it matter, thought Tonia miserably. They had begun to argue now. It was something about a handker-chief each claimed as her own, and Tonia listened to the heated controversy in amazement. She realized that their values were entirely different from hers—things she thought important did not interest them, and things they regarded as vital seemed to her of no account whatsoever. (This impression remained

with Tonia, and the more she saw of the Garlands the deeper it
became; they never gave her cause to alter it.) She would have
to bear with them as long as they wanted to stay because they
were Robert's relations, but how glad she would be when they
went away and left her in peace!

Nita had started to rummage through the drawers of Robert's
desk, and somehow this was more than Tonia could bear.

"Please don't," said Tonia, going over to her. "I can give
you some notepaper if that's what you want...and that's
Robert's pen!"

"I know," replied Nita in a casual tone. "I've lost my foun-
tain pen. This nib suits me rather well, which seems odd when
you think of Uncle Robert's queer writing. You had better give
it to me, Tonia; it won't suit you."

"I want to keep it," Tonia said.

"But it won't suit you. It's no use to you. Why on earth do
you want to keep it?"

"Because it was Robert's."

"It's rather selfish of you, dear," interposed Janet. "Robert
would have liked Nita to have it, I'm sure."

Tonia let her have it: she could not wrangle with them over
Robert's pen.

It was curious (Tonia thought) how one's whole life could fall
to pieces in a moment. She had lost not only Robert himself, his
love and kindness and companionship, but also the settled and
secure feeling his presence had given her. With Robert's death
everything had changed. The whole fabric of Tonia's life had
disintegrated. She was giving up the flat—that was settled—but
what was she to do? Should she return to Edinburgh and open up
the house in Belgrave Crescent? Could she bear it? Wouldn't it be
better to join one of the women's services and be useful and busy?
She decided that it would, and without telling Janet (who might
have tried to dissuade her) she made inquiries about the Auxiliary

Territorial Service. They wanted girls badly and almost immediately she was called up for an interview and a medical examination.

A woman doctor examined Tonia and turned her down. "You aren't fit," she said, looking at Tonia kindly. "There's nothing wrong organically, nothing that a few months' rest won't cure. I expect you've had a bad time lately, haven't you?"

"Yes, I suppose I have," admitted Tonia.

"You need rest and a strong tonic."

"Then…you don't want me?"

"I'm sorry," said the doctor. "I'm very sorry indeed. We want girls, of course, especially girls of your type who can take responsibility, but it wouldn't be the slightest use passing you because you would just break down. That wouldn't be much help, would it? Come back in six months—and don't worry. There's nothing serious the matter."

Tonia did not tell Janet about the interview because Janet fussed enough already. Janet was always telling her she was too thin and encouraging her to eat or exclaiming that she was pale and advising her to lie down. She fussed in other ways, too, for she always wanted to know where Tonia was going and when she would be back, and she kept on saying that Tonia would tire herself.

"I'm going to a symphony concert," said Tonia one day, when urged by Janet to give an account of her movements.

"A concert!" cried Janet in horrified tones. "Really Tonia, I can't understand you at all. Fancy *wanting* to go to a concert!"

"But why not?" asked Tonia. "Robert loved music. We always went to these symphony concerts together."

"Poor Robert," said Janet with a sigh.

"It's poor *me*," declared Tonia with unusual show of spirit. "It isn't 'poor Robert' at all. Robert was a saint and he's perfectly happy now. If I didn't know that for certain I couldn't bear it… but I *do* know that."

Janet was startled at this outburst and she answered softly, so softly that Tonia was sorry and felt she had been unkind. She must try to be more patient, she decided. As a matter of fact she was trying to be patient already, not only with Janet but with Nita...and how wearing it was! Nita turned on the wireless at all hours of the day and filled the flat with the voices of crooners or swing music; Nita borrowed silk stockings and forgot to return them. No, it wasn't easy to be patient. Tonia made allowances, of course, telling herself that Robert had spoiled her and that she must learn to rub shoulders with less understanding people.

Perhaps the thing that worried Tonia most was her guests' attitude to their friends. Both Janet and Nita had friends in or near London and issued cordial invitations to them to come and eat Tonia's food, and then, when these people had come and gone, Janet and Nita would set to work and pull them to pieces, criticizing their manners and their clothes, making fun of their conversation and discussing their private affairs without charity or understanding. It made Tonia miserable to hear them. Sometimes she could bear it no longer and was obliged to get up and leave the room. They discussed their hostess too, of course, and discussed her with the same lack of proper feeling. Tonia was sure of that, and her conviction was confirmed when one day she happened to be passing the door of the lounge and heard the tail end of a conversation. Nita had a loud penetrating voice and this voice was saying in dogmatic fashion, "Oh yes, I *know,* but any man would marry her with all that money."

How horrible! thought Tonia, hastening away with burning cheeks. How horrible to think of her marrying...anybody... now...after Robert...how beastly to discuss it like that...to imply that she was worth nothing in herself...that all men were fortune hunters.

There was so much nastiness in the remark, so many

unpleasant implications, that Tonia found it more difficult than ever to be patient and polite.

Soon after this Frank Melville came up from Oxford and spent the weekend at his club. He called at the flat to see Tonia and was very friendly and kind. Tonia liked Frank. They had had fun together, finding his rooms, and she and Robert had missed him when the ministry had moved to Oxford. She was glad to see him and welcomed him cordially, and they had tea together.

"You'll be giving up this flat, of course," said Frank, looking around.

"Yes," agreed Tonia. "I've decided to go back to Edinburgh and open up the house in Belgrave Crescent."

"Don't do that," said Frank earnestly. "I've thought of a much better plan. I can get you a job at Oxford, and we shall be able to see more of each other. You see, Tonia, you may be called up. That wouldn't suit us, would it?"

Tonia hesitated before replying, for Frank's air was too possessive and she did not like it much. She was aware that she would not be called up, for she had tried to join the ATS and failed, but somehow or other she did not want to tell Frank about it. She did not want to tell Frank anything; she only wanted him to go away. Nita's words came into her mind as she looked at him sitting there, smiling at her…*any man would marry her with all that money.*

"Well, what about it?" inquired Frank. "You'd like the work. It wouldn't be hard and we could see each other in our spare time. We could go up the river together and all that. We could have picnics. I'll fix up the whole thing; as a matter of fact, it's practically fixed already. I was sure you would say yes."

"I can't," declared Tonia. "No, honestly, Frank…"

"But why?"

"I've arranged to go back to Edinburgh."

"Oh, Tonia—why? Do think about it. Please think about it…"

He continued trying to persuade her until at last Tonia was forced to say she would think about it and let him know. Fortunately Janet came in at that moment and Frank got up and went away. Tonia had never been pleased to see Janet before; she was particularly nice to Janet all the evening.

This interview with Frank was worrying for several reasons but mainly because it underlined the words Tonia had over-heard. They were poisonous words; she knew that and tried to banish them from her mind, for she saw quite clearly that they might become an obsession. And if they became an obsession (if every time a man spoke to her in a friendly manner she began to think he wanted to marry her, and marry her for her money) life would soon become unbearable. It's nonsense, said Tonia to herself. Frank was only being friendly and kind. It was only because I heard Nita say that horrible thing that I imagined. Frank was different…

Chapter Fifteen
The Trustees' Meeting

The Garlands stayed on and made no mention of future plans. They were comfortable and happy and were living at Tonia's expense. She did not know how to get rid of them…but they would have to leave when she gave up the flat; that was something to look forward to. There was a good deal to do before giving up the flat—china and linen and silver to be packed up and sent home to the house in Edinburgh, and, to give Janet her due, she was helpful in these necessary preparations for removal, and was able to make sensible suggestions as to how things should be done. They worked together—she and Tonia—and once or twice Tonia tried to sound her about her plans, but Janet was evasive about the matter and would not be drawn.

One morning Tonia was obliged to attend a meeting of trustees to settle some business affairs, so she took a tube to the city and found her way, with some little difficulty, to the lawyer's office, and here she found three elderly gentlemen awaiting her arrival. They were Robert's friends, of course, and she had met them before: Mr. Macdonald, Mr. Phillips, and Mr. Wisdon. Mr. Phillips had come from Edinburgh to attend the meeting, which made it seem very important. After some preliminary conversation about the condition of the weather, they began to talk business and Tonia was informed that practically the whole of Robert's estate was left to her in trust without any conditions whatever.

"Whatever does that mean?" asked Tonia patiently.

"It means that you will derive the income from the estate but you cannot touch the capital," replied Mr. Macdonald, who seemed to be the spokesman. "The capital is to be held in trust for your children—if any."

"My children!"

"You may marry again," Mr. Macdonald pointed out. "The trust provides for that eventuality."

"What does that mean?" asked Tonia.

"It means," said Mr. Macdonald in patient tones. "It means that you forfeit nothing if you marry again. You continue to receive the same income. It is an unusual provision but Mr. Norman was determined upon it."

"I shall never marry again," declared Tonia.

There was a short silence and then Mr. Macdonald cleared his throat and continued. "The income is large. I can give you the figures, of course. Let me see now. Where did I put that paper…"

Tonia did not listen. She knew Robert was rich, and the figures, which Mr. Macdonald was reading out, did not seem to matter. She was wondering how long she would have to sit there in that dull, dusty room. She watched a bluebottle buzzing feebly on the windowpane.

"…she would share expenses, of course," said Mr. Macdonald and his voice ceased. They were all looking at Tonia expectantly.

"I'm sorry," said Tonia, blushing furiously. "I'm afraid—I'm afraid I wasn't listening."

Mr. Macdonald looked surprised and a trifle pained. He was not used to dealing with clients who did not listen to him. He cleared his throat again. "It was about Mrs. Garland," he said in reproachful tones. "Mrs. Garland made the suggestion that you should combine your households."

"You mean—you mean Janet wants to come and live with me!" exclaimed Tonia in dismay.

"And her daughter, of course."

"Oh no!" cried Tonia. "No, I couldn't possibly…"

There was a short silence. Mr. Macdonald glanced at Mr. Wisdon and gave an almost imperceptible shrug; Mr. Wisdon nodded, pursing his mouth; Mr. Phillips was looking at Tonia doubtfully.

"We think you should consider it," said Mr. Macdonald at last. "The arrangement seems sensible and beneficial to both parties. Mrs. Garland is not very well off. Your husband helped her a good deal. In fact, she spent a great part of her time beneath his roof."

"I know, but that was before Robert and I were married."

"She is a very charming lady," put in Mr. Wisdon.

"Oh yes," agreed Tonia. "Yes, of course, but—"

"And you would have the benefit of her experience."

"I know, but—"

"You don't propose to live alone, do you?"

"Of course I do," said Tonia firmly.

The trustees looked at her in dismay. There she sat, looking about seventeen years old and talking like it, too, Robert's widow, and so appallingly wealthy…a prey to fortune hunters, thought Robert's friends, remembering the unconventional conditions of the trust.

Mr. Macdonald drew a long breath. "My dear Mrs. Norman," he said. "You are so young and—and attractive (if you will allow me to say so), it would be so very much better if you would accept Mrs. Garland's suggestion and share your home with her and her daughter—at least for the duration of the war. We are all agreed that it would be best for all parties. Mrs. Garland would be able to act as chaperon, you would find her experience helpful, and the arrangement would solve her problems, which are largely financial."

"I could give her the house," suggested Tonia with sudden inspiration. "Yes, of course I could. The house in Belgrave Crescent is much too big for me…and it would remind me of Robert all the time. That's a splendid idea, isn't it?"

Apparently it was not. The idea Tonia hailed as an inspiration met with the unqualified disapproval of her trustees. She discovered that, for some reason or other, you could not give away houses even if you did not want to live in them yourself. It was all very difficult indeed.

It was so difficult that nothing was settled except that Mrs. Norman was to think about it and talk it over with her sister-in-law. The three elderly gentlemen put their faith in Mrs. Garland. They had done their best to prepare the way and they could do no more.

The remainder of their business was easily accomplished, papers were signed and witnessed—Mrs. Norman wrote her name, most obediently, exactly where she was told—and then they said good-bye and Mr. Macdonald showed her out.

Tonia found the sun shining; the street was very bright after the dimness of the lawyer's room. She hesitated on the doorstep and looked up and down. People were passing, hurrying off to lunch. They were free people; they could do what they liked; they wouldn't have to live with Janet, and Nita. Somehow or other Tonia felt like a mouse in a trap, the horrible sort of trap that doesn't hurt the mouse but just confines it so that it can't run away. But I'm *not* a mouse, thought Tonia.

Part Two

Chapter Sixteen

Homecoming

It was a very dark evening about the beginning of September. The London train drew into Ryddelton Station and one passenger alighted. She stood there, looking around in a dazed manner, for the sudden transition from the lighted compartment to the gloomy platform was blinding, and before she had time to recover her powers of vision a porter, carrying an oil lantern, loomed out of the darkness and began to collect her luggage and stack it on a handbarrow.

"Is there a taxi?" inquired the passenger anxiously.

"Are they not meeting you?" asked the porter, answering the question with another question, which happened to be his way.

"Who?" inquired the passenger, adding immediately, "No, nobody is meeting me. I want a taxi, please."

"But you'll be staying at one of the big houses—Dunnian, maybe."

"No," said the lady firmly.

The porter looked at her in perplexity. "You'll not get a taxi tonight," he told her.

"Then I suppose I shall have to walk."

"Are you going far?"

"I'm going to Melville House. I don't know how far it is, but—"

"But it's shut!" exclaimed the porter. "It's been shut since Miss Dalrymple died!"

"I can open it, I suppose," returned the lady a trifle impatiently, for she was finding the porter's interest in her affairs rather overwhelming.

"You can open it!"

"Yes, the people who live next door have charge of the key."

"Well now, who'd have thought it? You'll be Miss Antonia Melville, I shouldn't wonder?"

"Yes—at least I was."

"Mr. Henry's daughter!" exclaimed the man, and he held up his lantern and took a good look at her. "Aye, you're a Melville," he added in a satisfied tone of voice.

The light had revealed his face as well as Antonia's. He was a round, ruddy old man with snow-white hair and dimpled cheeks, a benevolent-looking old man who might easily have taken the part of Father Christmas at a children's party. She discovered a little later that his name was Mr. Smilie, and it certainly suited him.

"I mind Mr. Henry well," continued Mr. Smilie. "He was a likely young fellow—a bit younger than me, but not much. Is he well enough now?"

"Quite well, thank you."

It was very dark, and a chill wind was whistling through the station, a remarkably chill wind considering the time of year, and Tonia, who had come straight from London, where it had been warm and stuffy, was not very warmly clad. She was cold and tired and she did not know what to do—she could scarcely stand here all night listening to reminiscences of her father's boyhood.

"I think I had better go," she said at last. "It's very dark and I don't know the way. Could you tell me which way to go?"

"Why not? Our house is next door."

"Next door?" asked Tonia.

"Next door to Melville House. Mother has the key of it, you see. She's looked after the place since Miss Dalrymple died, like the lawyer asked her."

"How kind of her!"

"Na, na, it's a pleasure to her. It's no bother at all…but what will we do? You'd have a job finding the way in the dark."

"It would be rather difficult, but I dare say——"

"See here now, can you not wait a few minutes? I'll need to be here when the Edinburgh train comes in and then I'll be away home myself, so it'll be easy enough to show you the way and take your things along on the barra. Will that do now?"

"It would be splendid!"

"Come away, then," said Mr. Smilie, and without more ado he took Tonia by the arm in a friendly manner and led her into the lamp room.

It was warm in here, for a tremendous fire was burning in the high old-fashioned grate, and Tonia was extremely glad to see it, for her hands were numb with cold.

"There now," said Mr. Smilie. "You can sit doon here for a wee while and get warmed through. The train'll no be long now. Did you come from London? What like's London these days? It's difficult to think of London without lights…and the White Horse Whisky in Piccadilly Circus, they'll not have that on now?"

"No, I'm afraid not."

"And yon bottle that kept on pouring out. It was a neat thing. Many's the time I've stood and looked at yon bottle…"

Tonia felt as if she were dreaming. Only a bit of her was here, sitting on the wooden bench, inhaling the strong smell of lamp oil and listening to the stream of conversation with which Mr. Smilie was whiling away the period of waiting for the Edinburgh train. She was tired—perhaps that was the reason she felt so bewildered, or perhaps it was because everything was so different. Mr. Smilie himself was absolutely different from anyone she had ever met before.

"We went to London most time for our holidays," continued Mr. Smilie. "That was before the war of course. You see, it's cheap fares if you work on the railway and Mother likes London. I like it fine myself for a wee while, but it's just awful the way the money goes. We'd put aside as much as we could spare and when it was spent we'd come home—that was the way we did. Mother was all for London this year, but I got her off it and we went to Portobello instead."

"It would have been a long journey for an old lady," remarked Tonia, who felt some sort of remark was expected.

"Och, Mother's younger than me," said Mr. Smilie, smiling. "Maybe she's not as young as she was but she's very active on her pins—and she's all for adventure. Adventure's the breath of life to Mother. You'll not believe it but she had me over to France one year—baloney," said Mr. Smilie, nodding portentously. "Baloney it was. I tell you it made me open my eyes when I heard those Johnnies jabbering together. It's a queer thing. I knew they would talk French before I went, but it was not till I got there I really believed it…"

"It does seem…odd," agreed Tonia faintly.

"Maybe you can talk French?"

"A little," admitted Tonia.

"Mother can talk it like a Frenchie," declared Mr. Smilie, nodding. "I tell you it made me proud to hear the way Mother ordered yon fellows about—and they did what she said, too. Mind you, she had the opportunity. She was with a French lady before she married me. She was with her for five years as housemaid and looked after her when she was ill, and the lady would talk away to her and that, but it's not everybody would take the opportunity like Mother did."

"She must be very clever," said Tonia.

"She is that," agreed Mr. Smilie. "Now I'll tell you...Och, there's the train!"

Mr. Smilie hastened away, and when he had dealt kindly and competently with the small group of arrivals he pronounced himself ready to start.

"They were all just strangers," he declared in derogatory accents as he took up the handles of the barrow.

Tonia got the inference. They were all strangers and therefore to be pitied, almost to be despised, but she was a Melville. She had never set foot in Ryddelton before, but for all that she belonged here. She had come home. It gave her a curious feeling, a nice warm comforting sort of feeling to know that Mr. Smilie regarded her as a friend.

They set off together—Mr. Smilie still talking—though his conversation was difficult to follow owing to the rattle of the barrow on the cobblestones. It was not so dark now, or perhaps Tonia's eyes had adjusted themselves to the gloom. She could see the dark bulk of houses on either side and the pattern of their chimneys outlined against the sky. She could see trees with wildly waving branches, and here and there a tiny chink of light from some carelessly blacked-out window. The town was very quiet, the streets empty; there was not a creature to be seen. They passed up a very narrow street with little shops (shops with closed doors and shuttered windows), and here the rattle of the barrow sounded louder than ever, echoing from side to side. It was a relief when they left this street and debouched into a very wide one with trees down the middle and a war memorial among the trees.

"This is the High Street," said Mr. Smilie, raising his voice. "They used to have a market here on Wednesdays. We've not far to go now—a hundred yards or so. The house is just beyond the post office."

Tonia was quite exhausted by this time, and she was thankful when Mr. Smilie stopped and put down the barrow and intimated that this was Melville House.

"I'll need to get the key from Mother," he explained and left her standing there.

Tonia looked at her house. It was lighter here in the broad, open street so she could see the house fairly clearly. She could see that it was very old and solidly built of gray stone. On one side of it was a smaller house that seemed to be huddling against it in a friendly sort of way; on the other side was a dairy. The door of Melville House was on a level with the street. It was simply a door in the wall, and on each side of the door there were windows protected by iron railings. Above, there were three windows, each with a small iron balcony. The whole house was slightly uneven, slightly off the straight. It reminded Tonia of the bottles Robert had collected with so much enthusiasm. Yes, it was a handmade house, thought Tonia with satisfaction.

"Here's the key!" said Mr. Smilie. "I'll open the door for you," and slipping an enormous key into the lock, he turned it and threw the door open.

It was very dark inside, but Mr. Smilie led the way in with a confidence born of familiarity. "Bide here," he said. "There's electricity, but it's turned off at the main and I'll need to find the switch before we can see what's what."

"It's awfully good of you," said Tonia feebly.

He did not reply to this but disappeared into the back premises. She could hear him moving about, his heavy boots clumping on the stone floor. How kind he is! thought Tonia as she waited, leaning against a big oak chest that stood at one side of the hall. How lucky I was to meet him! What on earth should I have done if he hadn't been there!

She had no time to answer her own questions, for suddenly

the electricity went on in a blinding dazzle and lit up the hall, showing it to be three-cornered in shape with a low oak-beamed ceiling and paneled walls and paved with large gray flagstones. The stairs went up very steeply from the corner farthest from the door. She saw all this in a flash, and she also saw that the front door was standing wide open (it had been an oblong of faint light but had now become an oblong of complete blackness), and she shut it hastily for she was "blackout conscious" to a marked degree.

"That's right," said Mr. Smilie, emerging from the kitchen. "We'll not need to let Hitler see us. I wonder what Mother was thinking of to leave the switch on. I'll get on to her about it, you'll see," added Mr. Smilie with a chuckle. "Now, I'll just carry up the luggage and then you'll get tidied. Supper will be ready in ten minutes."

"Supper."

"Next door," said Mr. Smilie, pointing sideways with his thumb. "I told you our house was next door.

"Oh!" exclaimed Tonia in dismay. "Oh, but I don't think… you see, I'm so tired…I think I shall just go straight to bed. It's most awfully kind of you but you do understand, don't you?"

"I might, but Mother won't," replied Mr. Smilie, getting even redder in the face than he was before. "It's no good me saying she will. Mother will be in here before you can blink twice and you'll be brought around to our house for your supper. It would save a deal of trouble if you'd come quiet," added Mr. Smilie persuasively. "It would, really. Mother and me have been married for forty years, as near as makes no odds."

Tonia realized that the last sentence clinched the matter, betraying as it did a lifelong experience of Mrs. Smilie's forcefulness and strength of purpose, so after a few more feeble expostulations and expressions of gratitude she went upstairs to wash. It was quite a small house—or rather it gave the impression of being small. Tonia opened several of the doors on the upper landing and peeped into the rooms. They were small rooms with low ceilings and floors of dark wood that sloped a little from the windows toward the doors. The walls were uneven too; they bulged slightly here and there. The shutters were all tightly shut, but the house smelled quite fresh and there was very little dust upon the furniture. The bathroom was painted green and white. It boasted a silver towel rail that reminded Tonia that she wanted a towel, so she looked about and found the linen cupboard with neatly stacked piles of linen upon the shelves. It was all just as Nannie had left it. Dear Nannie, thought Tonia, as she took a towel from the cupboard (it had a crochet border, of course, and a big red D in the corner) and went into the bathroom to wash.

"There's no hot water," said a voice from the door—quite a soft, pleasant voice but for all that it made Tonia jump. She looked around and saw a small thin woman with red cheeks, like apples, and high cheekbones and gray smooth hair.

"If I'd known," declared the woman, standing in the doorway with her hands upon her hips. "If I'd known you were coming, if you'd postcarded me, I'd have had the fire on and a nice cup of tea waiting. It's not very nice to arrive at night in a cold empty house."

"But I didn't know—"

"I'll need to take the sheets and air them. They'll get the chill off while we're at our supper."

"Please don't bother—" began Tonia. "I mean, I can easily sleep in blankets tonight—"

"Miss Dalrymple would turn in her grave!" exclaimed the woman with such emphasis and such a horrified expression that the trite words seemed to reassume their original grisly meaning.

"Oh!" said Tonia in dismay.

"We'll go when you're ready," continued the woman, who

had suddenly dived into the linen cupboard and now emerged with an armful of snow-white linen. "It's sausages, that's all, but they're better eaten hot. I'd have killed a fowl if you'd postcarded me," she added, shaking her head reproachfully.

"But how could I!" cried Tonia, bursting into sudden peals of laughter that were just a shade hysterical, perhaps. "How could I—er, postcard you when I didn't know your name—not even that you existed? And why on earth should I bother you, Mrs. Smilie? I'm sure you must be Mrs. Smilie."

"I knew about you," returned Mrs. Smilie with a reluctant smile. "Miss Dalrymple talked about you, even on. It was Miss Tonia this and Miss Tonia that and pictures of you on the mantelshelf from six months old, naked on a cushion, and Miss Louise in a sailor suit with HMS *Victory* on the cap."

"Oh dear!" cried Tonia, sitting on the edge of the bath and laughing helplessly. "Oh, dear, I can't stop."

"You're starved, that's what—and there's little sense in us dandering here and the sausages cooling in the fat—or maybe burning to a cinder if Alec hasn't the gumption to take them off the fire. Come away now, Miss Tonia, you'll feel a different being when you've had a cup of tea."

Chapter Seventeen
Melville House

"Will you take mustard, Miss Tonia?" inquired Mr. Smilie politely.

"Do you take cream and sugar in your tea?" asked Mrs. Smilie, pausing with the round, fat cream jug in her hand.

Tonia replied that she did, but she was amazed when she saw real, thick cream pouring out of the jug.

"It's just a treat," explained Mrs. Smilie apologetically. "I just popped in next door when you and Alec were opening up the house, and Mrs. Wilson gave me a wee pickle of cream off the milk that was left over. Mrs. Wilson was dumbfounded when she heard you'd arrived."

"It'll be all over the town tomorrow," said Mr. Smilie.

"What of it!" returned his wife tartly. "Miss Tonia's not wanting to hide from folk. If the news goes around with the milk it'll be over and done with and less trouble for everybody."

"That's true," said Mr. Smilie, meekly. He was not so garrulous now; he was even a trifle embarrassed and was wearing party manners and playing the host to the best of his ability. Now and again his eyes sought the eyes of his wife to see if he was behaving as he should. After a little while, however, he began to feel more comfortable and to emerge from his shell, and the slight air of constraint that had hovered over the little party was dissipated.

"She's looking better, Mother," declared Mr. Smilie, rubbing his hands together. "She was awful peaky, I thought."

"Peaky!" exclaimed Mrs. Smilie. "Maybe you'd be peaky if you'd traveled all day long and were kept hanging about a cold platform and nobody to meet you."

"Mr. Smilie met me," said Tonia, smiling at him.

"You've a nice color now, anyway," declared Mr. Smilie. "Hasn't she, Mother? She's a nice color now."

Tonia felt a good deal better. The Smilies' kitchen was warm and comfortable and as clean and bright as a new pin. The sausages and bacon and fried potatoes, the scones and butter, and the strong sweet tea were just the sort of meal Tonia needed to revive her after her long journey. Some people might have found the meal trying to the digestion or refused the tea in case it should keep them awake, but Tonia had no qualms whatever; she ate and drank everything that was offered to her.

"I like to see folks enjoying their food," declared Mr. Smilie, handing his guest the honey and watching her demolish her third scone.

"Wheesht, Alec, Miss Tonia's eaten nothing at all," said his wife hastily. "Maybe she's had nothing to eat all day. You know as well as I do there's no food on the trains."

"I was just meaning—" began Alec, with a crestfallen air.

"Everything is so good," declared Tonia, laughing. "I've eaten an enormous supper, the best supper I've ever had in all my life."

They talked of other things after that. Mr. Smilie spoke of "the children" and produced photographs of his grown-up family for Tonia to admire.

"Here's Archie," he said, holding out a picture of a very smart sergeant. "He's in the King's Own Scottish Borderers. He's a great one for the girls is Archie…and this is Tom. He's in the Air Force… and Mary's in the Wrens. We've got one in all the services, you see."

"What a pretty girl," said Tonia.

"She's not bad," agreed her father, looking at the photograph with fond pride.

"Now, Alec, don't you go worrying Miss Tonia," said Mrs. Smilie. "Do you think she wants to look at photos of folks she's never seen?"

"Oh, I like it," declared Tonia. "But you know I'm not really Miss Tonia; I'm Mrs. Norman."

"You're Mrs. Norman!"

Tonia nodded. She had been trying to find an opportunity of making this announcement, but an opportunity had not occurred so she had been obliged to make one for herself. Perhaps if she told the Smilies the whole story there would be no need to tell anyone else—already Tonia had realized that Ryddelton was a self-contained community, a cozy sort of place, and that everybody here was interested in everybody else's affairs, not having much contact with the outside world. Besides, the Smilies deserved to hear her story; they deserved the best she could give them, and it was no part of Tonia's intention to conceal her identity. She told them about her marriage and the trip to India and touched lightly upon her experiences in the London raids, and finally she told them about her work in the office and about Robert's death last winter and her decision to come to Ryddelton and make it her home. She could not have had a more sympathetic audience. They did not say much, but what they said was exactly right.

"You're young to have had all that trouble," said Mr. Smilie at last.

"I thought you looked as if you'd been through a good deal," added Mrs. Smilie.

"You'll need to feed up a bit."

"And rest." Mrs. Smilie nodded. "Ryddelton's a fine place to rest. You'll get no bombs here; that's one thing. If you don't mind I'll just go on calling you Miss Tonia. It's easier somehow. I'd not know where I was if I had to start saying Mrs. Norman."

Tonia did not mind at all. It was rather pleasant, really, for it reminded her of Nannie and made her feel at home.

"And now," declared Mrs. Smilie in a different tone of voice. "Now it's high time you were in bed. The sheets are warmed through, and I'll make it up while you're getting undressed."

"I can do it myself," objected Tonia. "Really, Mrs. Smilie, there's no need for you to bother. Just give me the sheets—"

Mrs. Smilie took no notice. She said, "I've aired the house once a week ever since Miss Dalrymple died, so there's no fears of it being damp for you to sleep in, Miss Tonia…and there's no need to thank me for *that*; I was paid for doing it by yon lawyer in Edinburgh and I liked doing it forby. It's not often you get paid for doing a thing you like doing," she added with one of her rare smiles.

"And I've gotten paid for keeping an eye on the garden," added Mr. Smilie, nodding. "I'd like fine to show you the garden when you've time, Miss Tonia."

"You'll be sleeping in the back room," continued Mrs. Smilie, collecting the linen from the pulleys and folding it with swift capable movements. "It's the best room. Old Miss Melville had it as her own because it was quiet and looked out over the garden and got all the morning sun."

"She's like old Miss Melville," declared Mr. Smilie, starting to fill his pipe. "I thought as much when I saw her at the station. D'you see the likeness, Mother?"

"I saw it first thing."

"She was a grand lady," declared Mr. Smilie. "There was nobody like her. She was a good friend to me. It was old Miss Melville bought this house and let me buy it off her bit by bit."

"And that's how Alec and me got married," added Mrs. Smilie.

Mr. Smilie interrupted her, saying with a proud air, "Mother could have had anybody in the town, but it was me she took."

"And many's the day I've regretted it," returned his spouse, smiling at him affectionately.

❦

Tonia woke suddenly—the morning sun was streaming in through the uncurtained window, filling the room with golden yellow light. She had a feeling that she had dreamed something just before she woke, something friendly and pleasant, but the more she tried to remember the dream the quicker it faded. The room was low ceilinged, like all the other rooms in Melville House. The furniture was old-fashioned but it wore an air of elegance and refinement. Tonia recognized Nannie's hand in the crochet mats that decked the dressing table and the top of the chest of drawers, but otherwise (she was pretty sure) the room was exactly as Great-Aunt Antonia had left it.

As she looked around, noting these details with interest, Tonia's nostrils were suddenly assailed by a familiar odor—the smell of frying bacon—and her quick ears caught the sound of someone moving about downstairs. It was Mrs. Smilie, of course.

Goodness! thought Tonia (who had told her most distinctly that she was not to come). Goodness, what a woman! There isn't any way to keep her out unless I put a bolt on the back door. Tonia could not help smiling at the idea of putting up bolts and bars to keep out kindness. But really (she thought as she swung her feet out of bed and felt for her slippers) really and truly it can't go on...

There was a knock on the door. It opened wide and Mrs. Smilie staggered in with a tray. It was an enormous tray and on it was an enormous breakfast—a breakfast fit for a giantess, thought Tonia, looking at it in amazement.

"Oh, Mrs. Smilie!" she exclaimed with a curious blend of gratitude and reproach. "How kind of you—but I wish you wouldn't—"

Mrs. Smilie was impervious to gratitude and reproach. She

brushed them both aside and explained in a grumbling tone that the eggs were pickled and the bacon nothing but rubbish; tea, nowadays, was sweepings, that was all, and scones made with national flour were not worth eating; and, settling the tray carefully on Tonia's knees she departed.

The despised food seemed good to Tonia. She ate it with relish and, thus fortified, descended, prepared to have it out with Mrs. Smilie.

It was curious to feel that the house was really hers—her very own. She touched the mahogany banister rail and thought, with surprise, *it's mine*. She looked at the large Chinese jar that stood on the upper landing and wondered where it had come from. There were green dragons on it—dragons with red tongues and long, curly tails. Its new owner was extremely pleased with it. The whole house pleased Tonia enormously. It looked quite different in daylight with the sunshine streaming through the windows into the dark, paneled rooms. The mixture of dazzling brightness and dark corners was most intriguing. Intriguing, also, was the mixture of elegant old Melville furniture and modern Dalrymple. One could read the history of the house quite easily. The Dalrymples (mother and daughter) had intended to keep the house exactly as Miss Melville had left it, for they had the sense to realize its charm, but they had not been able to resist the lure of a pair of china vases, an occasional table made of wicker work, and one or two colored oleographs of mountain cattle and children with dogs. Nannie's mats were everywhere, of course. Her antimacassars were spread upon the backs of all the chairs, and these results of Nannie's labors brought back their maker to Tonia with positively astounding clearness. Tonia could *see* Nannie making them, her nimble fingers flickering quickly to and fro, her lips murmuring the intricate pattern as she waited for the children to finish their tea. I was always the slow one, thought Tonia, taking up an elaborately fashioned mat and holding it in her hands. I wonder when she made this one. I wish I had taken more interest in Nannie's crochet. Her heart was bursting with gratitude to Nannie for this splendid gift, this darling house. She loved it already, and she knew she would love it more dearly every day. It was a happy house; she felt that it had welcomed her and was prepared to cherish her. She would live here always.

The drawing room was the largest room in the house; it stretched from back to front with windows at each end. The back windows looked out on to the garden and were full of morning sunshine. In the evening the sun would shine into the room at the other end. Opposite the fireplace was an alcove that held an old-fashioned piano with yellowed ivory keys. Tonia was enchanted with the instrument, for she felt it would suit her exactly. Pianos, when they were new and shiny, had a lordly air. They were scornful of fingers that could not accomplish trills, but this piano would never be scornful. It had been neglected for so long that it had grown humble and wistful; this piano would like to be played. She struck a few chords and found that its voice was still sweet.

Mrs. Smilie was sweeping the kitchen floor when Tonia went in.

"Now, Mrs. Smilie—" began Tonia in a firm voice.

"Now, Miss Tonia," interrupted Mrs. Smilie perfectly seriously. "You and me had better have a talk. It's like this, you see, I can run this house with one hand and it will give me something to do. Time hangs pretty heavy now the children are away and Alec at his work—and I never was one for reading. You'll not get a girl in the place; they're all at ammunitions."

"I don't want a girl. I'm going to run the house myself."

"That's right, then," declared Mrs. Smilie beaming with pleasure. "You'll run the house yourself and I'll just look in and give a hand when I can spare the time. In the mornings, that is, and maybe an hour in the afternoons. I'm a good enough cook if you're not wanting fal-lals."

"I don't think I can afford it," said Tonia in desperation. "I mean, I don't quite know how much money I shall have. I came away without telling anyone where I was going, because they tried to make me do something I didn't want to do…so, you see, I don't know what will happen…and I must be very economical and try to make the money I've got in the bank go as far as I can…"

Mrs. Smilie could make very little of this halting explanation of Tonia's financial affairs, but that did not worry her at all. "I wouldn't take a penny," she declared. "It would just be a neighborly sort of arrangement. You're not used to cleaning and I am. Cleaning never tires me and to tell the truth I enjoy it more than the pictures."

"But I couldn't let you—"

"Och, nonsense. There's lots of little things you could do for me if you felt like it."

It was a long argument—almost heated at times—and Tonia was handicapped from the start by her sense of humor. Every now and then laughter rose within her like steam in a boiling kettle, and she was obliged to force it down.

"Well, that's settled, then," said Mrs. Smilie at last. "I'll not come in the afternoons but just the mornings. I'll get your breakfast and clean up a bit and maybe start the dinner and you'll manage the rest yourself."

When Mrs. Smilie had gone Tonia sat down at the piano and fell into a dream—slipped comfortably into her listening valley. It was a long time since she had been there, for life had been demanding and difficult, usurping all her thoughts and energies. Today listening valley was full of music; it was calm and bright and peaceful. And presently her fingers were on the keys and the music found its way out. There were soft chords that trembled in the air and a little tinkling tune, timid and hesitating.

Chapter Eighteen
Listening Valley

The town of Ryddelton was old; parts of it were very old indeed, with narrow winding streets paved with gray stone setts. No two houses were built on the same plan; some of them jutted out into the roadway while others looked as if they had stepped back a pace. Tonia had decided that her own house was homemade. She now decided that practically the whole of Ryddelton belonged to the same category. One could imagine coaches clattering down these streets, and gentlemen on horseback. A motor car, which was nosing its way carefully along, seemed a ridiculous anachronism.

People were staring at her (so Tonia thought, and perhaps she was right for everybody in Ryddelton knew everybody else and she was a stranger. She would not be a stranger long, of course, for she would soon find friends, but the feeling was slightly unpleasant). The feeling resembled a dream experience that most people have endured, the dream experience of being out of doors among a crowd of people and finding oneself insufficiently clad. Tonia smiled at the idea, but all the same she hastened her steps and turned into a lane that led steeply upward between solid stone houses and high garden walls.

Tonia climbed this lane without any idea where she was going and presently the walls stopped and the lane became a cart track leading to some woods that clothed a high ridge. There was a wall here, a dry stone dyke, and a gate of silver-gray weathered oak, but there were no notices to say that the woods were private or that trespassers would be prosecuted, so she opened the gate and went in. The path she chose—from two or three bridle paths that offered themselves for her selection—was the one along the crest of the ridge. The sun was shining brightly, but in the woods it was shady and very quiet. There was no sound except the cooing of pigeons and a sudden rustle of foliage as the birds took fright and flew away. The trees were mostly pine and fir and the ground was carpeted with brown needles, but here and there an oak stood, old and gnarled and sturdy, or a chestnut spread its branches, and beneath these trees there was mossy green turf.

The path wound up and down between rocks. In places it was so narrow that the fans of fir brushed her shoulders, and the roots of the trees straggled across it like friendly brown snakes (they were friendly snakes because everything in the wood was friendly, Tonia felt). The sunshine penetrated through the foliage here and there, falling across the path like a golden sword or sleeping in golden pools between the rocks. Suddenly she emerged from the trees into a little clearing that had once been a small quarry but was now overgrown with soft green turf, and here, all breathless from her haste, Tonia sat down and looked at the view.

There were trees below her, so that she looked out over the tops of them, and there were trees on both sides and above; the little quarry was a dimple in the hill, bathed in sunshine, redolent with the scent of sun-warmed pines. At the bottom of the hill the gray houses of Ryddelton clustered, with their gray slate roofs and curls of smoke rising from their chimneys. In the midst of the town rose the church spire. Beyond the town a road ran, curving away into the distance.

The valley itself stretched southward, shallow and sunlit, bounded by rolling hills clad with green grass and patches of brilliant purple heather and dark pine woods, and above the hills was the pale blue sky with fat white clouds floating in it. Along the floor of the valley wound the river, sparkling in the sunshine; it wound among woods and yellow cornfields and bright green meadows full of cattle that looked like toys, and over it all was a faint haze, an almost imperceptible opal-tinted haze that softened the brightness of the colors. Green it was, green and peaceful, an oasis of peace in a land at war.

The valley was familiar to Tonia. She knew it well. She knew each curve of the river, each patch of purple heather upon the hills. "Listening valley," said Tonia to herself, not in surprise at all, but simply with satisfaction and delight.

⚬⚬⚬⚬

It was a long time before Tonia rose to go home. There was no need to go home to lunch, for nobody would be waiting for her, nobody would be worried about her, nobody would be cross. The sun moved slowly behind a cloud. The shadows spread themselves and the coloring was dimmed; it moved out again and the valley smiled. Tonia thought of many things as she sat there watching (her knees up to her chin and her hands clasped around them). She thought of Robert—she could think of him now without pain. His life was complete. It had been a happy life, full and busy and worthwhile. Robert had made friends with life, and life had been good to him. It was for her to follow his example, to follow his advice: "Make friends with life." She had begun to see what he meant. Not to shut yourself up and grieve or dream but to go forward with your eyes wide open and accept what life offered.

Presently Tonia walked home. She had had a happy time, but she was glad to go home to her own darling house. It would be waiting for her, and she would make tea for herself and have it in the kitchen. She had taken the key of the back door because it was smaller. The back door opened into the garden and the garden into a lane, and the lane was quite enchanting; it was very narrow with high stone walls on either side with ferns growing in their crevices. Tonia found the lane, not without difficulty, and she found the garden door and opened it. Just inside the door was a lavender bush, and the moment she opened the door she smelled the lavender. She stood quite still enjoying it and feeling that she was home, for the smell of lavender was the keynote of the house. She thought of Nannie and of old Aunt Antonia—the house was a gift from them both (which was rather odd, really)—and then she walked up the gray-flagged path to the back door.

The back door had a doorstep, slightly raised, and on this step were set out two large brown eggs, a section of honey, and a paper bag containing four scones. They were quite apart from each other (the eggs on the left, the bag of scones on the right, and the honey in the middle) as if they had nothing to do with each other, Tonia thought. She picked them up and took them in and put them on the kitchen table. "This is the most extraordinary place," she said aloud.

"What's wrong with the place?" inquired Mrs. Smilie, appearing out of the coal cellar with two buckets of coal.

"And you're the most extraordinary person," declared Tonia.

"There's nothing very out-of-the-way in making up a person's fire. It would have been blackout in another minute... I see you found your presents. They were on the step when I came in."

"It's so kind. Why did they do it when they don't know me at all?"

"Maybe they didn't have their calling cards handy," suggested Mrs. Smilie with perfect gravity.

Tonia could not help smiling. She said, "Do you know who put the things there?"

"I might—and I might not. There's a woman I know that has Rhode Island hens and another that keeps bees," said Mrs. Smilie thoughtfully.

"And the scones?"

"A scone is a queer thing. Everybody has their own way with a scone. There's no two alike. You might write some other person's name on a scone, but it would give you away every time—to your friends, that is."

"Really?"

"M'hm," said Mrs. Smilie, nodding.

"Who?" asked Tonia eagerly.

Mrs. Smilie actually smiled. She said, "Well now, Miss Tonia, if they'd wanted you to know they'd have told you."

"But how can I thank them?"

"Maybe they're not wanting thanks."

Tonia could understand that. She hesitated and then said, "But I'd like to know, so that I could be nice to them."

"You could be nice to everybody."

"Oh, Mrs. Smilie, you have an answer to everything," declared Tonia, laughing.

Chapter Nineteen
Two Adventures

Melville House was a place of refuge to Tonia (the mouse had escaped from the trap), but she was aware that she would not be left in peace very long. She had told Janet that she was going to Ryddelton to see the house, and Janet had made no objections, for it seemed reasonable that Tonia should want to see that her house was in proper order. It had not occurred to Janet that her young sister-in-law intended to remain in Ryddelton, of course.

Tonia wrote to Janet. It was a difficult letter to compose, and she gave its composition a great deal of thought and care. She explained that she was comfortable and was enjoying the quiet country life and intended to remain here indefinitely. Janet and Nita were to consider the house in Belgrave Crescent as their home—it was theirs, rent free, for as long as they wanted it. She hoped they would be very happy there. She also wrote to her father and mother, to Frank and Lou and Mrs. Halley—all these people were interested in her and deserved to be told her plans. Having gotten this troublesome business over, Tonia gave a sigh of relief…but her relief was short-lived, for her correspondents, immediately on receipt of her letters, sat down and wrote back. Letters arrived from her father and mother, from Janet and Nita, and from Frank beseeching her to give up this mad idea of living alone, of burying herself in the country, and to take the writer's advice on the ordering of her life. Tonia wrote again—briefly this time—saying she intended to stay where she was.

It was the middle of September now, and Janet and Nita had moved to Belgrave Crescent. Janet wrote again, saying that she was sure Tonia must be tired of the country, her room was ready, and they would expect her at the end of the week. Tonia smiled when she read this. She was not in the least flattered by Janet's apparently overwhelming desire for her company, for she knew that the reason Janet wanted her was so that they could share expenses—and so that Tonia could pay the lion's share. Robert had settled quite a reasonable income on Janet—he had said so—but Janet was extravagant. Money ran through her fingers like sand, and she was always hard up. Tonia did not know what would happen—whether the Garlands would remain at Belgrave Crescent or move somewhere else—and she did not greatly care.

The question of money puzzled Tonia a little. She had flouted the advice of her trustees and had had no further communication with them, and as she was completely ignorant of business matters she had no idea how she stood. Could they withhold Robert's money unless she did what they told her?

I shall wait and see, thought Tonia. Fortunately she was able to wait, for (as she had told Mrs. Smilie) she had a little money in her own bank, which, with care, could be made to last some months. When it was finished she might be fit enough to join the ATS—those were her plans, quite good ones, really, and there were several advantages about her condition she realized to the full. She had no money now—or at least only barely sufficient for her needs—so if anyone was nice to her she need not suspect them of ulterior motives. The people who were nice to her were nice because they liked her, and the ugly specter Nita's poisonous words had brought to life was banished.

Meantime Tonia was not worrying at all. She was contented

and happy—much happier than she had thought possible. She cooked and cleaned under Mrs. Smilie's tuition; she read and played the piano and walked in the woods. Now that she had found the little quarry among the trees, from whence she could see and enjoy the beauties of her listening valley, Tonia went there quite often and sometimes took her lunch with her and had a solitary picnic. And, every day she went, the view was different, with changing colors and shadows and clouds. Autumn was on its way. The corn was being cut. Here and there a tree was touched by early frost.

One afternoon when she was on her way home Tonia met two young American airmen in the woods and this surprised her, for although she was aware that there was a camp near Ryddelton and a large airfield as well, she had no idea that there were any Americans at either place. She looked at them as they came toward her, noting that one was very young and tall and fair, and the other was older and stockier in build.

They stopped her as she was passing and asked if she could tell them the way back to the airfield, and Tonia told them as best she could, explaining that she had not been here very long and perhaps it might be safer to ask someone else.

"I shouldn't like you to get lost," said Tonia anxiously.

This seemed to amuse them a little, for they looked at each other and smiled, and the younger man explained their amusement by saying that his companion was a backwoodsman and pretty tough. It was now Tonia's turn to smile, for this information had given the show away. The question had been a ruse, that was all, and what they really wanted was a little chat. She was quite ready to cooperate and agreed at once when they pointed out a conveniently fallen tree and suggested she sit down. One of them gave her a cigarette and the other lighted it for her. It was all quite easy.

They introduced themselves as Chalmers T. Wood and

Robert Morgan but added that they were known to their friends as Teak and Bob.

"T. Wood," explained Teak. "That was the big idea."

"He's tough, too. I told you, didn't I?" added Bob.

Tonia liked them. They seemed very young to her, partly because of their naïveté and partly because she was used to people who were much older than herself. They seemed to be bursting with youth and vitality and enthusiasm. It gave her a very pleasant feeling of confidence to think that these men—and thousands of others like them—were fighting on our side.

"Have you been here long?" asked Tonia, starting to roll the ball.

"We left the States a couple of months ago," replied Bob, the younger of the two, who seemed to have constituted himself the spokesman. "We've been attached to the RAF for 'further instruction.'"

"We've got it," put in Teak in his gruffer voice.

"We've got it all right," agreed Bob. "They've been four years at the game, so they can put us wise to a good deal. You have to learn pretty fast or you don't live long, so we jumped at the chance of picking their brains."

"It's interesting, too," said Teak.

"Sure thing. I had a free trip to Cologne last night," declared Bob.

Teak leaned down and looked between his legs.

"All right, all right," said Bob, laughing. "What's the harm in saying I went to Cologne! D'you think Hitler doesn't know we were there? I'll say he does!"

Tonia laughed too. She realized that Teak's gesture was a signal to beware of careless talk, for she had seen the pictures in the railway stations, pictures of people discussing secrets and Hitler curled up beneath the seat, listening to them.

"I suppose you couldn't tell me about the flight?" inquired Tonia.

Bob agreed at once. He said, "I've been trying to write home and tell the folks about it, but I found it a bit difficult. Squadron Leader Coates was our pilot. He's a marvel. He was all through the Battle of Britain and then he changed over to bombers. There's nothing much he doesn't know about the wily Hun."

"They call him Socks," said Teak.

"Maybe because he gives the Huns socks," said Bob thoughtfully. He leaned back and blew a cloud of smoke into the still air and started his story.

They had taken off at dusk, climbing to about a thousand feet and then setting off straight for their objective, roaring along through the darkness like an express train. There were clouds in the sky but not very many, and there were no incidents at all. In fact, it was a bit dull—so Bob declared—until they neared the target. They were not the first on the scene and the city was burning already. The guns were crashing and the flak was pretty concentrated, and there were colored rockets. "Very pretty. Just like the rockets at a kid's party," said Bob. The Halifax was "jinking" now, weaving in and out to avoid the beams of the searchlights, and then, quite suddenly, they ran in and made their attack. The navigator and the pilot worked together. They had always flown together and knew each other's methods so well that they scarcely needed words, and this was lucky, for there was so much crackling on the intercom that no conversation was possible. They ran in and the bombs were dropped in a bunch right in the middle of the target area; the navigator called out, "Bombs gone," and they turned and made for home. It was all over in about five minutes, but it felt a good deal longer to Bob.

"Sounds easy when I tell it like that," declared Bob somewhat ruefully. "There was plenty I didn't see, but I saw enough to know it wasn't just so easy. The teamwork was fine—they were all on their toes, and they knew what to do themselves and what the other guys were doing. Coming home we got mixed up in a scrap and it was pretty hot for a minute or two, but Socks was right there on the job. He handled the Halifax like the master he is. It happened like this: the Huns came cracking through a bank of cloud thinking they'd take us unawares. We slipped sideways, dropping like a stone, and I thought we were done for. Maybe they thought the same, for they came after us a bit carelessly. The rear gunner got two of them, and the rest thought better of it and made off home."

"What happened then?" asked Tonia.

"Nothing much. We had coffee in a flask—I'll say I was glad of it—and the second pilot took over the controls so that Coates could have some too. I'll tell you one funny thing. It was when we had landed. Coates turned to me and he said, 'I hope you enjoyed the party.' He said it without a smile on his face, quite cool and calm and serious. I told him yes. Maybe I didn't enjoy every minute of it—there were times when I got that cold feeling in the pit of my stomach—but I wouldn't have missed it for a million dollars."

Bob was silent for a while and then he added, "Coates is a grand guy, and he isn't the only one, but they take a bit of knowing. Teak and I thought they were a bit soft at first, didn't we, Teak?"

"Maybe it's the way they talk makes them seem soft," said Teak thoughtfully.

"I guess that's what it is," agreed Bob. He chuckled suddenly and repeated under his breath, "I hope you enjoyed the party."

They talked of other things after that and became so friendly that Tonia asked them if they would like to come in some evening after dinner. She asked them in a tentative manner, for she felt she had nothing to offer them in the way of entertainment, but they accepted rapturously and inquired if they might bring two of their friends ("It's a bit dull in Ryddelton," explained Teak). No date could be fixed of course because they never knew when they would be off duty, but they promised to let her know. They walked home with Tonia and parted from her at her door the best of friends.

⁂

That evening, after supper, Tonia had quite a different sort of adventure. She was looking at Aunt Antonia's bureau, putting away some notepaper she had bought, and she happened to find a sliding panel that concealed a secret drawer. Tonia found it fairly easily because Robert had had a desk very like it, with a secret drawer in much the same place. The drawer contained a little pile of square books, bound in red leather. They were Great-Aunt Antonia's diaries.

Tonia took them out one by one and looked at them. She found that they were not really diaries (not the sort of diaries that are written up every day and contain uninteresting jottings of the owners' activities) but a record of important events in the life of Antonia Melville. The entries were partly in ink and partly in pencil and were difficult to read, but Tonia was interested in everything pertaining to her namesake, so she took the first book and sat down by the fire and began to turn over the pages.

> *...such a delightful party at Dunnian House. I wore my new dress Papa gave me for my birthday. Mama complimented me upon my appearance, which made me very happy. Dunnian is a house full of the spirit of hospitality, so that any party taking place beneath its roof must be enjoyable. We were a little late in arriving owing to the rain, which had turned the road into a sea of mud and when we*

*arrived the drawing room was already full of people. Old
Mr. Dunne received us very kindly. Celia and Arthur and
William were all dancing with their guests. I was interested
to meet Courtney Dale; he is an American and is engaged to
be married to Mary Dunne. They are to be married shortly
and will go to America together. Mr. Dale is very tall and
handsome. He spoke to me in a pleasant manner, and I must
admit I was delighted with him. It is no wonder that he has
won Mary's heart and that she is willing to leave her home
for his sake, but I could not help wondering why he had chosen Mary, who, although charming and elegant, is nothing
in comparison with her sister (in appearance and intelli-
gence and in all the spiritual graces, in her quick wit and
delightful humor Celia excels). Mr. Dale and Celia would
make an admirable couple—this was my first thought.
I discovered in conversation with Mr. Dale that he was
already engaged to be married to Mary before he saw Celia.
I saw his eyes follow Celia as she moved about the room,
speaking to her guests and creating a pleasant atmosphere of
cordiality and kindness, and suddenly I knew their secret as
surely as if I had been told.*

*Later when I spoke to Celia I found no cause to change
my mind, for Celia is unhappy. She is too gay and rattles on
in a manner that is foreign to her nature. She is the soul of
honor. I feel sure that no word has been spoken that all the
world might not hear. I feel sure that nobody except myself
has any idea of their secret. It is because Celia is so dear to
me that I have guessed it and because I, too, am in love.*

*How difficult it is to write what is in my heart! I have
known Arthur Dunne all my life and have always admired him and thought him perfect in every way. He is
Celia's favorite brother. She has spoken of him often, and
lately I have felt that he was not altogether indifferent to*

*me, so I was not very much surprised when he asked me
if he might speak to Papa. We were in the conservatory,
where Arthur had taken me to admire the camelias, but I
fear the camelias did not receive the admiration they deserve. Arthur was so gentle and considerate in his manner that I felt wonderfully easy and after a few moments I
was able to reply that I would be his wife and that I was
sure Papa would consent to our union. He took my hand
and thanked me, saying very earnestly that my happiness
would always be his first consideration. How fortunate I
am! How happy I am! My dear Arthur...*

Tonia could not help smiling at this glimpse into the past,
but her smile was a little sad, for she remembered that Antonia's
romance had ended in disaster. Antonia and her dear Arthur had
never been married—he had been lost at sea. These were the
words her father had used when he had spoken of the tragedy:
"lost at sea." There was a curiously forlorn sound about the
expression; its very vagueness excited the imagination. Had the
ship run upon a rock and been lost with all hands, or was it only
Arthur who had perished? Perhaps he had been swept overboard
in a storm and had sunk before his shipmates could rescue him.

Tonia sighed and turned over the page.

*It was late when the party was over. Celia accompa-
nied me to her bedroom, where I had left my wraps. She
kissed me very warmly and said: "Is it true that we are
to be sisters?" I told her that it was true and added that I
could not love her more. "I have always hoped for this," said
Celia with the sharp little nod that is so characteristic of her.
We kissed each other again and laughed—I fear we were a
little foolish but there was no one to see our foolishness...
Dunnian House will belong to Arthur when his father dies,*

for he is the eldest son, and we shall live there, which will be very pleasant indeed, not only because Dunnian is so beautiful, but also because I shall be near Papa and Mama. Arthur must make another voyage to the West Indies, but after that he will leave the sea and settle down at Dunnian. This is what Celia told me and I am writing as if all were settled. I feel sure Papa will welcome Arthur and agree to our marriage.

It was late and Tonia's eyes were tired, for Antonia's writing was small and faint and difficult to decipher. She put the book back where she had found it and went to bed.

Chapter Twenty

An Old Friend

By this time most of the people in Ryddelton knew Tonia, or at least knew who she was, so they had ceased to stare at her. She did the shopping every morning, not only her own shopping but Mrs. Smilie's as well. She had disliked shopping in London, but it was quite different here, for there were no queues and everyone was friendly and anxious to oblige. They were really sorry—one felt—when they were forced to deny one syrup, prunes, cookies, and onions, and usually held out strong hopes of being able to supply these commodities next week. How different from their counterparts in towns, where one was made to feel both foolish and greedy if one happened to ask for something unobtainable!

Tonia shopped with a large basket that grew heavier and heavier as she progressed. One day it became so heavy that she could scarcely carry it, and she was struggling home, feeling very thankful that she had not far to go, when she met an officer in the blue uniform of the RAF. There was nothing very odd about this, for, owing to the proximity of the airfield, the town was full of Air Force officers and men, but this particular officer engaged Tonia's attention because he seemed, in some way, familiar—almost as if she had met him in a dream. They passed each other and walked on, and then Tonia stopped and looked back. The officer had stopped, too, and was looking back at

Tonia. He began to walk toward her and Tonia waited. She saw that his eyes were very brown, so was his hair beneath his jauntily cocked cap, and his teeth gleamed with pearly whiteness in his suntanned face.

"Hallo, Butterfingers!" he said.

"Bay!" exclaimed Tonia in amazement.

Bay laughed. "You've missed your cue. You ought to say, 'You didn't do it!'"

"But I know you didn't, so I don't need to ask," replied Tonia smiling.

"Everyone else was sure I did it."

"They were silly. It was quite a different sort of thing."

"Not funny?"

"Not a bit funny," said Tonia firmly.

He took the basket from her and they walked along, talking as they went.

"Who did it?" Tonia asked. "Do you know who did it?"

"Yes, it was Nita," replied Bay. "I knew it was Nita because it was purple ink—the kind she always used."

"Nita!" said Tonia. "Goodness, how horrible! I wonder why she didn't put it in your bottle, Bay. I suppose she thought you would be blamed—how disgustingly clever of her."

"It wasn't cleverness. Dear me, no, Dr. Thorndyke. She didn't put it in my bottle because I had a case with a lock— funny how well I remember that case. It was the pride of my heart. I spent hours locking and unlocking it."

"Why didn't you tell them?"

"I wonder," said Bay thoughtfully. "I believe I was too proud. They thought I did it so I let them go on thinking it—that was my attitude as far as I can remember. Wasn't I a little beast?"

"Oh no," said Tonia hastily.

"Oh yes," returned Bay. "I certainly was. I remember putting fluff on the nib of your pen—"

"And a piece of wood under the leg of my desk."

"Why did I?" Bay wondered.

"I expect you hated me."

"No," said Bay, thinking back. "No, that's the queer thing. I believe I liked you quite a lot, but I didn't *want* to like you. I wanted to be bold and free like the Sea Hawk or some such blood and thunder fellow...and all the time I had a sort of sneaking affection for you. I don't suppose anybody on earth could understand it."

Tonia most certainly could not. She was no psychologist. But after all what did it matter...

"Come in, Bay," said Tonia, opening the door.

"Is this your house?"

"My very own. I'm living here by myself."

"It's nice," said Bay. "I've always admired this house. I find its crookedness very intriguing."

"Homemade," said Tonia, wondering if he would understand.

"Yes," said Bay, nodding. "Houses were homemade in those days, not turned out by the gross. They were solidly made by people who took a real interest in their work and laid every stone as well as they could do it. There's a different sort of feeling in a house built like that—I can't explain it."

He did not need to explain it, for it was exactly the feeling she had herself.

"Will you have some beer?" she asked. "You must have something to celebrate the occasion and beer is the only thing I've got."

Bay said he liked beer.

"Are you married or anything?" he inquired when she brought the tray into the drawing room.

"I was...he died. No, he wasn't killed in the war. What about you?"

"Engaged," said Bay. "Gosh, she's a great girl! As a matter of fact she's coming to Ryddelton for a bit so you'll meet her. I suppose you don't happen to know of any comfortable rooms."

"Mrs. Smilie would know," declared Tonia.

"Don't worry, I'll find something," replied Bay. "She's French, you know. Retta is French, I mean. Retta Delarge."

"She sounds—interesting."

"Interesting isn't the word," declared Bay. "She's tremendously amusing. I met her in France at the very beginning of the war when we were operating from an airfield near Dieppe, and then I lost sight of her completely until she wrote to me from London…but wait till you see her," said Bay, smiling. "Just wait."

"I shall have to, I suppose," said Tonia, smiling in sympathy.

Bay said no more about his fiancée. He had sat down in a chair near the window and was looking around with interest and appreciation, so Tonia told him the history of the house and how it had become hers.

"It *is* nice," he said. "So peaceful. You get awfully tired of living in a mess with big strong men sitting around and talking shop."

Now that he had taken off his cap she saw that he looked a good deal older than his years—and very tired. There were lines on his face that had no business to be there, and his mouth (when he was not smiling) was a trifle grim. She saw, too (now that she had time to look at him properly), that he was a squadron leader and was wearing a Distinguished Flying Cross and bar.

"You're Socks!" exclaimed Tonia suddenly.

"How on earth did you know?" inquired Bay in surprise.

"I just guessed," she replied, laughing.

He held up the glass of beer and said quite seriously, "Here's luck to Butterfingers Thorndyke and her homemade house."

Bay dropped in two days later at teatime and they played "Do you remember," which is a most enthralling game. Some things they both remembered very clearly: the mole on Mrs. Grant's wrist, which you looked at when she leaned over you to correct your exercise, and the way Miss Mann rapped on her desk and cried, "Now, children, *think* before you answer." But other things, which Tonia remembered clearly, Bay had forgotten—or thought he had.

"You *must* remember Mrs. Harris!" cried Tonia.

"Come off it," said Bay. "You're trying to pull my leg but I know that one. Mrs. Harris wasn't real."

"This one was," declared Tonia, laughing. "She was the charwoman and she was always washing the passage when we arrived. Mrs. Grant fell over her pail one day—surely you remember that!"

"Of course!" cried Bay. "I remember now. One of my very best jokes was when I put a stone on the floor beside her and took away the soap. You ought to have seen her rubbing the stone on her scrubbing brush."

"You were awful!"

"She had red hair—exactly the color of carrots—and her teeth stuck out," continued Bay, determined to show that he really did remember Mrs. Harris after all.

Tonia was enjoying the game for its own sake but perhaps more for Bay's. The lines around his mouth had softened and his laugh came more often and more easily. It's good for him, she thought. It's good for Bay to be silly with me.

"Come whenever you like," she told him as she saw him off at the door.

"Do you mean that? You aren't just saying it…"

"Of course I mean it."

"I never know when," said Bay, lingering at the door. "But if you really mean it, I should love to drop in. You get awfully tired of a mess."

It was getting dark. There was a pale green light in the sky. Between the houses the gloom seemed to lie in pools of darkness. It was very quiet and peaceful, and the sound of footsteps going past—click clack, click clack—on the other side of the street seemed to intensify the stillness rather than disturb it.

"Wooden soles," said Bay softly. "We're funny, aren't we? It's no wonder our enemies don't understand us."

"If we can't get leather we just wear wood—and wood becomes the fashion."

"That's what I meant," said Bay in a voice of surprise.

He still lingered, and Tonia did not mind, for it was pleasant standing at the door and watching the darkness deepen.

"Oh, look here," said Bay in a sudden sort of voice. "I nearly forgot, which seems odd because I came specially to ask you. We're having a sort of party at the mess; somebody's managed to raise some booze—don't ask how. You'll come, won't you? It's tomorrow. And could you possibly lend us a few glasses? I'll send for them, of course."

"Yes," said Tonia, a trifle breathlessly, for she was not used to such speed. "Yes, of course…glasses…sherry glasses, you mean."

"You don't have any flowers, do you? No, hold on, it doesn't matter about flowers; they're sending flowers from Dunnian."

"Dunnian!" cried Tonia. "Did you say Dunnian? Who lives there now?"

"The Dunnes," said Bay. "There's an awfully decent old admiral—and young Mrs. Dunne and her baby—and Celia, of course."

"Celia!"

"Nice," said Bay, nodding. "Not terribly young (she must be over thirty) but full of life and go. You'd like her. I must go, Butterfingers."

"Must you go? Are you flying tonight?"

He hesitated. "Don't ask me that," he said. "I mean, I should have to lie to you and I don't want to."

"I'm sorry. I didn't mean—"

"Oh, I know, but it's just one of those things."

Soon after that he went away, and Tonia had supper and thought about his visit and chuckled to herself at some of the foolish things they had said. And she thought of Celia Dunne and wished she had asked Bay more about her. It was odd to think that there was another Celia at Dunnian and another Antonia at Melville House. Perhaps I shan't like her *at all,* thought Tonia.

Presently Tonia went upstairs to bed and lay awake a long time, listening, but she heard no planes that night.

❧

The mess was decorated with flags. Flowers in tall glasses stood on tables in the corners of the room. They had been crammed into the glasses in tight bunches, and Tonia could not help wondering which of the sturdy red-faced mess waiters had been responsible for their arrangement. She was a little late and the room was crowded, but Bay saw her almost at once and pushed his way toward her with a glass of sherry in his hand.

"I began to think you weren't coming," said Bay. "Here's some sherry in one of your own glasses. I'll be back in a minute…"

Bob was the next person to speak to her. He appeared at her elbow with a plate of cookies. "Have a cracker, Mrs. Norman," he said, adding rather hastily, "I mean, a cookie. We call them crackers at home."

"Crackers is rather a good name. They crackle, don't they?" said Tonia, smiling. "You haven't been to see me yet, Bob."

"We've been busy," he replied. "We're coming all right. Here's Teak."

They chatted for a few minutes and then moved on and left her. She listened to the chatter all around her, the tinkle of glasses, the gay laughter. On the surface it seemed as if these boys had not a care in the world, yet every night (or nearly every night) they braved the elements, the crash of guns and shells, and played hide-and-seek with death.

Somebody behind her announced in a very English voice, *"Il n'est pas tout a fait juste dans la tête."*

There was a roar of laughter at this sally and Tonia looked around, smiling.

"He thinks he's funny, you know," explained a very young officer, smiling back at Tonia.

"He *is* funny," declared a girl who was one of the group, a small, neatly made girl dressed in tweeds, with dark hair and sparkling brown eyes. "He's very funny indeed. If he wants a job after the war I'll take him on as my jester." She did not wait for her offer to be accepted but pushed her way between the men who surrounded her and reached Tonia's side, smiling in a friendly manner. "I'm so glad you're here," she declared. "I wanted to meet you. We were all quite thrilled when we heard that a Melville had come back to live at Melville House."

Tonia liked the girl at once, and oddly enough she was not in the least surprised when the girl added, "I'm Celia Dunne."

"I thought you might be," Tonia said.

"Why?" inquired Miss Dunne. "Of course I knew you, because I know everybody else—if you see what I mean."

"I had heard about you."

"Nice things, I hope?"

"Very nice things," said Tonia laughing.

"Good," said Miss Dunne, giving a sharp little nod.

They chatted for a few minutes. "Dad knew your father," said Miss Dunne. "They met when they were boys, and he remembered Miss Antonia Melville very well indeed, so of course he wants to meet you. We should love to have you to lunch but it's rather a long way unless you have a bicycle."

Tonia had never bicycled in her life. She said rather shyly, "Perhaps you could come to lunch with me some day."

"I'd love to," replied Miss Dunne. "I'm often in Ryddelton, shopping and that sort of thing. Are you strong?"

"Strong!" echoed Tonia in surprise.

Miss Dunne chuckled. "Yes, it *does* sound mad, but I was just wondering if I could rope you in for war work. We need people very badly for gathering sphagnum moss."

Tonia had heard of sphagnum moss but she had never seen it.

"Wonderful stuff," said Miss Dunne. "They use it for front-line dressings because it's so absorbent—sixteen times more absorbent than cotton wool—and because it's full of iodine. They can't get enough of it, really; they're always shrieking for more. We get as much as we can, of course, but I could do with a lot more helpers. We go up the hill to the moor and wade about in bogs and gather great sacks of it. Some people like doing it and some don't," added Miss Dunne with a mischievous grin.

"I could try," said Tonia a little doubtfully.

"You need Wellington boots and a thermos," said Miss Dunne. "I'll let you know…"

She moved away before Tonia could answer. She was a very capable young woman, Tonia decided.

"This is Jim Mannering," said Bay, appearing with a young man in tow—a young man with very fair hair and a pink-and-white complexion. "Mannering is my navigator. He takes me by the hand and leads me there and back, don't you, Manners?"

"Usually," replied Mannering without turning a hair.

"Usually," agreed Bay. "There have been occasions when… but never mind. Mannering will get you another drink and talk to you nicely while I go and make myself pleasant to some of the bores."

"Do you always fly with Bay?" asked Tonia.

"Practically always," replied Mannering. "It's better to stick together because you get to know what the other fellow can do. You get the best results. I'm lucky, of course. I'd rather fly with Socks than anyone. He's so safe."

Safe seemed an odd word to use.

"He's brilliant, of course," said Mannering in a casual sort of voice. "He's brilliant and he's cautious. You don't often get the two together, but, when you do, you've got something pretty good."

"The American boy told me about his flight with you. He was tremendously impressed."

"Enthusiastic, aren't they?" said Mannering. "We rather distrusted that enthusiasm at first—seemed a bit odd, if you know what I mean—but they're all right. They take a bit of knowing, that's all."

"They said that about you," said Tonia, smiling.

"About us!" exclaimed Mannering in surprise. "But we're quite ordinary blokes." He looked thoughtful for a few moments, as if he were considering the matter carefully, and then continued, "They're all right, the Americans. Those daylight offensives of theirs are absolutely top-notch."

"Precision bombing," put in Tonia, who had begun to know quite a lot about the matter and made a point of reading all she could get hold of.

"That's the stuff. The RAF by night and the USA by day. That's what's going to bust the Hun," said Mannering in his quiet, casual sort of voice.

"Is it really worthwhile—I mean, we seem to lose so many—"

"Oh, rather," he replied. "It's worthwhile all right. Of course it's frightful when we lose a lot—too horrible for words—but even *then* it's worthwhile. We bust up their factories—everyone knows that—but there's another thing about it that everyone doesn't seem to realize. You see, the Hun keeps thousands of fighters specially for our benefit. These fighters ought to be providing air cover for the German armies in Russia and Italy, but they can't be in two places at once. So the German armies have to do the best they can without adequate protection. The troops don't enjoy getting bombed; it's bad for morale to say the least of it, and the staff doesn't enjoy it when the bridges and railways and ammo dumps go up sky high. Makes it pretty difficult. So, actually, we are helping our fellows directly as well as indirectly, if you see what I mean."

Tonia was about to reply in the affirmative and to ask for more information when Bay came back, remarking that he had polished off the bores and was ready to enjoy himself. Mannering took the hint and faded away.

Chapter Twenty-One
Music Hath Charms

Tonia was in bed when the planes began to thunder overhead, one after another at regular intervals. She counted them carefully...there were nine. Nine bombers on their way to Germany, and in one of those planes was Bay. Yes, Bay was sure to be there with Jim Mannering and Willard and the rest of the splendid men who made up the crew of seven that was the complement of the big Halifax. She would have liked to know which of the planes was G for George. This one perhaps, thought Tonia, as she heard the roar of engines passing overhead. The sound faded away in the distance as the plane flew over the hills. It would have reached the coast by this time, would be thundering along above the dark rolling sea, speeding east to the appointed place with its load of death, taking death to thousands of people in some German city. Ghastly thought! But that was war. We had to do it. We had to crush our enemies in every way we could. She reminded herself of London and Liverpool and Coventry; she thought of Warsaw and Rotterdam and Belgrade. The tables had been turned now, not in a spirit of revenge but merely as a wartime necessity. She thought of all that Jim Mannering had told her...

The hours crawled on. Would they have reached their target now? She tried to imagine what it would be like—the searchlights, the shells bursting all around the plane, the bombs falling, the colored lights Bob had said were so pretty—"just like rockets at a kid's party." And now the planes would be turning and making for home, and among them would be the nine that had gone out from Ryddelton—but would there be nine?

She slept a little, very lightly, and awoke to hear them coming back. Not at regular intervals but two or three together and then a long space and another single plane. It was difficult to count them when they came like this...there were seven, she thought, or perhaps eight...

Dawn was breaking now and Tonia rose, for she could stay in bed no longer. She dressed and leaned out of the window... how peaceful it was! The sun had not come up, but the sky was red; it looked as though it were on fire. There were clouds above the dark hills, fiery clouds with bright red fringes hanging above the hills. Above them were more layers of cloud, gray and golden, touched with fire; they floated peacefully in the pale blue sky. Gradually the red faded. The high ridge of hills was dark against the brightness of the sky, dark and smooth and rounded in outline. There was no red at all in the sky, only blue and gold when at last the sun looked over the top. The bright beams of light seemed to spill over the crest of the ridge; it was like molten gold spilling out of a cup. The gold spilled over and ran down the gray gloomy hillside, lighting first the little knolls and then the whole hillside. Tonia's room was flooded with golden light.

"Did you hear the planes?" asked Mrs. Smilie when Tonia went downstairs to have her breakfast. "One of them didn't come back."

"I thought...not," said Tonia faintly.

"It was not Mr. Coates's plane," declared Mrs. Smilie (who never bothered herself with ranks and titles but used plain mister for every man). "Mr. Coates is back all right, the postman says."

"How does the postman know?"

"Mr. Murray knows everything that goes on," declared Mrs. Smilie. "He knows about the airfield because there's an aircraftsman billeted on them. A wise-like lad, and no trouble in the house, Mrs. Murray says."

"Oh!" said Tonia.

Mrs. Smilie gave her a quick glance. "You're up early," she remarked. "Maybe the planes woke you, coming home."

"Yes," said Tonia.

The day passed slowly. It was wet and windy; the weather seemed to have broken, and Tonia employed herself doing things in the house. She was washing up the supper dishes when she heard Bay come in. He was now so much at home that he did not ring the bell—it was a loud jangling bell of the old-fashioned type and Tonia had told him that it startled her. Tonia dried her hands and went through to the drawing room. She knew at once that there was something wrong. Bay looked old—quite old and haggard. There was no light in him.

"What is it?" she asked. "What's the matter, Bay?"

"Only another one gone. That's all," he replied, lighting a cigarette with hands that trembled a little. "I ought to have gotten used to it by this time but it seems to get worse. Funny, isn't it?"

Tonia said nothing. She knelt down and began to blow up the fire with a pair of bellows.

"Damned funny, really," continued Bay in a grim sort of voice. "Damned war…they all go…one after another."

"Who?" asked Tonia.

"Wingford—a frightfully good fellow, one of my best pilots—and the crew, of course. You wouldn't know them. One of them was an American, who was attached to us for training—"

"Not Bob!" exclaimed Tonia.

"No, Wood. We called him Teak. Did you know him?"

"Yes," said Tonia. She sat back on her heels and looked up at Bay.

"It's—hellish, really," Bay said. "They were all tremendously good chaps but somehow I feel…I feel responsible for Teak. He wasn't actually one of our crowd but just attached to us. Of course it can't be helped. I mean, it isn't anyone's fault."

"No, of course not. What happened, Bay?"

"It was a crash. We were on the way home, and O for Orange was just ahead of us. I thought they were in difficulties, but of course one can't do anything—that's the worst of it—except just hang about in case somebody bales out and one can wireless his position…and then quite suddenly the starboard wing dropped off and the plane fell like a stone. That's all, really."

"Yes," said Tonia.

Bay sat down and leaned his head on his hand. "I've been trying to write to Teak's mother," he said. "It seems—I mean, she's such a long way off, isn't she?"

"Do you think she'd like me to write?" asked Tonia.

"Yes," said Bay. "Yes, do write. Of course she would like it. I'll give you her address."

They were silent for a long time after that. The fire was going well now; little tongues of flame, yellow and red and blue, were licking around the log Tonia had put on. A sudden squall sent rain, blattering against the window.

"Play something," said Bay at last.

"Play the piano, do you mean?" asked Tonia in surprise. "But I can't play, Bay."

"Of course you can," declared Bay, smiling down at her. "I remember you learning to play at school, and, as a matter of fact, I heard you playing the other night when I passed."

"But I only play to myself. Just to—to amuse myself."

"Play to yourself, then."

She saw that he did not want to talk, so she gave him the evening paper and sat down at the piano, but she was shy of playing when anyone was in the room. And for a little while she could not make up her mind to begin—there was no music in listening valley tonight. And then, quite suddenly, the music came; her hands strayed about the old yellowed keys, which had become so familiar and friendly, and she forgot Bay was there…

"What's that, Butterfingers?" said Bay suddenly.

"What's what?"

"That thing you were playing just now," he replied, putting down his paper and coming over to the piano. "I don't seem to know it and I thought I knew all the latest hums."

Tonia looked up. "It isn't anything…I mean, I just heard it."

"On the radio?"

"No, I heard it in a place—a place I go to—sometimes—"

"A place in Ryddelton?" asked Bay in amazement, for to him the word called up the vision of some pleasant little restaurant with an orchestra and shaded lights and soft-footed waiters appearing with succulent food. He gazed at Tonia (she did not reply) and saw that she was suddenly rosy with blushes and she was looking down so that her dark lashes were spread upon her cheeks like two small fans. "A place in Ryddelton," repeated Bay incredulously.

"A place—inside," she replied, laying her hand on her bosom.

"You don't mean you made it up!"

"Oh no…at least…it isn't like that at all," said Tonia in a very low voice. "I just…listen."

There was silence for a few moments and then Bay said, "I see. It's rather wonderful, isn't it? I mean, it must be wonderful."

She looked up and smiled, for he had understood and said exactly the right thing. "Of course it is," she said happily.

"Play it again," commanded Bay, leaning his elbows on the piano.

She played it softly, with variations. It was a haunting melody, and Bay, who had an extremely good ear, got the hang of it and began to hum it in a pleasant baritone.

"Lovely," he declared when they had finished.

Tonia thought so too. The voice had made all the difference, had made the little wandering melody into something more substantial.

"Could you write it down?" asked Bay. "I mean, write it out properly with the accompaniment and all the variations."

Tonia said she could.

"There's a fellow in the mess called Harrison," explained Bay. "I'd like to show it to him."

She had the manuscript ready next time he came. It had taken her quite a long time to do but was delightful work, absorbing and satisfying. She handed it to him when he came in and he saw that she had called it "Listening Valley."

"That's from Keats, isn't it?" he asked.

"Blake," replied Tonia.

"It's a lovely name—and a lovely tune. Let's play it again, shall we? I wish we could find words for it, don't you?"

They played it (and sang it) again, and it was quite as pleasant as before. Then they went on to other things, for there was a cabinet full of songs that had belonged to Great-Aunt Antonia. Bay sang "There Is a Tavern in the Town" and others of the same ilk and they finished up with "I'll Walk Beside Thee."

"That's all," said Bay, whose voice had suddenly become a little husky. "I mean, we can't have anything else after that."

He went away quite suddenly and hurriedly, glancing at the clock and murmuring that he didn't know it was so late. And it was still quite early; it was early enough for there to be a possibility of a raid on Germany tonight, and the moon was full...

She sat down at the piano and played "Abide with Me" very, very softly, whispering the words:

"Abide with me, fast falls the eventide.
The darkness deepens, Lord, with me abide.
When other helpers fail and comforts flee,
Help of the helpless, O, abide with me."

Tonia went to bed, feeling comforted. She lay awake listening, but no planes went over that night.

⚮

"Hi!" cried Bay, striding into the hall and throwing his cap down on the oak chest. "Hi there! Where are you, Butterfingers?"

She was upstairs making her bed, and she came running down the stairs in her pink overall with her hair all over the place.

"He says it's marvelous," cried Bay excitedly. "He says it's the goods—*absolutely*. I can't stay a moment but I had to rush in and tell you—"

"Who? What?"

"The song, of course. 'Listening Valley.' Harrison is sending it up to his firm. I told you he was a music publisher before the war."

"You didn't tell me anything."

"Didn't I? No, perhaps I didn't. I wanted to be sure, first. I was afraid you might be disappointed if it didn't come off. The money will be useful, won't it?"

"The money?" asked Tonia in perplexity.

"Gosh, yes! There's money in songs, you know. Especially if you make a hit, and Harrison says everyone will be singing 'Listening Valley.' As a matter of fact, the whole mess is humming it already, more or less in tune."

"No!"

"Yes, honestly. I knew you'd be pleased about the money."

"Oh, I am," declared Tonia, smiling at him. "It's most awfully good of you to have bothered, and the money will be very helpful. It isn't that I'm badly off, exactly," continued Tonia, trying to explain. "I mean, Robert left me plenty of money but I had a lot of bother with the trustees."

"Good Lord!" exclaimed Bay sympathetically. It was natural that Bay should misunderstand this statement, for Tonia was looking extremely wistful now, and "a lot of bother" sounded pretty serious. Bay imagined Robert Norman's trustees as blackguards of the deepest dye and visualized them absconding to Uruguay (or somewhere) with small black briefcase full of Bearer Bonds. He could not know—how could he—that the wistful expression on Tonia's face was due to the recollection of her interview with the three kind and eminently respectable, if somewhat misguided, gentlemen chosen by Robert Norman as trustees for his fortune. She was thinking of the lawyer's office, of the fly buzzing feebly on the dirty windowpane, and remembering her own feeling of horror and dismay at the prospect of living with the Garlands.

"Good Lord, how frightful!" repeated Bay, gazing at her.

"It was, rather," said Tonia. "There was a meeting, you see. They all talked about things I couldn't understand, except one who didn't talk at all. I think he was sorry for me."

"They made you sign papers, I suppose?" asked Bay anxiously.

"Oh yes," said Tonia. "Lots of papers. I just signed where they told me."

"Frightful!" said Bay. He was more than ever glad that the song was going to be a success. If by any chance it wasn't a success, thought Bay, one might be able to arrange something with Harrison (she would never suspect anything, for she was an absolute infant in money matters, one could see *that*). The only bother was that although one's pay seemed pretty good on paper it melted away in the most astounding manner…and there was Retta, of course.

"Oh, look here," he said. "I've found rooms for Retta. It's just across the street—quite decent, really. The woman seems a nice kindly sort of creature and she said she would do her best to make Retta comfortable. I've wired Retta to come next week—rather exciting, isn't it?"

"Yes, of course," agreed Tonia. "*Lovely* for you, Bay."

"I told you she was French, didn't I? I don't quite know how she managed to get away before the Bosche arrived at Dieppe. She just wrote from London and said she had escaped. I wrote back, of course, and arranged to meet her my next leave and we had a good time together and—well—we got engaged. That's how it was, you see."

"I see," said Tonia, nodding.

"She had a frightful time," said Bay. "She doesn't know whether her parents are dead or alive. Her brother managed to escape; he's doing some sort of job in London. She's devoted to her brother."

"I see," said Tonia, again.

"I'm awfully sorry for Retta," declared Bay with a sigh. He glanced at the clock, gave an exclamation of horror, and rushed wildly out of the door.

Chapter Twenty-Two
Miss Dunne

Celia Dunne sent a postcard to say she was taking Mrs. Norman at her word and would come to lunch tomorrow.

"And that's today," said Tonia to herself, half in delight and half in trepidation. The delight was due to the fact that she wanted to see Miss Dunne again, the trepidation to the difficulty of feeding her in a suitable manner.

Mrs. Smilie was quite excited when she heard the news and declared that it put her in mind of the old days when old Miss Dunne used to drive over in the carriage and have lunch with Miss Antonia. "Such a baking as there was," said Mrs. Smilie reminiscently. "Old Miss Dunne had a sweet tooth and Mrs. Fraser would put her best foot foremost when she heard Miss Dunne was coming. Mrs. Fraser was always a bit sharp, but when Miss Dunne was expected you couldn't put your nose inside the kitchen door without having it bitten off. There was a special pudding she made: a kind of basket with trifle in the middle and ratafia cookies all around, and I mind there was pigeons in aspic and clear soup with letters of the alphabet made of macaroni floating in it. Or if it was winter she'd make chicken in a casserole with mushrooms and whatnot, and maybe pancakes to follow with bits of lemon to squeeze over them…"

Tonia sighed heavily, for this description of the food with

which Great-Aunt Antonia had sustained her guest was somewhat depressing in view of present-day restrictions.

"Never you mind," said Mrs. Smilie, who perceived Tonia's gloom and divined the cause. "Miss Celia'll not expect very much, for she's a sensible young lady. I'll boil a drop of soup out of that bone and you can get some sliced sausage for patties. I can make some gravy to go with them and mashed potatoes and baked beetroot, and you can have baked apple and custard and then cheese and oatcakes and a nice cup of coffee to follow."

"Goodness, that's far too much!" exclaimed Tonia. "Nobody could eat all that—"

"It wouldn't have been too much before the war."

"I know, but one hasn't room for a lot of food nowadays. Our insides must have shrunk or something…besides I don't want you to trouble. I can easily manage."

"And be all hot and bothered when Miss Celia arrives!" exclaimed Mrs. Smilie with scorn. "*That* would be a nice thing! No, no, I'll see to the lunch myself. You can put on your things and do the shopping. I'll give you a list," declared Mrs. Smilie, diving into the cupboard and poking about to see what was there. "There'll be the sausage, of course, and mind you get sliced…and we'll need dried eggs for the custard…flour? No, you've plenty of flour and here's a tin of coffee. What about gravy powder?"

"I wish you wouldn't bother, Mrs. Smilie. You have your own work to do and I can manage—"

"I like doing it, fine," said Mrs. Smilie. "It's something I can do, and do well, and that's all there is to it…it's like this, Miss Tonia," she continued, laying down the tin of coffee and putting her hands on her hips—an attitude she invariably assumed when she had something important to say. "It's like this, you see: if it had not been for old Miss Antonia we never could have gotten married, Alec and me, not for years and years. We were saving up to buy a house, but Miss Antonia was all against waiting; maybe it was because of her own loss—Captain Dunne, who she was engaged to, having been drowned. Anyway, she was all against us waiting, and she gave Alec the money to buy the house. We paid back every penny of it, of course, for that was the way we wanted it—not to be beholden to anybody. We paid it back to her, bit by bit, all except the interest and Alec wanted to pay that, too, but Miss Antonia said no. To tell the truth, I never could understand about the interest, no matter how often Alec explained it, but anyway it didn't matter because Miss Antonia said nothing would make her take it.

"But it was not only that," continued Mrs. Smilie after a short pause. "It was not only the house. There were other things she did for me, off and on, all the time we were neighbors to her. Maybe you wouldn't think they were big things, but they meant a good deal to me. It was not so much the things she did as the way she did them. If you were ill Miss Antonia would come in and see you and she'd bring a few flowers. She wouldn't bring you a great armful of flowers that the gardener had picked, but just a few that she had picked herself, thinking about you…and she'd bring them all ready in a little glass. It would be one of her best glasses, too—not just a jam jar—and she'd put it on the table beside your bed for you to look at. Or maybe it would be soup she'd send you, and she'd send it straight from her own table in one of her own cups, and there'd be a message that Miss Melville thought the soup was specially good today and she hoped you'd fancy it."

Mrs. Smilie paused and looked at Tonia.

"I see," said Tonia slowly.

"You see," agreed Mrs. Smilie. "And so if there's anything I can do for you—"

"But I'm me—" began Tonia.

"You put me in mind of her," explained Mrs. Smilie. "It's

your voice, mostly—and your hands (she was never much use with her hands except doing kindnesses to folk that were in trouble), and you're like what she must have been when she was young. She was old when I knew her, of course…but it's not only *that*," declared Mrs. Smilie. "Even if you were not a bit like her, to look at, it would be just the same."

"Why?" asked Tonia.

"It was something she said to me once and I've never forgotten. Alec had been ill and I was run off my feet and nearly demented with the worry of it, and Miss Antonia had been like an angel straight from heaven, taking the children off my hands and sending in eggs and chickens and all. Well, I was trying to thank her and not making much of a job of it, and I said I wished I could do something for her but there was nothing I could do…and Miss Antonia said to me: 'Do it to somebody else.' I couldn't for the life of me see how *that* would help, but she just said, 'If you think you owe me a kindness, pass it on.' 'Who to?' I said, sharp-like, for to tell the truth I was not too keen on some of the folks that live roundabout us. (There was Mrs. MacBean, a feckless body if you like. Her house was like a midden and she was never out of the bit—and her man bringing in good money, too!) Then Miss Antonia said, 'Love your neighbor,' and it gave me quite a turn; it was like as if she could see what I was thinking. '*Love* your neighbor, Jean,' said Miss Antonia again. I said, 'We've to love our enemies, too, Miss Antonia.' So then she laughed and said, 'Why not start with your neighbors? It's easy enough to love your friends— even the devils do that—and it's very difficult to love your enemies, but there are plenty of people in between who are neither the one nor the other to practice on, and maybe when you've practiced a bit you'll get to loving your enemies.' She wasn't one to preach, mind you. In fact, that's the only religious talk we ever had—if you call it religious—and maybe that was the reason I heeded it more than if the minister had said it…or maybe it was because you could see she did it herself and was not just telling you what *you* ought to do. I'd have liked to ask her if *she'd* gotten to loving her enemies yet—not that she had any enemies as far as I knew, for everybody in the place loved her—but Miss Antonia was a great lady. She was friendly as you please but there was something—you could go so far with her and you could go no further—and I dursn't ask her that. Well, anyway, I thought about what she'd said and I've never forgotten it to this day."

There was a short silence.

"I thought about it," continued Mrs. Smilie. "And I tried it out and I was getting on none too badly until the war. The war put me back a good bit."

"Yes," said Tonia. "I don't wonder, really."

"For, to tell the truth," said Mrs. Smilie seriously. "To tell the truth it's difficult to believe that even the Almighty Himself could love Hitler and Goebbels and the rest of them."

"It *is* difficult," agreed Tonia.

"I asked the minister," said Mrs. Smilie, nodding. "M'hm, you'll maybe not believe I could be so brash, but he was in one day to see me and he took a cup of tea and suddenly it all came over me, and I asked him straight out. 'Mr. Torrance,' I said. 'Will you tell me this, for it's a trouble to me: Does God love Hitler?'"

"What did he say?" asked Tonia, hiding an involuntary smile.

"I could see he was put about," replied Mrs. Smilie. "But he's not one to be easily beaten, and off he went on a long tirade about the powers of good and the powers of evil fighting for a man's soul, and he brought in bits of the Bible every now and then to show what he meant. It was like having a sermon all to yourself; but to tell the truth, Miss Tonia, I knew no more at the end than I did at the start…and now," said Mrs. Smilie changing her tone, all in a moment, to the strictly practical tone of everyday life. "Now, away you go and get the sausages, for I'll need all my time."

⁂

Miss Dunne arrived on a bicycle at the appointed hour. "Here I am!" she said. "I hope to goodness you really meant it when you said come to lunch. Deb thought it was frightful of me to take you at your word—but Deb hadn't seen you."

Tonia was pleased at the implied compliment. She replied very cordially and with complete sincerity that she was delighted to have Miss Dunne. At first Tonia was just a trifle shy (Miss Dunne was a good deal older than herself) but nobody could continue to be shy with Celia Dunne, for she was so amusing and not self-conscious. They went upstairs together, and Miss Dunne washed and talked and admired the house and everything in it in a way that won its owner's heart.

Mrs. Smilie was carrying in the soup when they came downstairs.

"Mrs. Smilie!" cried Celia. "I didn't know *you* were here."

"I'm not," replied Mrs. Smilie, standing foursquare in the hall with the tray in her hands and looking as pleased as Punch. "I'm *not* here, Miss Celia. I just come in and give a wee help now and then when I can spare the time. Is the admiral keeping well, Miss Celia?"

Celia replied that her father was in excellent health and returned the compliment by inquiring after Tom and Archie and Mary. By this time they had seated themselves at the table and Mrs. Smilie had served the soup.

"You're engaged, aren't you?" said Tonia, glancing at the diamond ring that sparkled on her guest's engagement finger.

"Yes, to Courtney Dale. He's—"

"Courtney Dale!" exclaimed Tonia in amazement.

"You know him?"

"No, of course not, but—"

Celia laughed. She said, "Why do you say 'Of course not'? You seem to know his name. I'm beginning to think you're rather a mysterious person, Mrs. Norman."

"Oh," said Tonia, blushing. "I meant—I mean, it's so extraordinary. It all happened a hundred years ago."

"So you've heard the old story! My Courtney is a great-grandson of the first Courtney Dale who came to Dunnian a hundred years ago and married Mary Dunne."

"He married Mary but he loved Celia."

"Not really? How do you know?" inquired the modern Celia, looking at her hostess in surprise.

"From the diary…my Great-Aunt Antonia's diary. Oh, isn't it exciting? Yes, he loved Celia and she loved him…" and with that Tonia plunged into the story.

Celia was interested, of course—who wouldn't have been?—and after lunch the diary was produced and parts of it were read and discussed very thoroughly.

"I wonder if Dad knows," said Celia thoughtfully. "It would be just like Dad to keep it under his hat—"

"How could he know?" asked Tonia. "Nobody knew except Antonia. She knew because she was Celia's friend. Celia was older, of course, but age doesn't matter, does it?"

"Not really," agreed the present-day Celia, looking at the present-day Antonia in a thoughtful way. "Why should it matter if you like the same things?"

"If you have the same values," said Tonia, nodding.

"And the odd thing is," continued Miss Dunne, following out her own train of thought. "The odd thing is that if Arthur hadn't been drowned they would have been sisters-in-law and we should be connected."

"Rather distantly," said Tonia with a regretful smile.

Time had passed quickly and Miss Dunne rose and said she was due at a Red Cross meeting and must go. "You must come over to Dunnian," she declared. "Dad would love to talk to you—and so would Deb. Deb is my sister-in-law. She's staying with us for the duration, also her son, a most attractive person aged six months or so. Deb thinks he's like his father—my brother, Mark—but I think he's like Bill."

Tonia received the impression that it was most satisfactory to be like Bill. "Another brother?" she asked.

"My favorite brother," admitted Miss Dunne.

"Bill and I used to do all sorts of wicked things together. We understand each other, somehow. You will come, won't you, Mrs. Norman?"

"Not Mrs. Norman, *please*," said Tonia quickly.

"And not Miss Dunne," said Celia, smiling and gathering up her belongings and hastening away.

Chapter Twenty-Three
Old Witch

Tonia had asked some of the young officers to come in after dinner. She had asked them in a tentative manner, for she had very little to offer them in the way of entertainment, but far from refusing her invitation they had accepted with alacrity and asked if they might bring some friends. Five of them came. Jim Mannering and Bob were the only two she knew. The other three were introduced to her in rather an airy fashion as George, Edward, and Douglas-Begge. (She had asked Bay too, of course, but he refused, saying that he would rather come when she was alone.) There was another who should have been there—Teak, of course. She had asked him that very first day when they met in the woods. Tonia was very conscious of Teak's absence when she shook hands with Bob, for in her mind, the two were linked together. She gave Bob a very special smile and Bob smiled back bravely, but there was a shadow in his eyes that had not been there before.

"Thank you for writing to Mrs. Wood," said Bob in a low voice as he followed her into the drawing room.

Nothing more was said—nothing *could* be said in a crowd like this—but Tonia knew that Bob had felt her sympathy.

The fire was bright and the chairs were comfortable and there was coffee and cigarettes. Tonia's guests sat down and began to talk, at first a trifle shyly, but soon with greater freedom. Tonia did not say very much herself, once she had started the ball rolling; she plied them with coffee and cigarettes and listened with all her ears. Unfortunately they had all begun to talk at once so it was impossible to follow the conversation, and this was a pity because it was "shop" and therefore intensely interesting.

"You were at Fornebu, weren't you? Frightfully difficult target to find…"

"I like marshaling yards. Such fun to upset Jerry's traffic schedules!"

"Marvelous fellow; he managed the whole trip without a wireless fix."

"Two holes appeared suddenly in the tailplane…"

"Four bandits appeared right out of the sun, and…"

"…that new American plane-mounted seventy-five cannon sounds pretty useful…sink a warship, can't it?"

"And then we went down to rooftop level and gunned the barrack square. You should have seen…"

Tonia listened and watched and tried to remember the names that had been mentioned to her when they arrived. She was almost sure that the tall, forceful-looking group captain had been introduced as George, but everyone seemed to be calling him Jeefer—it sounded like that. The small, dapper flight lieutenant was Douglas-Begge. Bob was addressed as "Carolina" more often than not and Mannering as "Manners." Her fifth guest was neither tall nor short and had mouse-colored hair; he was the sort of person you don't notice and cannot describe. She could not remember his name.

After a bit someone suggested a game and, as Great-Aunt Antonia had been fond of whist, there was no difficulty in producing cards and a table.

"What's it to be?" inquired Jeefer, sitting down and beginning to shuffle the cards, shooting them from one hand to the other in an exceedingly expert manner.

"Poker," suggested Douglas-Begge.

"I don't suppose Tony knows Poker," objected Jim Mannering.

Tonia realized that he was referring to her and replied that she would be perfectly happy looking on, but her guests declared unanimously that it would be no fun unless she played.

"I don't know anything—except Old Maid," said Tonia laughing.

"In that case we'll play Old Maid," declared Jeefer with perfect gravity. "Take your seats, gentlemen—Old Maid it is."

"Can you play for money?" inquired Douglas-Begge as he maneuvered dexterously for the chair next to his hostess.

"My dear Double Bed you can play anything for money," retorted Jeefer. "You can play kiss-in-the-ring for money if you put your mind to it."

"*Let's* play kiss-in-the-ring," Mannering said.

Jeefer took no notice of this frivolous suggestion. He asked for chips, adding that Tony probably called them counters, and when some had been found he divided them evenly into six heaps.

"I'll stand Tony her chips," said Bob.

There was a chorus of disapproval. Everybody wanted to stand Tony her chips and the argument became quite heated until Mannering made the suggestion that Tony should get her chips free, which would mean that everybody would be paying for them.

"Nobody," said Douglas-Begge.

"Everybody," declared Mannering firmly. "If nobody pays for them everybody pays—it's as clear as crystal."

"All set?" asked Jeefer. "Now then, pin back your ears. We deal the cards first and you look at your hand and make your bet—something like blackjack. You throw out your pairs on the rubbish heap and then each bloke in turn draws a card from his right-hand neighbor. The first to get rid of all his cards gets paid double his stake by the bank. The bloke who is left with the Old Maid—namely the Queen of Spades—pays double his stake to the bank. I'm the bank to start with. Got that, everybody?"

They argued a little about the finer points but Jeefer had his way. "We can alter the rules a bit as we go along," said Jeefer firmly.

"Why Jeefer?" asked Tonia as she took up her cards and began to pair them.

"G for George, of course. His name is George," said Mannering. "Go on, Double Bed, you start by drawing from Tony."

They played. It was quite a good game, really, but it became more and more complicated with each round because everybody suggested modifications. At last Jeefer put his foot down.

"No more mods," said Jeefer. "Mods retard production."

It was fun because everybody was keen. Tonia realized that it was a "very gambling" game, for dozens of chips changed hands after every round. She hoped sincerely that the chips did not represent large sums of money, but obviously there was nothing she could do about it. The fun grew fast and furious. Shouts of derision rent the air when Douglas-Begge was left with the Queen of Spades three times in succession, and the fifth guest, who had been extraordinarily silent, remarked *sotto voce* that Double Bed had better change his name.

"She isn't an Old Maid, she's an old—er—witch," declared Douglas-Begge, throwing the offending card upon the table with an air of disgust.

Tonia had beer and sandwiches ready on a tray in the kitchen; she went to fetch the tray, but her intention was foiled by her guests, who pursued in a body, offering assistance, and since they were all there and the kitchen was warm and comfortable it seemed more sensible to remain.

"Gosh, it *is* nice!" said Jeefer, looking around. "I like a kitchen, don't you? Seems so matey."

They agreed that it did, and perching themselves upon the table and the dresser they consumed the refreshments with apparent satisfaction.

"Did you ever meet Phelps?" inquired Jeefer.

"He was a prune," declared Mannering in a judicial voice.

"A waffling prune," agreed Jeefer solemnly.

"What became of him? Was he pranged?"

"He was not. Prunes are scarcely ever pranged. Waffling prunes never. Waffling prunes get lovely cushy jobs in nice safe places where the nasty Germans never come…"

"Tony!" said Bob, holding up his glass and smiling at his hostess.

The others immediately followed his example, saying, "Chin-chin, Tony!" or "Here's how!" and Tonia returned the compliment, saying, "All the best, Jeefer!" and "Happy landings, Bob!" as if she had known them all her life.

It was midnight when they left. Tonia saw them off at the door.

"Come back soon," she told them.

"You bet!"

"It's been a tremendous party."

"Absolutely wizard."

"We must have another go at Old Witch."

"The only thing is we never quite know…"

She watched them down the street. They were still talking and laughing, pranking like schoolboys, jockeying each other. Bob turned and waved, calling out, "So long, Tony!" and Tonia waved back.

"The only thing is we never quite know…" said Tonia to herself

as she turned back into the house. They never quite knew whether they would be able to come and play foolish games with her, or whether they would be spending the hours flying over enemy territory. They never quite knew whether, the next time she asked them, they would still be alive. And they were so friendly and natural; they were just boys.

As she straightened the furniture and made the drawing room tidy, she found to her surprise that her eyes were full of tears.

⚬⚬⚬

"You had a fine party last night," said Mrs. Smilie.

"I hope the noise didn't disturb you," Tonia replied.

"It takes more than that to disturb *me*; I like fine to hear folks enjoying themselves. To tell the truth I'm sorry for the officers, here. The men have plenty of friends in the town and dances every Friday, but there's not much for the officers to do. I'm going to clean the windows this morning, Miss Tonia."

Tonia started off to do the shopping with the big basket on her arm, and Mrs. Smilie carried out the steps and two pails of water and various cloths and "shammies" that she needed for the job. She was looking forward to a pleasant hour, for, although she liked all sorts of cleaning, she liked cleaning windows best. You saw your work—as Mrs. Smilie put it, you saw the results of your labors—when the crystal clear windowpanes winked and blinked and shone in the sunshine; and the front windows were by far the most amusing, for you were actually in the street—without any of the bother of dressing to go out—and you could see the world go by and glean the latest gossip from your friends.

The postman was the first to pass. He commented upon the weather, which was mild and pleasant for the end of October if somewhat damp. He also remarked that the war would be over by Christmas, which Mrs. Smilie considered superoptimistic.

"It'll be June before we're through with them," declared Mrs. Smilie, looking down at him and nodding. "You mark my words, Willie. It'll be June."

Mrs. MacBean was the next. "Och, you're cleaning windows!" she exclaimed. "It's wasted wurrk in saft weather like this. You'd be as well to leave it alone."

"Some folks likes to see out of their windows," replied Mrs. Smilie ironically.

"John does mine," continued Mrs. MacBean. "John says it's man's wurrk, cleaning windows."

"Alec has enough to do at the station," retorted Mrs. Smilie.

Mrs. Wilson's Annie had her baby in a baby carriage. She stopped beneath the ladder and Mrs. Smilie came down to admire him properly, for she adored babies. Annie had several tidbits of news about the girls who were working with her at the aircraft factory; she detailed these to Mrs. Smilie before she moved on. After this, quite a number of people passed and they all stopped for a wee chat. Some of them had interesting information and Mrs. Smilie paid them the honor of descending from her perch; others were not worth bothering about and were sent about their business.

In spite of the interruptions the work progressed fairly rapidly and Mrs. Smilie had finished with Melville House and started upon her own front windows when a stranger came up the street. A stranger was always an interesting sight in Ryddelton. This particular stranger was tall and thin and very smartly dressed in a blue cloth coat and expensive-looking furs and a hat with a feather in it. The stranger paused and inquired if this was Melville House, and Mrs. Smilie, looking down at her, saw that she was quite young but rather plain. It's her nose, thought Mrs. Smilie, gazing at her and forgetting to reply.

"Is this Melville House?" repeated the young lady.

"You'll be from London?" said Mrs. Smilie. "You'll be staying at the Arms, I shouldn't wonder."

"The Arms?"

"The Rydd Arms," explained Mrs. Smilie, pointing to the hotel that flaunted its sign several hundred yards down the street.

The young lady was about to reply that she had just that moment arrived from Edinburgh by train, but she thought better of it. Surely it was nobody's business but her own (it was certainly no business of this extraordinary-looking woman with the yellow duster tied around her head), so she ignored the question, and seeing that "Melville House" was engraved upon a brass plate on the door, she pulled the bell and waited for the door to open.

Mrs. Smilie smiled at the arrogant-looking back and continued her task; the bell jangled forlornly in the distance—it jangled several times before the young lady gave up the struggle in disgust. When she was tired of ringing the bell she returned to Mrs. Smilie and asked in haughty accents if Mrs. Norman were at home.

"Mrs. Norman is out," replied Mrs. Smilie, polishing industriously.

"Why doesn't somebody answer the door?"

"Maybe the butler is sleeping," suggested Mrs. Smilie gravely.

The young lady did not smile. She said crossly, "Surely there's someone whose duty it is to answer the door. I can't stand here all morning. I've come from Edinburgh to see Mrs. Norman on business."

The joke had gone far enough (perhaps a little too far, thought Mrs. Smilie remorsefully; she was aware that her sense of humor was liable to run away with her), so she climbed down the ladder, opened the door of Melville House, and showed the young lady into the drawing room.

"What name shall I say?" she inquired, turning most unexpectedly into a well-trained housemaid.

"Miss Garland," was the reply.

Nita Garland sat down in the drawing room and waited. She was surprised at the room. The house was a common sort of house in the High Street with no garden—just the sort of house she had expected—but the room was quite lovely and full of valuable things. The cabinet was a gem, and so was the bureau…really old and beautifully preserved. Everything in the room was of the same period, Nita decided, and everything blended harmoniously.

She was still sitting there, admiring it and trying to make up her mind how much you would get for it at Sotheby's, when the door opened and an air force officer walked into the room. He was very young and fair with pink cheeks and blue eyes. Nice-looking, too, thought Nita, eyeing him appraisingly.

"Oh, I'm sorry!" he exclaimed in embarrassment and surprise. "I didn't know anyone was here. I met Tony—Mrs. Norman, I mean—in the town and she said just to come in and look for it. My name's Jim Mannering, and—"

"Look for what?" asked Nita.

"My pocketbook," he replied, starting to search around the room, moving chairs and feeling down the sides of them. "It's sort of brown. You haven't seen it, I suppose?"

"No."

"I must have dropped it last night when we were playing Old Witch," declared Mannering continuing to hunt with feverish intensity. "It must have fallen out of my pocket when…but no, it must have been *afterward*, really, because of course I had it when we were settling up—Jeefer took twenty-two bob off me—so perhaps it's in the kitchen. Yes, it must be…"

He disappeared. Nita could hear him moving about in the back premises. She was smiling to herself in a slightly unpleasant manner when the door opened again and another young man came in. This one was carrying a bouquet of roses done up with tissue paper (Nita saw at a glance that he was a pilot in the American Air Force, for she was well up on the uniforms and insignia of our allies). Unlike his predecessor, he was neither surprised nor embarrassed to find a stranger in the room but smiled at Nita in a friendly manner and asked if Tony happened to be around.

"I believe Mrs. Norman is out," said Nita coldly.

"I say, that's just too bad," he declared with a crestfallen air.

A short silence ensued. He stood there, irresolutely, with the flowers in his hands, trying to make up his mind what to do with them. Finally he put them down on the piano.

"Maybe you would tell her," he said, looking at Nita doubtfully (for her attitude was not cooperative). "Just say they're from Bob, that's all. I guess Tony will understand." He vanished.

The RAF officer put his head around the door and said, "I say, would you mind telling Tony I found it?"

"I'll tell her," said Nita grimly.

The front door banged and she heard him running down the street.

Nita waited for quite a long time after that, but she did not mind waiting. Not only had she plenty to think about, but also plenty to do. The bureau, which she had admired as a period piece, was discovered by Nita to be unlocked; there were letters tucked away in the cubbyholes. Unfortunately they were not very interesting. There was a postcard, signed Celia Dunne, announcing that its author was coming to lunch; there was a letter from Frank, couched in a reproachful vein, asking why Tonia had not answered his previous letter and what she was doing with herself in Ryddelton. There were several letters from Lou, but these were so long and so closely written that Nita could not be bothered with them. The remainder were from Janet, and these Nita had helped to compose so nothing was to be gained by rereading them.

When Tonia came in she found Nita sitting upon the sofa with an expression of resigned patience upon her face.

"Nita!" exclaimed Tonia in anything but cordial tones.

"Yes, it's me. I came to see what on earth you were doing. Mother was worried about you."

"I'm perfectly all right. I wrote to Janet. I'm very well and I like living alone. Listen, Nita, I *like* being here. You wouldn't like it, I know, because you would find it dull. I don't feel dull. I'm not in the least lonely."

"Lonely!" exclaimed Nita. "No, I shouldn't think you were *lonely*. I can reassure Mother about *that*."

"Yes, please do," said Tonia, but she said it doubtfully, for there was an unpleasant sort of feeling in the air.

"You're a hermit, I suppose. That's what you'd like to make out."

"I'm not very sociable, I'm afraid," said Tonia, thinking of her life with the Garlands and how glad she had been to get away.

"What a hypocrite you are!" cried Nita. "I always knew you were a dark horse, but Mother was completely taken in."

"I don't understand—"

"I'm fed up with you! I'm not a spoilsport—as a matter of fact I like having a good time, myself—but I can't stand anything underhand," declared Nita. "If you had said you wanted to enjoy yourself and have a good time, I wouldn't have blamed you. It's all this talk about liking a quiet country life that annoys *me*."

"It's a nice change," declared Tonia, trying to be patient.

Nita laughed. "Oh, it *must* be a nice change," she agreed. "It must be a big change from living with Uncle Robert to running a sort of gambling den."

"You're mad," said Tonia in bewilderment.

"I shall go home and tell Mother *everything*."

"I don't have anything to hide."

"You had better be careful."

"Careful of what?"

"Of men," said Nita, rising and putting on her furs. "I suppose you don't care about your reputation…what a fool you are, Tonia."

They were silent for a moment. Tonia's bosom was heaving. Her eyes were very bright. "I can look after myself," she said at last. "I don't know what you mean, but anyhow it has nothing to do with you."

"I wonder," said Nita. "We'll see what Mother says." She was ready to go now (Tonia did not ask her to stay to lunch) and suddenly her eyes fell on the roses lying on the piano. "From Bob," said Nita, pointing to them. "To dear little Tony from Bob…and your other young man found his pocketbook in the kitchen. I nearly forgot to tell you."

"Oh!" exclaimed Tonia, somewhat taken aback. "Oh…yes, some of them came in last night…"

Nita said nothing. She just smiled.

They were in the hall now, and Tonia opened the front door very wide. She would have liked to push Nita out, but she managed to refrain.

"Good-bye," said Nita, nastily. "I shall tell Mother *all* about the merry widow." She turned to go…and almost collided with another member of the Royal Air Force, a squadron leader this time.

They both said "Oh!" and stepped back a pace.

Tonia was so enraged with Nita that caution fled, and she introduced them, adding with dangerous sweetness, "You *must* remember each other at Miss Mann's school, when Nita put some of that violet ink of hers in our milk." And with that she turned and went back into the house and left them to it, for she could bear no more.

༄

"Well, I sent her away," said Bay, entering the kitchen some minutes later and hoisting himself onto the dresser. "I gathered that was your intention, Butterfingers."

"Yes…no," said Tonia, half laughing and half crying and peeling potatoes with reckless speed. "I mean, I don't really know what I wanted. I was just—angry—"

"You look angry," agreed Bay. "It suits you, Butterfingers."

"It makes me feel sick," declared Tonia.

"Don't cut your fingers."

"Oh, Bay!" she exclaimed, laying down the knife.

"You *have* cut your fingers!"

"No, I haven't. It was only—it made me remember something."

"Something nasty?"

"Something *horrible*," she declared, looking at him wide-eyed. "Something that makes all this fuss seem childish and absurd. Let's not think about it anymore."

"We ought to, really," replied Bay. "I mean, Nita seems to think you're going to live with them, but you couldn't. Good Lord, I'd rather live with an asp! Surely you can manage to live here. It can't be costing you very much."

"Oh, yes," said Tonia. "I mean, it isn't costing much." She hesitated. Bay seemed to have gotten hold of the wrong idea.

"There will be money coming in from that song," said Bay earnestly. "It won't be long now, so if you can manage for a week or two… I'm awfully glad I showed it to Harrison and got him to take it up," added Bay with satisfaction.

He looked so pleased at the idea, pleased that he had been able to help her, that she had not the heart to undeceive him.

"Light your pipe, Bay," said Tonia, taking up the knife and resuming her task, but more carefully.

"In the kitchen?"

"Anywhere. I like to see you smoking. You look so nice and comfortable smoking your pipe."

"I've lost it," said Bay.

"Oh, Bay, I'm so sorry. Do you think you left it here, or—"

"Don't worry," he said, smiling at her. "It often goes a-missing, but it always turns up like a bad penny."

Chapter Twenty-Four
The Poet of the Hills

It was the day Celia had appointed for gathering sphagnum moss, and, fortunately for everyone concerned, it was an exceedingly fine day, with crisp, cool air and pale yellow sunshine and a light haze upon the hills. Since Tonia's arrival at Ryddelton the scene had changed. The heather was dark brown now, and the bracken was bright brown, tangled like a child's hair when it comes in from play. The trees had lost their leaves, except the conifers, which stood like tall green sentinels upon the slopes of the hills. Far in the distance a wood of larches looked like wreaths of soft brown smoke streaming up the hill between plow and pasture land.

Celia and Tonia were walking along a cart track winding through gorse bushes and trees. The leaves crackled underfoot and a startled rabbit scuttled across the path and vanished down his hole. There were squirrels here, too, little red ones with white waistcoats and long bushy tails. Behind the girls came the other pickers in twos and threes. They were all dressed in their very oldest clothes, shabby tweeds or slacks, and they all wore rubber boots and carried haversacks. Tonia had been surprised to see that they were middle-aged women, for it seemed to her that this sort of war work was more suited to the young, but Celia explained that all the young people of Ryddelton were in the Services, or munitions, or else so busy that they could not get away.

"I ought to be in the Wrens or something, myself," continued Celia. "As a matter of fact I feel a bit of a slacker sometimes, but they exempted me because Dad is so old and Deb (my sister-in-law) isn't strong and has her work cut out looking after little Humphrey…and of course I don't know what would happen to all the voluntary work in Ryddelton if they took me away. There isn't anyone else left—anyone able-bodied, I mean—so it all seems to devolve on me. I run the VCP and the WVS and now they want me to be secretary of the local branch of the Red Cross. The sphagnum moss takes a good deal of time. We have quite a good depot where we dry and clean it."

"Perhaps I could help you," Tonia suggested.

"That would be splendid," Celia replied. "You might do some collecting for the penny a week fund, and you could come to the work party once a week and help to clean the moss."

They had reached their objective by this time. It was a bog that lay in a bowl-shaped depression among the hills. There was heather growing in places, and there were masses of tumbled gray rocks, but for the most part the terrain consisted of long, yellowish-green grass and boggy land. There were hills all around (the ground rising gradually from the boggy floor of the depression), and the hills were all much about the same height so that the tops of them, which were outlined against the pale sky, presented a definite wavy appearance. And these tops were powdered with snow, but very lightly powdered, as if an economical hand had been using the sugar sifter. The hills themselves were pale fawn and looked smooth as velvet.

"I love this country," said Tonia with a sigh.

Celia agreed. "It satisfies something inside me. I like it better than trees or rocks or plains. Yet I've heard people say it was ugly and depressing—funny, isn't it?—but we must get to work now."

They were all getting to work and wasting no time about it; each picker provided herself with a basket and a sack and set forth in a determined manner, wading through the bog. Tonia took a basket and a sack and attached herself to Celia, for Celia had promised to instruct her and show her the right stuff to pick.

"It's a bit difficult, at first," said Celia. "There are so many different kinds of sphagnum, and some of them aren't much use, but you'll soon get into it, so don't worry. You can leave your haversack here. We usually pick all the afternoon and have tea when we've finished."

The sphagnum moss grew in the wettest parts of the bog: it grew in old cuttings from which peat had been taken, it grew in banks among the heather, and it grew in pools. From a distance it looked like a smooth green carpet, but when you got closer, you saw that the carpet was made of millions of little star-shaped heads—green and brown and pink and fawn. When you picked the moss you found that each little head had a feathery stem reaching down into the bog.

"Look," said Celia, digging her fingers into the bog and pulling out a handful. "That's the stuff we want. Look how feathery it is! You squeeze it hard...like that...and put it into your basket."

"What about this?" asked Tonia, following her instructor's example and clawing up a handful of pale green moss.

"Well, no," said Celia. "That isn't quite right, really. It *is* sphagnum but it isn't mature. Look how thin and skinny the stems are...see what I mean?"

Tonia saw the difference. She picked several handfuls. Some of the moss was red, some green, and some fawn. Some of the stems were woody and sparsely clothed with tiny boat-shaped leaves; others were thickly clothed, quite furry from their little heads to their roots.

"It's the furry kind we want," said Celia. "Its proper name

is *cymbifolia papillosum*, but we call it Teddy Bear. You can feel how spongy it is when you squeeze it. Are your hands cold?"

"Simply frozen," replied Tonia smiling.

"They'll recover if you persevere. We'll pick for an hour and then you can come with me up the hill. The shepherd is a friend of mine and he promised to have a look around and find another bog for us to pick, so I want to get hold of him if I can. Do you think you can manage now?"

Tonia was doubtful. The sphagnum looked much the same to her and it was only when she had picked a handful and squeezed it that she was able to discover whether or not it was the proper "Teddy Bear" variety. Celia seemed to know, from looking at the heads, what the stems would be like.

It's experience, I suppose, thought Tonia as she waded about, grubbing up handfuls and looking at them carefully and trying to decide whether to put them in her basket or throw them away. Her hands were warm now, and it was pleasant work. The moss was so pretty; the coloring of the moor was magnificent. The blue sky was reflected in the peaty pools, but at the end of an hour the new recruit was very thankful to straighten her back and follow her leader up the hill.

Celia found a sheep track that led upward between thick heather, and Tonia came behind. They did not talk much, for it was fairly steep; here and there an outcrop of rock rose in their path and they were forced to climb. Tonia was not used to mountaineering and she was very glad when she saw that they had nearly reached the top, but her joy was somewhat damped when she discovered that another hill, much higher, lay ahead of them.

"Don't worry," said Celia, laughing. "We aren't going very far. In fact, we needn't go a step farther because there he is—there's Jock Tod!"

The shepherd appeared from behind the shoulder of the hill

with his dog at his heels. He was an enormous man, tall and broad in proportion. Perhaps he looked even larger than he really was, for he came down the hill to meet them, striding over the heather and the tussocks of grass as if the whole countryside belonged to him. He was clad in very ancient tweeds that blended with the coloring of the moors. He had a plaid over his shoulder and a shepherd's crook in his hand.

Celia waved to him. "He's rather a wonderful person," she said. "He's a poet. We must get him to talk. He reminds me of Noah."

Tonia had never seen Noah, but she realized what Celia meant, for the shepherd seemed wild and free and more than life-size. His hair was long and white; it lifted in the breeze. His face was lined and weather-beaten and his eyes had the far-seeing look of men who spend their lives upon the mountains or the sea.

Celia introduced him to her companion and they shook hands.

"Aye," said Mr. Tod, giving her a piercing glance. "Aye, you're a Melville. Ah wis hearing aboot ye."

"You hear everything!" Celia exclaimed. "How do you hear things when you're always on the hills?"

"Och, you'd wonder," said Mr. Tod (he had a slow deep resonant voice, and his R's came rolling out with a soft burring sound). "There's aye folks aboot, an' where there's folks there's clash." He sat down as he spoke, settling himself upon a convenient rock, with his knees wide apart and his feet firmly placed upon the ground. The girls sat down too, for they were glad to rest after their stiff climb.

"Ah kennt yer faither," continued Mr. Tod, looking at Tonia. "He was a grand shot when he wis a lad. It wis an ill day when the Melvilles sold the castle." Then he turned to Celia. "I saw ye from the tops," he said. "Those'll be your folks at the foot of Blaegill."

"Yes, they're my moss-hags," said Celia, smiling.

"Moass-hags!" remarked Mr. Tod with a quiet rumble of laughter. "Is that whit ye ca' yersel's? It's no' a bad name for ye, Miss Celia. Weel, noo, see here, Ah've bin keepin' ma eyes open for yon moass, an' Ah've found twa, three places where ye could get it." He took some specimens of sphagnum moss from his pocket and laid them out on the ground. "See here," he said gravely. "Yon's the wee bit ye gave me as a patteran, an' yon's the wee bits Ah found masel'."

"It's the right stuff," declared Celia, nodding.

"Och, it's the right stuff," he agreed. "There's a wheen o' it high up on the hillside—over by Souden Gap, but ye'd not get the cairts up near it. There's a guid enough boag at Carles Knowe. D'ye ken yon wee burn, Roab's Burn, they ca' it? Weel, ye could get the cairts up there easy enough…"

Celia listened and made notes of the different places and how to get to them. It was not until the business talk was over and she had all the information she required that she turned the conversation into a different channel and asked if Mr. Tod had been making any poems lately.

"Makin'!" he said, smiling at her. "Yon's a guid auld wurrd. It was 'makars' the auld poets were ca'ed…but Ah dinna make poems, Miss Celia. They come intae ma heid when Ah luik at the hills an' the muirs an' Ah hear the wee burns tinklin'."

Tonia looked at him with even more interest now, for she understood exactly what he meant. Mr. Tod was a listener. She was thinking of this and wondering about it, when she heard Celia ask him for a poem; somewhat to her surprise, Mr. Tod made no trouble about granting the request. To judge from his demeanor one would have thought it the most natural request in the world; he was neither proud nor shy.

"If ye would like it, Miss Celia—" he said, and launched forth into his poem without more ado, pronouncing the lines slowly and clearly in his deep resonant voice.

The Rydd Water

Amangst the everlastin' hills
Winds doon the quiet Rydd;
The burns splash through verdant gills
Wi' sunbeams in their snid.

An' here the black-faced sheep an' lambs
Are weel content to dream;
Their meat the wiry mountain grass
Their drink the siller stream.

A thoosand floo-ers o' golden sheen
Are scattered o'er the lowes;
In caller moass-hags, pink an' green,
The starry sphagnum grows.

The lav'rock lilts abune the muir
An' shrill the curlew cries,
Wi' soochin' wind an' trinn'lin' burn
Their voices harmonize.

Man, like cloud-shadows on the braes,
Is skliffed wi' winds o' Ware;
But Rydd, amang her quiet ways
Rins on like evermair.

There was a little silence when he had finished. Celia broke it. She said, "It's the real thing. It's beautiful and—and true. Thank you very much indeed."

"You're welcome," said Mr. Tod gravely. He called his dog and they went away together up the hill.

Tonia said nothing. She scarcely knew whether the poem

was good or bad. She only knew that in this setting it seemed quite perfect and was deeply moving. This was what he heard as he strode about on the hills he knew so well. He heard the birds call and the tinkle of the burns and the "sooch" of the wind in the grass. He heard it as poetry, and she as music. She would have liked to sit and think about it quietly for a long time, but Celia was stirring.

"Sometimes I wonder about Jock Tod," said Celia thoughtfully. "Is his poetry really first-class or is it just everything together that makes it sound so wonderful? The man himself is so grand. And his marvelous voice...and the hills all around..."

"You can't judge dispassionately."

Celia nodded. "Sometimes I think we ought to get the poems written down, and then I begin to wonder if that would spoil them...I should hate to be disillusioned." She hesitated, and then continued, "I'm a prosaic sort of person but even I feel poetical when I look at the hills. I could sit here all day and watch the shadows of the clouds moving over them and the light changing. I like them even better now than when the heather is in bloom. There's something so garish about heather—it's unbelievably purple—but now, when the hills are bare, they're smooth and velvety and the color of a lion's pelt."

"Almost," agreed Tonia, smiling at the simile.

"Deb laughs at me, too," said Celia, smiling back. "Deb says I'm quite mad about the hills—and to tell the truth I get madder about them every year. I don't know what I would do if I had to go to America with Courtney. Fortunately I don't have to choose between them because he's quite made up his mind to stay here with me."

"Are you going to be married soon?" Tonia asked.

Celia did not reply for a few moments and then she said, "That depends. It depends on whether or not I can make Courtney understand my point of view. I want to be married now, but Courtney thinks we should wait until after the war. It sounds a bit odd, doesn't it?"

Tonia said nothing. She waited while Celia took out a cigarette and lit it. She had a feeling that Celia was going to tell her more.

"It sounds very odd," continued Celia. "We've talked about it a bit—Courtney and I—but we haven't really gotten down to brass tacks because I find it a bit difficult. I suppose I'm old-fashioned or something."

Tonia nodded understandingly.

"Courtney's idea is that it wouldn't be fair to me to be married now. He says that he doesn't want me to be tied to him. This frightful invasion is supposed to be coming off pretty soon and of course he'll be in it. He seems to think," said Celia, knocking the ash off her cigarette with elaborate care. "He seems to think it wouldn't matter so much if he were killed outright, but it would matter quite a lot if he were maimed. That's his idea, you see," said Celia in a voice that tried very hard to be quite steady but shook just a little in spite of itself. "That's *his* idea. My idea is—is different."

"Yes," said Tonia a trifle huskily. "Yes, I see."

"My idea is *quite* different," continued Celia in stronger tones. "I *want* to be tied to Courtney. I want to be tied to him tight and fast, hand and foot, *now*, this very minute. I want him to belong to me when he lands in France or Belgium or wherever it is, when he goes roaring up the beach in his tank. If he comes through all right—then it will be—marvelous, and if—if he doesn't—at any rate I shall have been his wife; and if he's wounded, or—or blinded—then I ask nothing better than to spend my life taking care of him. That's all, really."

Tonia said nothing, because she couldn't speak.

"That's what I feel," explained Celia. "It's quite—sensible, really, and I feel it more strongly than anything I've ever felt before. But the silly thing is I can't explain it to Courtney. I can't tell anybody about it... I haven't the least idea why I'm telling *you*."

"Because we're friends," said Tonia, who had managed to find her voice. "Because we're old friends, Celia. That's why."

"You mean...yes, I see," said Celia, smiling. "Our friendship is a hundred years' old."

They were silent for a little while.

"It *does* make a difference," said Celia at last in thoughtful tones. "I think we should have been friends anyway, but it would have taken longer. It's as if we were building a house and the foundations were laid already."

"It's *exactly* like that!" cried Tonia joyfully.

Celia smiled at her. "You are a dear," she said.

Chapter Twenty-Five
Reinforcements Arrive

When Celia and Tonia got back to the bog the picking was over and the "moss-hags" were thinking about tea. The picked moss was in large sacks, which were scattered far and wide over the moor, just where the pickers had filled them, and the next thing to be done was to collect the sacks and bring them over to the road where two pony carts were waiting to take them to the depot. This was the most unpopular part of moss gathering, for the sacks were full of wet moss and therefore incredibly heavy, and the ground was boggy and seamed with deep fissures full of peaty water. There were bushes of bog myrtle, with tough wiry stems, and patches of heather and rocks—all these presented formidable obstacles to a woman with a sack of moss upon her back. Some of the pickers suggested that they should have tea before tackling the job, and others were anxious to finish the job before sitting down to tea. They appealed to Celia for a casting vote and Celia was about to give her opinion when two men appeared from behind a rocky knoll, leaping over the bog from tussock to tussock and waving their arms. One of them was well in advance of the other and seemed to be making better progress.

"Soldiers!" exclaimed Celia in surprise.

"It's Bay!" exclaimed Tonia.

"Hold hard!" cried Bay when he got within speaking distance. "We've come to give you a hand, Bob and I. We couldn't find you or we'd have been here ages ago…and Bob kept on falling into holes."

"Your moors…take a bit of knowing," declared Bob, arriving breathless and muddy. "That green stuff looks OK, but when you jump on it there's nothing solid. It's like a nightmare…"

"That sinking feeling," said Bay, nodding gravely. "You ought to take something for it. I'll speak to the M.O."

"And the ditches are full of molasses," added Bob.

"I wish they were," declared Celia.

"Never mind, Bob," said Bay. "It's a new experience for you. When you go back to Carolina you can tell the old folks at home that you've sampled Macbeth's blasted heath."

"Blasted is the word," agreed Bob with a grin. "I guess the old folks at home will want to know if I saw the witches, too."

"Tell them you met the moss-hags," suggested Celia.

"Enough of this!" exclaimed Bay. "We've come to work, not to bandy words. You want these sacks carried over to the carts, don't you, Celia? Come on, Bob. Get a move on. You take these two sacks and I'll get those two over there."

"Easy," agreed Bob cheerfully. He bent to lift the sack nearest to him and then looked up in surprise. "Did you say take *two*?" he inquired.

"Of course," replied Bay. "Save you another journey. Much better take two at a time." He also bent to lift the sack; he also looked up in surprise.

There was a peal of laughter from the pickers, who had been watching with bated breath.

"All right, all right," said Bay, smiling. "I thought there was moss in the bags—not coal. We'll take them one by one. Come on, Bob, remember this is the stuff to cure you when you get that Jerry bullet through your—through your leg."

"I get you," agreed Bob. "Just give me a lift with this onto my back." He hoisted it up and staggered off, remarking, cheerfully that if he happened to fall into another hole he would sink to the bottom and never be seen again.

"Don't worry," cried Bay. "There isn't a bottom. You'll come out in Australia."

In spite of this backchat the work went forward rapidly, much more rapidly than it would have without the reinforcements. The sacks were hoisted into the pony carts and the workers sat down to have their well-earned tea. They found a sheltered spot in a disused quarry and spread their rugs and produced sandwiches and thermos flasks. It was cold now, and the sun was declining. It was sinking into a group of larches whose bare branches showed red against the pale turquoise blue of the sky. There was a faint haze on the ground, tinged with reddish gold.

Everybody was tired and hungry and conscious of good work well done; there was not much talk, but the silence was friendly and intimate.

"It might be a summer evening," said Bay suddenly. "I mean, it *looks* like a summer evening if you forget that it's so cold."

Some of the party agreed with Bay and some did not. It depended upon whether the person in question had sufficient imagination.

"I suppose it's quite different from America," somebody asked Bob.

Tonia thought this rather a foolish remark, but Bob answered it quite cheerfully, saying that he came from South Carolina and the country there was completely different—not to speak of the climate.

"I meant the people," explained his interlocutor.

"Our women are a bit smarter," replied Bob frankly.

Everybody laughed at this, for it seemed a miracle of understatement.

"You forget that we're moss-hags," said somebody.

"No," replied Bob quite seriously. "That's the whole thing. I guess an American woman would be dressed up a bit even if she was on a dirty job."

"Old clothes look best on the moors," declared Bay, glancing at Tonia's shabby tweeds.

"But we don't have moors," said Bob, frowning a little. "To tell the truth I just can't see this happening in the States. It would all be different. Our women do chores in the house but I can't see them wading in bogs. Maybe they would if they had to."

"Of course they would," said Celia. "And I know exactly what you mean. They would wear marvelous skiing suits and colored berets."

"Not if they had to do it on clothes coupons," objected one of the hags.

"We have picnics, of course," continued Bob, who seemed to be interested in the discussion. "But if this was the States there would be a lot more talk and wisecracking."

"Wisecracking?" somebody inquired.

Bob nodded and explained. "I say something pretty smart and you say something a bit smarter."

Celia remarked that America was not the place for her because she could never think of anything smart at the right moment. "Long afterward I think of it," said Celia sadly. "I think of the most marvelous wisecrack, but of course it's too late."

"I'm not much good at it myself," said Bob comfortingly.

They did not dawdle over their tea, for it was too cold and the light was beginning to fail. The rugs and haversacks were piled into the carts and the workers started for home. It was very quiet, the shadows of the trees stretched across the road, and wisps of fleecy white mist lay in the hollows.

"Bay is in good form today," said Celia, as she and Tonia

walked along together. "He's looking ever so much fitter and happier, somehow."

"His fiancée is coming tomorrow," explained Tonia.

"I didn't know he was engaged!" cried Celia in surprise.

"Oh, yes, he's been engaged for a long time. She's French and very pretty and smart. Her name is Retta Delarge."

"Where did Bay meet her?"

"At Dieppe," replied Tonia. "It was at the beginning of the war, and then she managed to escape and came over here."

"I see," said Celia in a very thoughtful voice.

"I'm so glad she's coming," continued Tonia cheerfully. "It will be nice for Bay, won't it? He has taken rooms for her at Mrs. MacBean's. I do hope she will be comfortable there—and not find it dull. Of course Bay can go and see her whenever he can get away but, as a matter of fact, he's pretty busy and doesn't get off much…" Tonia continued to babble in this cheerful, but somewhat unnatural manner, until their ways parted.

Chapter Twenty-Six
Retta Delarge

Retta Delarge arrived at Ryddelton by the morning train (Bay could not meet her because he was busy) and walked up the High Street to her rooms, causing a good deal of interest by reason of her exotic appearance. She left her suitcase there and crossed the street to Melville House and rang the bell.

"Bay did tell me about you," said Miss Delarge, when Tonia opened the door. "Bay's letters were all about the good, kind Mrs. Norman who took pittee upon his lonely condition. I feel I must come and say thank you the very first moment I am here."

"I hope the rooms are comfortable," said Tonia, showing her guest into the drawing room.

"Comfortable!" cried Miss Delarge. "*O, mon Dieu!* They are so small one could swing a cat and the roof comes down at the sides!"

"The roof comes down!"

"It slopes," she explained, gesticulating wildly. "It slopes so that only in the middle can one stand erect. O, how you are fortunate to have this beautiful house all of your own! My home it is beautiful too but, alas, the dirty Bosche is there and who knows what he is doing to it. Who knows whether my beautiful home is still in its place or burnt to ruins!"

"Oh, *no*," said Tonia faintly.

"But this," cried Miss Delarge, throwing out her arms. "But this, how beautiful it is! So very peaceful, *n'est-ce pas?* You do not know there is any war at all. Ah, how peaceful!" Miss Delarge sighed, sinking gracefully into a chair.

"You must come here," said Tonia, trying to sound more hospitable than she felt.

"Oh, I could not trouble you!"

"Of course you must come. I can easily give you a room."

Miss Delarge protested and exclaimed, but she was so easily persuaded that it was obvious she had intended to come from the very beginning, but it could not be helped. Tonia had felt bound to ask her, and perhaps she would not stay very long— perhaps she would be bored. This seemed all the more likely because she was so out of place in Ryddelton, so smart and colorful—exactly like an illustration in *Vogue,* thought Tonia, eyeing the elegant figure with reluctant admiration. Although she had been traveling all night she was full of life and vivacity.

"And if I come," cried Miss Delarge. "If then I accept this so delightful and warm invitation there is no need of delay. I come now, *n'est-ce pas?* I go queek and fetch my suitcase across the street and I tell the fat lady with the beard that I do not stay to knock my head against her roof."

"Yes, of course," agreed Tonia, smiling. "I'll get the bed aired—"

"No, no, you leave it to me. *All that* I will do and not you at all. You will see I am a useful person and no bother."

She moved across the street that afternoon, bringing one suitcase and explaining that it contained all that she possessed. "But me, I am clevaire," she added. "One does not need much clothes if one is clevaire. It is the little touch that counts, the little blouse that makes the whole ensemble a different appearance, the red scarf or the green that is put around the neck or the head."

It was true, of course. She had a flair for clothes and every-thing she wore suited her and expressed her personality. It was true, also, that she was useful in the house; she helped to get the room ready and when that was done she insisted on cooking the supper.

"You will call me Retta," she announced, as she took Tonia's apron and tied it around her waist. "And I will call you Antonia. It is a lovely name and a pittee to spoil it... And now I will make the omelet with some dry eggs that are so very strange but not at all bad when they are cooked the right way, and we will look in the larder for a little something to put inside…and there will be coffee."

"It sounds lovely," said Tonia.

"It will taste lovely," declared Retta. "There is nobody can make an omelet like me, my husband says—"

"Your husband?"

"O, how I am stupid!" cried Retta, throwing up her hands and laughing. "*Mon frère*—it is my brother, I mean. This *so* diffi-cult language of yours, I shall never learn it proper, but perhaps you can speak French?"

Tonia shook her head. She was much too shy to attempt to speak French to Retta.

"*Quel dommage!*" said Retta sadly. "What a pittee! We must do the best we can and you shall tell me when I say things all wrong. *N'est-ce pas, chère* Antonia? You shall say, 'No, stupid Retta, that is not the way we say,' and then you will tell me how."

"I think you're very clever," declared Tonia, with sincerity, for although Retta's English was a bit peculiar, she had a fine flow of words and was never at a loss to explain what she meant.

"O, clevaire!" said Retta. "It is not that. It is just that I *must* learn how to talk or else I burst. At first when I come to England there is nobody I know and I am like a fish on straw gasping to breathe…and then I learn to talk and it is not so bad…and then my brother come and it is better. We take a little flat together in London and we get on all right though all the time our hearts are sore for *La France*. You do not understand that."

"But of course I do!"

"You do not understand," repeated Retta. "*La France* is everything to us and now she has no friend in all the world. There are people who laugh and say bad things about her. That makes me mad. Yes, I am mad when I hear what people say. You do not know there is a war. You are happy and comfortable. It is not fair."

Tonia did not know what to say to this, so she said nothing—and perhaps this was best, for it is impossible to argue with a person who will not argue back.

Retta had made her omelet by this time and had gotten it in the pan. She was bending over it and watching it with anxious care.

"When the omelet is ready we must eat it queek," said Retta. "You have the plate hot? That is right. Where is the fork?"

"Spoon," said Tonia, smiling and handing it.

"I make mistakes all the time!" exclaimed Retta, laughing heartily—so heartily that Tonia was obliged to laugh too.

They were still laughing when the door opened and Bay walked in. "What a row!" he exclaimed with a delighted smile, for to tell the truth he was more than pleased to find the two girls getting on so well.

"O, Bay!" cried Retta excitedly. "What brings *you* here, may one ask? Who is wanting great big ugly men in a kitchen! And why you come in whenever you like and not to ring the door knocker!" She flung herself into his arms as she spoke and raised her face to kiss him.

Bay kissed her lightly. He was very red and embarrassed, and Tonia was embarrassed too. She busied herself dishing the omelet Retta had abandoned in her excitement. Retta was speaking French now; streams of it were pouring from her lips, and this embarrassed Tonia still more, for she could understand every word. *I never meant I couldn't understand French,* thought Tonia, trying to shut her ears. *Goodness, how awful this is!*

It was more than awful, for Retta was giving Bay a long account of her arrival at the rooms and of her conversation with Tonia. Tonia learned to her surprise that she had visited Retta at Mrs. MacBean's and had looked around in horror and had insisted on Retta repacking her suitcase and coming to Melville House, that she had refused to accept any excuses or denials but had declared she was lonely and *"triste"* and she would go mad if she did not have company in the long evenings. "So you see," continued Retta, in her rapid flowing French. "So what could I do, tell me that, dear one. Could I do other than come here and be with her and cheer her? She has been so kind to you that I felt I owed her a little consideration, for anyone who is kind to my dearest one is kind to me. Of course it would be better to be on our own, and you know that your Retta does not care where she is—whether she is comfortable or not—if only she can be near you. We should have had more freedom if I could have remained in the rooms—*ça va sans dire*—but she will be *convenant,* the poor little thing; she will not embarrass us with her company…"

Tonia did not embarrass them with her company more than she could help. They had supper together, of course (the omelet was extremely good), and then she sent her two guests into the drawing room and shut the door upon them and proceeded to wash up the dishes. For some reason or other she felt lonely and miserable—it was the first time she had felt lonely since she came to Ryddelton—and this was rather strange when you came to think of it. Tonia would have liked somebody to talk to. She half thought of going in and seeing the Smilies (she had a standing invitation to go in and see them whenever she felt dull) but that would be silly, thought Tonia, hesitating. I'm *not* lonely, really. I expect I'm just tired or something so I had better go to bed.

She got into bed and there, beside her on the table, was Great-Aunt Antonia's diary. Tonia settled herself comfortably and began to read the delightful account of Arthur's visit to Ryddelton Castle to ask for Antonia's hand.

How splendid he looked, riding up the drive, wrote Antonia. I had been watching for him from my bedroom window, for I was aware that he would ride over in the afternoon. When he reached the corner by the rhododendron bushes, he raised his hat so I knew he had seen me and I waved my handkerchief. I fear Mama might have thought this conduct unmaidenly, but I was glad to have the opportunity to encourage Arthur and nerve him for the interview, and I have known Arthur all my life, which makes it seem less bold. He was with Papa for more than an hour, and I confess I was restless and impatient, though I tried to compose myself with my sewing, but when I was sent for to go down to Papa's library, my mood changed and I was reluctant to leave my room. I realized that this was an important moment in my life. I loved Arthur dearly, but I felt young and awkward, unwilling to advance and to leave my childhood behind. However, I managed to encourage myself and I went downstairs, as boldly as I could. Mama and Papa and Arthur were all in the library. Arthur came to me at once and took me by the hand and smiled at me. There was no need to ask the result of his interview with Papa—all was settled. Papa was kind enough to say I had been a good daughter and Mama kissed me with great affection, saying she would miss my help with the little ones but that she was overjoyed that I would be settled so conveniently near. I was overcome with so much kindness, which I feel I have done little to deserve...

Arthur and I walked in the garden together. It was a beautiful spring day and the clouds were moving across the sky like stately galleons, casting their shadows upon the hills. Arthur told me that Papa had been most kind and approved of the marriage heartily...Arthur asked me if it would be possible for us to be married before he sails. He asked it very modestly and diffidently, saying that he was aware the time was short but it would make him very happy if I would agree. I was somewhat alarmed, for the time is short indeed. I am devoted to Arthur and would do anything to give him pleasure but I have not become used to the idea. It will take time for me to adjust myself. I explained this as best I could but I could see he was disappointed and eventually I agreed to talk to Mama and see what could be done. "You will persuade her," Arthur said, and he looked at me so lovingly that I felt I could deny him nothing...

Today I spoke to Mama and asked her if she and Papa would allow us to be married before Arthur sails, but Mama was very much against the proposal, declaring that we should have no time to prepare my trousseau, to buy the linen and mark it and a hundred and one other things. It will be better, Mama says, to wait until Arthur's return when everything will be prepared. I told her that Arthur wished it and that I should like to conform to his wishes, to which Mama replied that marriage should not be entered upon hastily or inadvisedly. She embraced me fondly and added that I was very young and had much to learn before becoming Arthur's wife. This is true, and although Arthur will be disappointed, he will realize that I can do nothing to distress Mama...

Arthur rode over today. He brought me a magnificent

Chinese jar, which he had bought in China the last time he was there. It is a most delightful shape and has green dragons on it. I am charmed with it and have put it on a little stand in the corner of my bedroom so that I may see it when I wake. Arthur was a little sad when I told him what Mama said about our marriage...

Today Mary and Courtney Dale were married. They were married in the drawing room at Dunnian and the room was crowded with friends and relations who had come to Ryddelton for the occasion. It was a gay scene. The room was decorated most beautifully with flowers from the Dunnian greenhouses. The cake was the largest I have seen. I must admit that Mary looked extremely well in white satin with orange blossoms in her hair. Celia was in pink, a color that becomes her mightily. Everyone seemed happy, and there was a great deal of talk and laughter, but I could not help feeling that the gaiety was false. Celia should have been the bride. Celia should have been standing beside Mr. Dale and receiving the good wishes and congratulations. This conviction was so strong that I could hardly believe the other guests did not share it. Arthur noticed my preoccupation and rallied me upon it. "I know what you are thinking," he declared (and for a moment I believed that it was true and that he had become aware of the secret). Before I could answer he continued. "You are thinking what a terrible ordeal it is to be married like this with the whole clan looking on, and I must admit I agree with you. I should find it impossible to emulate Courtney's courage and cool demeanor. Give me a naval battle and I warrant I shall be as cool as a cucumber, but this sort of affair tries a man too high." I laughed, but Arthur was perfectly serious. "I shall run away with you," he said. "We shall be married privately and only our nearest and dearest shall be present to hear us

*take our vows. Say you agree with this, my dearest one." I
told him that his pleasure was mine and that we should be
married exactly as he wished. "But not when I wish," said
Arthur with a sigh. This distressed me, and distressed me all
the more because he has been very good and patient and has
not tried to hurry me in any way but has taken the decision
to wait as final.*

*Arthur came over today to say good-bye. Nothing could
be worse than this parting. As I gazed at his dear face I had
a terrible premonition that I might never see him again. It
was more than I could bear. I wish I were his wife. I wish
it with all my heart and soul. I know now that it is my
own fault we are not married, for if I had urged the matter
strongly Mama would have agreed. The truth is I was glad
when Mama counseled delay. I was a coward. I felt young
and awkward and ignorant. My fate came upon me too
suddenly, and I was not ready to go forward and meet the
challenge. Yes, I am a coward and not fit to be the wife of a
brave man. Mama and I were both wrong. I see that now,
when it is too late. I should have married Arthur and given
him all the happiness I could. I feel very strongly—though
perhaps unreasonably—that he would be safer if we had
been married, that the bond would shelter him in the midst
of danger and bring him back to me. Arthur kissed me tenderly, and I clung to him, for I felt I could not let him go. I
felt as if my heart were breaking. He whispered to me that a
year is not long, but I know he feels it will be an eternity—
just as I do…*

Tonia put down the diary and sighed. She understood so well
what Antonia meant when she had written that she was not ready
to go forward into life, for she (Tonia) was of the same nature—or
had been until she met Robert. She had very nearly missed her

chance of marrying Robert because she was a coward and not ready. If *they* had not quarreled over the fish, thought Tonia, looking back on that evening that seemed so long ago, if they had not been so horrid about Lou, I might be at home now, growing up into a soured old spinster. It was unpleasant and more than a little alarming to think that the whole of one's life could hang in the balance and the balance be tipped by a piece of fried sole.

She took up the diary again and turned over a good many pages, for she did not want to read about Arthur's death tonight—she was sad enough already—and presently she came to a list of furniture Antonia had brought with her when she came to live at Melville House. This interested the present owner a good deal, for the things were still here in much the same places. There was the Chinese jar, of course, which had been Arthur's parting present to Antonia and which still stood upon its ebony plinth on the upper landing, and there was the cabinet in the drawing room and the writing bureau and a score of other pieces that had become Tonia's friends…for if you dust and polish your own furniture, as Tonia was obliged to do, you get to know it intimately in a very short time.

Below this list of furniture Antonia had written an explanation of her desire to leave her home.

> *Papa understands my feelings, but Mama is a little hurt and this distresses me. However, I am sure she will soon get used to the idea of my leaving home, and Louise is now quite old enough to help her. Perhaps it seems strange that I should wish to leave my home where everyone has been so kind to me, but my heart is sad and will never recover its lightness. I cannot join in the gay talk, and my presence casts a constraint upon the spirits of my younger sisters and brothers. At Melville House I shall be my own mistress and able to do as I feel inclined; I can be quiet and read and sew. I shall practice*

my music daily. Mama has insisted that I must have Mrs.
Thomson to live with me and I have consented, for I do not
want to go against Mama's wishes in the matter, but I have a
feeling that Mrs. Thomson will find it somewhat dull after her
gay life in Edinburgh. Perhaps she will not stay...

Tonia put down the diary and listened. Yes, Bay was going
away; she could hear his voice in the hall, and Retta's voice
protesting that it was early and inquiring whether he was going
out over Germany tonight and, if so, where he was going.
She could not hear Bay's answer, but it must have been quite
short, for almost immediately the door was shut and Retta
came upstairs.

"My poor little one," said Retta, looking in at the door.
"You have a migraine? If you had told Retta she would have
given a powder that takes it away directly—whoof, it is gone!"

"No," said Tonia. "I just thought you and Bay would like a
little chat all by yourselves."

"*Chérie!*" cried Retta. "How sweet! How very, very kind! I
will not pretend it is not true. Bay is so fond, so lover-like, you
would not think it when you see him and other peoples are
there, but when we are alone he is *quite* different."

"Yes," said Tonia.

"Bay is dreadful," declared Retta with a little laugh. "He is
so strong and forceful. I say to him, 'O, Bay, you must not eat
me,' but what is the good?"

"He hasn't seen you for a long time."

"It is a thousand years," agreed Retta. She yawned luxuri-
ously and added, "And now I must go to bed. How nice to
think of it! That *so* comfortable bed that is not at all like the one
at Mrs. MacBean's house. Ugh, what a bed! I feel it with my
hand and it is lumpy like potatoes..."

She blew a kiss in Tonia's direction and went away.

Chapter Twenty-Seven
Tea for Five

Retta settled down comfortably at Melville House. She was a very easy guest. The odd thing was Tonia could not make up her mind about Retta. Sometimes she liked her very much indeed, and sometimes she did not like her at all. On the credit side Retta was always pleasant and smiling and often amusing; she admired the house and was most appreciative of anything Tonia did for her comfort; she did most of the cooking and did it extremely well—far better than Tonia, of course—and she was amazingly unobtrusive and did not expect attention nor entertainment. On the debit side Retta was just a shade untruthful, though perhaps untruthful was too hard and definite a word; it was more as if her exuberance ran away with her and she turned things roundabout to make a better story or to put things in a better light.

At one time the mere fact of a person deviating from strict truthfulness would have shocked Tonia and put her off completely, but since living with the Garlands Tonia had become more broadminded and she was prepared to make allowances for Retta.

Tonia thought of all this as she prepared tea in the drawing room, putting the little table near the fire and spreading upon it one of Nannie's best tea cloths edged with crochet lace. Retta had

been out all the afternoon but would soon be home, and Celia
Dunne was coming and bringing Courtney, who was on leave at
the moment. Bay might look in if he could get away—and that
made five. Quite a nice little tea party, thought Tonia.

Retta was the first to appear; she came in with glowing cheeks
and was full of apologies for not having gotten back earlier. She
had been in the woods and had lost her way and had run all the
way home.

"What a view!" declared Retta, standing near the fire with
her hands in the pockets of her slacks she had put on for her
walk. "From the woods one can see for miles—the airfield and
the town and the hills—and I was fortunate to meet a very nice
man, who did tell me so many interesting things…and then it
was late," said Retta, laughing and shaking her head. "It was late
quite suddenly, and I ran and ran. So now I must go and get tidy
and put on a skirt before the guests arrive."

"You look very nice in slacks," said Tonia.

"It is because my legs are long," agreed Retta. "To wear
slacks one must have long slim legs and not much behind."

Tonia laughed.

"That is another joke?" inquired Retta, smiling. "Again I
make a clevaire joke without meaning. So clevaire I am! But
it is true about the legs and the behind. When I was little I
sometimes put on the trousers of my brother and dance about
and have fun. You have a brother, Antonia?"

"No, just a sister."

"But that is lovely!" cried Retta. "It is what I have wanted,
always—to have a sister. It is quite different, the two things,
n'est-ce pas? To have a brother—*lovely*—he take you about and
introduce his friends and you make a gay time together. To
have a sister, she share your secrets and you talk your heads off."

"Yes," agreed Tonia. "Yes, when Lou and I get together we
talk all the time."

"Tell me about this Lou. She is like you?"

"I'll tell you another time," replied Tonia. "If you want to change before the others come you had better go now."

"O gosh!" exclaimed Retta (who had picked up this expression from Bay and used it with intense feeling). "O gosh, it is true, I will have to be queek."

The three guests arrived all together just as Retta was coming downstairs and when the buzz of greetings and introductions had subsided Tonia found herself sitting at the tea table with Courtney Dale beside her. She was glad of this, for she had not met him before and she had heard a great deal about him. At first she was too busy pouring out tea to have much time to talk, but she noticed that he was extremely helpful in an unobtrusive way, passing the cups and offering the scones and making himself generally useful. When everyone had been served they settled down to talk and, as the others were fully occupied in listening to Retta, their conversation was as private as any *tête-a-tête*. He talked about Celia—it was obvious that he adored her and thought her perfect in every way—and Tonia was only too ready to listen to Celia's praises, so they got on very well indeed. Celia had told him about the diary, and he asked about it and was quite awed when it was put into his hands.

"History repeats itself," he said. "But I guess this Courtney is going to marry the right girl."

"I'm sure he is," agreed Tonia.

"I'd like to read this little book," continued Courtney. "Maybe someday I could come over and read it."

"You can take it with you if you like."

"Take it!" he exclaimed. "That's very good of you. I'll read it and fetch it back on Monday. I promise I'll take great care of it, Mrs. Norman."

He was so earnest about it and seemed so impressed by the antiquity of the book that Tonia could not help laughing; and

Courtney, who was always ready to laugh, joined in. Whereupon the other members of the party turned around and inquired if they might share the joke.

"It's private," replied Courtney, taking the book and stowing it away safely in an inner pocket. "It's between Mrs. Norman and me."

Retta was somewhat annoyed, for she liked being the center of attraction. She decided that Courtney Dale was worth cultivating and having ascertained that, like most Americans, he could speak French, she proceeded to talk to him volubly in that language, complimenting him upon his accent, his nationality and the outstanding courage of his compatriots. Courtney could do nothing to stem the torrent of words. He smiled in a somewhat embarrassed manner and allowed himself to drift.

This was one of the times when Tonia did not like Retta at all. She left them to it and retired to the kitchen to prepare some vegetables for a pie she and Retta intended to have for supper.

"Bay," said Celia in a low voice completely covered by the rattle of Retta's conversation. "Bay, you've read old Antonia's diary, haven't you?"

"Bits of it," replied Bay.

"You know about old Courtney Dale and Mary and Celia?"

"Yes," said Bay, nodding.

"He married the wrong girl, Bay."

"I know," said Bay, taking out his pipe and polishing it carefully.

"It's a pity when that happens," said Celia earnestly. "It's a pity for everyone."

"We're more sensible nowadays," declared Bay.

"Are we, Bay?"

Bay had begun to fill his pipe. He did not speak for a few moments and then he said, "Courtney was engaged to Mary before he met Celia—that's what the diary says."

"But, Bay—"

"So what could he do? He couldn't do anything, could he?"

"Listen, Bay—"

"Personally," said Bay in a casual sort of voice. "Personally I think old Courtney did the right thing."

"Oh, no, I don't agree with you at all."

"We must agree to differ, then," declared Bay, firmly.

Celia rose. She said, "Are you ready, Courtney?"

Courtney was perfectly ready—almost eager—to depart. He said good-bye to Miss Delarge and followed Celia out of the room.

"She has him well in hand, that one," declared Retta when they had gone and she and Bay were alone.

"They're engaged," replied Bay.

"I know, and so are we," said Retta, smiling. "Come then, we are alone at last and all the tiresome peoples gone." She patted the sofa with her hand, inviting him to sit down beside her.

Bay did not seem to notice. He was lighting his pipe with a spill from the fire. "I don't know what you mean by *tiresome*," he said. "You seemed to be getting on all right with Dale."

"O, la la!" cried Retta, laughing. "He is jealous now, my big Bay. But he must not be jealous—that is *too* stupid. Come and sit here and I will tell you how nice you are, how much nicer than the tiresome American…but you must put your pipe away first, for the smoke is not nice at all."

"The smoke is very nice," declared Bay, standing on the hearth rug and smiling down at her.

"Nicer than kisses, perhaps?"

"Sometimes," said Bay, smoking with rather too obvious enjoyment.

Her eyes flashed and she opened her mouth to make a spirited retort…and then closed it again. There was a short silence.

"Cher ami," said Retta at last in a low husky voice. *"Cher ami,*

let us not say unkind things to each other. Let us not be unkind even in little ways, for I have no one else to love me, no one at all…"

"Oh, Retta—" exclaimed Bay.

"No," said Retta, taking out her handkerchief and dabbing her eyes. "No, I have no one. I am a stupid girl and not very patient but how can one be patient when one loves…so you will be kind and forgive, *n'est-ce pas, mon ami?*"

"Of course," said Bay uncomfortably. "I mean, there's nothing to forgive. It's absolutely all right. I was rather a beast—"

"It is all forgotten!" cried Retta, smiling at him with dewy eyes. "I was a little bit naughty, too. I was flirting just a little bit with the American…so now it is all right as you say."

"Of course," agreed Bay, putting his pipe on the mantelpiece and sitting down beside her.

"Dear Bay," said Retta, laying her head on his shoulder and relapsing into her native tongue. "It is so dull when you are not here; I think of you all the time. I should like to see your quarters, the room where you sleep, so that I can think of you better."

"Perhaps we could manage it," said Bay.

"And the airfield," continued Retta. "I have never seen an airfield."

"I don't know about that," said Bay, smiling. "Why do you want to see these things, Retta?"

"But is it not natural!" cried Retta. "All that you do interests me, because I love you so much. It is a woman's way to want to know all about the man she loves and all the little things in his life. I should like to sit in the big bomber, in your seat and put my hands on the controls. I should like to walk around the airfield with you so that I could imagine you whenever I shut my eyes."

"I'm afraid that's impossible," said Bay. "I could show you my quarters of course but nobody is allowed in the hangars."

"Tell me," said Retta, snuggling against him, "are you going out tonight. I get so anxious and worried about you. It would make me happy if I knew you were not going tonight."

"It would make the Germans happy, too," replied Bay grimly.

"What do you mean?"

"Just exactly what I say. It can't be much fun for the Germans to have their cities bombed. I know what it was like in London."

"You use much bigger bombs," said Retta thoughtfully.

"Yes, of course. Everybody knows that."

"Bay," said Retta. "Sometimes I have wondered—sometimes I have felt a little frightened to think of those big bombs so near the town of Ryddelton. What would happen to the town if they went off suddenly?"

"They are not likely to do that."

"Why?" asked Retta, turning to look at him. "If you keep them at the airfield—hundreds of them! But perhaps they come in small quantities, just when you need them?"

"You need not worry," declared Bay. "We take every precaution."

Retta pouted at him. She said, "You tell me nothing. Why is that, dear one? Do you not trust me? Will you tell me more when we are married?"

"What a lot of questions all at once!" he exclaimed, smiling at her. "I'll tell you something if you promise not to tell anyone else."

"But yes," declared Retta earnestly.

Bay assumed a very serious expression and lowered his voice to a whisper. "You are very pretty," he said. "Very elegant, and also very inquisitive…"

Chapter Twenty-Eight
Another Visitor

The next morning when Tonia was dusting her bedroom she heard the front doorbell jangle fiercely and came out onto the landing. Retta had gone to the door and was talking to someone in her usual voluble style. Tonia smiled to herself, for she had discovered that people calling at Melville House were usually somewhat scared when Retta answered the door; her colorful appearance and exuberant personality were unexpected and unusual. Perhaps I had better go down, thought Tonia; so she went down, still with her duster in her hand, and met Retta coming up to find her.

"He is in the drawing room," said Retta in a stage whisper. "It is a gentleman, quite old, with a fat red face and no hair. He say his name but I cannot remember…no, it is gone from my mind…but he is come from Edinburgh to see you so we must give him lunch, and it is not very easy because we have outrun our ration and no more from the butcher this week. Look you, Antonia, I will make egg cutlets and a vegetable pie and I will talk very hard so then he will not notice no meat…and we will have *souffle au gratin* and a cup of coffee, what do you say to that?"

"It sounds excellent," said Tonia, laughing, "but perhaps I had better see who he is before we make such elaborate preparations for him. He may be the electrician to look at the electric grill."

"He is a gentleman, I tell you," declared Retta. "He have a gold watch and chain across his stomach and his clothes is made of good stuff."

Tonia was giggling feebly when she reached the drawing room door. She had to pause for a few moments and straighten her face before going in to meet her unexpected visitor. She paused and looked back at Retta, and Retta informed her by pantomime that she (Retta) would start to prepare the meal, so that Tonia need have no qualms about tendering an invitation to her friend.

Tonia nodded and smiled and opened the door...and *there was Mr. Phillips* standing on the hearth rug.

Mr. Phillips held out his hand and Tonia shook it gravely. The sight of her trustee had banished her giggles completely, for it took her straight back to the last time she had seen him in the lawyer's office in London; it revived the miseries she had endured and reminded her of the worries she had tried to forget.

"I've found you," said Mr. Phillips, smiling at her.

"I wasn't hiding," replied Tonia quickly.

"Not hiding, exactly. Just in retreat. That's the correct term, isn't it?"

Tonia could not help smiling. He was quite nice really. She had been thinking of her trustees as three ogres, but Mr. Phillips was the best of them; he wasn't really an ogre at all.

"I suppose Nita told you things about me," Tonia said.

Mr. Phillips allowed this to be the case, but he did not go into details; he did not tell Tonia about his interview with the Garlands, mother and daughter. It had been a most unpleasant interview, for the Garlands were in a thoroughly excited condition and had iterated and reiterated their conviction that Tonia was in danger of being married offhand to three different young men, and that these young men were "after her money" and were pursuing her for no other reason. Mr. Phillips might have believed in one young man, but three was a little too much for him to swallow and the Garlands had found him somewhat unsympathetic. "You must go down there and see her," Mrs. Garland had said. "You're her trustee and you're responsible. You must make her come to Edinburgh and live with us so that I can keep an eye on her."

Mr. Phillips had agreed to go to Ryddelton, but he had not agreed to carry out the second half of Mrs. Garland's command. He had never thought it a good plan to make people live together if they did not want to (even if they thought they wanted to, it did not always work), and now that he had seen the Garlands in full fling he thought a good deal less of the plan than before. All this passed through Mr. Phillips's mind very rapidly.

"It's no use," Tonia was saying. "I'm not going to Edinburgh. I'm going to live here. Won't you sit down?"

Mr. Phillips sat down gratefully. He looked around and said, "This seems a very good place to live."

"Oh!" exclaimed Tonia in surprise. "But I thought...but of course you didn't say anything, did you?"

"I didn't say anything?"

"At the meeting, you know. You came all the way from Edinburgh to be at the meeting and you never said a word."

"Didn't I?"

"No," said Tonia, shaking her head.

"And you paid my fare," said Mr. Phillips regretfully.

They smiled at each other.

"You have a friend living with you," said Mr. Phillips after a moment's silence.

"Just for a short time," replied Tonia. "I'm really living alone, and I like it. I'm not dull or lonely."

"No, Mrs. Garland thought—"

"It's nonsense," declared Tonia, getting rather pink. "I'm not a child. I'm perfectly capable of looking after myself."

"Robert was one of my greatest friends," said Mr. Phillips. "He asked me to look after you in the event of his death and I want to carry out his wishes. I don't want to interfere or bother you in any way, but I should like you to regard me as a friend. I hope you will feel that you can appeal to me in case of need—if anything goes wrong or if you want help or advice. Will you promise that, Mrs. Norman?"

"Yes, thank you," said Tonia promptly.

"Good. Now then, what about money? Are you living on air?"

"On air?"

"You don't seem to be spending anything," explained Mr. Phillips.

"Oh," said Tonia understandingly. "Oh, that's all right. I had some money in my own bank."

"Why haven't you drawn any of your income?"

"I didn't know I could. I mean, I thought—I thought if I didn't do as the trustees said I couldn't have the money."

"Great Scott!"

"And anyhow I don't have a checkbook for Robert's bank," added Tonia as if that settled the matter for good and all...

"Great Scott!" exclaimed Mr. Phillips again.

"I don't want it, really," continued Tonia. "It would be far too much—just a bother to me—there's nothing to spend it on, you see."

Mr. Phillips opened his mouth to say "Great Scott" for the third time, but no sound came.

"Can't you do something about it?" inquired Tonia with a frown. "I don't want a lot of money—honestly I don't—I would much rather have a little."

"Why?" asked Mr. Phillips.

"Oh, there are all sorts of reasons."

"Ah, there *are* reasons?"

"Yes."

"But you aren't going to tell me them?"

"Well—no."

"I see," said Mr. Phillips, nodding.

"And you couldn't guess," added Tonia hastily.

"I shouldn't dream of trying. You see I have four daughters and I never try to guess what they are thinking—never. It wouldn't be the least use."

Tonia looked at him rather hard but he seemed perfectly serious.

"About the money," continued Mr. Phillips. "We'll put most of it into a War Loan, shall we? And I will interview the bank agent and ask him to send you a checkbook. If you want the money you can have it, and if not it can help to buy tanks. How about that?"

"I shan't want it," said Tonia firmly. "I've got all I want. I'm perfectly happy and comfortable as I am."

He looked at her and decided it was true. She looked well and happy. She was certainly a little fatter—or less thin—than the last time he had seen her. She was a trifle shabby, of course; her tweed skirt was well-worn and there was a darn in the elbow of her cardigan, but that was no unusual sight in these days of clothes coupons.

"I suppose Janet is very angry," Tonia was saying.

"Very." Mr. Phillips nodded. "But that doesn't affect you much, does it?"

"Not very much, really," replied Tonia with a smile.

"And what about Mrs. Smilie?" asked Mr. Phillips. "I've been paying her to keep the house aired, but now she has written to say she isn't keeping the house aired and doesn't want the money."

"She does a *lot*," declared Tonia earnestly. "Please go on paying her. I don't suppose it's half enough, really."

"You could use some of your despised money to give her more," suggested Mr. Phillips.

"But she wouldn't take it," replied Tonia. "I know she wouldn't—and it would spoil everything if she thought I was rich. It would spoil the whole—the whole *balance*," said Tonia earnestly. "It would alter the whole atmosphere of my life."

"Very well," agreed Mr. Phillips. "We'll maintain the *status quo*—in the meantime, at any rate."

Having settled this business Tonia offered Mr. Phillips some beer or coffee or a cup of tea, adding that she hoped he would stay to lunch. Mr. Phillips said he had a train to catch but he would like some coffee now—if it wasn't a bother—and his hostess went away to fetch it. He was sitting quietly in the drawing room, musing on all that had been said, when the door opened and a young man in Air Force uniform walked into the room. He walked in (Mr. Phillips noticed) as if the place belonged to him—not arrogantly, but just as a man walks into his own home.

"Hallo!" he exclaimed, looking at Mr. Phillips in surprise.

Mr. Phillips introduced himself and learned in return that the young man's name was Coates.

"I know your father," said Mr. Phillips holding out his hand. "Coates of West Drumford, isn't it?"

"That's right," agreed Coates. "But look here, you're one of Mrs. Norman's trustees, aren't you? I want to speak to you if you are."

Mr. Phillips said that he was and added that he was prepared to listen.

"We don't have much time," said Coates, pulling forward a chair and sitting down. "I mean, she may come back any minute. It's about this money business."

"What about it?" asked Mr. Phillips warily.

"I think it's a beastly shame. Surely there must be something saved out of the crash."

"What crash?"

"Oh, I don't know the details," declared Coates. "Butter—I mean, Mrs. Norman doesn't talk about it."

"She didn't actually tell you there had been a crash."

"No," said Coates, thinking back. "No, not actually. I put two and two together and—"

"What was the answer?" inquired Mr. Phillips with a touch of irony.

"The answer? Oh, I see. You think I got five."

"Did Mrs. Norman tell you that her trustees had let her down?"

"Not exactly, but it's obvious there's been some funny business. Everyone knows that Robert Norman had pots of money—and here's Butterfingers without a penny. You can't get over that."

Mr. Phillips shook his head sadly.

"I'm not accusing *you*," continued Coates in earnest tones. "She told me that you weren't in with the others; she said you seemed sorry for her."

"I was—really," said Mr. Phillips, turning his head away and coughing into his handkerchief.

"Surely something could be saved out of the wreck," continued Coates, more earnestly than ever. "I mean, Butterfingers isn't at all strong. She can't possibly turn to and earn her own living, and she can't rely upon her songs—"

"Her songs!"

"She composes," explained Coates. "At least she wouldn't put it like that, but—but anyhow she has written a song that is going to bring in some cash pretty soon now. She may write others, of course, but it's rather a hand to mouth sort of game."

"You think she ought to have a settled income?"

"Well, don't you?" asked Coates. "Surely you could scrape up something."

"You're worried about Mrs. Norman?"

"Yes, I am, rather. That's why I'm butting in."

"How much do you think she would need to live on?"

"Oh well—say two hundred," suggested Coates.

"Two hundred a year!" exclaimed Mr. Phillips in amazement.

"She could manage on that," said Coates thoughtfully. "It wouldn't be luxury, of course, but she has the house and she isn't—she isn't an *expensive* sort of girl, if you know what I mean. She likes simple things."

"I gathered that," admitted Mr. Phillips.

"You'll see what you can do, won't you?"

"I'll see what I can do," agreed Mr. Phillips. He was smiling now. He looked satisfied, as if he had solved a problem that had been teasing him—and perhaps he had, for although he had told Tonia that he never tried to guess his daughters' secrets it was not entirely true. He had a legal mind and liked to have things neatly docketed and put away in the right pigeonholes.

Mr. Phillips was still smiling complacently when Tonia came in with the tray. Coates looked at Mr. Phillips and shook his head, and Mr. Phillips nodded to show that he would maintain silence. He was amused to see an expression of anxiety on Mrs. Norman's face but allayed it by winking at her behind the young man's back. He was not going to tell anybody anything; he was going home, leaving little Mrs. Norman to manage her affairs in her own way. She knew what she was doing.

Miss Delarge also appeared and they all had coffee together. Mr. Phillips had met Miss Delarge before—she had opened the door to him—and he had admired her tremendously. She was a damned fine-looking girl with plenty of go in her. He saw no reason to change his opinion now, for Retta was in good form and only too ready for a little amiable persiflage. Anything in trousers was fair game to Retta.

"You speak French?" inquired Retta as she handed him his cup and smiled at him with widely opened eyes.

"Oui," replied Mr. Phillips solemnly, adding with an atrocious accent. *"Défense de cracher. Défense de se pencher sur la rampe quand l'ascenseur est en marche."*

They all laughed at this essay, and Retta inquired where he had learned it. She inquired in English, for it was obvious that Mr. Phillips's knowledge of her native tongue was extremely limited.

"I learned it in Paree," replied Mr. Phillips, who had begun to enjoy himself tremendously. "It was written up in the lift at the hotel where I used to stay when I went to see my daughters at their finishing school."

"Do you know any more, sir?" asked Bay.

"Deux bouteilles de Veuve Cliquot," replied Mr. Phillips promptly. *"J'ai faim. Où est le cabinet de toilette?"*

When the laughter had subsided Mr. Phillips remarked that they could laugh if they liked, but with these three phrases at one's command it was possible to travel in comfort all over France—before the war, of course.

Retta said she would come with him if he liked—after the war, of course—and Mr. Phillips accepted the offer rapturously.

It was now discovered that Mr. Phillips had missed his train, and, as he had an appointment in the afternoon, he was very much disturbed about it. His round pink face, which a moment ago had been wreathed in smiles, was suddenly creased with frowns, so that he looked exactly like a very large baby about to burst into tears. Fortunately, however, Bay came to the rescue, saying that he had to go over to Timperton immediately to see a man at the hospital, and he would take Mr. Phillips, and Mr. Phillips could catch the express and be in Edinburgh in half no time. He rose as he spoke, and Mr. Phillips rose too—all smiles again—and they all went into the hall and opened the front door. A very large and extremely powerful-looking motorcycle with a sidecar attached to it was waiting in the street.

"In that?" asked Mr. Phillips, somewhat doubtfully.

Bay did not hear. He was rooting about in the sidecar and now he produced a leather helmet, an extremely old trench coat covered with oil, and a pair of dark goggles. "I'm afraid you must," said Bay apologetically. "You see we aren't allowed to take civilians, not really…"

Mr. Phillips hesitated. But his appointment was important and this seemed the only way. He allowed himself to be attired in the evil-smelling garments and climbed into the sidecar.

"This is a beastly old bike," declared Bay, kicking the self-starter violently. "It isn't really meant for a sidecar and has a sort of list to port…as a matter of fact I hate driving on the roads. Damn, why won't it start?"

"Why do you hate driving on the roads?" asked Mr. Phillips a little anxiously.

"They're so dangerous," complained Bay, taking out a wrench and tinkering with the engine. "I mean, compared with the air. You come zooming around a blind corner and find yourself bumping into a tank or something. There aren't any blind corners in the air, of course. The percentage of collisions in the air is infinitesimal," added Bay gravely.

Mr. Phillips opened his lips to say that after all his appointment was not so very important and he would put it off by wire and take the afternoon train, but at that moment the engine burst into life, stuttering like a machine gun, and Bay leaped into the saddle and they were off.

Chapter Twenty-Nine
Retta's Visitor

Retta and Tonia were having breakfast together in the dining room, for since the arrival of her guest Tonia had abjured her luxurious habit of breakfasting in bed. Mrs. Smilie still came in every morning, but it was too much to expect her to carry up two trays.

"My brother is coming," said Retta, looking up from a letter that had just arrived by post. "He is going to Glasgow to do some business and he will pass here on the way. It would be so very nice if he could be here for a night."

Tonia did not rise. Somehow or other she did not want Retta's brother at Melville House. She had not wanted Retta, of course, but she had been forced to ask her.

"Perhaps he could get a room at the Rydd Arms," suggested Tonia. "Or perhaps they could take him at Mrs. MacBean's—"

"Of course!" cried Retta, simulating delight. "How clever you are, *chère* Antonia! Those rooms that Bay found for me will be the best for Henri. I will see about it at once. Henri will not give a sou for the so lumpy bed and the sloping down roof—he has been sleeping in a lot worse places in his life. Ah, poor Henri, what he has suffered before he has escape from *La France!* He has been sleeping in a pig house and a stack of hay and *le bon Dieu* knows where. And then at last he escape at night in a little boat no bigger as this table—and the waves as big as mountains."

"How dreadful!" said Tonia, who was convinced that Henri's sufferings were being exaggerated in order to melt her heart.

Retta sighed and gave up the attempt. "But I must not waste time," she declared. "You will excuse me that I go and leave the breakfast dishes to be washed, for it is necessary that I talk to the big fat woman with the beard and the glassy eyes so she have the room prepared for my Henri."

"Is he coming today?"

"Tonight," replied Retta, rising and making for the door. "I will take your coat off the hall peg—*n'est-ce pas?*—and run across the street."

"Yes, of course," agreed Tonia, by this time thoroughly ashamed of her inhospitality to Retta's brother. "Of course you can wear my coat, and you must ask him to come over and have supper with you. I shall be out."

"You will be out!" exclaimed Retta incredulously.

"It's that whist drive tonight," Tonia reminded her. "You said you didn't want to come, but I had to take a ticket for it, because it's for the Red Cross."

"Of course! It did go out of my mind—so you will be out."

"Yes."

"And you will win the prize—and I will have my dear Henri and make an omelet for him."

"Yes," said Tonia again. "At least you will have Henri and you can make anything you like for him. There isn't the slightest chance of my winning a prize."

Mrs. Smilie was in the kitchen when Tonia carried in the tray of breakfast dishes, and they greeted each other in a casual manner that hid a very real affection.

"How long is *she* staying?" asked Mrs. Smilie as she began to wash up.

"Her brother is coming," said Tonia, without answering the question. As a matter of fact she could not answer it, for Retta had made no reference to her future plans.

"He's not coming here, I hope!"

"No...I suppose I should have asked him." She took up a dish towel as she spoke and began to dry the plates, which Mrs. Smilie was piling on the board.

"Why should you? It's your own house," returned Mrs. Smilie grimly. "Maybe you're forgetting it's your own house—"

"I don't mind having her," protested Tonia.

There was a silence for a few moments, broken by the chink of crockery; it was a friendly sort of silence.

"She'll be having him to supper," said Mrs. Smilie at last. "And you're going out to the whist drive, so the two of them will be here alone."

"It will be nice for them. They can talk much better if I'm not here."

"So they can," agreed Mrs. Smilie thoughtfully.

"You're coming to the whist drive, of course."

"Well, I don't know. Maybe I will and maybe I won't."

Tonia laughed. She was always amused when Mrs. Smilie became enigmatic. "I expect you will," she said.

From the very first moment Mrs. Smilie and Retta had disapproved of each other. They did not understand each other and made no attempt to do so. Tonia had tried to persuade Mrs. Smilie that Retta was really very good-natured, but without avail; she had tried to explain to Retta that Mrs. Smilie was not a servant and must not be ordered about.

"Mrs. Smilie is a friend," Tonia had said. "I don't pay her anything. She comes in to help because she is so kind."

Retta had replied, "She loses nothing, that one. She has her pickings."

"Oh no, Retta—"

"But yes, my dear little cabbage. You are too innocent, too trustful. She come in and out and who knows when she is there and when she is not!"

∽∾

Henri had not appeared at Melville House when Tonia was ready to go out to the whist drive. He had arrived at Ryddelton about five o'clock and Retta had met him at the station and settled him in his rooms. Retta was now in the kitchen, and savory smells came wafting through the house whenever the kitchen door was opened. It was obvious that Henri was going to have a most enjoyable repast.

"Dear one," said Retta, appearing at the kitchen door as Tonia came downstairs. "Dear one, you will come home very late, isn't it?"

"I expect so," replied Tonia.

"You will be late, and Henri and I we are early worms. He will be tired after his so long journey and he will go back across the street to his little room with the lumpy bed. Very early, he will go, so you will not see him."

"No, of course not. But I shall see him tomorrow."

"But that is the trouble; he must go away by the early train!"

"What a pity!" exclaimed Tonia, trying to sound suitably disappointed.

"What a pittee, indeed," agreed Retta in sorrowful accents. "*Le pauvre Henri,* he will be desolated, but what can we? It is this so annoying wheest that has upset the apple tree."

"Yes," said Tonia, but she said it doubtfully, for it was not the whist drive that had upset their plans. To be strictly accurate, no plans had been upset and everything was for the best. Retta was delighted at the prospect of having Henri to herself and Tonia was more than reconciled to the fact that she would not meet him…but this was just Retta's way. She had a habit of turning things around and presenting them in a false light.

"It cannot be helped," continued Retta, heaving a tremendous sigh. "I have hoped and prayed for you and Henri to meet, but it cannot be—not this time. So Henri and me will spend the evening—brother and sister together—and Henri will go away early, and I will go to bed. I will be fast asleep when you come home from the wheest—and the house will be very quiet."

"I shan't disturb you," promised Tonia, who had grasped the point.

"Ah, dear one!" cried Retta. "So always considerate for other peoples!"

"You have everything you want?" asked Tonia, preparing to go.

"But *everything*," declared Retta. "The supper is almost ready and I have nothing more except to powder my nose."

Tonia smiled. It was obvious that Retta had put on her best clothes to do honor to her brother and had taken extra trouble with her hair. Although she was in the midst of cooking the supper she looked cool and *soignee*—fit for a mannequin parade.

"*Bonsoir,*" said Tonia. "Have a good time."

"*Et toi, chère petite,*" replied Retta, kissing the tips of her fingers. "We meet at breakfast, *n'est-ce pas?*"

∽≫

There was plenty to talk about when they met at breakfast next morning, for they had both enjoyed themselves. Tonia was cajoled into giving an account of the "wheest" and did so amusingly, for Retta was an appreciative audience. An aircraftsman had won the prize, which was just as it should be, and Tonia had escaped winning the booby prize by a few points. This had not surprised her, for she had never played whist in her life until she came to Ryddelton. The Smilies had invited her to supper on two occasions and had instructed her in the rudiments of the game.

"And Mrs. Smilie was there?" asked Retta casually.

"No, she wasn't," Tonia replied. "I thought she was going, but she must have changed her mind."

"How odd!" said Retta with a thoughtful look.

"And your party, Retta. How did your party go off?"

"It was nice," declared Retta. "Henri was so pleased at his supper and send a thousand messages to his kind hostess he has never seen. We talk and talk about when we were little children and *La France* was free and happy. O, what happy times! How much one wish that one was a little child again!"

Tonia had never wished that, for her childhood had not been particularly happy. When she looked back it was her married life with Robert that seemed her happiest time. The voyage to India and the visit to Jack and Lou shone with bright colors in her memory. She explained this, somewhat haltingly, and was surprised to find that Retta understood.

"O, yes," cried Retta, alight in a moment. "But it is true— those first days of being married to the dearest one, those are the wonderfullest days of all! The sunsets so gay with all the colors of the artist's palette, the food tasting so good! It is my sister tell me all this, of course. For me, I have never known it yet...for me the first days of being married are in the future."

"Yes, but I didn't know you had a sister, Retta."

"I do not speak about her," said Retta in a low voice, taking out her handkerchief and dabbing her eyes. "Yes, she is...dead. I cannot speak about her, no, not even to you, *chère petite*. It make me too sad to think about her...and the little baby that is dead, too. No, we must speak of something else..."

"I'm so sorry, Retta—"

"*Mais non, mais non*—I am foolish, that is all. Look, Antonia,

I will take the tray and wash all the dishes and be so busy I will not think about it anymore."

"Wait, Retta, Mrs. Smilie will be there."

"But what matter? I will be very nice to Mrs. Smilee," said Retta, nodding gravely. "It is necessary for me to speak to Mrs. Smilee for I gave her my slacks to press and she has not brought them back."

"Oh, Retta, I would have done them for you! I wish you wouldn't ask Mrs. Smilie—"

"But she will do them so much better, dear one," laughed Retta. "She will not make the two railway lines down the front. And they needed to be pressed after my long walk up the hill and through the woods...so do not disturb yourself."

Tonia followed Retta into the kitchen, for she did not want Retta and Mrs. Smilie to be alone. Someday there would be a flare-up (she was sure of that), but there would be no serious trouble as long as she was there to smooth things over.

Today things were worse than usual; in fact, there was an undercurrent of real hostility in the kitchen. Mrs. Smilie was quite unlike herself; her eyes smoldered when she looked at Retta and she seemed on the verge of an outbreak.

"I'd like to speak to you for a moment, Miss Tonia," said Mrs. Smilie in an undertone.

"Later on," replied Tonia, who was all for peace and hoped that Mrs. Smilie might settle down and become more amenable to reason.

"Have you pressed my slacks yet?" asked Retta, in the haughty tone she always affected when she had cause to address Mrs. Smilie.

"No, I've not ironed your trousers yet," was the uncompromising reply. "I've ironed men's trousers often enough but I've never ironed trousers for a woman...I'll *do* them for you," she added in grudging tones. "I said I'd do them and so I will when

I can find the time. You'll get them this afternoon, or maybe in the morning..."

"We can manage now, Mrs. Smilie," said Tonia, interposing before Retta could speak. "Thank you so much for your help. You know how much I appreciate all you do."

When she had gone Retta danced around the kitchen. "O, what relief!" she cried ecstatically. "That so dreadful woman with her self-righteous face! How can you bear her is what I cannot understand. How can you *bear* her?"

"She's so kindhearted. If only you would try to understand her instead of rubbing her the wrong way!"

"But it is she who rubs me the wrong way—*vraiment*—she gives me the *creeps*," declared Retta earnestly. "There is something about her...yes, there is something...and I cannot bear that she come out and in as she will, with her red and blue carpet shoes that make no noise."

"Why should I mind?" asked Tonia in surprise. "I don't mind her coming in and out. I've nothing to hide."

"To hide—no. One has nothing to hide...but you would do well to look to your purse when that one is about."

This accusation was so utterly ridiculous that Tonia laughed; she would as soon have suspected the Archbishop of Canterbury of rifling her purse!

The morning passed without incident worthy of note and immediately after lunch Bay appeared, for they had arranged to walk over to Dunnian House to tea, with Bay as escort. Retta had been the instigator of this expedition (she wanted to see Dunnian), but the day had clouded over and the skies were heavy and Retta was as allergic to rain as a tabby cat.

"You two can go," declared Retta. "The English are so hardy and do not care a sou if the wet rain pours down their necks. For me, I shall remain by the fire and mend my delicates that are falling into pieces because I have worn them so long and have no coupons for new ones…and there will be no need to hurry back, for I will be happy and warm and comfortable, and I will make me the five o'clock when it is time. So then you two will go…and you will put on your thick shoes, *chère* Antonia, and your old skirt and a mackintosh and on your head a beret, and the rain will not bother you at all—no, not one little bit."

"It isn't raining," said Bay, who seemed annoyed at the change of plan.

"But it will rain," replied Retta with a shudder. "Me, I know when the rain is coming, and I like to stay inside."

Tonia did not take long to array herself. She came downstairs to find Bay and Retta in the hall. "I wish you were coming, Retta," she said.

"That is nice," declared Retta with a slightly sarcastic inflection in her voice. "It pleases me that you wish I was coming—"

"We'll be late if we don't start," interrupted Bay. "Come along, Mrs. Dundas."

"Mrs. Dundas!" echoed Tonia in surprise.

Bay smiled at her. "I've been reading *The Life of Piny*," explained Bay. "Dundas was a friend of Pitt's and this is what Pitt said about him: 'Dundas is not an orator…but he will go out with you in any weather.'"

They laughed at that—Retta a little less heartily than usual—and Tonia chose an ash stick from the stand and announced that Mrs. Dundas was ready.

Retta watched the two figures walk away down the street and then she went in and shut the door.

Chapter Thirty
Mrs. Smilie's Discovery

About four o'clock the rain started. Mrs. Smilie was pressing the navy-blue slacks, bumping and thumping with her iron and muttering to herself—but making a very good job of them nevertheless. When she had finished she slipped her hand into the pocket and discovered a small piece of paper. She smoothed it out and looked at it with knitted brows, for she could not think what it was. It seemed to be some sort of map, roughly sketched in pencil, with a small red cross in one of the corners. Mrs. Smilie was not versed in map reading so she could not make much of it. For all she knew it might be important. She folded it again and put it in the pocket of her apron; and taking the trousers, which were now neatly pressed, she went in next door. The kitchen fire was pretty low, so Mrs. Smilie attended to it. They were all out, she knew, for she had heard them discussing the expedition to Dunnian House.

By this time it was raining pretty hard, and the rain was beating against the kitchen window. It would be beating in at the bedroom window, too, decided Mrs. Smilie, who knew and disapproved of her neighbor's passion for fresh air. She went upstairs, taking a towel with her to mop up the mess.

The house was very quiet and Mrs. Smilie paused for a moment on the upper landing; she always paused at the bedroom door because there was an odd sort of feeling about old Miss Antonia's bedroom. Mrs. Smilie was not an imaginative person, but she could not overcome the conviction that someday when she opened the door she would see old Miss Antonia sitting up in bed with her fleecy bed jacket around her shoulders and her lace cap framing her kind old face. Mrs. Smilie did not have this feeling when Miss Tonia was here, but today Miss Tonia was out.

She paused and looked at the door, which was slightly ajar, and then she heard a noise, a rustle of paper and the scrape of a drawer being shut. *There was somebody in the room.* Yes, somebody was there, and it could not be Miss Tonia because they were all out. Mrs. Smilie turned to go home, and then she stopped. If she went home now, without seeing who was there, she would never be able to look herself in the face again—never as long as she lived. It couldn't be old Miss Antonia because there were no such things as ghosts. Besides, ghosts did not rustle paper and open drawers…

Mrs. Smilie looked in very quietly through the half-open door. It was no ghost, no burglar either. At least it was not an ordinary burglar.

"Miss Delarge," said Mrs. Smilie in honeyed tones. "I'll trouble you to leave Mrs. Norman's things alone."

Miss Delarge sprang to her feet with a gasp of dismay…and then she laughed. "O, it is you!" she exclaimed. "What a fright you gave me!"

"Is that so?" said Mrs. Smilie sarcastically.

"Such a fright," declared Retta, holding her hand to her heart. "But it is all right now, and no harm done. I was just looking in Mrs. Norman's drawer for a pair of gloves I lent her, because they have a little hole and need mending." She pushed in the drawer as she spoke and walked toward the door.

"It's time you and me had a wee talk together," said Mrs. Smilie, blocking the way.

"But no. Not just now," returned Retta. "There is a letter I must write for the post. Some other time we will talk."

"We'll talk now."

"I do not want any impertinence, Mrs. Smilee. You will move away from the door and let me pass."

"Not till I've done…and as for impertinence I've had enough of that from you. But this is the end of it. I know all about you and your carryings on, *Miss Delarge*."

"That is my name——" began Retta.

"It's not. You're a married woman. It was your husband that had supper with you last night…"

"You are mad!"

"…and spent the night with you," added Mrs. Smilie.

They looked at each other. There was a strange gleam in Retta's eyes. "And how is that your business, Mrs. Smilee?" she inquired in dangerously smooth tones.

"It's not," replied Mrs. Smilie promptly. "It's none of my business who you sleep with, but maybe Mr. Coates would think it was *his*."

Retta laughed. She said, "You have been dreaming. My brother was here last night; he had his supper with me. We talk together about when we were little children. We talk about our home."

"You talked about your marriage," replied Mrs. Smilie. "You talked about your life together; you talked about——"

"*Mon Dieu!* You were listening at the door—but how——"

"But how did I understand?" said Mrs. Smilie, raising her voice. "It's queer, isn't it? A woman in my position was not worth your notice, no more than a bit of dust on the carpet, but it just so happens that I was with a French lady before I was married, and it amused her to talk to me and teach me. I thought I'd forgotten it," said Mrs. Smilie, nodding. "But I found I remembered a good deal."

"You listened—at the door," repeated Retta in choking tones. "I did think I heard someone—"

"It was me," said Mrs. Smilie.

Retta was shaking with rage. She burst out into rapid French with a short but vitriolic exposition of Mrs. Smilie's character and the nature of her immediate forebears. Most of the words used were strange to Mrs. Smilie, for her former mistress had omitted them from her instruction, but the drift of Retta's remarks was fairly clear.

"Umphm," said Mrs. Smilie thoughtfully when Retta paused for breath. "Maybe you're right. It's not a very nice thing to listen at doors but I'd do the same again if I had the chance, for I never would have known you were married if I'd not listened… and there's more to it than that. You're up to no good, you and that man of yours."

"I do not know what you mean."

"Why were you masquerading as an unmarried woman? Answer me that."

"I do not choose to answer."

"I thought as much. Here's another question, then. Does this wee piece of paper belong to you?" Mrs. Smilie produced the little sketch from the pocket of her apron as she spoke.

"That!" cried Retta. "But yes, it is mine. Give it to me, please."

"I was wondering what it was."

"It is nothing. Just a little picture of my home; a little plan of the country roundabout—"

"To keep you in mind of it?"

"But yes, of course. My memory is so bad—"

"So bad that you need to make a map of your home?"

"You will give it back to me, please," said Retta; holding out her hand and speaking in authoritative tones.

"You can have it back later on. I'll just let Mr. Coates have a wee look at it first. You'll not object to that."

"He would not be interested."

"Are you sure of it?" asked Mrs. Smilie, folding the paper and putting it inside her blouse. "I'm not so sure. We'll see which of us is right."

Retta hesitated, biting her lip. Then she said in quite a different tone. "Come then, Mrs. Smilee, you have won. I will give you ten pounds for that silly bit of paper."

"Ten pounds!" cried Mrs. Smilie. "What sort of person do you take me for—"

"Twenty pounds, then," said Retta persuasively. "I do not want Squadron Leader Coates to see that paper. He would think I was so foolish, and I do not like him to think me foolish. Look, Mrs. Smilee, you will burn that little bit of paper and I will give you twenty pounds."

"Not for a hundred pounds," replied Mrs. Smilie forcefully.

Retta saw her mistake, but it was too late now. The words had been said, and she could not unsay them. She saw that the game was up. She was angry but she was not frightened, not yet. "What will you do, Mrs. Smilee?" she inquired sweetly.

There was no answer. As a matter of fact Mrs. Smilie had been wondering for the last five minutes what she had better do. She had not planned this interview; it had come upon her suddenly and taken her unawares. She was alone in the house with Retta. Mrs. Smilie considered several plans and rejected them.

"You do not speak," said Retta at last. "You can think of nothing, eh? You would like to shut me in the coal cellar but you are not strong enough. It is a pittee, yes? I would like to have that piece of paper. I wonder if I am strong enough to get it...?"

Retta was much younger than Mrs. Smilie, and although thin and willowy she looked wiry. She advanced upon Mrs. Smilie, her mouth smiling a little, her eyes glittering danger-ously...and quite suddenly Mrs. Smilie's nerve failed her. A moment ago she had been perfectly calm—somewhat puzzled as to what she had better do, but without any apprehensions as to her personal safety—but now she was suddenly panic-stricken. Before she knew what she was doing she had taken to her heels and was out of the door and running down the stairs like a rabbit. Her fear and haste were justified, for, as she ran, the big Chinese jar that stood upon the upper landing came hurtling over the banisters and crashed into a thousand pieces behind her on the stairs. Mrs. Smilie was out of the back door, through the hedge, and into her own house with the door barred behind her in a matter of seconds; she was panting and puffing, and her heart was thumping like a steam engine as she sank into the comfortable chair in her own comfortable kitchen and looked about her with a dazed stare. *There* were the onions, boiling away in the pot—the onions for Alec's supper—and *there* was the kettle, singing on the hob, and all her pots and pans and lids were gleaming and winking and twinkling in the firelight…

"In the name of goodness!" whispered Mrs. Smilie to herself.

∞

Tonia opened her front door and entered her house, thinking of something else—thinking vaguely of the party at Dunnian and her walk with Bay—and the first thing she saw was the Chinese jar in pieces, scattered all over the stairs.

"Oh!" cried Tonia in distress and dismay, for this jar was one of her most treasured possessions, not on account of its intrinsic value but because of its sentimental associations.

She was standing in the hall, looking at the pieces and wondering how on earth the disaster could have occurred, when Retta came downstairs, dressed in her hat and coat and carrying her suitcase in her hand.

Retta picked her way carefully among the fragments and arrived in the hall. "I am going away," she said in a casual voice.

"Going away!" echoed Tonia in amazement. She had been about to ask Retta about the jar, but Retta's extraordinary statement put the jar into second place.

"I am going," said Retta, pushing past her hostess without ceremony. "I am so very tired of here, so very tired of you and of Bay and of this so dull town. That is why I am going," declared Retta, struggling to open the door.

"But, Retta—"

"But, Retta," said Retta, mimicking Tonia's voice. "But, Retta, you are mad to say such things. But, Retta, do you not love me and Bay and this so lovely Ryddelton? But, Retta—"

"What on earth is the matter with you?" asked Tonia, loudly.

"There is nothing the matter except I am bored—bored to tears. I have borne it a long time, but now I bear it no more; so you will open the door and let me out."

"Retta, listen," said Tonia earnestly. "You can't go tonight. Wait till the morning. What will Bay think if you go off like this without saying good-bye to him?"

"It matters not what Bay thinks," declared Retta, wrenching the door open and pushing Tonia aside.

"I am done with Bay...so you can tell Bay I am going to my husband and I do not want another husband because one is enough. It will be nice for Bay to hear these things from you," added Retta as she seized her suitcase and ran out into the street.

Tonia started after her, but it was too dark to see. Retta had vanished completely in the gloom. And what was the use, thought Tonia, turning back into the house. What was the use of pursuing Retta? Retta was quite capable of looking after herself.

Tonia shut the door and stood quite still, utterly bewildered. It had all happened so suddenly that she could hardly believe her eyes and ears. It can't be true, thought Tonia, it *isn't* true. How can Retta have a husband, already—she's going to marry Bay. Retta was angry and just said the first thing that came into her head. But after a few moments' reflection Tonia began to think it might be true, and the more she thought about it the more she became convinced that it *was* true. She remembered several odd things about Retta, things Retta had said and done…

Goodness, how awful! said Tonia to herself. What will Bay feel when he hears about it? Why on earth did she deceive Bay?

All sorts of thoughts whirled through Tonia's brain, mixed up together like the colors in a kaleidoscope. Retta had vanished. She had been angry, of course, furiously angry, and she *had* said the first thing that came into her head, but the thing happened to be true. Why had she suddenly decided to go? She had been perfectly friendly when they left her to walk over to Dunnian, so something must have happened. What *could* have happened to enrage her and send her tearing off into the darkness like a madwoman? Could she have had a row with Mrs. Smilie? That was quite likely, of course, but even that would not account for her sudden departure. No, thought Tonia, Retta was not that sort. If she and Mrs. Smilie had had words Retta would stay and brave it out. She would never let Mrs. Smilie get the better of her. And the jar, thought Tonia (looking sorrowfully at the remains of her treasured possession). How could the jar have gotten broken?

It was not much use asking all these questions, for she could find no answers to them, so she fetched a pail and began to collect the fragments of the jar, though without much idea of what she was doing. The task took some time and helped her to recover from the shock. She began to wonder what she had better do next. Should she get hold of Mrs. Smilie and see if she could help to clear up the mystery, or should she get hold of Bay?

Bay must be told, of course, but not tonight. Bad news can

always wait, thought Tonia…and then she hesitated. Perhaps it was her duty to tell Bay at once. Perhaps it was cowardice that counseled delay. It *is* cowardice, thought Tonia. Bay ought to be told at once. This isn't the sort of bad news that can wait… and I'm the person to tell him. Yes, she was the person; even Retta had realized that. "It will be nice for Bay to hear these things from you," Retta had cried as she burst wildly out of the door. Nice, thought Tonia in dismay, but all the same she was aware that it would be a good deal nastier for Bay to hear the news from someone else.

Having made up her mind upon this Tonia wasted no more time.

She took two pennies out of her purse and went along to the telephone box at the corner, and, being unversed in this manner of telephoning, she read the rules carefully, lifted the receiver, and inserted the pennies in the slot. She got through to the camp almost immediately and asked for Squadron Leader Coates. Bay must have been quite near the telephone, for he came at once—and Tonia, who had expected a long wait while he was being found, was so startled that she did not know what to say.

"Who's that?" asked Bay, in a sharp, decisive tone, quite unlike his usual voice.

"It's Tonia," said Tonia faintly.

"Who?"

"Tonia…Butterfingers. I want to see you."

"Do you mean tonight?" asked Bay's voice in surprised accents.

"Yes."

"Nothing wrong, is there?"

Tonia hesitated.

"Are you still there?" inquired Bay loudly. "Hallo, Butterfingers, are you there? *Is anything the matter?*"

Tonia found to her dismay that she was dumb. There was

an enormous lump in her throat that precluded speech, and she was shaking all over so that she had to lean against the side of the box. It was some moments before she found enough strength to replace the receiver and walk slowly home.

Bay arrived some ten minutes later upon a motorbike. Tonia was upstairs when she heard him come in, and she began to go down. Bay had looked for her downstairs and now he was coming up, so they met halfway.

"What on earth!" exclaimed Bay. "You scared me to death! You're ill!"

"No."

"You look awful. I'll get the doctor—"

"No, I'm all right—"

"Well, *what?*" asked Bay. "I mean, I ought to be at a lecture, but I just leaped on MacLean's bike. There's something wrong."

"Yes." She sat down rather suddenly on the stairs, for her knees felt as if they were made of wet cardboard, and, as the stairs were very steep, this brought her face on a level with Bay's.

"You *are* ill," said Bay with conviction.

"No, honestly—"

"Tell me, Butterfingers," said Bay, laying a hand on her knee. "For heaven's sake tell me what's the matter. It can't be as bad as all that—"

"It's Retta," said Tonia faintly. "Retta's gone."

"Oh, is that all!" said Bay, with a relieved air. "Well, it's a bit sudden, but she's a sudden sort of person. Good Lord, I thought it was something much worse than that. I suppose she got into one of her rages and scared you," continued Bay, patting Tonia's knee. "She's a bit of a Tartar when she's roused, but it soon blows over—"

"It isn't that. I mean, she *was* in a rage, but—"

"But what?"

"She said she was married," replied Tonia in a very low voice.

Bay drew back and leaned against the banisters.

"I'm afraid it's true," added Tonia. "I mean, there were several things…but of course I never thought…and then—then when she was going away she said she was going to her husband—"

"How funny!" said Bay.

"Not—funny."

"I think it's damn funny," declared Bay with a very unmirthful sort of laugh. "I think it's the funniest thing I've heard for months."

"Let's go downstairs," said Tonia.

They went downstairs and into the drawing room. The fire was almost dead, which was rather fortunate, for it gave Tonia something to do. She knelt on the hearth rug and began to coax it gently with the bellows. Bay walked to the end of the room and back.

"Why!" said Bay. "I mean, what was the object? She didn't tell you that, I suppose."

"No. Oh, Bay, I'm sorry…it seems ridiculous to say I'm sorry. It seems futile. I said I was sorry when you lost your pipe!"

"I'm not sorry," declared Bay. "I'm—angry. I want to know why she set out to make a fool of me."

"I don't know *anything*," declared Tonia. "I don't, really. She was just going when I got back. I've been trying to think what could have happened."

At this moment the door opened and Mrs. Smilie appeared. Tonia was usually quite pleased to see Mrs. Smilie—but not now. It was bad enough to have Bay here, walking up and down the room like a caged lion; Mrs. Smilie's appearance on the scene was the last straw.

"Not now, Mrs. Smilie," said Tonia. "Perhaps you would come back later if you want to talk to me."

"There's things I'd like to say," began Mrs. Smilie, hesitating at the door.

"You know something," said Bay, looking at her. "Come on, Mrs. Smilie, out with it. Give us the works."

"It's about Miss Delarge—as she calls herself."

Bay nodded. "Go on," he said.

"It wasn't her brother that was here last night; it was her husband," declared Mrs. Smilie. "They were talking away together as man and wife. They were arguing, too. He was wanting her to come away with him, but she was all for staying on a bit longer and finishing the job."

"What job?" asked Bay.

"I'm not very sure but maybe this has something to do with it," and so saying Mrs. Smilie took the piece of paper out of her pocket and handed it to Bay.

"What's this?" he asked, looking at it in a puzzled way. "It seems to be a sort of map."

"Umphm, that's what I was thinking myself. A map of Ryddelton and the airfield. Maybe you'll know what the wee red cross means, Mr. Coates."

"Hell!" exclaimed Bay, gazing at the piece of paper as if it were a viper.

"I thought you might be interested in it," said Mrs. Smilie.

"This is frightful," declared Bay. "This is simply appalling. Where on earth did you find it?"

"It was in the pocket of yon woman's trousers. Maybe I shouldn't have rummaged in her pockets, but I just thought I'd have a look—and that's what I found. She was a wee bit put out when I showed her it."

"But what does it mean?" cried Tonia. "I don't understand. Why did Retta make a map of Ryddelton?"

"Exactly," agreed Bay in grim tones. "That's what we must find out."

"Anybody could make a map," said Tonia earnestly. "I mean, from the wood you can see the whole place spread out and the airfield and everything. There's no harm in that."

"None whatever," said Bay. "But there's something in this

map that you can't see from the woods…or rather something that looks quite ordinary and uninteresting, but isn't."

"It'll be your bomb dump," said Mrs. Smilie in a matter-of-fact voice. "There, where she put the wee red cross. That's what I was thinking. I may be wrong, of course," added Mrs. Smilie modestly. "It was just an idea I had. Maybe the Germans would like to know the place—and I knew it was important, for she offered me twenty pounds if I'd burn it."

"Twenty pounds!" cried Tonia.

"She'd have given me more," said Mrs. Smilie, nodding. "She'd have given pretty well anything to see that wee bit of paper burned."

"I expect she would," declared Bay.

"Oh, Bay!" Tonia cried. "You don't mean she was going to give it to the Germans!"

"Sell it, probably," he replied. "She was always short of money—but we mustn't waste time. It's just possible she's still in Ryddelton, unless she managed to get a train. I must go straight down to the police station—"

"There's no need for that, Mr. Coates," said Mrs. Smilie comfortably. "You'll just sit down by the fire and take a cup of tea. Sergeant Duncan will be here any minute now."

"Here!" exclaimed Bay.

Mrs. Smilie nodded. "It was this way," she said. "I felt bothered about the affair, for it was my blame, you see. If I'd held my tongue and showed you the paper you could have managed the whole affair a lot better. That was what I *should* have done. I saw that when it was too late. Well, I felt pretty bad about it and Alec was out and there was nobody to ask, so when I had gotten my breath a bit I put on my hat and away I went to the police station and told Willie the whole thing, and—"

"Willie?" asked Bay in bewilderment.

"Willie Duncan. He's the sergeant, and he's a sensible man (you'd never think, to talk to him, he was a policeman). We had a wee crack and I showed him the paper. He wanted me to let him keep it but I thought I would just give it you myself... and there he is," added Mrs. Smilie, as the front doorbell did its usual wild jangle in the back premises. "There's Willie, himself, to see you. I'll just let him in and then I'll infuse the tea. You can send Willie into the kitchen when you've done with him and he'll take his tea with me. It'll be more comfortable for everybody."

"What a woman!" said Bay in a dazed voice.

Tonia had started to laugh hysterically. "I know it's silly," she declared, shaking all over and wiping her eyes. "I know there's nothing to laugh at...but I can't help it...somehow."

"Don't, Butterfingers," implored Bay, patting her on the back. "Don't shake like that. It's all right—honestly. Don't worry."

"Bay—"

"Go upstairs," said Bay wildly. "Go to bed; there's a dear. You look absolutely all in. I'll come and tell you all about it when he's gone."

❧

Mrs. Smilie followed Tonia upstairs and turned down the bed and put on the electric radiator.

"There's a bottle in the bed and you'll just get straight in," said Mrs. Smilie firmly. "I'll bring you a cup of tea and your supper later."

"You're a darling," declared Tonia in rather a shaky voice, and she put her arms around Mrs. Smilie and kissed her (her cheek was hard and smooth like an apple).

"Hoots, that's a silly kind of carry-on," said Mrs. Smilie, turning away.

Tonia was not in the least put out by this reception of her embrace, for she understood Mrs. Smilie quite well by this time.

"I suppose this is your nightdress," continued Mrs. Smilie, in scornful tones, as she shook out the pale pink silk garment she had found beneath the pillow. "There's not much warmth in *that*. I prefer flannel, myself."

It was very comfortable in bed. Tonia was tired—what a long day it had been! She went over the incidents as she lay there with the hot water bottle cuddled in her arms. Breakfast first—that odd conversation with Retta had taken place only this morning, though it felt like a week ago—that odd conversation in which Retta had described the joys of being married to "the dearest one" and had added that her sister had told her about it. If Tonia had had a grain of sense she would have known at the time that it was Retta's own experience and not a secondhand account of someone else's (and all that talk of her sister! That was untrue...Retta had no sister and had never had one). Then, after breakfast, the barely averted row with Mrs. Smilie over the slacks... Queer about the slacks, thought Tonia. Retta had worn them the day she went up to the woods and had met "the nice man" who had told her "interesting things." This might be important, for it was *that* day she must have sketched the map, and she must have gotten the information she wanted from the man, worming it out of him, perhaps without his knowledge (for she was clever in some ways, though rather foolish in other ways, thought Tonia). The man might have been from the airfield—probably was. What a pity Tonia had not asked Retta about him! Retta had made the little map and put it in her pocket and forgotten about it—what an extraordinary thing to do! Or had she made two maps and given one to Henri? That seemed more probable.

Tonia's thoughts strayed on. She thought of Bay's arrival after lunch and their walk to Dunnian, a walk that should have been enjoyable but somehow or other was very uncomfortable and odd. They had started off well, with Bay's joke about Mrs. Dundas, but soon a silence had fallen and they had been obliged to make trite remarks to break it. "It feels thundery," Tonia had said, and Bay had replied, "Too cold for thunder." Then Bay had remarked, "River seems pretty full today," and Tonia had replied, "It rained in the night."

Tonia had been thankful when they reached Dunnian, and not only because of the heavy shower that was threatening. The tea party had been very pleasant. First of all, she had talked to Admiral Dunne (Celia's father) and had found him very easy to get on with. He had told her a great deal about old Miss Celia Dunne. Then Captain Dale had gotten hold of her and given back the diary, saying somewhat cryptically that it had made him see things in a different light. Tonia had inquired further and Courtney Dale had replied that that old story about Arthur and Antonia was very, very sad. Courtney looked as if he were going to say more but their conversation was interrupted.

The rain had cleared off for the walk home. Bay and Tonia, Celia and Courtney had all set out together, but after a few minutes they separated into pairs, Celia and Tonia going ahead and the two men coming along behind and carrying on a spirited conversation on the subject of Lend Lease commitments.

"You're very silent," Celia had declared, linking her arm in Tonia's. "What's the matter with my hundred-years'-old friend, I wonder."

Tonia did not know what was the matter with her. She felt rather miserable, that was all.

"I want to tell you something," Celia had continued. "It's about Courtney and me—we're going to be married quite soon."

"Celia!" cried Tonia in delight.

"Yes," said Celia, nodding. "Yes, Courtney has changed his mind; he seems to understand my feelings. It's all *your* doing," said Celia, squeezing Tonia's arm. "It was you who gave him the diary…"

They had talked a lot more about it as they walked along, and Tonia had felt a good deal cheered, for it was so nice to think that she had been able to smooth Celia's path and make her happy. So much for the walk home, and now Tonia's thoughts moved on; she saw herself entering the house and reviewed her conversation with Retta. The mystery of Retta's flight was cleared up now, for Mrs. Smilie had discovered her secret, but the accident to the Chinese jar was still unexplained; it seemed unimportant compared with the other occurrences.

Tonia had gotten thus far in her reconstruction of the day's events when she heard a very timid knock on the door and in answer to her invitation to enter a voice said humbly, "But it's me."

"Come in, Bay," said Tonia cheerfully. "I'm in bed, but you can pretend you're the doctor. I must hear what happened. What was Willie like?"

Bay entered and shut the door. "Willie was grand," he said. "Willie understands the whole thing and he's willing to cooperate. He's coming up to headquarters with me."

"Will they catch Retta?" asked Tonia anxiously.

"They'll catch her if they want to," replied Bay. "Willie seems to have no doubts about that, but he thinks the London people will put someone on to shadow her. He says she's very small fry but she might be the means of catching a bigger fish."

"She's rather silly in some ways," said Tonia. "I don't think she can have had much experience. She made several slips talking to me."

"I feel such a fool," declared Bay. "I feel… Gosh, I can't tell you what an idiot I feel!"

Tonia was glad to observe that whatever else he might feel

he was not heartbroken. "You didn't tell her anything," said Tonia comfortingly.

"Not a thing," agreed Bay. "I really am careful. I don't even tell *you* things, do I?"

This remark pleased Tonia a good deal, but she hid her pleasure. "You were sorry for Retta," she pointed out.

"Yes, and of course she *was* attractive. I mean, when I first met her at Dieppe I fell for her with an almighty crash…and then, afterward, when I began—began—well, it sounds frightfully caddish, but I began to—to—"

"Yes, but you couldn't let her down."

"That was it," agreed Bay with a sigh of relief. "I simply couldn't. She had lost everything, her parents and her home and her country, so how could I possibly let her down?"

"You couldn't," agreed Tonia. She hesitated and then asked, "What will they do to her?"

"Not much, unless there's something else against her. It would be difficult to prove that she intended to hand over the information to the enemy."

"Why did she?" asked Tonia, frowning. "It seems so extraordinary. She hated the Germans, didn't she?"

"I'm not sure about that," he replied in a thoughtful voice. "She hated the Germans, but I believe she hated us even more. I've been thinking back and remembering things she said—nothing definite, you know, just odd remarks. She thought we had deserted France and left her to face the music; she thought we were taking things too easily…I remember one day we were talking about Vichy and she got quite rabid on the subject and stood up for Pétain like anything. I didn't think much of it at the time, because she often gets excited and says things she doesn't mean, but it all comes back to me now and it all fits in."

"I know," said Tonia, who had had much the same experience.

"I want to find out how she got the information," continued

Bay. "That's the important thing. She asked *me* about it, of course, but I was jolly careful not to tell her anything. Somebody must have told her. We keep all our bombs in an underground store near a little cottage—a perfectly innocent-looking little cottage—and there's enough stuff there to blow the whole of Ryddelton sky-high. It doesn't matter telling you now, because we shall move it, of course."

"The cottage was marked with a cross?"

"Yes. I can tell you it gave me a shock when I saw that sketch with the cross on it. A well-aimed bomb would set off the whole bag of tricks."

"I'll tell you all I know," said Tonia, and she began to tell Bay about Retta's expedition to the woods.

Chapter Thirty-One
Marriage A La Mode

Celia's wedding was to be "very quiet." Everyone said so. Admiral Dunne said so, and young Mrs. Dunne (who was Mark's wife) and Courtney Dale and Celia herself.

"*Quite* quiet," said Celia. "But we must have Tonia, of course—and Bay Coates."

"I'd like to have Bob," said Courtney a trifle diffidently.

"Of course!" cried the others. It was natural that Courtney should want his fellow countryman to keep him in countenance.

Bill was coming on leave, but not Mark. Then there was Mrs. Rewden (who was Celia's eldest sister) and her husband and their two girls, and there was Joyce (another sister) and her two boys. There was Mrs. Raeworth (their nearest neighbor) and Mrs. Murray from Timperton. The list grew and grew (for if you asked one person it seemed that you must ask another); it grew to alarming proportions—alarming because of the food question and the lack of domestic staff.

"What on earth are you going to give them to drink?" asked the admiral anxiously.

"Coffee, I suppose," said Celia after a moment's thought. "We can't give them wine of any sort. We can't make lemonade, nor tea."

"They'll have to drink their coffee without sugar," added Deb, who was the housekeeper.

"We'll give them sandwiches," put in Celia.

"I might raise some beer," suggested Courtney.

Admiral Dunne shuddered. He remembered Edith's wedding, a tremendous affair with champagne and wedding cake and the whole county invited, and the more he thought about it the more he disliked the idea of marrying Celia on coffee and sandwiches. Nobody else seemed to be worrying about it, but they were all young and therefore more adaptable; he, alone, was old and tired and sad.

Dunnian House had been shrouded in dust sheets for several years, but now it was being spruced up for the great occasion and decorated with late chrysanthemums and shiny rhododendron leaves in tall vases. It was Deb who was the prime mover in all these activities. Perhaps Deb was thinking of Edith's wedding, too, thought the admiral as he watched her at work and helped her to polish the brasses and to move the furniture.

"It can't be the same, of course," said Deb suddenly, looking up into her father-in-law's face and smiling gravely.

Admiral Dunne was a little startled, but he need not have been, for Deb had always possessed the faculty of reading one's thoughts.

"It seems—shoddy," he said unhappily.

"Oh no," replied Deb, shaking her head. "Not shoddy, really. Celia and Courtney have the principal thing—champagne and wedding cake are just unimportant details."

The admiral was comforted, for of course it was true. Celia and Courtney had the principal thing, the thing upon which marriage ought to be built, the thing he had shared with Alice—now long dead—which Deb shared with Mark, but which had been totally lacking in the marriage of Edith and Douglas Rewden.

The day was fine and clear and frosty, and when the wedding party arrived at Ryddelton Church they found it full of people. Everybody in the town knew Celia and everybody wanted to see her marry her American. Mrs. Smilie was there in her best hat—a fearsome concoction—and Mrs. Wilson (who kept Rhode Island hens) and Mrs. MacBean and a host of others. Of course everybody had heard the romantic story; people said to one another, "He's a Dunne, really. He's no stranger. He's Miss Mary Dunne's great-grandson, and they'll be living at Dunnian after the war so we'll not be losing Miss Celia…"

The Air Force was well represented, not only Bay and Bob had turned up, but Mannering and Jeefer and dozens of others. Some of them knew Celia and thought Dale was a lucky fellow and others knew Dale and thought Celia a lucky girl. The wedding went off well—as weddings always do—and the congregation emerged from the church and stood about in the street. There was one taxi in Ryddelton, and this had been engaged to convey the bride and bridegroom home to Dunnian for the reception. Their immediate relatives climbed in beside them and filled the taxi to bursting point.

"It's frightful," declared the admiral, looking out of the window at the crowds of people in the road. "How on earth are they going to get to Dunnian? We ought to have engaged a bus."

"I tried," said Bill. "You can't engage buses."

"They'll find their way out, somehow," declared Deb.

"I don't see how—without wings," said the admiral with a sigh.

Tonia had no wings, she had not even a bicycle, but she managed to get a lift to Dunnian House in the baker's van. Bay had borrowed MacLean's motorcycle, which was strictly illegal, of course. He took Bob on the pillion and Mannering hung on with his arms around Bob's neck. Some of the guests bicycled.

Some walked. Jeefer and Douglas-Begge got a lift in a tank that happened to be going in the right direction.

It was quite amazing how many people had managed to make the grade (as Bob put it). They trickled into the house and, far from being annoyed at the discomforts they had endured, they seemed proud of themselves for having overcome the difficulties of wartime transport. Even Bob, who had attached himself to Tonia, could find no fault with the appearance of the guests. It was obvious that they had put on their best clothes for the occasion.

"Maybe she's a duchess," remarked Bob, pointing out an elderly lady who was wearing a magnificent diamond brooch and a cloak of Russian sable.

"She may be, for all I know," replied Tonia with a smile.

At this moment another old lady bore down upon Tonia with a purposeful air. "You're Mrs. Norman," she said. "I know everybody else, so you must be Mrs. Norman. I'm Mrs. Raeworth. I would have called but I'm seventy-six and I can't walk as far as I used to… Yes, I know everyone. I could tell you who everybody is and who married who—and why. I could tell you quite a lot of things but I'm not going to, because you would be horribly bored."

Tonia smiled. She introduced Bob to Mrs. Raeworth and explained that he was anxious to know whether the lady in the sable cloak was a duchess.

"No," replied Mrs. Raeworth. "There's only one duchess here and she's wearing a WVS uniform…there she is, talking to the admiral. Perhaps you'd like to be introduced to her, Captain—er—"

"Me?" exclaimed Bob. "I wouldn't know what to say!"

Mrs. Raeworth laughed at this and assured him that he need have no qualms, adding that she would make the introduction presently when she had finished talking to Mrs. Norman.

"I wanted to ask you about the Skenes," she continued. "Edmund Skene's son married a Melville."

"My sister," said Tonia, nodding.

"I thought it might be. I shan't say it's a small world because that would be tiresome of me. Edmund Skene was a nice creature but deadly dull. As a matter of fact, I never blamed his young wife for going off with Philip Halley. It created a bit of a stir at the time, but Edmund behaved very sensibly and people soon forgot about it. What is the son like?"

Tonia told her about Jack and Lou.

"Very interesting," said Mrs. Raeworth, nodding. "Very interesting to me because I used to know old Lady Skene. She was a great character. She was at Edith's wedding and I sat beside her and told her what everybody was doing. She was very shortsighted, but she kept tabs on everything that was going on. Some people were frightened of her but she was a good friend to me. Edith's wedding was a marvelous affair. The whole county turned up in its best clothes and the drive was packed with cars—but I don't believe the guests enjoyed themselves any better than today. Their clothes look just as nice in spite of the fact that they had to come on bicycles. I can't bicycle so I came in the laundry van. The man was most kind and said he would pick me up on the way back. I wonder what Lady Skene would have thought of it," added Mrs. Raeworth thoughtfully.

"And old Miss Celia Dunne," suggested Tonia.

"Did you know her!" cried Mrs. Raeworth. "No, of course you couldn't have known her. She died long before you were born."

"Did you know her?" asked Tonia.

"Very well indeed. She was a delightful old lady, full of life and energy and interested in everyone and everything. I did a portrait of her once—I used to paint when I was young. It was the best portrait I ever did. Perhaps you'd like to see it."

Tonia said she would.

"This house is full of ghosts," continued Mrs. Raeworth. "Nice friendly ghosts, you know, and it seems to me that they're all here today. The Dunnes have always liked parties. Dunnian House likes parties; it welcomes you when you come in at the door."

The drawing room had filled up rapidly and the buzz of talk had grown louder. A young man appeared suddenly at Tonia's elbow with a tray of cups. He was a very nice-looking young man and was wearing a naval uniform, so there was not much doubt as to his identity.

"Do you know Bill?" asked Mrs. Raeworth.

"Not really," replied Tonia, smiling at him. "I've heard about him, of course."

"How do you do, Mrs. Norman," said Bill. "Will you have coffee in a white cup or a blue one? The white cups are bigger but the blue ones aren't quite so thick."

Tonia smiled and chose a blue cup, but Mrs. Raeworth took a white one, remarking that coffee tasted better in a thick cup. She had brought a small bottle of saccharine tablets in her handbag and she offered one to Tonia. "I never go anywhere without them," she declared. "It's positively criminal to eat people's sugar and I like sweet things…"

"Look at Monkey-Face," said Bill. "She's happy, isn't she?"

"Monkey-Face!" cried Mrs. Raeworth. "How often have I told you to stop calling Celia by that absurd name?"

"Dozens of times," admitted Bill with a grin. "But she *is* like a monkey. She's like a very pretty little monkey, of course…"

"You're incorrigible," said Mrs. Raeworth. "I shan't waste my time upon you. I shall find that nice young American and introduce him to the duchess."

"She's a dear, isn't she?" said Bill, looking at Mrs. Raeworth's retreating figure. He added, "Well, everyone seems to have coffee now so my job's finished. Come and sit on the stairs."

They sat on the stairs together and watched the people. There was an odd sort of feeling about this party, Tonia decided. She felt as if it had all happened before and she had watched it happening, but there was a difference, for this time it was happening right—the right people had been married to each other. There was no doubt of that. Celia and her husband had begun to move about among their guests; Celia's face was shining with happiness, and Courtney bore himself like a conqueror. He bowed and smiled as he was introduced first to one person and then to another (and he seemed to have the faculty of saying exactly the right thing), but his eyes always strayed back to Celia and dwelt upon her with almost incredulous joy.

"It's nice," said Bill, after a little silence. "But it's sad, too. Sad for me, I mean. Celia and I have always been very special friends."

"It will make less difference than you think," replied Tonia in a thoughtful voice. "One kind of love doesn't interfere with another."

He looked at her in surprise, for he had not expected that she would understand, still less had he expected grave words of wisdom from her. She was so very young and so exceedingly pretty, and Bill (who was a connoisseur of pretty girls) had formed the opinion that if a girl was easy on the eye she was performing her role in life. You could not ask for more—even if you asked for more, you seldom got it.

"I say, that's interesting," said Bill, moving a step nearer to her and beginning to get down to it in a workmanlike fashion. "You seem to have thought out things…"

They were still talking, comparing notes on the things they thought of, when Bay came out of the dining room with Jim Mannering and found them sitting there.

"I've been looking for you everywhere," declared Bay, frowning.

"It's nice and cool here," replied Tonia, making room for him on the step.

He sat down. So did Mannering and Jeefer and several others who happened to come along. There was quite a crowd—and a gay crowd at that—sitting on the stairs or leaning against the banisters before many minutes had passed.

❧

Tonia had hoped that Bay would walk part of the way home with her, but when the time came to go home he had disappeared so she walked home by herself feeling a little flat after all the excitement. She made an omelet for supper—as Retta had shown her—with dried eggs and mixed herbs. And as she ate it she thought of Retta and wondered where she was and what had happened to her, for since her disappearance nothing had been heard of her and even Bay did not seem to know anything about her. Tonia had not asked Bay, for she felt it was better to leave the subject alone, but she had a feeling that Bay would have told her if he had had anything to tell.

After supper Tonia took the last installment of Great-Aunt Antonia's diary and settled herself comfortably in front of the drawing room fire. There was just a chance that Bay might come in and see her, but it was no use expecting him because he never knew whether he could come or not. It was difficult not to expect him, of course, and every time she heard a step on the pavement she found herself listening and wondering if it was Bay. But the diary was very interesting, and presently she became absorbed and the time passed without her noticing it.

This last book of the diary was more modern in tone, and there were little touches of humor in it—as if Miss Antonia had recovered from the sorrow of her youth and made friends with life. It had been written by an old woman, but a woman who had moved with the times and was vitally interested in people and affairs. There was a short account of the relief of Mafeking and Miss Antonia's reaction to the wave of excitement that had swept over the country. *People seem to have gone mad. They have made the occasion an excuse for a riot of pleasure. There is shouting and singing in the streets and much drunkenness. Is this the way to celebrate the relief of that handful of brave men who have held out for seven long months against hunger and their enemies? Too much excitement and too little gratitude to God,* wrote Miss Antonia, underlining her verdict with a firm hand.

There was a great deal in this diary about the people in Ryddelton and their affairs. It was obvious that Miss Antonia was a confidential friend and had a beneficent finger in many pies; and her great-niece decided—after reading some of the entries—that this particular book must not be shown to anybody. Later on, among the chronicles of everyday life, which included details of jam making and lists of shrubs being planted in the garden, Tonia came upon her father's name.

Henry came to see me, wrote Miss Antonia. *He has grown a great deal and is a very good-looking young fellow, but I can see evidences of a hasty temper I fear he has inherited from his father. Henry is too old now to be offered sugar cookies. He took a glass of sherry with me and accepted a "tip" with evident pleasure. There is no nonsense about Henry—that is one thing in his favor—I look forward to his next visit in the summer holidays."*

And now Tonia came upon another name she knew. *Jean Smilie is unwell so I went in to see her and took her a book and some calves' foot jelly, which Mrs. Fraser made this morning. Jean is a dear, good creature and her heart is in the right place, but she has not learned tolerance. She expects her neighbors to live up to her standards and judges them by the shine on their brasses.* Tonia laughed at this, for Jean Smilie had not altered much in the forty odd years since this little character sketch was penned.

"Celia" figured largely in this diary. There were constant references to her: *Celia came to tea but could not stay long because it was so cold for the horses. Thomson walked them up and down the streets for half an hour… I drove over to Dunnian to see Celia. She has been ill but is much better and Becky says she will be allowed up tomorrow… Celia came to lunch. She arranged for Thomson to put up at the Rydd Arms so that we might have longer together. We talked of old times. We are both so old now and it is quite true that old people remember their youth clearly and in detail. I asked Celia if she ever heard from Courtney Dale and she replied that she had lost touch with him since Mary died. I told her I had always known that she and Courtney were fond of each other: Celia did not deny it but smiled and said it was a very old story. My poor little romance is a very old story, too. Sometimes I try to imagine what my life would have been if Arthur had lived and we had been married and if Celia had married Courtney Dale and gone to America with him. How strange to think of these "might have beens" and what small incidents shape one's destiny! I can look back and see the gay colored pictures of my childhood, and the dark tunnel through which I wandered after Arthur's death. It was a long tunnel, but I came through it and emerged into the sunshine, the mellower sunshine of the afternoon…and Celia has suffered too, perhaps in a harder way, though it is difficult to measure suffering. Here we are, two old ladies who sit and talk in the firelight. We have been friends all our lives, nearer than sisters. We have lived long and seen much. Some people might think our lives dull and uneventful, but it does not seem so to us. We talked of this and agreed that it is not travel and adventure that make a full life. There are adventures of the spirit, and one can travel in books and interest oneself in people and affairs. One need never be dull as long as one has friends to help, gardens to enjoy, and books in the long winter evenings. "And the hills!" exclaimed Celia. "The hills are always different. I could look at the hills forever, and I thank God every night that I can still see them clearly." I could not help laughing at this. Celia's bright brown eyes see most things—I remember her annoyance when she was forced to take to spectacles for reading...*

It was at this moment that Tonia heard the planes. So that was why Bay had not come! It was still early, which probably meant they were going far afield—perhaps to Berlin. She sat and listened to them, zooming over the town, the heavy beat of their engines sounding loud in the stillness. She heard them pass and the sound of them die away as they flew over the hills.

Tonia rose and went to bed. She decided not to think about the planes, not to think of Bay. She would think about the wedding and go over every incident, and that would send her to sleep. But somehow or other it was more difficult than usual to get off to sleep, and, when at last she slept, her dreams were troubled and uneasy.

Chapter Thirty-Two
Unhappy Landing

Mrs. Smilie appeared at the usual hour with Tonia's breakfast, for now that Retta had gone they had returned to this pleasant custom. She settled the tray upon Tonia's knees and turned to go without saying anything…and this was so unusual that Tonia was quite startled.

"Is anything the matter?" inquired Tonia.

"What should be the matter?" said Mrs. Smilie, making for the door.

"Mrs. Smilie, *please!*" cried Tonia. "Please don't go away. Have I done something—something to offend you?"

"It's nothing like that," said Mrs. Smilie, and she disappeared, closing the door behind her.

Tonia pushed aside the tray and leaped out of bed and was out on the landing in a moment. "Wait!" she cried. "Please wait, Mrs. Smilie. You *must* tell me what's the matter. Come up here at once. There's something wrong and I must know what it is."

"It'll do after you've had your breakfast—or later."

"It won't," declared Tonia. "I shan't start my breakfast until you've told me."

Mrs. Smilie hesitated on the stairs, and then came up slowly… and now that Tonia could see her face clearly she knew it was something serious.

"It isn't—" began Tonia, holding on to the banisters. "Oh no, it can't be—it can't be—Bay."

"Now don't take on, Miss Tonia," said Mrs. Smilie, seizing her arm and leading her back into her bedroom. "We don't know anything. He may be perfectly all right…and that's why I wasn't wanting to tell you."

"Missing!"

"Not really," declared Mrs. Smilie. "They didn't come back, that's all. Maybe they've had to come down somewhere else; that's what's happened, you may be sure. Mr. Coates is a very clever pilot. The Germans are not likely to get *him* in a hurry—"

"They didn't come back," said Tonia, interrupting the babble of talk. "I suppose the postman told you."

"That was all he knew—just that they didn't come back. Now, don't worry yourself, Miss Tonia. There's time enough to worry when—"

"I'm all right," declared Tonia, sitting down on the stool in front of the dressing table. "I'll come down soon. Don't wait, Mrs. Smilie."

"You'll take your breakfast?" asked Mrs. Smilie anxiously.

"Yes, of course. Don't wait."

Mrs. Smilie went to the door, somewhat reluctantly. She paused and looked at Tonia, and then she went away.

"They didn't come back," said Tonia to herself. She leaned her elbow on the dressing table and her cheek on her hand. She had no inclination to cry. She just felt a sense of utter desolation. I might have known, she thought. I did know, really. I knew this would happen some day. Oh, Bay, where are you! What has become of you! Oh, Bay!

It was harder because she knew so little, and because she had no right to know. She had no right to grieve for Bay—except as a friend. She had no right to ask for news of him, to ring up the airfield and find out what was known. They would tell her later, perhaps. Somebody might think of telling her. Some of the others might have seen what had happened to Bay's plane. Bay had seen the end of O for Orange and had told her about it, and so it was possible that one of the other pilots had seen what had happened…and would tell her about it.

She rose and began to dress. It was impossible to think of eating anything, but she poured out a little tea and drank it thirstily. Presently she was ready to go downstairs. She went down and sat in the drawing room. Somebody would come; somebody would come and tell her. She would have to wait.

Mrs. Smilie came in from the kitchen and looked at her and repeated all she had said before. Mr. Coates was very clever— everybody said so. He had come down somewhere; there was no need to worry.

Tonia nodded and agreed with all she said.

"Maybe you'd do the silver this morning," suggested Mrs. Smilie. "The silver needs doing and I don't have the time."

"I cleaned the silver yesterday," replied Tonia, trying to smile.

"You could cut up the vegetables for the soup."

"Yes, I will—presently," said Tonia.

Mrs. Smilie went away and Tonia sat quite still and waited and thought about Bay. She remembered the first day she saw him, here, in Ryddelton and how they had passed each other and then turned back. She thought of the evening they had stood at the door and watched the light fade and the darkness gather in pools of gloom upon the street, and a girl had walked past on the other side, and Bay had said, "Wooden soles!" Such a trifle to remember, but it was trifles like this that made up your life, and if there was somebody who could share them with you, understandingly, it made your life a paradise. She remembered other things: Nita's visit and how Bay had come into the kitchen and announced with satisfaction that he had sent her away." She remembered Bay humming "Listening

Valley" in his clear, deep voice and saying, "It's a lovely tune.
Let's play it again, shall we?" and she remembered him singing
"I'll Walk Beside Thee" and the strange pain she had felt in her
heart... Then Retta had come, but even Retta had not spoiled
the queer companionable feeling that existed between them, for
Retta had been outside it and had not understood. Last, but not
least, Tonia remembered Bay saying in a serious voice: "I really
am careful. I don't even tell *you* things, do I?"

Tonia had been happy here, but now that she looked back
she saw that all her happiness had come from Bay. Yes, every
bit of it, for even when Bay was not with her the thought of
him made a pleasant warmth in her heart. She knew him so
well, inside and out, that she could guess his thoughts, and
when she shut her eyes she could see his tall, loosely built figure
lounging in a chair; she could see his long-fingered hands that
looked big and clumsy but were really neat and capable and
well controlled she could see his bright brown hair and his
clear-complexioned face and his straight lips that suddenly
curved into smiles.

If that had gone—all of it, suddenly and completely—would
she be able to bear it? Could she go on without it? Antonia
had faced the same ordeal when Arthur was drowned and had
struggled through and come out at the other end of the tunnel
with her courage and sweetness and kindness unimpaired.
Antonia had made friends with life and had been able to say
at the end of it, "One need never be dull as long as one has
friends to help."

Tonia twisted her hands together and looked at them...
useless sort of hands, but Bay liked them. It was because he
liked them that he called her Butterfingers—it was just a silly,
tender joke.

It was four o'clock and Tonia was making herself a cup of tea when the front doorbell rang. She had almost ceased to expect news by this time, and the bell scared her so much that it took real courage to go and open the door.

It was Jim Mannering.

"Hallo, Tony!" he said with a false jauntiness that was somehow very pathetic. "Hallo, old thing, I thought I'd look in and see you—"

"But how—" began Tonia. "Weren't you there? What happened?"

He came into the hall and threw his cap on the chest, and now she saw that he was very pale, with dark shadows around his eyes.

"Of course I was there," he said. "At least I suppose you mean in the plane."

"But it didn't come back!" cried Tonia.

"How on earth did you hear that? Gosh, how extraordinary! Everybody seems to know everything in this blinking place."

She tried to frame the words, to ask him about Bay, but she couldn't.

"How beastly for you!" added Mannering, looking at her sympathetically.

"It was, rather," said Tonia in a faint voice.

"Coates is OK," said Mannering. He was hanging up his belt as he spoke and, very carefully, did not look at her.

Tonia heard someone say, "Oh, that's good!" and realized afterward it was herself.

"Yes," said Mannering. "He's perfectly all right. He asked me to tell you. He couldn't come himself because he's broken his arm."

"Oh!" said Tonia. She sat down on the stairs, chiefly because her legs felt so very peculiar.

"But there's no need to worry," continued Mannering in the

same casual sort of voice. "Socks said I was to tell you not to worry. He'll be out of the hospital in no time."

"Really?" asked Tonia. "I mean, you aren't just—just breaking it gently or something?"

"Good Lord, no," replied Mannering in horrified tones. "What a frightful idea! He's broken his arm, and of course he got a bit of a shake, but he's absolutely OK."

"You had better tell me the whole thing," said Tonia.

"There isn't much to tell. We had a forced landing, that's all."

"Go on, Jim."

"Socks said not to tell you too much," said Mannering doubtfully. "It's all over and he's perfectly OK, so why worry? It was quite an ordinary sort of thing—not even a crash."

"But it might have been—"

"If you begin to think about what might have been—"

"That's just why you must tell me exactly what happened," said Tonia earnestly. "We'll have tea, shall we? As a matter of fact the kettle is boiling and it's all ready if you don't mind having it in the kitchen."

Mannering was only too pleased to have tea in the kitchen; it was warm and cozy and, to tell the truth, he was not feeling too good. They sat down opposite one another at the table and began their meal. Tonia was extremely anxious to hear the story, but she noticed that her guest seemed hungry. He cut a large chunk off the loaf and spread it with honey.

"I hope I shan't eat you out of house and home," he said, smiling at her. "As a matter of fact I didn't know I was hungry or I'd have had a snack at the mess before I came."

"I'm glad you didn't."

"Yes—well, so am I. It's nice here," he replied. She waited as patiently as she could and presently Mannering began to talk. He started somewhat lamely, for he was hampered by the fact that he was talking to a person who did not know the first thing about flying, but after a bit he warmed up to the tale. They had dropped their bombs on the target, Mannering said. There was a good deal of flak but nothing out of the ordinary; in fact, it had been rather a dull sort of trip until they were well on their way home. One of the engines packed up, and this slowed down their speed so that they dropped behind, but that was nothing either; it just meant they would be late. Then, quite suddenly, somebody called out that there were bandits coming up from the south. The moon was pretty bright, but they had been lurking in an innocent-looking cloud—four Me 109's—nasty brutes to encounter without fighter protection. They made a determined attack, coming in from both sides at once but Socks jinked pretty successfully and the port gunner gave them a burst and sent one down. There were only three now, but they came on again. It was a pretty hectic moment, said Mannering. Tracer bullets whizzing past and cannon shells exploding all around. The Halifax shuddered all over when the shells got her but no real damage was done. Socks was dodging about all over the sky in his usual masterly style and puzzling the Jerries a lot. In fact, they were beginning to get a bit sick of it—a bit halfhearted. Most people would have left it at that, said Mannering, but Socks liked to down all the bandits he could. "I know Socks," explained Mannering. "So I wasn't surprised when he played his little trick; he's done the same thing before." Sock's little trick consisted of side-slipping and dropping like a stone for several hundred feet. It gave you a bit of a scare if you weren't prepared for it, but it usually worked.

"It worked all right," said Mannering, smiling reminiscently. "Jerry thought we were done for and came after us, careless-like, to finish us off—but it doesn't do to be careless. Jenkins put in some pretty useful work with the tail gun and they decided to call it a day. Two of them were smoking nicely as they made off. I put them down as probables.

"We had lost a good deal of height and the plane felt a bit sluggish. I looked down and saw we weren't more than thirty feet above the sea. The wireless gear had been damaged but I managed to work out where we were, more or less, and I told Coates. He chirped back that some of the controls had come unstuck so we'd better set a course for the nearest coastline, and he had to make enough height for the crew to bale out. I said why bale out and he said, have a look at the undercarriage. Gosh, I got a bit of a shock when I looked. It was hanging down all tangled and twisted... It wasn't too cheerful inside the plane. It had started to rain pretty hard and the rain was blowing in through the smashed windows. The second pilot was wounded and we were all feeling pretty blue, but we felt a good deal better when we began to climb and better still when we saw the English coast. Dawn was breaking now. It was a gray sort of light and hadn't much effect upon the visibility, but still it was dawn. It meant that if we could struggle on we'd soon have a bit more light. Well, we had no sooner crossed the coast than Socks gave the order to bail out. I was a bit doubtful about Peters—I told you he was wounded, didn't I? But he wasn't too bad and he thought he could make it, so we got him ready and dropped him out. The others all dropped too—except me. I thought I'd stay put."

"Why?" asked Tonia, who had been following the story closely.

"Oh, well," said Mannering. "There were several reasons, really. Socks and I have flown together for ages. I mean, if he was going down the drain I'd just as soon go too, but as a matter of fact I was pretty certain he'd bring it off all right—I know him, you see. Besides, it isn't much fun baling out on a cold dark morning, or at any time for that matter. Anyhow, I made up my mind that if he was going to stick to the old crate so was I."

"I see," said Tonia.

"You see," agreed Mannering. "Of course I didn't think it all out at the time, you know. One doesn't, really. The plane was a good deal lighter when they'd gone. It made quite an appreciable difference and another thing happened—it was our first bit of luck; there was a horrible sort of tearing sound and the Halifax gave a bound. I tell you what it was like," said Mannering. "It was like the feeling when you let your bombs go and you're too low and the blast gets under your wings. Or, look here, it was like when you're in a lift and it starts to go up with a jerk. I couldn't think what had happened and then I saw that the whole undercarriage had gone. It had just dropped off and disappeared. That was all to the good. You see that, don't you?"

"Not really," said Tonia doubtfully.

"Oh yes, because it made it easier to land, because there was nothing hanging down to catch on to things. I was so bucked that I hooted down the intercom. Quite forgetting I was supposed to have baled out. Socks sounded a bit snooty. He wanted to know why the devil I hadn't gone. I said I was frightened. I hated baling out at the best of times—he knew that. He said I'd be more frightened before he'd done with me. We were losing height rapidly now, and the country didn't look too good. There were a lot of trees about. But on the other hand it had stopped raining and was quite light—the sun was coming up behind us. We scraped over a thick wood—yes, literally scraped; I could hear the top branches scratching against the plane—and then, suddenly, there was a meadow full of sheep. We had to land, of course. There was no choice and we were lucky it wasn't plow. Socks stalled and pancaked. There was a frightful jerk. The plane seemed to stand on her tail (just for a moment I thought we were going to flip over), but she came down right side up... It was pretty good work, you know. I don't believe anybody else could have done it with the controls all anyhow and no undercarriage, but Socks is pretty good—I told you that, didn't I?

"That's all, really," said Mannering, helping himself to another cup of tea in an absentminded manner. "Except that Socks had gotten a bullet through his arm. He'd gotten it in the scrap but he hadn't said a word, just tied his handkerchief around it and carried on. He'd lost a good deal of blood and he was pretty well all in. I got him out of the plane and tied him up as best I could and left him in a sheltered sort of place while I went to the farm to get help. I was glad I'd stuck to Socks. All the way to the farm I kept on feeling pretty glad about it. The farmer was a decent soul; he took Socks to the hospital while I phoned up headquarters and told them what had happened. As a matter of fact they knew a good deal about it already because Jenkins had phoned. They're all right—I mean, the rest of the crew—except Willard who broke his ankle…Well, I've told you now," said Mannering after a pause. "That's absolutely all. Socks is absolutely OK so you needn't worry about him. We'll be phoning up the hospital tonight—it's in Yorkshire—and I'll let you know what they say. You aren't worrying, are you?"

Chapter Thirty-Three
Mrs. Dundas Again

It was a cold frosty night in December; Tonia was sitting reading by the fire when the door opened and Bay walked in.

"Bay!" cried Tonia in amazement.

"Yes, it's me," declared Bay. "I got out of that bl-blinking hospital this morning, and here I am. Lord, I was tired of the place! They've given me three weeks' leave and then I've got to be boarded…"

He looked thinner and paler and was carrying his left arm in a sling, but otherwise he seemed much as usual, quite fit and cheery.

"Come and sit down," said Tonia, piling cushions into a chair and arranging it near the fire. "I'll make you some tea—or would you rather have hot chocolate? I'm sure you shouldn't be out in the cold…"

Bay laughed. "Don't fuss, Butterfingers," he said. "I've had enough fussing to last me for years, and I'm perfectly fit now. Let's go out, shall we?"

"Out?"

"Yes, come out for a walk. It's cold but you don't mind that, do you? I've been shut up in that wretched hospital and I want some fresh air."

"But, Bay—"

"It's all right," he assured her. "Why shouldn't we go out? I've often wondered why people make a habit of sleeping all night. It seems such a waste. Sometimes you get a soaking wet day followed by a beautiful night."

"So then you should sleep all day and go out all night," put in Tonia, smiling. "It sounds splendid, but what about house-keeping? The shops don't remain open all night."

"They ought to," declared Bay. "I mean, it's an idea. It has tremendous possibilities. If half the population were night birds the British Isles wouldn't be so overcrowded."

Tonia got her coat and wrapped a scarf around her head and they went out together, locking the front door behind them with the enormous iron key.

"It's like the key of a jail," said Bay, looking at it with interest. "And what a weight it is! Cast iron, I suppose."

"I like it," said Tonia.

"I like it, too. I like everything about your house."

The moon was almost full, sailing placidly in a cloudless sky, and there was a crispness in the air, a touch of frost, but it did not feel very cold, for there was no wind. Tonia and Bay turned up the steep lane that led to the woods and began to climb. They said very little to each other but there was no constraint about their silence. It was quite different from the day they had walked over to Dunnian together.

Quite soon they reached the woods, and the woods were silver with moonlight and dark where the shadows fell. The firs had a light sprinkling of frost upon their fanlike branches. The bare branches of the chestnuts seemed to be hung with stars. If Tonia had been alone she might have been a little frightened, for there was something very eerie about these black and silver trees, and it was so still—not a sound broke the stillness except the soft thud of their footsteps on the bone-hard ground. They had come pretty fast, and Tonia was quite breathless when they reached the little quarry on the hillside. Bay spread his waterproof and they sat down and looked across the valley without saying a word. The valley looked quite different tonight—all black and silver, with the river and the little lochs shining like pieces of looking glass.

"Listening Valley," said Bay, in a low voice. "Are you listening tonight, Butterfingers?"

"Not really," she replied—nor was she, for her thoughts were too full of Bay.

"I'm listening," he said. "But I only hear things secondhand. I don't have words for them myself. So I have to use other people's words."

"Tell me, Bay."

He hesitated and then said, "'How sweet the moonlight sleeps upon this bank! Here let us sit and let the sound of music creep in our ears.'"

"It might have been written especially for us!" exclaimed Tonia.

"I think it was," said Bay, and he put his arm around her.

She leaned against him without speaking.

"Tonia, I love you awfully," said Bay.

"I know, darling."

He kissed her.

❧

Quite a long time after that Bay said, "Let's be married soon."

"Why?" asked Tonia.

"Because—oh, well, there are several reasons. First of all, you're such a darling."

"And second?"

"It would be sensible," said Bay in a thoughtful voice. "We've got to face things, Butterfingers. I might have another crash and I might not be so lucky."

"Bay!"

"It's no use shirking, darling. If we were married you would get a pension—see?"

Tonia clasped her hands together. She said in a carefully controlled voice, "But you aren't just marrying me for *that*—to protect me? No, listen, Bay. I've got quite enough money to live on comfortably, *more* than enough, so—"

"Oh, Butterfingers, do be quiet!" cried Bay. "How silly you are! I've been in love with you since I was seven years old."

They laughed then, both of them—it was a relief to laugh—and Tonia declared that she did not believe him. If he had loved her when he was seven years old he had shown it in a funny way.

"That's the way it took me," replied Bay. "I was a wild little devil. Of course I didn't know what was the matter with me."

"When did you know?"

"Not until that night when I sang 'I'll Walk Beside Thee,'" replied Bay promptly. "I knew then, quite suddenly. I knew I wanted to walk beside you for the rest of my life...*and there was Retta!* But let's not talk about that. Let's talk about getting married. When shall we put up the banns? That's the first thing to do, isn't it?"

"No," said Tonia, firmly.

"No?"

"We can get a special license and be married next week."

"Butterfingers!" exclaimed Bay incredulously.

"Oh, this is awful," said Tonia, turning her head away. "It sounds so—so queer, doesn't it? I ought to be like dear old Antonia, all coy and maidenly—"

"And I ought to come riding up to Ryddelton Castle on a white horse to ask Papa's consent," added Bay, laughing.

"You can laugh if you like, but there was something *nice* about it, Bay. Honestly there was. I would much rather have it like that, with everything done slowly and in proper order...but there isn't time, nowadays. We have to take things when we can get them. We have to gulp them down instead of sipping them."

"I know," said Bay, tightening his arm around her.

"It spoils the flavor," declared Tonia with a sigh.

"No—no I don't think so."

"I think it does, a little, but we can't help that. You see, Bay, if you're having three weeks' sick leave we could be married and spend our honeymoon at Melville House."

"It's a marvelous idea!"

"And quite sensible?"

"Very sensible."

"Bay, listen. Perhaps you would rather wait...wait till after the war," suggested Tonia anxiously.

"Perhaps I wouldn't," replied Bay in firm accents. "You can't do that, you know. It isn't fair. You can't offer a man a piece of cake and then snatch it away again. It just isn't done. Your idea is the most marvelous and sensible idea I ever heard in all my life. I don't know why I didn't think of it myself. Of course it would be a frightful waste not to get married... but perhaps you're regretting it," continued Bay, thoughtfully. "You may have changed your mind, suddenly, and decided you don't want me to come and hang up my Sam Browne on the peg in your hall."

"Oh, Bay, you know perfectly well—"

"Darling," said Bay.

❧

"There's just one other thing," said Bay after a little silence. "I hope you don't mind my asking. It's about—Robert."

"Yes," said Tonia slowly. "No, I don't mind. In fact, I'd like to tell you. I've been thinking about Robert a good deal,

myself, wondering whether I had been—well, unfaithful, if
you know what I mean. But I believe Robert would be glad
about us. I believe he *is* glad. Robert was a splendid person.
He was wonderful. When I married him I was a miserable
sort of object—scarcely human, really," said Tonia smiling
rather sadly.

"Butterfingers, surely—"

"Honestly, Bay. I was all tangled up inside and frightened
of everything...almost frightened to *breathe*. I don't know
what Robert saw in me, I'm sure. He undid all the tangles and
showed me how to live. He loved me and believed in me. I
loved Robert very, very dearly, and I shall always love him, but
that doesn't interfere with what I feel for you."

"Are you sure?" asked Bay anxiously.

"Quite sure, because it's a different feeling—not less nor
more but just completely different."

"I think I see."

"You *must* see," urged Tonia. "We're partners, Bay. I'm
your Mrs. Dundas. I'll go out with you in any weather."

"Oh, darling, that's perfect!" he exclaimed. "You're always
doing that—saying things that I feel but can't express. I'll go out
with you in any weather, too."

"Mr. and Mrs. Dundas," said Tonia, smiling at him, her small
face very white in the moonlight.

"Mr. and Mrs. Dundas," repeated Bay.

They shook hands quite solemnly—and then laughed.

❧

Bay had to go back to the airfield, so they walked as far as
the gate together and there they said good night. There was a
little shower as they came through the woods, a silvery moonlit
shower, very beautiful, and then the cloud passed and it was

fine and clear. Tonia paused at the gate, for she need not hurry. Nobody was waiting for her. She could stay here all night if she liked. The moon had moved across the sky and was setting behind a group of pine trees. It looked like a big lantern hung upon the branches. The silver light flooded the whole land; trees and walls stood out dark against its brightness. The roofs of the little town were silver too, for they were still wet from the shower. She leaned her arms upon the gate and looked down. Dear friendly little town, thought Tonia.

She was happy, and yet she was sad; for Bay loved her and she would have him for three weeks. He would be perfectly safe for three weeks, and her very own. After that…but some people didn't even have three weeks. She ought to be grateful. She *was* grateful. But if only the war could end, thought Tonia, pressing her hands against the rough, wet surface of the weathered wood. If only something could happen now, this very minute, so that the war would be over and all the misery of it; so that you could enjoy the beauty of the world without this burden of sadness, this racking anxiety that turned your bones to water; so that you could go to bed and sleep in peace without wondering how many splendid men had been killed today, and how many more would meet their deaths tonight, and how many mothers and wives would be carrying hearts of lead in their bosoms. It was not only on Bay's account that she feared and sorrowed—though of course Bay was nearest to her. It was not for Courtney, either—though Courtney meant everything to Celia, and Celia was her friend. It was the sorrow of the whole world that moved Tonia's heart tonight. It seemed to her that the world was tired and sick, that the whole of creation was suffering.

The clock in the town struck ten and immediately a bugle rang out, playing the Last Post. The silver notes floated in the air, clear and cold and otherworldly—silver notes in the silver moonlight. It was unbearably perfect. As the last questioning notes died away in the stillness (whither, whither, they seemed to ask), Tonia's eyes were full of tears. Her cheeks were wet.

About the Author

D. E. Stevenson (1892–1973) had an enormously successful writing career: between 1923 and 1970, four million copies of her books were sold in Britain and three million in the States. Her books include *Miss Buncle's Book, Miss Buncle Married, The Young Clementina, The Two Mrs. Abbotts,* and *The Four Graces.* D. E. Stevenson was born in Edinburgh in 1892; she lived in Scotland all her life. She wrote her first book in 1923, but her second did not appear for nine years. She published *Listening Valley* in 1944.